WICKED BY DESIGN

Katy Moran is the author of *False Lights*, published by Head of Zeus in 2017 under the pseudonym K.J. Whittaker and published as *Hester and Crow* on Kindle. After a career in publishing, Katy now works as a bookseller, and lives with her husband and three children in a ramshackle house in the Welsh borders.

Visit Katy's website to sign up for her newsletter and enjoy exclusive short stories set in the world of *Wicked by Design*.

katymoran.co.uk

@KatyjaMoran
@KatyjaMoran

BY THE SAME AUTHOR

False Lights (as K.J. Whittaker)

WICKED BY DESIGN

Katy Moran

HEAD of ZEUS

First published in the UK in 2019 by Head of Zeus Ltd

9 7 5 3 1 2 4 6 8

A catalogue record for this book is available from the British Library.

ISBN (HB): 9781786695383
ISBN (XTPB): 9781786695390
ISBN (E): 9781786695376

Typeset by NewGen

Printed and bound in Great Britain by CPI Group (UK) Ltd, Croydon CRO 4YY

Head of Zeus Ltd
First Floor East
5–8 Hardwick Street
London EC1R 4RG
WWW.HEADOFZEUS.COM

For Will

They hang the man and flog the woman
That steal the goose from off the common
Yet they let the greater villain loose
That steals the common from the goose

Anon.

Pele ero whei ow mos, mos fettow teg
Gen agas pedn du ha gas blew melyn?

Edward Chirgwin, *Cân an Delkyow Sevy*, 1698

The events in this book take place during a period of history that never happened.

Several years after Napoleon defeated the Duke of Wellington at the Battle of Waterloo, the French Occupation has at last been expelled from Britain. The country is on the brink of revolution – and the English throne is still empty.

Note on the text: in Cornish dialect, 'little maid' makes affectionate and familiar reference to a young girl. The Russian name Nadezhda is pronounced exactly as it is spelt. The 'zh' sound is the same as the 's' in pleasure, or treasure.

Part I

LAMORNA, 1819

1

Not far from Lamorna Cove, the ancient manor house of Nansmornow lay in a curl of wooded parkland. Shards of glowing window stood bright against the moonlit granite bulk of the hall, all nestled like a cultivated pearl between rain-lashed Cornish moorland, sea-cliffs and the wild Atlantic. Here the garden lad's spade would often turn up human bones or Roman tiles decorated with mosaic fish scales, once even a rust-caked sword and a clay dish of green beads. In the drawing-room, candlelight glanced off the silver dish of honey on the tray and long shadows were cast across the faded Turkish carpet. It was late, but four women still remained at the fireside and Hester Lamorna was quite unable to decide which she hated or mistrusted the most, even as she smiled and poured the tea. The rumours had reached a lethal temperature: before long, someone would boil like a lobster on a Tuesday in Lent. Most of the Cabinet, including the prime minister Lord Castlereagh, were now ensconced in Nansmornow's various oak-panelled guest-chambers, which meant that the servants' quarters teemed with scornful London valets, opinionated ladies' maids and bitter grievances, and that Hester must deal with the wives.

Wielding the teapot as a man might a rifle, Hester observed them all from beneath lowered lashes. Close to sixty and clad in quantities of lace, Martha Mulgrave laid claim to more than forty years' scheming passage through the shark-strewn waters of high society. She was absorbed in netting a purse, but hadn't survived this long without using girlhood accomplishments as a cover for acute observation. Nestling beside her on the chaise longue the Russian ambassador's wife, Dorothea Lieven, tucked a dark ringlet behind one pearl-strung ear, unfolding the letter received from Tsar Alexander only that morning. Ensconced in a damask Queen Anne chair, Emily Stewart, Lady Castlereagh, accepted her cup and smiled with brazen insincerity. They all had a way of looking at one that made Hester uncomfortably aware of both her light brown skin and those spirals of sand-dark hair springing loose from the bundle of weightless curls pinned atop her head. Straightening her back in unspoken defiance, she adjusted the Kashmiri shawl tucked around her shoulders and passed Dorothea the milk jug. She could not help fearing that this gathering of vultures would be her husband's undoing, but when had Crow ever contented himself with anything other than playing for high stakes? It was so exactly like him to invite the men most suspicious of his motives to drink the contents of the cellar.

'A penny for your thoughts, Lady Lamorna?' Emily said to her. 'Do you suppose the men ever plan to rejoin us? I only hope they've stopped boring on about that irrelevant Boscobel person and his trading-frigate or caravel or whatever it was. I can't conceive of a more unsuitable topic of conversation, quite as though they were all so many chicken-nabobs.' She sipped her tea. 'But then your dear Lord Lamorna does seem *so* very concerned with trade these days – I'm sure his father would have been quite appalled. Beau Lamorna was a person of the old style, don't you think?' Her eyes lingered on Hester. 'I would imagine darling Beau spinning in his grave if he only knew the half of how we live now.'

'Well,' Hester said calmly, 'considering my husband's lands are so rich in copper and coastline, it would be a little foolish of him not to take advantage of both. And as for the *Deliverance*, it was her unseaworthiness my husband took issue with. Unlike Hawkins Boscobel, Lord Lamorna would never send men from his own land to sea in a vessel that ought to have been condemned – or any man at all, for that matter.'

Emily's smile froze. 'Well, it's hardly our place to understand the complexities of commerce. I can't hope to have an informed opinion on such issues, although with your background, my dear, I do appreciate that matters might be quite otherwise.' She spoke as if trade were akin to the procurement of prostitutes. Had Emily confused Hester's father's naval career with that of a merchant seaman? Or did she allude to the fact that he himself had once been traded as cargo? Emily had been speaking French, so continued her sentence even as Mr Hughes opened the double doors, resplendent in his sober butler's garb, and then Hester's husband, Lord Lamorna, came into the drawing-room. He'd long since shelved the title Viscount Crowlas in favour of his dead father's ancient name, but those who knew him well still called him Crow. He wore a white shirt and a jacket of midnight-blue superfine, silencing all feminine chatter with his presence alone, with his black hair in its perpetual state of disarray, those lashes always so very dark against such white skin, and his pale, oyster-grey eyes gifted with the ability to privately communicate his quite disreputable intentions without the need for so much as a word.

'You women have outlasted us,' Crow said, with a slight bow to Emily, Dorothea and Lady Mulgrave. 'Castlereagh and Mulgrave have just gone up to bed. I go too, my lady.' He stood just close enough that he would not shame Hester with his touch in public as though she were his concubine and not his wife, and Hester longed for the moment she could reach for him beneath the crisp linen sheets, aired and lavender scented; knowing it, he gave her one of his quick smiles, all the more precious for their rarity.

'Well, really, Lamorna,' Lady Mulgrave said, laying down her netting at last. 'Are we not to drink our tea before you summon your wife to bed? I'm appalled at such medieval behaviour, even if I am surprised to see it among your mealy-mouthed generation.'

'Drink all the tea you wish, ma'am, but I'm going to bolt the door,' Crow said; he wasn't one to wither before a woman who was old, white and rich enough to be just as outrageous as she pleased. With another smile, Crow bowed and went out, and Mr Hughes remained entirely expressionless as he closed the doors behind him, leaving the four women alone in their enclave once more.

'Dear me, what a disgracefully beautiful young man he is,' Lady Mulgrave went on, as if she were discussing new curtains for the breakfast-parlour. 'They're always the worst.'

Emily smiled from the depths of the Queen Anne chair. 'Indeed,' she said, 'we all think you're being so amazingly dignified about it, darling Hester.'

With considerable effort, Hester stopped the honey-spoon rattling against the inside of her teacup. 'Dignified about what?'

'Emily, is this really the moment?' Dorothea said quickly, glancing away from her letter.

Lady Mulgrave spoke without looking up from her netting. 'Is there ever a good moment?'

Taking that as her invitation, Emily treated Hester to her most condescending smile. 'Oh, Hester, I do admire you for treating the entire affair with the contempt it deserves. In my view, Lord Burford's so-called daughter ought to be sent to some quiet place in the country and forgotten about.'

Hester fought for breath. It was an open secret that Lady Burford had once been not only her husband's stepmother but also his mistress.

Lady Mulgrave stirred a spoonful of honey into her own tea, which by judicious application from a small flask in her reticule was at this point mostly brandy, anyway. 'Oh, don't bore us with Louisa and her supposed seven-months child, Emily. Burford's mother says the man is a damned fool, and so he is. The girl must be well above a year old by now, and may survive. I shouldn't wonder they'll bring it to town so that some nursemaid might parade Louisa's downright cheek through the park.'

Hester held the china jug in both hands, staring at the creamy yellow milk. *Her seven-months child.* And over a year old? A child who could then be Crow's: that's what they were saying. That's what they meant, and to share the gossip so publicly was to humiliate her, to put her in her place. Hester's eyes burned: it took every last shred of willpower not to let tears gather.

'According to my cousin,' Emily went on, 'the darling thing has a very fine pair of grey eyes, and an absolute mop of black hair.' She turned to Hester with manufactured affection. 'Only think, the child must be scarcely a few months older than your own dear little creature. It'll seem five minutes before they're both debutantes in the same Season. Louisa's daughter will be quite devastating, I'm sure, if she lives, God willing.'

Hester forced herself to speak with a lightness of tone she wasn't even close to feeling as she thought of her year-old daughter asleep in milky contentment upstairs. 'Well, Louisa herself was a diamond of the first water in her day. Crow's father wouldn't have married her, otherwise.'

'Either way, I'm sure it'll all soon blow over,' Dorothea said, watching Hester over the rim of her teacup. 'It wouldn't be a real Season if someone didn't bring a miscellaneous bastard up from the country.'

'Well, that much hasn't changed since I was a green girl,' Lady Mulgrave said, and it was not until they had all finished their tea and kissed each other upon the cheek at the top of the stairs amid the clove-oil scent of Lady Mulgrave's face-powder that Hester knew she was at last within reach of indulging in a shamefully unrestrained display of emotion.

Blessed with an ability shared only with Crow's deceased parents to tell when he was lying, she was quite sure that he really had given Louisa up before they married: the child must have been conceived before that date, but her existence was still a betrayal of their own daughter. Louisa Burford's child would suffer no jibes about her black grandfather. Hester was infinitely proud of her African forebears, who had endured so much that she might exist, but there was no point in pretending those sidelong glances and whispered remarks did not happen. She had accepted Crow's proposal to save her honour and her life. She would never have chosen to live among these white aristocrats. Closing the bedroom door behind her, she sat rigid as Lizzy unbuttoned her gown, lifting the creased silk over her head, before unlacing her stays and sweeping the chemise over her head. Hester brushed her teeth with coral powder, breathing in the earthy, liquorice scent of myrrh and Havannah snuff. Lizzy passed her the folded linen cloth soaked in warm water, and Hester washed her face and under her arms and between her legs. Once she was dry, Lizzy gently tugged the nightgown over her head, and Hester sat to have her curls unpinned, waiting while Lizzy carefully unteased them.

'I think we must oil your scalp in the morning, milady,' Lizzy said. 'Mrs Rescorla has some of the rose treatment ready, I think.' Tying Hester's hair atop with a ribbon, she wrapped her head in a silk scarf, employing a firm knot. 'Is there anything more I can do, ma'am? I venture to say that you don't look quite well.'

Hester shook her head, longing to scream and hurl the lead-glass decanter of orange-flower paste across the room. 'Nothing, thank you, Lizzy. I've kept you awake long enough. Do go to bed. I shan't need anything else tonight.'

She waited until Lizzy had closed the door behind her, before getting to her feet and walking with restrained ire to the dressing-room, which in turn led to the master bedchamber. First, she passed through Crow's own dressing-room, past his valet's neatly folded piles of starched muslin neckcloths and tomorrow's fine lawn shirt hanging from the outside of the armoire, and the faint, enticing cucumber scent of Crow's shaving-water. After so many years in the navy and then the army, Crow was surprisingly precise with his grooming habits, never leaving his shirts on the floor for Hoby to pick up. By God, he would answer to her for Louisa Burford's grey-eyed daughter. Hester twitched back heavy crimson bed-curtains, faded to a peachy pink where light from the mullioned windows had shafted into the room for the past four hundred years, and found her husband's bed quite empty.

2

Many hours later, Lord Lamorna came home again. Crow closed the front door behind himself, barring the dregs of the night and all its danger and disorder. For him, the drawn bolt had presented no great difficulty. The hall was lit only by embers sulking in a fireplace large enough to roast a pig in, just as Hester had said with her usual asperity when he first brought her home to Nansmornow as his wife. Every sense rendered unbearably acute, he knew immediately that he was not alone. It was not Hughes: Crow's butler was over six feet tall and, standing on these ancient floorboards, Crow felt the counterweight of a much lighter intruder right through the soles of his boots. The interloper was behind him, concealed by the velvet drape always drawn across the front door once it had been locked, the folds of heavy fabric now still bunched at one end of the brass curtain rod. He reached for the knife at his belt, but even as his fingers closed around the ivory hilt a frozen prickling sensation shot down his spine, and through the curtain he felt the hard steel nub of a pistol pressed into his side just above the waist. The shot would pulverise his liver: a messy route to oblivion. With one swift jerk he closed his hand over the velvet-covered pistol-barrel and jerked it to one side. With a crack, a shot was fired. The ball dislodged a gilded boss from the ancient wall-panelling, which crashed to the floorboards. Crow was just conscious of admiring the burst of white plaster that sprang up like ocean spray before he tore aside the curtain with the knife at his side and came face to face with Hester, clad only in a thin linen nightgown and an expression of simmering fury, a blue silk scarf bound around her curls. He had been holding her wrist but let go with a swift curse as if her skin were red-hot, allowing her to back him up against the door so that they were just inches apart. He thought his wife beautiful always, but anger lent such compelling animation to her features – the flash of fire in her liquid dark eyes, the set of her lips. She knew about Louisa Burford's child.

'You have approximately two minutes to tell me where in heaven's name you've been before you do so in front of an audience,' Hester said. 'I shan't imagine it'll be long before the servants and possibly our guests come to investigate all this commotion.'

'Really?' he said, not daring to smile while she was still so angry with him. 'Are you to deliver ultimatums?'

'You had better believe it, my lord.' Hester spoke with what he felt was unnecessary sarcasm. The front of her nightgown clung to her, a little damp with breast-milk; she was no less desirable for it. 'Where have you been? For all I knew, you were a house-breaker.' Her voice cracked infinitesimally as she looked him up and down in rising disbelief. 'Is that a *crossbow*?'

'Yes, and good Christ, you've quite ruined the wall.' He wanted badly to kiss her, but in this present mood she would likely skin him if he tried it, and indeed he could not blame her. 'Hughes is a fool – where is he?'

'I sent him to bed once I'd discovered that you'd absconded for the evening. Why should the poor man wait up for dilettantes and criminals?'

'Because this particular dilettante and criminal pays his annual eighty pounds?'

They were standing so close that Crow felt crackling heat in the air between them, and genuine anger shot through him: markswoman though she was it had been the work of moments to disarm her. 'Give me that pistol.' He took it from her unresisting hand, setting it on the mantelpiece even as Hughes himself came in with a pair of nightgown-clad footmen holding lamps, and Lord Castlereagh's sharp-eyed valet. 'Go back to bed, all of you,' Crow said. 'I have relieved my wife of the night-watch, that's all, which my own servants – I need not add – ought to have been keeping.' A single glance at her face was enough to inform him that when they were alone she would make him sorry for his own evening's work. He had a reckoning to pay, and he would waste no more time. In one movement he lifted Hester, ignoring her stunned intake of breath and a whispered furious blasphemy; bearing her in his arms like a bride crossing the threshold for the first time he carried her up the stairs as Hughes, the footmen, and Castlereagh's man melted silently back into the servants' quarters.

'That was Castlereagh's valet – did you not see?' Hester hissed into his ear as they passed portraits of one Lamorna ancestor after another. 'Are they not all suspicious enough as it is without you creeping about in the night like a common criminal? You'll break your neck heaving me about like this, and very well it will serve you.'

'I shall do no such thing. Do you think I have never walked around this house in darkness before, Het?'

She made no reply; she was actually too angry now to speak, and by the time he set her down in his own bedchamber her eyes were swimming with furious tears that made him feel so extraordinarily ashamed that for a moment he too was lost for words. 'You've heard about Louisa's daughter, haven't you? Het, I'm sorry,' he said. He was sorry, too, for everyone's sake, that a child of his own blood would be brought up by that wet-eyed deviant Lord Burford.

'Oh, as to that I'm only surprised you don't have more bastards,' she said with scalding scorn. 'Don't apologise to me! I have sufficient skill in mathematics to understand that the child was conceived before you and I were married, and probably before I even had the misfortune to be washed up on your beach. And I suppose you found out this evening, too. I wouldn't put it past Lord Castlereagh and Emily to plan the timing of that little revelation between them. I don't even particularly care about it. *Where have you been?*'

He knew he could do little but tell her the truth, even though she now did not trust him enough to tell him how devastated she clearly was about the base-born child, and how humiliated she felt. He lifted the crossbow and the sling over his head, setting them both down on the ancient walnut chest of drawers that had stood in this room for as long as he remembered. 'I've been lamping for rabbits in Reverend Tregarthen's garden.'

She took two quick paces away from him, her eyes narrowed. 'With a crossbow, not a rifle. Quietly, so no one could hear you?'

She was right. He couldn't help himself, although Christ only knew that killing on the battlefield and killing in other, quieter places had infected both his sleeping and waking hours with unmentionable nightmares. How did she always know immediately what he had been thinking when her own thought processes were still so often a mystery to him?

'You fool,' Hester said, stepping forward now. He stepped back, just once. 'After *everything*, you miss the excitement of it all so much that you go out stalking rabbits in the middle of the night when your gamekeeper's boy could perfectly well do it himself?'

He found himself completely unable to explain that there had been no choice – that he couldn't stand the battened-down strain of entertaining half the Cabinet here in his own hall when Castlereagh was only waiting for the chance to prove him a traitor. He knew how to hunt quietly in the darkness, and how to kill: such waters were easier to navigate. Out beneath the silent moon, crouching in the shelter of the Tregarthens' rose bushes and snuffing out life after life in the dark, one felt in control. Why could he not simply tell her that? He couldn't frame the words.

'Well?' Hester demanded. 'Is that it? You miss the war?'

And because, despite everything, she was right about that, Crow said simply, 'Yes.' He took her gently by the shoulders, hardly able to bear the shame of the tears still streaking her face. Her nightgown had slipped down so that it barely concealed her breasts. 'Het,' he said, 'I'm sorry. God knows, I'm sorry for it all.'

'Have you forgotten what it does to you, fighting in wars?' she demanded, and now fresh anger rose up in him, too.

'How can you ask me that?' he replied. 'I'm sorry about the child – about Louisa's child.'

'So you keep saying. But think of your little adventure tonight, and the way you drank your own weight in brandy through all those years of fighting and subterfuge. What about the child who actually lives under your own roof? What if our daughter were to vex you in the way your brother once did? What then?'

Crow briefly closed his eyes, turning to walk rapidly to the window. 'Kitto did more than vex me, although God knows I didn't deal with him as I should have. Do you think I don't wonder why he kept refusing his leave, and why he hasn't come home, even though MacArthur said he ought to be here by Christmas? It shouldn't have taken him more than one month to sail from St Petersburg, and it's been two.' He sensed Hester standing close behind him, knowing that the moonlight would be shining through the fine linen of her nightgown. 'You must know that I would never hurt the maid,' he said to her in Cornish, holding on hard to the windowsill. He had done so much that was wrong. He didn't deserve this woman; he didn't deserve their child, asleep in the nursery. He turned and against all odds she put her hands behind his head and kissed him, her fingers light against the sweat-damp skin at the nape of his neck. He ran his hands down her back, with only that gossamer layer of linen between his fingers and her naked skin. Lifting his wife again, he carried her to the bed, and the curtains at the windows and around the bed had all been left undrawn, heavy velvet shifting in an easterly wind coming in through the casement he always left open; he'd never been able to sleep in an airless room. At last, he laid her on the bed and knelt before her in supplication, sliding that profligate nightgown up around her waist and brushing the inside of her thigh with kiss after kiss, higher and higher, until her fingers curled in his hair, pulling it tight.

'I love you,' he said, and then kissed her there again so that she arched her back as she lay on the bed, 'you and only you, Hester.'

'You are so shockingly badly behaved—' She broke off, liquescent and incoherent, clutching at his hair again when he cupped the round warmth of her rear in his hands, and as he did so, there was a knock on the door that persisted even after his imperious dismissal, but she had already curled away from him, tugging down her nightgown.

Hester sighed. 'You must go – whatever it can be at this time of night.'

By the time Crow reached the door and turned the handle, still dizzy with desire but his every sense now also surging with the urge to fight or to flee, he found Hughes once more, still dressed, holding a glowing Davy lamp, his face alive with alarming panic, dark skin sheened with sweat.

'It's the *Deliverance*, your honour – that caravel of Sir Hawkins Boscobel's,' Hughes said. 'They say she foundered for some reason right out beyond the cove, and the tide and the wind will soon have her smashed into pieces against Carn Du.'

And for the briefest moment Crow remembered lying on the *Belle*'s bowsprit when he was a midshipman at twelve years old, watching the sea sparkle and heave far below, knowing even as dolphins played in the spray as they crossed Biscay that this same ocean might easily one day be his grave. He turned to Hester: there was no choice.

'I know,' she said, tears standing in her eyes. 'I know you must go, but be careful. Do you understand?'

She came to take his hands and he loved her with all the force of his being. 'Of course,' he said, knowing this might well be the last thing he said to her, 'I'm ever your obedient servant, my dear.'

'The chance would be a fine thing,' Hester said, and kissed him. 'Now go.'

He reached the top of the stairs at a run, knowing that he was almost certainly too late to save a single life on board the *Deliverance*, and that he might be lost himself in the attempt, but that he still must try.

3

Crow rode before them all, right along the headland to Lamorna Cove, every manservant in the house roused and a number of them mounted, and to hell with what the so-called noblemen still asleep in their beds thought of their horseflesh requisitioned. A good number of females and stable-boys followed on foot, at a desperate run, and he prayed that Hester was not among them; he wouldn't put it past her to dress herself and to come, but not for the world did he want her to witness the devastation of a foundering ship. He tasted salt on the air even as rain and wind lashed his face: the storm was rising, not abating. As they thundered away from the gates of the park at Nansmornow and down towards the village of Nantewas, he glimpsed lamplit windows among the trees and knew that the men of Rosemerryn had already gone down to the cove. As they rode on he found that the same was true in Nantewas – windows bright with lamplight, front doors flung open to the rain, and no one to be seen. Everyone had gathered on the beach. Goading his mare, he left the fern-hung slopes of Nantewas behind, setting her hard down the hill towards the shore and passed the villagers there, a rain-soaked huddle of women and children, watching the grey, foam-splashed fury of ocean and sky, waves like walls of black water overtopping the great stone quay, smashing against it in great clouds of thick white spray.

The cove was a mess of lashing wind and white-tipped waves, and he could see now that by the look of it the *Deliverance* had come to grief outside the bay, and was by the strength of tide and wind forced against Carn Du, the great tusk of granite guarding the seaward entrance to the cove. With a jolt of horror Crow realised that she was in point of fact actually sinking before his eyes, sliding inexorably beneath the waves, and that he could see desperate figures still clinging to the tilting yards – crewmen waving, but as yet unreachable, even so close to the carn. He heard one of the Trewarthen women say, 'Lord Lamorna is here!' as if it were in his power to personally save all seventy men aboard the unseaworthy bath-tub that the unscrupulous lapdog of the English Hawkins Boscobel had put out from Newlyn. After six years in the navy, Crow could imagine all too clearly the panic – sails flapping and useless, masts leaning at sickening angles. Squinting against the rain, he saw that one of the Trewarthen gigs had already gone out, battling a filthy swell, his own men rowing hard towards the wreck in the hope of picking up survivors. God, they would be lucky to return alive. Still in the saddle, Crow knew there was no one left on the beach who could row well enough to crew for him, and no time to send word up the coast and have the breeches buoy and line-throwing cannon brought around.

Shouting to those of his men still on horseback, Crow called on them all to dismount. If he could not reach the *Deliverance* by sea, he must reach her from Carn Du itself: there was nothing to do but to send a rope-team into the water, himself at the fore. There was just a chance that men could be pulled from the water so close to the wreck, even if the gig could never reach them without also being smashed against the rocks. Whisking the coiled rope from his saddlebag, Crow slung it over his shoulder and sprinted to the narrow, winding path that led away from the beach and up towards the cliff-top, along to Carn Du. He snatched at handfuls of broom to steady himself, careless of the needles tearing into the palms of his hands. Once he reached the cliff-top, wind tearing at his face, his hair, he saw waves and spray smashing against the cliffs, against the rocks, and the spars of the *Deliverance* again, still sliding beneath the waves, with now only two figures clinging to them.

'*Run!*' Crow shouted at the men behind him. 'With me, come on!' And where in hell's name were Castlereagh, Mulgrave, Vansittart or any of the others? Peers of the realm still asleep in bed, leaving servants and fishermen to save lives? Reaching the outcrop of Carn Du, the heap of vast grey rocks rearing up against a sodden sky, Crow tore off his coat and jacket and unshouldered the rope. He lashed it around his waist with swift expertise, leaving one long end for his men to belay him with, and the rest to throw. This he coiled for now, and slung over his shoulder. Looking again, there was but a single man still clinging to the yards of the *Deliverance*. Squinting through spray and rain, Crow saw that the survivor was not even a man, but a boy. If he climbed down the seaward face of Carn Du as far as he could, there was a chance he could toss the rope to him, and failing that to anyone still clinging to wreckage below even as it was flung at the rocks. Amid the thundering roar of the surf and the hideous crunch of wood against rock as the top spars of the *Deliverance* were smashed against granite by the force of the ocean, he shouted to Hughes to take up the belaying end of the line.

'My lord,' Hughes said, his face rigid with emotion, rain streaming down his dark skin from grizzled, short-cropped hair, 'if you will permit me to speak? This is suicide. The waves are too high – you'll be washed away yourself.'

Crow turned to his assembled servants and tenants, rain-soaked, hair splattered across their faces as they passed the rope from one man to the next. 'What then must I do? Stand here on my own land and watch people die? Just for Christ's sake don't let go of the line.'

He ran light-footed to the great carn; he had climbed down it many times as a boy, clinging to fissures in the rock and leaping from narrow, algae-speckled ledges into the ocean twenty feet below, and he had clouted his young brother for doing the same too, but even then there had not been waves almost as high as the rock itself. Amid the roar of water and the groan of failing timber, Crow glanced over his shoulder as he climbed and saw the boy still clinging to a spar like kelp splattered against the upright timber of a jetty. What remained of the mast leaned at a heart-stopping angle. Wave-soaked, Crow clung to the rock, the rope taut above him, digging into the spare flesh of his midriff through his wet shirt. One boy out of a crew of seventy: was that really to be all? Another wave crashed into him, and he dug the fingers of one hand into a fissure in the rock, grasping a heaven-sent handful of sprouting marram grass with the other as he yelled over his shoulder at the boy, '*Hold on.*' Crow could see now that he was really very young, perhaps only eight or nine, his face familiar – one of the many urchins one saw on the cobbled streets of St Erth. Crow knew in the same instant that the child was losing the will to hold on, that he was too cold, and too afraid, his face white and pinched with exhaustion and terror.

'I'm going to throw this rope,' Crow shouted, clinging with one hand as he unshouldered the coil. 'And you must catch it, do you understand—' He broke off as another wave crashed into him, and it took every ounce of willpower not to let go. By some miracle, the boy was still there too. 'I'll climb back up the rock,' Crow went on, 'and we'll pull you up the cliff, do you hear?'

If this gambit failed – if the boy didn't catch the rope, or if he panicked and tried to jump with it before Crow had reached the cliff-top himself – they would both plummet down into the hellish cauldron below, and Crow knew he would have rendered his own child fatherless for the sake of another man's son.

Hester's hood flew back as she reached the headland after scrambling hand over hand up the steep cliff-path, tripping over the hem of a gown hastily pulled on top of her nightdress, even as she'd ignored Lizzy's protestations. Everyone gathered on the rain-lashed beach had looked at her with such horror that she knew immediately Crow had done something quite idiotic. She ran along the wind- and rain-blasted cliff-top to Mr Hughes, who was wrapping his coat around a single, shivering boy, as a knot of men she knew from the village – Crow's men – belayed a taut-stretched rope that ran right along the cliff-edge and to the rising granite mound of Carn Du itself. Blaspheming under her breath and every shred of flesh alive with terror, she ran to the rock, ignoring the men from Nantewas, Crow's men, who were gently trying to steer her away.

'*John!*' Held back by them all, she hurled Crow's Christian name into the storm, into the great cloud of spray that flew up, splattering her face, her hair – she had never called him Jack, as his brother used to, and as his father had done. As Louisa Burford had done. '*John!*' Only the ocean replied, booming waves, along with a grinding rush of timber against rock, and she heard someone say that was the foremast of the *Deliverance* going down at last with the rest of the ship. Hester dropped to her knees, snatching handfuls of wet grass. Crow was not gone, his life given in exchange for this poor boy's. He could not be gone. And then, as she watched, on her knees in the wet grass, rain streaming down her face, the taut rope quivered and a white hand appeared around the edge of the shouldering granite bulk of Carn Du. Getting to her feet, Hester was just aware of Mr Hughes at her side. 'Wait now, my lady. Let him come around the rock.'

Even as Hughes spoke, Hester's voice died in her throat as a vast grey wave reared up behind Carn Du, exploding against it in a burst of creamy white spray that soaked them all. With a cry, when the maelstrom of water had fallen away, she saw that there was no sign of Crow, or his hand, and Hester surged towards the cliff-edge, held back by her own servants. He was gone, simply gone.

'John!' she called. '*John, John, John!*'

At the edge of her hearing, she was dimly aware of the rope-team heaving, calling out a rhythm, counting in Cornish, in the old language, as they hauled, just like fishermen pulling up the nets. *Un, dew, trei, pajar*; *un, dew, trei, pajar*— And then here Crow was, hauling himself over the wind-whipped cliff-edge, his black hair dripping water. Shaking off Mr Hughes and the other men, Hester ran to her husband, snatching handfuls of his sodden shirt as he slung one long leg over the edge, rolling on to the grass as she pulled, and after lying flat on his back for one moment he got to his feet, the shirt plastered to his chest, wet breeches clinging to the lean length of his thighs, and he looked at her with stark hopelessness.

'Oh my God, come here!' Hester said quietly, and she felt the crushing strength in Crow's arms as he enveloped her in his embrace, his soaking wet hair sending runnels of water down the back of her neck.

'Het, they are all gone.' He spoke with his face buried in her hair. 'Just one boy, that's all. I went back. One other man I tried to reach, but he went under, and it was too late. That ship should never have left Newlyn. Boscobel should never have allowed her to be put out.'

'You tried your best.'

'What if it had been the boy?' Crow said. 'What if he's down there at the bottom of the cove with the rest of them?'

Hester pulled away, watching him with unease. 'Crow, you saved the boy.' Even as she spoke Hester knew he was not talking about that shivering creature now wrapped in Mr Hughes's greatcoat, but about his own brother, who should have been home a month ago at least. She seized Crow's shirt, twisting a handful of it, pulling him closer still. 'No. Think properly. *Think*.'

'You know as well as I do it's the kind of thing he would do,' Crow said, 'idiotic young spendthrift that he is – with no money for a coach or doubtless even a horse, he'd soon enough sweet-talk his way into getting passage all the way down the coast. God damn his eyes, I'll thrash him from here to Newlyn.'

'No, think,' Hester said again, 'the *Deliverance* left Newlyn. It's not as if she came down the coast from up-country. It doesn't make sense. Kitto was never on that boat, Crow, he simply can't have been.'

He pulled away, raking back the hair from his eyes as he mastered himself. 'God forgive me, Hester. I'm a fool, and I failed those men today.'

'You didn't,' she said, holding him again. 'It was not your fault that Hawkins Boscobel put out an unseaworthy vessel. You tried your best to save the crew.' Hester knew even as she spoke that her words would not be enough to convince him that there was nothing he could have – should have – done. She shook him a little. 'You're still a fool, though.'

He said nothing to that, but only held her close to his chest, and they clung to each other on the cliff-top even as the seawater soaked into her own clothes, unnoticed by them both.

4

One night after the *Deliverance* went down with seventy-two souls aboard, Captain the Honourable Christopher Helford stood up to his waist in the frigid black waters of Lamorna Cove, wondering if it were possible to be hanged by one's own brother for stealing shipwrecked cargo on his land. Lamorna Bay spread out towards a sliver of moon; the sea was quiet now, all her temper spent when the wreck of the *Deliverance* had been smashed against Carn Du. Another dead man floated past, rolling over in the swell with the slow grace of a breaching whale, hair spreading like seaweed, mouth wide in his wax-white face. Twenty-four hours after the wreck, and the sea surrendered those it had been impossible to save. Captain Helford caught sight of another bobbing shape; it was too high in the water to be another victim. Wading, he grasped the hogshead with both hands, soaked wood slippery beneath his fingertips. The *Deliverance*'s crew might all be long past help, but there were those on land whose continued existence depended on how much coin the Cornish resistance could get for French brandy, whale oil and sodden bales of ruined muslin: the shadowy trade networks of An Gostel would make short work of this haul.

'Take this!' Captain Helford passed the hogshead to the girl beside him, wet, copper-red hair sticking wild across her cheeks. As he turned inland, he caught a faint glimmer of light on the headland by Carn Du, out towards Mousehole and Newlyn.

'Is that Lord Lamorna or the English, sir?' The girl was unnecessarily sarcastic, as if she'd always known this mission would end at Bodmin Assizes and the gallows, and Captain Helford wished to encounter Lord Lamorna here for the first time in almost two years as little as he hoped to meet a battalion of English troops. As if this had even been his damned notion, anyway.

'Let's not find out either way. *Enough!*' Raising his voice, Captain Helford called a halt; the girl turned to look out to sea where the *Deliverance* had gone down. He didn't know her: like the rest of the starved and ragged criminals herding bobbing flotsam shoreward, she wasn't local. Likely she'd had father, brother or lover among the drowned crew. They'd all been from St Erth, so it was said. She'd have come across the moor in the hope of retrieving corpse and contraband alike. His hand closed over her narrow wrist. 'Get up the beach unless you want to swing. Trust me, it's not a pretty way to go.' She turned her back on him, tails of sodden hair plastered to the back of her gown, shoulder-deep in the water, surging towards land.

Captain Helford forced himself through the swell, cursing. He raised his voice above the crash of surf and moaning wind, shouting so that the rest could hear. 'Go for the top of the valley! *Now.* I'll show you where to make the drop.' He'd been an idiot to involve himself in this, but what choice had there been, really?

The lights on the headland shifted, shuddering: they'd been seen. Beached and heavily laden with barrels and bales of wet Rajasthani muslin, the women of St Erth ran and staggered up the cobbled slip, passing the quay where his brother's caravels were so often moored, heading for a steep path that led away from the cove and through the fern-hung valley. A cry rose up, and the pinpricks of light on the headland began to shift again: whoever they were, they'd soon reach the tree-lined Mousehole lane slicing above the valley, putting an end to any chance of getting clean away from here. Turning to glance back at wet sand and lapping tide, Captain Helford saw figures still huddled around a dark shape on the rocks, a woman hunching at the side of a drowned man, her cloak trailing in a barnacle-studded pool. She made a low, inhuman noise akin to the cattle-lowing cry of childbirth.

'Move,' he shouted, 'or we'll none of us see the end of the week.'

Her companion turned to him – the only other living man among them. 'It's her boy, your honour. Young Thomas.' Middle-aged, sparsely bearded, those fingers nervously grasping the woman's shoulder were ink-stained. Captain Helford recognised him with a jolt: Nathaniel Edwards, count-man at the Boscobel mine, and devout Methodist. So Edwards had come as escort to the women of St Erth, but he was stoop-shouldered and weak, a man of ledgers, ink and quill feathers, no more able to plan a raid on shipwrecked cargo than the bal-maids he was here to protect.

Suppressing a flash of irritation, Captain Helford spoke with the measured fury he'd perfected in the sleet-filled trenches at Novgorod, a tone that made even the surliest private shift. 'Edwards, help me get her up that damned fucking valley. Now.'

They ran, hauling the prostrate woman between them, slipping on the rocks at the mouth of the steep path. Sweating through wet clothes at the weight of a sodden bale heaved on to his back, Captain Helford led his unlikely troop of smugglers past the scattered houses of Nantewas and the Wink, tavern windows shuttered against small-hour darkness.

He really could hear horses now, hoofbeats pounding. One of the would-be smugglers stumbled, dropping her barrel, and he stopped it with his feet. He bent beneath the weight of the bale and took up the hogshead, too, forcing himself to run up the hill, sweat streaming beneath his shirt. It was at least a mile of hard and desperate sprinting past silent, scattered houses, snowdrops and wild garlic flowers pale in the moonlit dark, already flowering among moss-covered rocks hidden by the darkness. Sandy tinning-streams criss-crossed the gullies, and the sound of rushing water roared in his ears; galloping horses bore down from the Mousehole road, louder every moment.

Crossing the mud-ridged lane and leaving it behind, Captain Helford splashed through standing water, dodging moss-covered stones and low branches, his chest tight with the exertion of running with such a burden, the muscles in his left arm and shoulders screaming. If he didn't lead, no one would find the way to the fogou, and yet he had no way of knowing what was happening behind him. He reached the tunnel at last, sensing, as he always did, the sheer age of this place, a souterrain excavated and lined with great flagstones before men even knew God. Gasping with relief, he set down both bale and barrel, bundling and rolling them one after the other over dead leaves and stones into the dark, concealing mouth of the tunnel. The strongest and fastest of the women were the first to join him, bal-maids from the Boscobel pit and hard-faced fishermen's wives, all weaving through moss-shrouded trees, laden with their stolen cargo.

'Get in!' Captain Helford waved them on into the fogou; wide-eyed, straggle-haired, the women crossed themselves as they ducked and went underground, bundling barrels and bales into the pitch-dark creep-tunnel that led away from the main chamber. Emerging into the night, he ran back down the valley to bring up the rear, jumping over streams and sidestepping trailing ivy. Passing the stragglers, he urged them on, and reaching the lane saw the girl with copper-bright curls supporting a limping Edwards, sparse hair in stringy disarray across his balding scalp.

'He's turned his ankle,' she gasped, 'he can't run, let alone carry anything.'

The hammering of hoofbeats now filled the air, and without discussion Captain Helford heaved the injured man over his shoulder. He snatched at the girl's thin arm, tugging her along in his wake. They reached the shelter of the trees moments before the first of the horsemen passed on the lane – steaming horse-breath, red jackets, white breeches, shining black boots: English troops, men of the 11th Northumbrian, a crack cavalry regiment. Helford frowned, watching them pass. Why were the Northumbrians patrolling in Cornwall, instead of the 31st Cornish? His own regiment recruited in Cornwall but both Coldstream battalions had been abroad since the French were expelled from British soil in 1818. As far as he knew, the 31st Cornish still had men in Britain – but they weren't here on Cornish land where one would expect to find them. None of this made sense.

He signalled to the girl to wait and they crouched in silence, all Edwards's weight still across his shoulder. His neck pulsed with agony. The girl shivered at his side, wet hair plastered across her forehead, and they watched through the trees as the soldiers rode by in a blast of iron-shod hooves and the sweat of horses and men and the bright glitter of a silver gorget hanging across an officer's chest. At last, the Northumbrians bore off abruptly to the right, turning downhill towards the cove. When they had gone, Captain Helford signalled at the girl to get up and make for the tunnel, his shoulder muscles now screaming with the effort of bearing the injured man's weight. The sour stink of Edwards's breath turned his stomach. They picked through undergrowth, the girl's breathing rapid and ragged with the effort of bearing the barrel she carried. They reached the tunnel in desperate, sweating silence, and Captain Helford gave up Edwards to the care of the women, shrugging off their clasping hands and their thanks. Edwards could stand now, gingerly testing his weight as he leaned against the moss-covered rock.

'Where will you go?' Captain Helford demanded of them all. 'For God's sake, do nothing so foolish again. If I'd not found you dithering on that beach, who'd be waiting for the gallows now? Next time you want to steal wrecked cargo, make a proper job of it.'

The women stared back at him in obstinate silence, hard-faced, hard-eyed.

It was the copper-haired girl who spoke. 'Hawkins Boscobel is in the pocket of the English. He hiked the rents and laid men off at the mine, and put out the *Deliverance* knowing she was hardly seaworthy, so what choice did our men have except to sail in her and take his wages? Now we've nothing left at all, and our children are hungry already.'

'Next time, apply to Lord Lamorna before you risk your own necks. Why on earth did you not?'

'St Erth lies in duchy land, not the earldom, that's why, *Captain*. And last we heard, the duchy's English-controlled, for all we're in Cornwall.' The girl spoke with a marked lack of respect, her eyes sparkling, chin tilted. 'So Lord Lamorna is entertaining the English at Nansmornow even as we speak, with Bloody Castlereagh himself as his guest. Some say my lord should be King of Cornwall; I say he's after striking deals with England, not feeding his own starved countrymen.'

'Oh, the devil take it!' Captain Helford retorted. 'You can't get back to St Erth tonight. Where will you go?'

'There's a prayer meeting at Sancreed, sir,' Edwards said, the whites of his eyes bright in the dark as he glanced out at the woodland. 'We'll be safe there. The patrols never ride inland when there's so little moon – they don't know where the old mineshafts are.'

'Go then,' Captain Helford said, forcing off a wave of exhaustion. Leaning against a tree, he watched them all flit away into the darkness, through the trees, Edwards limping and glancing back over one narrow, stooped shoulder.

The copper-haired girl turned to face him, defiant. Still there. 'I suppose you think we ought to be grateful.' Somehow, she was only inches away.

'I don't know what to think,' Captain Helford said truthfully, and when he kissed her, it was because he was glad to be alive out there in the night, and the warm curves of her body were proof of it, and together they lay down in the ferns and the dead leaves, cheating death in the darkness.

By the time he heard footsteps, it was too late.

5

The girl screamed as she lay beneath him, strands of spittle between her wide-apart lips. With a leaping crouch, Captain Helford reached for the knife strapped to the inside of his boot, rearranging his clothes in panicked, battle-ready haste as he turned to face the night-roaming newcomer who stood watching him, two pistols at his belt. Crow was so devastatingly familiar a sight that the captain felt like a child again in his presence, as if all those months of snow, boredom, near-starvation and occasional bloody melee in Russia had melted quite away. With the detachment of a cat toying with prey, Crow watched the girl flee. She disappeared into the trees, still sobbing with fear, and only then did Captain Helford suffer his brother's full attention. It was damnably odd how much smaller Crow seemed to have got since they had last met. He was barely an inch the taller now, with that scent of cigarillo smoke and rosemary laundry soap, and the attendant familiar hostility. The captain found it quite impossible to speak, an affliction that did not appear to affect his brother, who addressed him as if they'd recently encountered one another at a ball.

'*Bonsoir, Christophe*,' Crow said in idle, laconic French. 'Do forgive the interruption. How extraordinary to encounter you here. We were expecting you for Christmas and it's January: I must own I'd quite given you up.'

'Oh, never mind that! Have you *any* idea what everyone's saying about you in every tavern between here and Plymouth?' Captain Helford demanded. 'I don't know what kind of game you're playing, Crow, but they're calling you the King of Cornwall, when we still don't even have a King of England. Everyone's saying you're as good as a traitor.'

'Have you finished?' Crow asked. 'Because I take it the legal property of Hawkins Boscobel is now concealed in the creep-tunnel and you've just aided and abetted the theft of a cargo from another man's boat wrecked on my beach. Naturally you'll explain the entire situation in your own good time.'

Captain Helford mastered himself, wrestling with the particularly acute fury that only his brother could induce, with that high-handed way of talking as though one were a servant, or a child. 'I landed at Plymouth a week ago,' he said. 'When I got to Fowey, one of your caravels was putting out – the *Brieuze*. Captain Douglas took me aboard. Everyone's saying you've turned against England – that you're leading Cornwall into allegiance with France, or the Russians—'

Crow interrupted him with complete lack of ceremony. 'A day after the *Deliverance* went down with over seventy men, all lost save a single boy, and you order the crew of one of my ships to make an unscheduled stop in an onshore wind? Jesus fucking Christ, have they been teaching you inexcusable stupidity in Russia as well as how to kill Frenchmen?'

Captain Helford fought for words, and he wanted to sink through the ground. 'I didn't know about the *Deliverance* then,' he said, 'none of us did. Word hadn't got that far north by the time we left Fowey. We didn't go alongside the quay – I ordered Douglas to drop anchor well beyond Carn Du. We rowed in.'

'How I do love my merchantmen to waste their time ferrying spoilt young officers up and down the coast,' Crow said, obviously prepared to concede nothing. 'Go on, I'm listening.'

'I found them on the beach – all the women from St Erth. They're starving, and they were making a mull of recovering the cargo; they'd have been caught with it if I hadn't helped them. What should I have done – leave them to be captured and to hang?'

With absent-minded expertise and his usual complete and total disregard for any justification of one's actions, Crow loaded one of his pistols, tipping powder down the barrel from the ox-horn that hung around his neck, followed by a wadded ball and a deft shove with the ramrod. 'Thank you, I'm conversant with the current miserable state of affairs in my own county, thanks to the constant efforts of the English. Did I miss the moment when you told me why you're here a month late? And don't tell me your leave was postponed, because I know it was not. I had a letter from Wellington wishing me a merry Christmas with my heroic young brother.'

'I went to Paris,' Captain Helford said, defiance emerging from eye-watering mortification. 'There was a girl. You know how it is.'

'England is still at war with France and you're a commissioned officer in the British army, but never mind, Kitto.'

It was a very long time since anyone had called the captain by his childhood name, and although Crow smiled only rarely, when he did, it was almost impossible to remain angry with him. The blow struck Kitto's shoulder from behind with stunning force. It was not for a long time that he knew he had been shot. First, he heard Crow swear – a tangle of Cornish and French obscenity – and dropped to his knees at his brother's side in the shelter of a long-fallen horse chestnut tree overgrown with ivy. It was hard to breathe, and a queer, cold wave swept through him. Expressionless, Crow handed him one of the two pistols, and Kitto closed his fingers around the polished cherry-wood stock, feeling by the weight of it that the pistol was already loaded. He didn't understand why his hands were wet, his fingers slipping against polished steel, against wood.

'Show yourselves!' The voice rang out beneath the silent tangle of branches overhead with a slight north-country tilt: not all the 11th Northumbrians had ridden down to the cove, then, and Kitto knew he had led English soldiers straight to where the goods were hidden, so very illegally, on his traitorous brother's land. Beside him, Crow was quite still, crouching behind the fallen tree. They waited, watching. The cavalry officer appeared through the trees, picking his way quietly through the mess of bracken and dead leaves, the silver gorget on his chest glinting in the darkness. His face was open and unremarkable. He looked like the type of fellow one might drink with all night back in Petersburg, if not precisely the sort one might have been at Eton with. Except that he was clearly afraid, not knowing who or what he was going to face out here in the woods. Kitto's head spun, and thick warm liquid seeped beneath his shirt and jacket.

The cavalry officer sang out again. 'Declare yourselves!'

Beside him, pistol aimed, Crow touched the trigger. The soldier crashed to the ground on his back, stirring up a dance of dead leaves. Without a word, Crow got to his feet and walked over to look at him as though he had just shot a pheasant overhead, not a man on the ground. Breathing the tang of smoke, Kitto forced himself to his feet. Crow really had just killed an English soldier. Crow, who had once been a lieutenant colonel in Kitto's own regiment, and aide-de-camp to the Duke of Wellington himself. Crow, whom everyone called King of Cornwall when there was still no King of England. Kitto tried to follow his brother to the dead man's side, but after a few steps he dropped to his knees, unable to feel his feet. Why would his body not obey? What was the matter with him? Kitto had never seen anyone move so quickly or so quietly as Crow did then, picking his way back through the undergrowth to crouch at his side.

He opened his mouth to speak, but with one brief gesture Crow signalled for silence. 'Not now, my boy,' he said, in Cornish, *A-der lebmyn, boya,* and then pain exploded through Kitto's shoulder with catastrophic force. He'd taken a hit. The agony was now overwhelming; it was like being at the centre of a dark whirlwind, trees and the night spinning around him. Crow took his hand, and the one constant at the centre of it all was the hard grasp of Crow's fingers gripping his own. Kitto knew the wooded valley might still be seeded with English soldiers running towards the sound of the gunshot, the smell of the smoke, and that for Crow to talk his way out of this as only he could do they must get to Nansmornow alive, and in silence, entirely unobserved, and so he held the pain inside himself and made no sound, as he had seen the village women do in childbed, and using all his strength he managed not to cry out.

6

At Nansmornow, Hester sat up in bed, alone once more. Her breasts were heavy with milk that had dampened the front of her fine lawn nightgown, but that wasn't why she'd woken. Leaning back against the pillows, she glanced at the shaft of moonlight pouring in through the lead-latticed window, right on to the unoccupied acreage of linen beside her. Crow had come with her to bed after a sombre supper, but now he was out roaming at night again: restless, unable to sleep, haunted by the catastrophic loss of life in the bay. It was long past midnight. What had woken her with that peculiar muffled thud? Someone stumbling up the stairs, perhaps, or dropping a candle-dish? Old Lord Vansittart had been exchanging yet more incendiary glances with Dorothea Lieven over the veal with olives and nutmeg tarts. And yet Hester couldn't shake off the certainty that she must get out of bed and investigate – that this was more than just her guests swapping bedchambers late at night. Crow always moved in silence: it could not be him, she knew.

Hester gasped at the cold as she groped for the heavy brocaded dressing gown Lizzy had left folded across the end of her bed, praying that she wouldn't come face to face with a pair of her guests in the middle of an indiscretion. She stepped out into the hallway, the old Turkey rug hard beneath her bare feet, her eyes growing used to the dark. The door to the master bedroom was open, and without even going in she could see that her husband had not uncharacteristically chosen to sleep without her – the bed-curtains were undrawn, the coverlet smooth and untouched. Surely he had not gone out? Surely it was quite clear to Crow that roaming the cliff-tops and moorlands in darkness was only going to make the English more suspicious of him?

'Damn your eyes, Lord Lamorna.' Trying to ignore rising unease, Hester trod silently towards the far end of the hallway. At the top of the stairs, she came face to face with her housekeeper and just managed not to scream. Catlin Rescorla wore a patchwork bedspread wrapped around her nightgown, hair hanging over her shoulder in a thick braid. Without discussion, they moved as one, and Hester followed Catlin downstairs, clutching the bannister. The great hall was silent and dark, lit only by odd, silvery shapes cast on to ancient flagstones by the light of a sickle moon trickling through mullioned windows. Together, they froze at the sound of footsteps.

'Lady Lamorna? Up so late? I thought the entire household had retired.'

Hester bristled at Lord Castlereagh's prying inflection as he stepped into the hall from the drawing-room, holding a candle in a pewter dish. In his fifties now, the prime minister was tall, fair and well made, and it was true that his wife Emily still had many frustrated rivals, but Hester felt a chill of disgust as he looked her up and down, near enough to touch her. He smiled, as though he could see through both dressing gown and scant linen.

'I'm so sorry, my lord,' Hester said mildly. 'Have you rung, only to find no servant? I'm afraid that my housekeeper and I were only just roused by hearing you move about. How may we help?'

Catlin smoothed the dressing gown around Hester's shoulders.

Castlereagh inclined his head in imitation of a bow. 'Allow me to escort you to the library, Lady Lamorna. After yesterday's tragedy I can quite understand why your nerves are overset. A shipwreck is a dreadful thing – a reminder of the ocean's wrath, and God's judgement.' He nodded curtly in Catlin's direction. 'I'm sure your servant will accompany us if you feel it necessary to observe the niceties.'

Hester had no choice in the matter, regardless of how deeply improper it was for Castlereagh even to have issued the invitation. Ignoring her panic, she followed him across the cavernous hall towards the library. Castlereagh was plainly waiting for Catlin to open the door, in the absence of a butler to do it for him.

'Perhaps,' Catlin said, 'her ladyship would prefer to go back to bed?'

Castlereagh stared at her with as much surprise as if the stair carpet had addressed him, and Hester felt a shiver of fear slide down her back. He knew they couldn't afford to antagonise him: not with the delicate nature of negotiations between Crow and the Cabinet.

'Mrs Rescorla,' she said to Catlin, carefully not looking at her, 'do bring tea and make up the fire. I'll wait with Lord Castlereagh for my husband.'

Catlin left, exuding silent disapproval, and Hester had no choice but to lead Castlereagh into the library. The candles in the chandelier had not yet been put out, and warm light glanced from the gilded spines of row after row of leather-bound volumes. He settled himself in Crow's father's old armchair by the still-glowing fire, light from the embers burnishing his fair hair, watching as Hester took her seat on the leather-upholstered fire surround. It was in truth one of her favourite places to perch, leafing through calf-bound Aeschylus or the works of Thomas Malory, but she knew Castlereagh should have offered her the chair. He didn't.

'Your housekeeper seems to enjoy a remarkable amount of authority in this house,' he commented. 'I wonder Lord Lamorna allows it.'

With the ease born of life-long practice, Hester smiled, forcing herself to suppress her annoyance. 'Mrs Rescorla's mother was my wet-nurse, in fact. Lord Lamorna has servants here at Nansmornow who have known him equally as long – I'm sure you know how it is with such people. They obey, of course, but they never quite forget the sight of one as an undignified toddler. You live so far away from Ireland, Lord Castlereagh. Perhaps you have no servants at home who have been with your family so long a time.' Mention of his birth country was as close as Hester dared get to the barbed rejoinder she longed to make. It was in Ireland that he'd earned the sobriquet Bloody Castlereagh for the insurrection he had so brutally suppressed; even a bishop had been hanged, still in his vestments.

Castlereagh smiled. 'Let's not play foolish games. Securing the house is so inarguably the preserve of a master, not a mistress. Surely there is no possible reason to investigate footsteps in the darkness unless you believe Lord Lamorna is not here? Does your husband often wander abroad at night? How odd that he should retire to bed, and then go out.' With one well-shaped finger, he outlined circular patterns on the brocade arm of his chair, never taking his eyes from Hester's face. 'Jack always did have an odd kick to his gallop. I was the last one up – even Lord Vansittart had gone to bed. How lowering to discover my conversation is really that unedifying.'

What was it that Crow had taught Kitto, time and again, much to her disapproval? She'd been reared in conditions of far stricter propriety than her husband and his young brother. *If you must lie, stay close to the truth.*

She chose her words with care. 'I confess, I'm rather worried myself.'

Castlereagh reached out as if to touch her hair, which was unbraided, a light cloud of spirals loose about her shoulders. 'You confess? Surely you have nothing to confess. Such pretty tresses you have, my lady. So unusual.'

Confess. Why had she said that? It sounded so guilty. She refrained from remarking that her hair was far from unusual, as he called it. How dared he touch her?

'Indeed I'm a goose, and I'm ashamed of myself. Lord Lamorna is a fitful sleeper. He fairly regularly walks outside at night. It's often so with men who've been at war: many of them do sleep very badly. And, as you say, the shipwreck has distressed him beyond measure. I believe that men who have been at sea themselves find such things particularly harrowing.'

'How terrible, then, that both you and your housekeeper should be moved to get out of bed at the merest noise downstairs. Is it really so unusual that you should hear something with a house full of guests, and so many valets and ladies' maids unfamiliar with their surroundings?' Castlereagh smiled again. His eyes were extremely blue, stark against his weatherworn, hawkish face; not days before, he had ridden to hounds with Crow in the winter sun. 'Really,

Lady Lamorna, it's almost as if you were expectant of some intrusion or other unlawful activity. Were you?' He leaned so close that she felt the heat of his body.

'Hardly, sir. We should grow used to shipwreck, living on such a coast as this,' Hester said, 'but I must admit that one never does. The loss of the *Deliverance* was a dreadful tragedy, was it not? When I think of those poor men lying dead in our chapel it's impossible to be sanguine. All those children in St Erth who will never see their fathers alive again. I'm not surprised Lord Lamorna has found it hard to rest.'

'Oh, naturally it's all very unsettling.' She caught the scent of clove pastilles in the warmth of his breath as he spoke. 'Could it be, perhaps, that your husband has gone to the Methodist meeting? I believe there is a large one nearby, and that such affairs take all night to reach a conclusion. So devout. One wonders how adherents to the Methodist faith attend to their work the following day.'

She knew quite well that he was toying with her, leading the conversation off at tangent after tangent. He was waiting for her to trip: to betray something she would rather have kept to herself.

'My husband pays lip service only to religious proprieties, and of course when he worships, it's in the Church of England,' Hester said lightly.

'Methodism does seem to attract such large crowds among the mining and fishing communities,' Lord Castlereagh went on, crossing his legs. 'I wonder that your husband allows these meetings on his land. Unless of course he actually sympathises with dissenters. I don't know about you, Lady Lamorna, but I find large crowds so unnerving.'

'I thought as much, my lord, considering that just two weeks ago a Methodist leader was hanged at your command in Exeter for sedition, and a crowd protesting the price of bread trampled by yeomanry. How unfortunate that so many children were also killed.'

Hester knew she had made a terrible mistake in losing her temper. Lord Castlereagh simply sat and watched her, that slight smile lingering. 'Ah, but you have so much spirit,' he said. 'Just like Lord Lamorna's mother. You know, Claire de la Saint-Maure had a delicious frankness of manner, too. Alas, Lamorna only had to crook his finger and she came running. But I can see why their son desired you so much that he took the quite extraordinary step of making you his lawful wife – Hester.'

In silent and furious dismay, she could hardly believe his sheer insolence, entirely trapped as she sat on that fireside surround. The silence between them stretched on again, and her eyes rested on a tall, highly polished grandfather clock recessed between two abutting bookshelves. It was half past two: they were well beyond social nicety. This was an interrogation, and Hester wished beyond anything that she had the means in her power to make this man pay for his brutality. Instead, he was prime minister.

He smiled. 'So, Lady Lamorna, since we're in a position to exchange confidences, what do you make of all these rumours about your husband? So many that he invited us here to quell them – although one does find that an invitation from Jack so often carries the air of a summons. But all these remarkable tales of a king in Cornwall? I should wonder that you don't laugh.'

He had moved in for the kill. 'My lord,' she said, forcing her voice not to shake, 'how could we do anything but laugh? Cornwall is not Scotland. We are a mere county in England, no more a nation in our own right than Hampshire.'

'And yet,' Lord Castlereagh went on, 'I have sources who tell me that at those Methodist meetings which wear on through the night hours, a Cornish king is all they speak of. Lord Lamorna is the rightful King of Cornwall, they say. So I think it rather strange and unsettling that your husband has apparently left the house after claiming the need for a good night's sleep, and on precisely the evening such a meeting takes place. What do *you* say, Lady Lamorna? Hester – if I may.' He smiled. 'Queen Hester. Now that would be a thing. An African queen, no less.'

Hester returned the smile, even though she felt quite sick with fear. 'I think it's more than possible your sources don't understand how much our country people here enjoy telling old stories and folk tales.'

Castlereagh took his chance and stood, leaning over her, crooking his forefinger beneath her chin, tilting her face up towards his so that she could not look away. 'Oh, don't show me that false modesty, Lady Lamorna – you're hot for it, with all that African blood.' He stood back, turning her face from side to side even as she was too terrified to move, admiring the swell of her breasts. 'I fancy I might admire you just as much I once did the previous Lady Lamorna. You know, my dear, it would be easy for you to make me forget all these difficulties about your husband's questionable loyalty to England. It must be so very frightening, wondering every moment when and if your husband will be accused of high treason and sent to London to die on the scaffold, as we both know he deserves.' With one swift, shocking movement he released her and as though unwrapping a parcel he flung aside the heavy silk folds of her wrap, and with a jerk of his finger tugged down the front of her nightgown so that the dark brown bud of her nipple was revealed. 'Beautiful,' he said. 'Let me possess you, Hester, and all this fear and suspicion might just go away.'

Hester sat frozen with horror and waves of cold shame, unable to move, to speak. The door swung open, and Catlin came in again with a tea-tray: Hester could have wept with relief. Lord Castlereagh stepped away, quite unconcerned by her state of undress, as though he had just been interrupted by a concubine's footman. Steam issued gently from the spout of the pot, and Hester tugged up her nightgown and stood to take the tray, suppressing another wild surge of terror. Catlin's face was an impassive mask, but when Hester glanced down at the two porcelain teacups arrayed on the gilded tray, she saw a faint slick of shimmering, oily liquid in the bottom of one. She poured a golden stream of tea into it, and handed the cup to Castlereagh.

'Milk, my lord?'

'I thank you, no.'

Pouring for herself, Hester forced herself not to look at the prime minister as he sipped his tea. After drinking that much tincture of opium, Castlereagh would soon be quite asleep, which could only mean that Catlin, who had prepared it, was now certain that the possible consequences of drugging the most powerful man in Britain were less appalling than his discovery of Crow's whereabouts. It wasn't until Catlin gently removed the cup and saucer from her hand that Hester realised how much she was shaking, and that hot tea had splashed all over her wrist.

7

Arm in arm, Hester and Catlin hurried down the whitewashed servants' passage; as soon as they were out of earshot of the library, Catlin stopped, taking Hester by the shoulders and giving her a slight shake as though they were still girls fleeing some childhood crime on the island of Bryher.

'Get a hold on yourself, my lady,' Catlin hissed. 'I saw what he did but if Lord Lamorna finds out there'll be bloodshed in this house. *Het.*'

'I know—' Hester fought for breath, both sickened and shamed at the memory of Castlereagh's touch, of his unclothing her. 'Crow would kill him if he ever found out. I know he would. God, I should like to kill him myself. But what am I to do?'

'I don't see what you can do, but you must come with me, my lady, *please*—'

She was begging. Even as a servant, Catlin had never begged anyone for anything – but this was no respectful request, either. Flying along beside her, Hester smelled the blood before she saw it: the hot, sickly scent of raw meat. A thick, dark red trail lay along the well-scrubbed flagstones. She followed Catlin in silent horror; closer to the kitchen, it was smeared into footprints. She pushed open the heavy oak door, gaining a hurried impression of the familiar iron range, the long table, the neat arrangement of white crockery on the dresser. It was impossible at first to tell who was actually bleeding: Crow, or the tall, hunched figure he was supporting. She let out a small, involuntary noise as she realised the blood was not Crow's after all. Even wounded, the stranger moved with a familiar coltish grace that she couldn't place, his head bowed, black hair dripping on to the flagstones. Her breasts were tingling again and leaking milk; with rising and profound irritation, she felt it soaking into the linen of her nightgown. Arms folded across her chest, she watched in appraising silence as together Crow and the injured young officer stepped unsteadily towards the kitchen table.

'The young sir has been shot, my lady,' Catlin said. 'I thought it best Lord Castlereagh shouldn't know.'

'About what? Who has been shot – who is he?' Hester demanded, pushing away another memory of Castlereagh's smile as he had revealed her nakedness; Crow must never, ever learn of it. Catlin just shook her head. It was quite clear that Crow had slipped into the mode of a soldier, and would take no notice of anyone. He swept an array of terracotta pudding bowls off the table, and they shattered on the flagstones. Next to follow was the remains of the Twelfth Night cake – thick white icing and marchpane exploded like parts of a grenado, scattering cake and fat orange sultanas across the floor.

'Lie down,' Crow ordered the injured man in a tone Hester had only ever heard him use with his brother. The command was quite unnecessary: the young soldier could barely stand. Now face down on the table, he turned his head as gobbets of blood dripped on to the rag rug. Only then did Hester recognise Kitto, no longer a boy, and her vision blurred with tears of shocked relief and joy.

'For God's sake, help me get his jacket and shirt off.' With one bloodstained hand, Crow snatched a flask of brandy from the dresser. As he drank, he met her gaze at last with a kindling, fiery glance that she chose to ignore. One of his arching cheekbones was smeared with blood and rust-brown leaf mould, his black hair stiff with blood. In furious denunciation of Castlereagh's violation, Hester forced herself to shatter an intense desire to shake and then kiss her husband by focusing her attention on his brother. She instantly recognised Kitto's expression: stubborn refusal to submit, precisely the look he'd worn so often as a boy, to no one's benefit. She knew it was costing him every shred of strength he possessed not to cry out in pain, which was just as well, with every bedchamber in the house occupied by a scion of the top ten thousand and the prime minister in an opium-induced waking dream on a chaise in the library.

With a sharp intake of breath, Crow set down the brandy, gripping the edge of the table, and Hester knew it was because his hands would otherwise shake. She took a kitchen knife and began to cut away Kitto's blood-blackened shirt herself. 'Well, you certainly know how to make an entrance,' she said austerely. 'No, don't tell me – I'd rather not hear about the comprehensive tour of London's finest fleshpots you elected over keeping Christmas with your family. How long has it been since we saw you? *A year and a half?*'

'The fleshpots were in Paris, I believe. The rest of the story I mean to have later.' Crow turned to Hester. 'Just trust me, if Castlereagh hears of this, we'll all swing. It needs to look like none of it ever happened.'

'Which will be no trouble at all, with the entire house full of guests and their prying servants!' Even had she capitulated to Castlereagh, it would not have been enough, she knew.

Crow merely raised his eyebrows, and Hester understood it would be useless to question him now: Lord Lamorna had given his orders and merely expected them to be followed. Kitto set his teeth and closed his eyes as she peeled the bloody linen away from his shoulder. Although Kitto had taken an equal share in black hair, pale grey eyes and soot-dark eyelashes, he was surprisingly different to his brother. Even in this wholly shocking and unshaven adult incarnation, and severely injured, there was still a sweetness to his mouth, the *fossette* at his cheek. Just below his shoulder blade, bruising flowered where the musket-ball had penetrated, and his skin was singed in a ring around the entry wound. Thick, dark blood oozed from the wound.

'That ball will have to come out.' Crow selected a long, thin fish knife from the selection Catlin held out, draining on to a clean cloth. Holding it up to the light, he ran the edge of his thumb along the blade. 'Are you ready, boy?'

Kitto made no reply. Hester said tightly, 'He's swooning.'

'*Wait!*'

They both turned, incredulous, to stare at Catlin, who had gone white, and Hester knew she was already imagining being turned out of doors for speaking so to Crow. 'Sir,' Catlin went on, a little breathless. 'Sir, you ought to wash your hands.'

He ignored her, turning to inspect the wound.

'Catlin, what do you mean?' Hester prompted. 'Can't you see we have so little time?'

Catlin shook her head. 'Have you never noticed that babies delivered by washerwomen always thrive, and the mothers don't die so quick, whereas one look at a fancy London doctor with filthy hands and blood all over his apron, and they drop like flies?' As she spoke, addressing Crow's straight back, she ladled steaming water from the pot on the fire into a deep earthenware bowl, then held it out towards him. Turning, expressionless, Crow washed the blood and grime from his hands, drying them on her clean linen cloth. He drank from the brandy flask again and Hester reached across, taking hold of his wrist as he held the knife. 'Will half a pint of cognac make your hand more steady, or less?'

Crow looked up at her, his eyes so pale and stark against his blood-splattered face. Without a word, he waited for her to release his wrist. She knew quite well that he would have killed anyone who threatened to harm her: she'd seen him do it; he would kill Castlereagh here in this house if he ever learned what had just happened in the library. And yet to criticise him in the presence of others was to transgress. How she longed to be alone with him.

Kitto opened his eyes; they were dark with shock and oddly lightless.

'*Now!*' Crow entirely failed to conceal his alarm. 'Catlin, we must do this now.'

Catlin took hold of Kitto's unresisting hand, turning to Hester. 'We're going to need more linen, my lady – quickly—'

Hester backed out of the kitchen, and even as she ran down the narrow, whitewashed passage towards the laundry-room, she heard only horrifying silence. Gasping for breath and trying and failing to piece together what in the world had just happened, she paused in the laundry-room; it was misty with lavender-soap-scented steam rising from a selection of the small nightgowns and napkins that had been set to dry on a rack before the banked-down fire. Hester snatched a folded sheet from a basket resting on the flagstones by the hearth and heard the unmistakable creak of door-hinges. Releasing a strangled, terrified gasp, she froze. Crow, Kitto and Catlin were all in the kitchen. Who, so close to morning, could possibly be coming into the house from the laundry-yard, right through the servants' entrance? Even the earliest-rising kitchen-maid would approach from the attics, not from outside. Hester watched her own shaking hand reach for one of the irons resting by the grate. Her fingers closed around the cold metal as she listened to heavy footfalls. Flattening herself against the wall, she glanced sideways through the doorway and saw the broad-shouldered form of Captain Wentworth of the 11th Northumbrian regiment as he moved towards the kitchen. Just days before she'd handed him a stirrup cup as the hunt gathered on the lawn and had poured his tea in the drawing-room afterwards. Crow had been quite clear on the matter: if Wentworth reached the kitchen, not even he would be able to save them all. Without question, they would hang or be transported.

Hester thought of her child asleep upstairs and set down the basket with quiet precision. She stepped out into the corridor, suddenly overwhelmed by the physical immediacy of Wentworth's as-yet unheeding presence – his grimy scarlet uniform jacket, the grubby white leather of his kit-belts, his shoulders dusted faintly with flakes of dead skin, the sharp scent of his sweat. She brought the iron down on the back of his skull with as much force as she could muster. It wasn't enough. With a strangled shout, he turned to face her and Hester screamed. Wentworth was in no position to reply. Crouching on his haunches, he rocked silently back and forth, clutching his head. His carefully combed fair hair was now thick with dark, oozing blood. Leaving him there, like a child fleeing a broken pie-dish, Hester ran to the kitchen to find no sign of Kitto or Crow, and only Catlin frantically wiping blood from the flagstones by the door.

'He's outside!' Hester gasped, in Cornish. 'Wentworth! He came in through the scullery, Catlin. I hit his head. Keep him downstairs, for God's sake!'

'The ball's out,' Catlin said, quickly. 'His lordship took the boy upstairs. I'll hide the sheets in your bedchamber – I don't believe even Lord Castlereagh or that prying valet of his would dare go in. But I heard the little maid stirring – Beatie Simmens won't be able to keep her quiet for long.'

Hester didn't need to be told. Her breasts were agonisingly full, her nightgown sodden with milk. Clutching her arms around her chest, she ran up the back stairs, hissing, 'I'm coming, I'm coming.' She stepped out on to the polished parquet floor, her ears full of the child's cries, and reached the nursery door just as Beatie opened it from the other side, clutching an angry, squirming bundle.

'Oh, mistress, thank heavens you've come—'

'It's all right, Beatie, just go back to bed for now.' Hester took the warm, damp weight of her daughter and sank into the nursing chair by the window, frantically loosening her nightgown and leaning her head back against the windowsill with relief as her daughter began to suckle. Morwenna's name had come to them both the moment she was born on a sun-soaked Azores morning, still wrapped in the caul. *A sea-maid,* Crow had said, seeing the face of his child for the first time, the old legend of his childhood coming to his lips. *You're alive,* he said to Hester, and for the first time ever she had seen him weep. Smiling and exhausted, relieved that such pain as she'd never known had at last come to an end, Hester had lain back against her pillows and said, *Yes, Morwenna.* A year old and now replete with milk, Lady Morwenna

Helford sank into sleep once more. Her skin was lighter in tone than Hester's, close to white, her eyelashes so long and delicate, and her fine, golden-brown spirals of hair glistened with a faint sheen of almond-oil. Hester kissed her daughter's rounded forehead and handed her back to Beatie.

'Stay in the room, do you understand?' she demanded. Eyes wide, Beatie nodded, and opened her mouth as if to speak. '*No,*' Hester interrupted before she had a chance to begin. 'No questions. Just listen. No matter what you hear, don't open that door to anyone. If anyone tries to come in, take the back stairs and hide in the attics with the child. Will you do that, Beatie? Will you do that for me?'

Beatie nodded, and Hester fled to the door, unable to stay another moment in her daughter's company, knowing it might be their last together. Not half an hour earlier, she'd struck and injured an English officer, and Kitto and Crow had both been covered in blood; Kitto might even have bled to death. She could make no sense of what had happened: it was only clear that all of it was deeply incriminating.

8

Long after they'd given up expecting Kitto to come and keep Christmas with his family, Hester had still been adamant that no guest was to occupy the blue room. Crow silently thanked her now as he let his brother collapse on to the unoccupied bed. Kitto sprawled on his front, stripped to the waist save for the bandages, the wound salved with Catlin's ointment of honey and comfrey. He was here, and for now he still lived, but Crow saw that his face was grey with shock and the inconceivable effort it had taken to stumble back to Nansmornow. Even so injured, the boy had appraised every stand of gorse bushes and every bank of heather as though each might conceal French partisan troops, even though there were none left in Britain. Kitto was a soldier now. He had endured the extraction of the musket-ball in hideous quiet, save his agonised vomiting of bile on to the kitchen flagstones. Crow pushed away memories of a glistening vein twitching deep within the wound that he knew he must not sever lest his brother bleed to death in minutes. God, the sickening relief when his probing finger found the shoulder blade intact, not shattered. With all the instinct of a partisan soldier, Kitto must have started to duck before the shot was fired, the lead ball meeting his flesh with enough force to slam into it, but not pass through him or to strike precious bone. Unable to go any further without a moment of rest, Crow sat in the worn cerulean brocade chair at the side of his brother's bed, watching the frost patterns that had formed on the windowpanes like the shadows of fallen autumn leaves.

Hayl Marya, leun a ras. He silently recited the Cornish prayer, so exhausted that shadows slithered and the edge of the Turkey rug shifted of its own accord. He was getting old; he was losing condition like an under-exercised hunter even as his young brother had become the consummate predator he himself had once been. Kitto's eyes were closed but he was conscious, Crow realised, as well as drenched in sweat. His arm was starting to swell: Crow had not forgotten the vile discomfort of that, although it was better not to think of Waterloo, or the injuries he'd suffered there: shot, sword-hacked, trampled by horses. By rights, he should be dead and his father still the earl; he should not be sitting here beside his brother in their father's place.

Kitto interrupted this maudlin train of thought with painful urgency. 'Oh, Christ,' he said. 'Jack, *Jack—*'

Crow held the basin, just in time.

'Don't let that butcher Dr Bolitho have my arm off,' Kitto said, between heaving and spitting. 'Don't let them, will you?' He was descending into fever already, his dark hair stiff with filth and sweat, his face hot against the pillow. 'You'll look after the whole thing, won't you?'

'Don't worry on that score,' Crow said, trying to forget the amputations he'd witnessed: the tortured clenching of teeth, spurting blood, metal grating against bone. 'Bolitho will come nowhere near this house. Mrs Rescorla will have to tend you unless we want the entire Cabinet to know what you were doing on my land, you bloody young fool.'

'Why couldn't you just stay out of it? As if I needed any help from you.' Carelessly and furiously inaccurate, Kitto spoke into the pillow, his shoulders now rigid with fury and pain in equal measure. 'You crazy bastard. You shot him. You *shot* him. God, you never change.'

Setting down the basin, Crow leaned over to the japanned tray Catlin had put on the bedside table and poured ale into a tin cup. 'Cast aside your scruples and drink this – just a little.' In no mood for insubordination, he eased Kitto into a sitting position and held the the cup to the boy's mouth, taking his weight as he drank. Crow's throat was parched and aching, too – the first physical consequence of a dogfight had always been this almost unbearable thirst. 'There's something I must tell you,' Crow said in Cornish, 'before you hear of it elsewhere.'

Kitto leaned on Crow's arm, looking at him with a distinctly fiery expression. 'If it's that Louisa Burford has spawned a brat, don't bother. I heard of that in Petersburg. No one said it was yours, but I expect they soon will. Is that it? Jesus Christ, Jack, poor Hester. What a perfectly hideous cross for her to bear.'

Crow was unexpectedly floored by the revelation that after the best part of two years at war, Kitto still retained his complete lack of acceptance that the world was harsh and unfair, and likely to remain that way whatever one did. 'Save the dressing-down for when you're feeling more the thing,' he said.

'As if it would make the blindest bit of difference. As if I would even dare, anyway. I should rather face a dozen cuirassiers.' Kitto closed his eyes again as he finished the ale in the cup, and then his anger suddenly receded like a wave on wet sand. 'Jack, it hurts abominably.'

'I know, but you'll be better directly.' Crow fell silent, wanting to tell him it had been a long time not to come home, to not meet his niece. And sooner or later he would have to demand an account of his brother's ill-advised detour via Paris with some French courtesan. Surely Kitto was too inexperienced to be deployed in any sort of manner by the Corps of Guides? And, despite Crow's differences with Wellington, it would have been a matter of honour with the man to have told him. Which could only mean that instead of being sent on an intelligence mission, Kitto had likely been the subject of one.

He looked up, his lips white with pain. 'You can tell Mrs Rescorla that I'm not having any of her concoctions – none of that filthy laudanum.'

Crow took the cup from him and set it back on the tray. 'Oh, naturally.' Easing his brother back on to the pillow, propping him on to his side, he watched him sink into deep unconsciousness, which was scarcely surprising considering his own order to Catlin not to stint on the laudanum in the ale Kitto had just drunk. The door swung open and Catlin herself came in, still in her dressing gown and cap, clinging to a bundle of clean clothing which she dropped on the end of the bed.

'With respect, my lord, but you ought to change that jacket and do it now. Captain Wentworth is downstairs. I can only thank God that I had a moment to push a mop along the passage and across the kitchen floor, there was that much blood. I'm afraid Lady Hester hit him before she realised who it was, but if he'd seen the boy in that state we'd all be on our way to Bodmin gaol.'

Wentworth. That could only mean Crow now had to explain to an upstart of an English soldier why one of his men was dead. Or even why the cargo of a wrecked ship had been stolen from a beach on his own land and hidden in an ancient tunnel, also on his own land. He forced himself up out of the chair and held out a hand to Catlin, taking the jacket she held.

'No shirt?' he asked, coolly. 'This one is pretty well bloodstained.'

Catlin shook her head. 'There was no time to find one, my lord, and I daren't risk waking Mr Hoby. I thought your lordship would say that the fewer who know of all this, the better, no matter how close-mouthed they might be.'

'No, you did right – the shock would finish Hoby anyway,' Crow said, tugging on the close-fitting jacket and buttoning it over his bloodstained shirt and waistcoat. His valet was cut from far more fragile cloth than his housekeeper. He spoke with a lightness he didn't feel, instinctively wishing not to frighten her. Catlin Rescorla had nerves of iron, but she was still a woman under his protection.

'If we rearrange your cravat, I dare say you'll look no more dishevelled than you ought.' Catlin twitched the muslin at his throat with a few deft touches of her blunt, work-worn fingers. 'I left Captain Wentworth in the library – there was still just about a fire, and Lord Castlereagh won't know anything about any of it, believe me.'

'Do what you can with the boy – keep his fever down,' Crow said, glancing at Kitto's sleeping form, forcing himself to sound reasonable and even-tempered. 'It's likely to go badly with him, I fear.' With a brief nod, he turned and made for the door. Running downstairs in the dark, he could only hope Wentworth wouldn't look too closely in the candlelight – he had washed his hands again, but his nails were still black with his brother's blood. Not for the first time. There was, after all, a reason that Kitto had stayed away.

He found Captain Wentworth standing with his back to the fire in the library, and Castlereagh still unconscious on the chaise. Like most men, Wentworth was short enough for Crow to look down on, with the well-fed look of a cherished second son of a minor baronet. Still, Crow was very sure there was more to Wentworth than these obvious parts. It was easy for a man to make his reputation in a theatre of war, less so when one's regiment had been deployed in Britain since Napoleon's brother had been sent running from England. Crow scented in Wentworth the desperation of a man in search of glory. His father would have offered the man port before excoriating him. Crow dispensed with the port.

'I'm extremely sorry about your head, Captain Wentworth. What do you mean by frightening my wife so that she went downstairs alone, in the middle of the night, only to find you coming into the house through the servants' entrance?'

Wentworth opened his mouth and then closed it again. 'I'm surprised that Lady Lamorna is so nervous.'

'Are you?' Crow watched him. Wentworth wilted beneath his gaze, but only a little. Crow took a cigarillo from the case on his desk and leaned across to light it at the candle-flame, smoking and waiting for Wentworth to take aim. He exhaled smoke. 'What is that you actually want, Wentworth, apart from a promotion?'

'I find it odd, my lord, to say the least, that you were out on the night when I am informed all the cargo from the *Deliverance* was stolen. The beach at your very own cove has been picked quite clean.'

'Has it all gone already? People are so unscrupulous.' Crow didn't bother to disguise his boredom. He had faced far worthier opponents than this well-upholstered suckling pig. 'I went to bring home my brother, as it happens. He's dangerously ill, and could travel no further unaccompanied.' Crow smiled, beginning to enjoy himself. 'The rigours of the Russian campaign appear to be catching up with the poor child. He's entirely done in, but I should say he's earned the right to a little recuperation. Not even seventeen, and Wellington has mentioned him in despatches, and of course he got his captaincy after Novgorod – just the start of a long and brilliant military career, one hopes. Will you do me the honour of staying here tonight, Wentworth? The house is rather full, but I'm sure we can find a chaise or a spare attic. Otherwise you may close the door on your way out. I'm afraid that at this extraordinary hour of the night I lack servants. If you'll excuse me, my brother is extremely unwell.'

Wentworth bowed and turned to go. Crow stopped him with a single look. 'Before I forget, I'm afraid I had to kill one of your men.'

Taken off guard, Wentworth stared at him.

'No one can regret it more than I do – except his people, of course, if he has any. We met on the road from Newlyn, and for some reason your man refused to identify himself when I called out. I'm sure you'll agree that in these times one can't be too careful, Captain. You'll find him on the lane near the cove.' Crow was quite sure that nothing in his expression betrayed the half-hour spent running through the wooded valley with a corpse over his shoulder, never sure whether Kitto would still be alive when he returned to him, if the ball fired by Wentworth's man had punctured some vital organ or severed some vein. There had been no choice: it was impossible to risk leaving the body so close to the hidden cargo.

For a moment, Wentworth did nothing but blink behind Crow's skein of cigarillo smoke. Finally, he saluted with one clenched fist held to his forehead, as he was bound to do. 'Very good, Lord Lamorna.' He bowed and walked out of the library, leaving Crow with the slumped, unconscious form of Lord Castlereagh, and Crow knew that England and Cornwall were now at war, if Captain Wentworth of the 11th Northumbrians had anything to do with it.

Leaving Beatie with the child, Hester closed the nursery door, only to find her husband leaning on the wall opposite. Crow stood with a cocked pistol against one shoulder, his hair in wild disarray, his bloodstained shirt half undone, revealing the swirling Otaheitan tattoos on his chest.

'The little maid?' he said, meaning their daughter. Hester had only ever heard him speak their child's name once, on the sunlit morning they had chosen it. And why was the certain knowledge that Morwenna was not his only child so very hard to bear, when every branch of the peerage in Britain budded with children of indeterminate origin?

'She's gone back to sleep,' Hester said, 'praise heaven. What about Kitto? Where's Captain Wentworth?'

'The boy is fevered, but Catlin's with him. Wentworth's on his way back to Newlyn. I asked what the devil he meant by frightening my wife.' Crow's face was tight with tension and dark with new beard, and Hester knew that in his current state of mind he would stand guard outside their daughter's room all day and all night, in his own ancestral hall, unless she stopped him.

'Come,' she said. 'If you're seen like this, we're finished.' He submitted to her and, side by side, they went to her bedchamber. Crow closed the door behind them, leaning on it with his eyes closed again, still holding the pistol. Gently, she took it from him, setting it with practised care on the carved oak blanket chest at the end of the bed. A steaming bowl had been set on her dressing table: Catlin must have brought up the water, and Hester felt a flash of guilt for all the extra work she had been put to. 'You're covered in blood.'

Crossing to the warm water, she soaked the folded cloth lying across the edge of the earthenware bowl and watched as her husband took off his shirt, pulling the ruined fine lawn over his head. Stripped now to the waist, he reached out, tucking a stray spiral of hair behind her ear before taking the steaming cloth. She let out a long, shuddering breath, watching as he wiped the blood from his tattooed belly and chest, and praying that Crow would never know Lord Castlereagh had touched her as though she were a whore. Letting out a brief, exhausted sigh, Crow bent low to kiss her; he carried with him a faint aroma of cucumber and mint shaving water, dizzying when mingled with his own faint, salty scent. She couldn't help pulling away. *No,* she told herself, furious. *Don't let Castlereagh do that. Don't let him spoil this.*

'I'm sorry,' Crow said, not understanding, because how could he? 'I'm so sorry about Louisa's child.'

Louisa's child; your child. She took the warm cloth in her own hands, watching bloodied, still-steaming water drip down the illustrated expanse of his lean torso. There was so much Hester knew she must find a way of telling him, but she couldn't see her way to doing it. She spoke without looking up at him: 'Crow, what have you done?'

He laid his hand over hers, one of the richest men in Britain, with an iron-hard grip on trade going out of every Cornish port, and fifty mines still seamed with tin while English coffers were empty after years of bloody and expensive conflict with France. Warm water trickled through their entwined fingers as he looked down at her. 'I killed the English soldier who shot my brother.' And Hester knew that here was the start of yet another war.

9

Two days later, Hester was arranging early narcissi, hellebore and freesias in the stillroom with Catlin and two of the young maidservants when Dorothea Lieven came in. At a single glance from Catlin, all three servants curtseyed and left, making for the scullery. It was said that Dorothea's influence spread far beyond the ballrooms and drawing-rooms of Mayfair. She was as much of a Russian emissary as her husband: the tsar himself tasked her with the most delicate of diplomatic missions, soothing fractious relationships between those who mattered in the English government as much as in the Russian court.

She smiled with all her usual assurance. 'Oh, please don't allow me to interrupt you, Hester darling. In fact, I know just what it's like when one has reached the tail-end of a house party, and one only wants to be alone, frankly, so I'm sorry to intrude on all your quiet. But may I join you, all the same?'

Hester gestured at the heap of greenery and pale petals tumbled across the scrubbed wooden tabletop. 'Of course. But please let me call my housekeeper back, and she'll bring you something. Some tea?'

'Oh no. I really do know how it is with so many guests – I couldn't possibly trouble your woman any further. Indeed I'm sorry for hurrying her away from the sort of job that just allows one to sit down for five minutes, especially with sickness in the house.'

'Not at all.' Mildly surprised that a cosseted daughter of Baltic German nobility brought up by the Russian tsar's own mother should possess even the concept of an overworked servant, Hester picked up a spray of narcissi; there was a fire licking at the grate with tongues of bright flame, and the warmth in the room had brought out the scent of the flowers.

'How is dear young Captain Helford?' Dorothea went on, stripping fresh green fronds from a curling branch of ivy. 'Weren't we fortunate that it wasn't an infectious disorder, with so many people in the house?' She laughed. 'Only think, you might have finished the entire Cabinet with a single dose of typhus. No doubt the papers would call it a plot.'

'Indeed,' Hester said lightly. 'Kitto is much better, thank you. Young men do so often succumb to feverish complaints after the rigours of campaigning, and then of London with their friends. We're thankful it seems nothing more serious than that.'

Dorothea spoke without looking up from the tangle of ivy in her hands. 'Well, he's been quite the sensation in Petersburg, as I'm sure you'll know. It was exactly the same when your husband was first on the town in London – I remember it very well.'

Hester knew she hadn't quite managed to conceal her surprise at that first revelation. Kitto rarely wrote to his brother, except for stiff, formal notes to request an advance upon his allowance or to announce his survival after the Siege of Novgorod or the victorious but punishing retreat from Grezhny in which so many men had died. Even her own letters from him were few and far between, and limited to commonplace remarks about the Russian princess whose foot he had trodden on as she taught him the mazurka, and the blood sausage he'd spent an afternoon bartering for in some remote outpost, only to cut it open and find a nest of dead flies. He often sent her his watercolours and sketches, though: the latest had been *Countess N. Pushkina*, a charcoal and pastel portrait of a woman in her middle forties, with quite as much obvious African ancestry as Hester herself – Kitto's way of telling her that she was not alone in the world, she supposed. She pictured him on the stairs here at Nansmornow as a confiding nine-year-old when she'd been a sea captain's daughter and a guest of his father, and he was all tousled black hair and grass-stained linen, and neither of them had ever imagined that they would one day be related. *Miss Harewood, I know you'll want to see my tadpoles. They're all so particularly interesting.*

'You're so quiet, Hester.' Dorothea twined a strand of ivy around one fingertip. 'One has no wish to pry, of course, but am I right in sensing a rift between Lord Lamorna and his brother?'

Hester hesitated. Dorothea saw too much, and would easily find a way of using any such information to the benefit of Russia. She herself was only too well aware that Kitto and Crow were scarcely speaking to one another, and that Crow's usual energy and decisiveness of movement were now interspersed with long periods of standing in silent contemplation at the window whenever he thought he was alone. Hester knew just how much Kitto loathed his former stepmother, and could only guess at the temperature of his feelings now he knew his brother had fathered her child, but by the same token Crow had killed an English soldier to save not only Kitto's life but his reputation, and that was the least of the unmentionable history between them. In his own infuriating fashion, Crow had rebuffed her every attempt to discuss this frigid stalemate – and Dorothea's interest in it must at all cost be diverted.

In the end, she chose her words with care. 'My husband is eleven years Kitto's senior, and you must recall that he was absent for most of Kitto's life, first at sea under my father's command, and then later in the army. They have no shared childhood, and it's very difficult to remain on the sort of pedestal on which an unhappy child will place a glamorous older brother seen only occasionally. Lord Lamorna became Kitto's guardian at a trying time, and when he was at a particularly trying age.'

'Oh, I do understand,' Dorothea said. 'Too old to really enjoy being a child, and too young to go on the town, with a fit of the sullens every five minutes. The army is really the best place for youths of that age, when education is not a possibility.'

'I entirely agree.' Hester wondered just how much Dorothea knew about Kitto: he'd been expelled from Eton, and then almost hanged twice during the French Occupation for insurrection against the Napoleonic authorities then in control. Yes, Kitto had been more than capable of the youthful fits of melodrama Dorothea spoke of – slamming doors and hostile speechlessness – but he'd also been equally adept at laying gunpowder. Hester smiled. 'I'm happy to hear he's been a success in St Petersburg, although I confess it's hard to imagine him in a ballroom. In my mind, he's still collecting grasshoppers and keeping ants in a bottle.'

'Well, if they can be brought to discussion, Lord Lamorna

might wish to drop a hint in Captain Helford's ear about Countess Tatyana Orlova,' Dorothea said, now looking directly across the table at Hester. 'She's quite the Petersburg society hostess, but one does hear that some of her closest associates have links to the Green Lamp. I've known her for years, of course – we were educated at the convent together – and Tatyana's star is so ascendant at the moment that no gossip seems able to touch her, but these things can change so rapidly.'

'The Green Lamp?' Hester let the question hang between them.

'A most insalubrious organisation – poets and silly, romantic young revolutionaries questioning the power of the tsar himself,' Dorothea went on. 'I do realise that in England you are still without a monarch, and that parliament exercised some powers here even before Napoleon's fool of a brother executed the regent, but you must understand that in Russia even the mildest hint of such views is abhorrent. The tsar rules as our father, but the Green Lamp question the legitimacy of his power at every turn. If it were only emancipation of the serfs they wanted, one might reason with them – as if we could survive without indentured labour in a country the size of Russia! – but more than that, it's said they plan to actually kill the tsar.'

Hester picked up a spray of narcissi, examining the pale petals, wondering how Dorothea dared speak so lightly of serfdom to the daughter of a man who had been enslaved. 'Honestly, please rest assured that Kitto hasn't a political bone in his body, but I'll speak to my husband.' It was simply too dangerous to discuss Kitto with a woman of Dorothea's unusual insight: she'd spent the best part of twenty years as the wife of a diplomat, watching men and women smile and lie to one another. Hester continued without looking up from her narcissi. 'Actually, I'm glad to have you alone, Dorothea – in all these weeks, we haven't yet had the opportunity to speak privately. I'm quite aware that your intervention made matters a great deal easier when Crow and I were in town for the Little Season before Christmas. In truth, you contrived to make me sought out rather than only tolerated and gossiped about. You should know that I've actually no wish to be pursued by society, but the fact is I can't escape my husband's position. So I want to thank you for making something I'm unable to avoid marginally less unpleasant. And the fact is that any social success I meet with now, regardless of how little I care for it or wish it for myself, will certainly make life easier for my daughter in fifteen years' time.'

Dorothea looked up from arranging a trio of white hellebore in a pewter bowl of water, accepting the change of subject without flinching. 'You know, Hester, when one is in the sort of social position I've contrived for myself, one gets used to dishonesty. It's refreshing to be simply told the truth, and you're wise to think of your daughter. Are you really dreading the Season to come? We'll all shortly be in London, will we not?'

'Will we?' Hester countered.

'You know, in Russia you would be far less remarkable,' Dorothea said, sidestepping her question. 'You must have heard of our most promising young poet? Pushkin's great-grandfather was an Abyssinian Moor adopted by Peter the Great, and Alexei's African ancestry is quite clear to look at him and his mother, although far less so with his siblings. Nevertheless, they were all brought up at court.'

'I've heard of him, of course,' Hester said, 'although I don't doubt this black but socially acceptable poet has been made to suffer in ways you may find hard to imagine, and his mother before him. But that isn't what you came to talk to me about, is it? We could, after all, have discussed your Pushkin or even Kitto in the drawing-room with everyone else.'

Dorothea smiled. 'Oh, indeed. We are only women, Hester, and as such we may discuss the sort of affairs of real interest to me in privacy, or not at all. Soon I do think we will all be in London for the start of the Season proper, but there's something I wish you to consider in the meantime.'

'And what's that?' Hester added a tendril of ivy to an arrangement of narcissi and freesias, leaning back in her seat to judge the effect.

'Your husband,' Dorothea said. 'We all know the fact is that he controls every port in Cornwall, and his lands are rich in tin – for now. But even without the Lamorna mineral wealth, one has to wonder how much you stand to gain from allying yourselves solely to England.'

Hester looked down at the narcissi in her hands. 'Well, if we're to be political, where will Russia's allegiances ultimately lie, Dorothea? To Britain as a whole, or to Napoleon and France?'

Dorothea adjusted the position of a fragrant spray of lily of the valley. 'France is still strong under Napoleon even now he's been expelled from England, true. He's a threat to Russia, plain and simple. But the simple fact is that although Britain claims to be our natural ally, all Britain really wants is control of Russian trading routes to the east, right through the Ottoman ports and into India. Your troops came to our aid at Grezhny and Novgorod, but at what cost? What price will be demanded in the future?' Dorothea twined another strand of ivy between her fingertips. 'Martha Mulgrave was quite right when she said that Castlereagh is only waiting for a reason to destroy Lord Lamorna completely. The question your husband must ask, Hester, is whether England is his most beneficial partner these days. His wisest ally? Or would he be better off serving Cornish interests alone?'

Hester smiled. 'Cornish and Russian interests entwined together, I presume?' She glanced up at the clock above the mantelpiece. 'It's gone half past four. We really ought to dress for dinner, Dorothea.'

10

A week later and well into February, sweet white cyclamen were in flower along the carriage drive at Nansmornow and Kitto lay still fevered on the chaise in the library, his eyes half closed. It was late afternoon, and the curtains had not yet been drawn. Immediately outside the mullioned window, frozen parkland spread beyond the hard-shorn form of a hydrangea, and with the wind in this quarter, he heard the far-off rhythm of waves crashing against the cliffs. Even so close to the fire, he was alternately freezing and sweating, and the wound in his shoulder throbbed with a dull, relentless ache. He watched the door open and Crow came in with Count Lieven, both still dressed for shooting, Crow in their father's old tweed jacket, the Russian ambassador grey-haired and flushed from the cold outside.

'All I ask is that you use your common sense, Lamorna,' he said, and Kitto wondered how on earth the man could have known Crow for so long and still expect anything like it. Lieven seemed about to say more before he noticed Kitto in the candlelit gloom.

'Save your machinations, sir, unless you wish to edify my brother with them,' Crow said carelessly. 'Perhaps we can go at it again over champagne before supper?'

'One day, Jack,' Lieven said, 'it's just possible that you might learn a little humility, and the worth of valuing your friends.' He turned and left, closing the door behind him with a sharp snap. Crow poured himself a glass of brandy from the decanter on his desk, drained it, and then walked over to the chaise and rested his hand on Kitto's forehead.

'Dear God, you ought still to be in bed, but then you'd be deprived of the pleasure of seeing me comprehensively put in my place by our father's friends. That arm should still be in a sling.'

'Mrs Rescorla said I'd do as well to try without.' Kitto sat up. 'I'm damned bored of staying in bed. I'll go, though. The house is so infernally full of people.' The room spun around him as he stood, ready to leave.

Crow lazily tilted his glass, holding it up to the light. 'If I thought you were intruding you wouldn't still be here. Sit. There is only so long we can circle each other like a pair of spitting alley cats, as Hester puts it. I want to talk to you. I heard that you brought twenty of your regiment back to Petersburg alive after Novgorod,' he said, 'that you walked with them for more than a hundred miles through French occupied territory instead of riding like an officer. *Sit.*'

Kitto obeyed: he had been expecting censure, not this – the closest his brother was likely to get to praise, not that anyone would have guessed it. 'We had to eat my horse,' he said, wondering who had told him, even as he did his best to ignore a vivid memory of the wide-open hazel eyes of the young French artillery officer he'd stepped across in frozen mud. He forced himself to look out of the window at the darkening parkland as a flock of starlings rose up, tossed in an easterly wind. 'Are you expecting someone?'

Crow had a disarming habit of occasionally treating pretension with amusement rather than hauteur. He didn't smile, but there was a particular expression in his eyes. He went to his seat at the desk before answering. 'Nathaniel Edwards and Mr Gloyne.'

'An Gostel? You can't be serious. Surely it's not safe to receive the resistance here?' Kitto hadn't spoken Cornish, his first language, since joining the army but somehow it was easier to say what he meant when he did, especially to Crow. 'Castlereagh and the others suspect you enough as it is: if you think Captain Wentworth's satisfied with that story about only firing after the fellow refused to identify himself, you're way out. *You killed an Englishman in the woods.*' And Crow had done it for him, to save his life, his reputation.

'Never mind that. What do you know of the Green Lamp?' Crow leaned forward in his chair; he lit a cigarillo from the candle, looking up at Kitto with an expression he recognised from his earlier youth, and which told him he was about to find it impossible to lie to his brother.

'One hears rumours, that sort of thing. Poets and dissidents. The tsar used to talk of freeing the serfs, but now all that's been forgotten. For my own part, I don't see how they can go on the way they are without revolution – not in a country that stretches from Europe to China and most of the population not even free.'

'And I trust you haven't said such a foolish thing to anyone, here or in Russia?'

'Of course not!'

'Then I also trust that if I tell you Countess Tatyana Orlova has rumoured links to the Green Lamp, then you will ensure that you have no remarkable connection with her?'

Kitto forced himself not to flinch. Sometimes it really was as if Crow saw all, and knew all. ‘She hosts half the balls in Petersburg – what do you wish me to do, never to go out?’

Crow poured another glassful of brandy and got up again, moving with the lazy, restless grace of a cat waking from sleep on a sunny windowsill; he could never be content for long. ‘I leave you to be the judge of that. But if I hear the slightest rumour of any connection between you and anyone involved in the Green Lamp, I will have you not only out of Russia, but out of the army entirely. You know, of course, that I can and I will do this, and that any such rumour reaches me quickly, even here. I'm sure you realise that this is not all I have to say to you, either. There is the matter of your trip to Paris.’

Kitto had not survived the filthiest campaign since Borodino only to wait in humble silence for one of Crow's blistering reprimands. ‘You're the worst hypocrite I've ever met, you do realise that, don't you? Saying that, and then receiving the Cornish resistance in here with most of the English Cabinet staying, and half society's worst gossips? You've got some nerve.’

‘My God, so have you, indeed,’ Crow remarked, and Kitto felt it would be beneath his dignity to reply. At a knock, the door opened, and Nathaniel Edwards came in with Mr Gloyne, who ran the circulating library in Penzance and had always seemed to Kitto to be the most unlikely revolutionary, with his old-fashioned tricorn and the same faded embroidered waistcoat he had worn for ever. Both removed their hats in Crow's presence, and each directed a swift, questioning glance at Kitto, answered by Crow with a nod. He was to stay: to Gloyne and Edwards he was still no more than a child, but for now Crow had decided that he was a man, and could listen.

Mr Gloyne accepted a glass of brandy with a nod of thanks. 'Your lordship will be pleased to know all cargo retrieved from the *Deliverance* safely reached Birmingham.'

'Good,' Crow said. 'Where it was then swiftly and efficiently fenced, I trust?'

Mr Gloyne nodded. 'The funds have been distributed across the usual channels, my lord.' He glanced at Kitto. 'It was a risky venture, if you don't mind my saying, even if it did end well. God knows we need what money we can lay our hands on when half the duchy villages are starving under English rule, but if that coin's seen to touch Lord Lamorna, we'll all suffer for it. The English government needs to think your brother really neutral, Captain Helford. They're suspicious enough of him as it is.'

Kitto said nothing, but the room seemed to spin around him – bookshelves, those so-familiar oil-painted landscapes in heavy gilded frames. It wasn't only the lingering fever, he knew. Yes, it had been a crime to help steal the *Deliverance*'s cargo, but it was one thing to assist starving and desperate Cornishwomen, and quite another to engage in deliberate and premeditated insurrection against England amidst a war with France. In truth, he had come home after all this time to find himself commissioned as an officer in an army at war against his own brother, who had the nerve to order him to beware of his acquaintances in Petersburg.

'Are you even actually loyal to anyone at all except to the notion of wringing as much profit from this situation as you possibly can?' Kitto demanded.

'Have you quite done?' Crow asked calmly. 'You might have a fever, but if you annoy me enough, you'll know about it. And you do begin to.'

'Don't be hard on the boy, I beg you, my lord,' Nathaniel Edwards said, not understanding anything at all. 'It's thanks to the captain we got away as we did – we were lucky he chanced on us. I was loath to go with the women, but go they would. I might have been little enough use, as the captain knows, but it seemed wrong to let the maids attempt to retrieve all that cargo alone. Things are come to such an evil pass in duchy-owned Cornwall that there seemed little choice. Castlereagh has filled it with either English landlords or men like Boscobel – new money, who'd do anything to join the aristocratic set, and see their tenants as little better than animals.'

'All the same, be very careful,' Crow said. 'Let no one gather in the streets. It's far too dangerous at the moment.' He lit another cigarillo, blowing out tendrils of smoke. 'For my own part, neither Wentworth nor even Lord Castlereagh will meddle any further while they still wish me to suppress all insurrection, but Captain Wentworth hates Cornwall, and he hates the Cornish. Do you think Castlereagh wouldn't sanction calling in the captain's men to take action against even the smallest perceived threat, and do you think he would not obey?'

'I'm in agreement with you, my lord,' Mr Gloyne said. 'An Gostel will remain quiet this while, at least. But with everyone from Scilly to the Tamar calling you King of Cornwall, your honour, I'm afraid there'll be trouble no matter how much care we all take.'

Mr Gloyne and Nathaniel Edwards bowed their way out, leaving Crow and Kitto alone again.

'You should be careful!' Kitto said, standing again despite the fact that the fever sent the room spinning around him like a child's top, Crow was the head of this family and still his guardian: he had really no right to offer his opinion on any matter whatsoever. 'You think that no one can touch you, but you're wrong.'

'And you're commissioned into the British army,' Crow said, watching him with what appeared to be little more than cold detachment. 'You'd be better off having nothing to do with the King of Cornwall, you know. Go back to bed and keep the spleen to yourself – all things considered, it would have been better had you continued with the melodrama of your self-imposed exile, would it not?'

Always, there was a sting. Kitto watched him with a sudden, breathless rage. 'I couldn't agree more. One has to go quite a long way to stay out of your shadow. But I suppose you think I can still be made to obey your every command, even though you're well on the way to being a gazetted traitor?'

Crow only smiled. 'Oh, I'm quite sure of that.'

Summoning all his strength, his head aching abominably, Kitto got up and walked out, leaning on the door as he closed it behind him. He couldn't help thinking of the linen-wrapped, wriggling bundle Hester had brought to his bedside, the cannon-ball round head covered with a pale green knitted cap, the fat wrists and dark, liquid eyes, a child born to face obstacles Crow no doubt refused to even consider. He wondered if Crow's daughter would share his own ability to make her father entirely lose control of his temper.

11

Several days later, Hester stood at the open door of the nursery, leaning on the doorframe. Morwenna was sitting in her bath before the fire, and Beatie stood at the dresser, folding nightgowns, shifts and small knitted caps, watching Kitto sprawl on the floor as he leaned against the faded cherry-striped chaise beneath the window. He sat with his long legs spread out before him, crossed at the ankle, just as Crow did. He held a ball, pretending to throw it to Morwenna, and then tossed it high into the air as she laughed.

'You'll have her splashing half the bathwater on to the floor, your honour,' Beatie said, looking more at peace than Hester had ever seen her.

'Oh good Lord, don't be so stuffy, Beats,' Kitto said lightly, and Hester realised that he must have roamed Nantewas with Beatie as a child, quite disregarded by his father in the days when no respectable female servant would have set foot at Nansmornow. The loyalty of local families to the Lamornas had not stretched to allowing their daughters to be dishonoured by serving in such a household as Crow and Kitto's father had kept for so long. Kitto looked up at Hester with this new restlessness of his and she remembered how, even just two years before, he might have been so absorbed in sketching the seeds of a gourd that he wouldn't have noticed a piano concerto with full orchestral accompaniment. He smiled – that at least hadn't changed – and tossed the ball to Morwenna so that it splashed in front of her, throwing up bright beads of water that clung in the soft, fine curls of her hair.

'Het, tell Beatie Simmens that she is not to force Mrs Rescorla's revolting tisanes upon me.'

'I'm sure I should never do such a thing, my lady,' Beatie said, ducking her head to hide a smile of her own.

'You may leave us, Beatie,' Hester said. 'Mrs Rescorla tells me you haven't yet had your tea. I'll take the child out of the bath myself – she'll soon want me to feed her, anyway.'

Still failing to hide her smile, Beatie dropped a little curtsey and went out of the servants' door set into the wainscoting. When she had gone, and there was no longer a need to maintain the appearance of dignity, Hester sat on the floor beside Kitto and caught the ball, tossing it to Morwenna herself who began thoughtfully to chew it.

'And do you make all the young servants fall in love with you, Christopher Helford?' Hester went on, in French, so that there was no way Beatie or any other servant passing in the passage might understand.

Kitto flushed, leaning his head against her shoulder. 'I've known Beatie for ever, Hets.'

'That only makes it worse, you silly boy. Be careful. I must admit this was the last place I expected to find you – a young soldier at home on leave when everyone else has been out shooting. You're still not feeling altogether well, are you?'

'Trust me, I'll likely get enough shooting when my leave is over – Marshal Davout is still manoeuvring around Russia like a terrier looking for a fight, don't forget. There'll be plenty of fun and games for me before the year is out.' Kitto laughed again as Morwenna threw the ball at him, leaving a watery trail across the ancient waxed floorboards, and Hester passed him the tissue-wrapped packet she had been holding.

'It's your Twelfth Night present,' she said. It had been sitting on the edge of the wash-stand in Crow's bedchamber for weeks, an unspoken presence.

Kitto flushed again. 'I'm sure I don't deserve one.'

'Why should you think of presents for your ageing family while you disport yourself in Paris? *Paris!* I don't know how you had the nerve. When I think of the silk alone, never mind the gloves, I could honestly crown you, Kitto.' Hester smiled because Kitto was irresistible in his rare moments of penitence, but surely Crow must speak to him about escorting some young person of compromised virtue right into the heart of enemy territory, in the middle of a war?

'You're not ageing *that* much.' He folded back the tissue revealing a medal of St Christopher struck from Cornish gold. He had the hands of a horseman now, she noticed, his long fingers tanned by wind and sun. He kissed her dutifully and she hung the medal around his neck, endowing him with the blessing of the patron saint of all travellers as she clasped the fine golden chain.

'Crow had it commissioned, you know.'

Kitto looked away, the gold glinting against the white of his shirt. He rolled the ball back to Morwenna, who gripped the sides of the bath with her small, fat hands and began to caw like a young rook. 'I'll take her out,' Kitto said, 'you'll only get your gown wet. Yes, little maid, I'm coming.' Facing Morwenna with the firm, unthinking confidence of one who had grown up handling the young of most creatures in the

Lamorna Valley, from chickens and lambs to squalling, ash-smudged babies crawling too near the hearth, Kitto lifted his niece out of the bath and folded her into the linen towel spread along the chaise, and Hester's eyes scalded with unexpected tears. Soon he would be going back to Russia, and he might never ride with Morwenna too fast along the beach, or come up to the schoolroom to show her how to paint the interior parts of a ripe, sweet-smelling quince, or lead her down a dance in a London ballroom when inevitably there would be whispered jibes about her grandfather, who had been born enslaved on a Jamaican plantation and died a captain in the British navy.

'Here!' Kitto thrust Morwenna into her arms, a struggling bundle of linen and strong, angry small limbs. 'Don't be maudlin, Hets.' And then his expression changed completely, the smile quite vanishing from his eyes, and Hester turned to see Crow leaning in the doorway; he had already dressed for dinner, and his hair was wet. He was holding three glasses of champagne.

'Can we drink,' he said in Cornish, 'to the fact that all of our guests will be gone by the end of the week, praise be? *Meur ras dhe Dhuw.*'

Hester settled with Morwenna into the nursing chair, and Crow set the glass down on the window-ledge beside her; as ever, she was so very aware of the heat of his presence. He glanced at Kitto. 'Are you certain you're quite well enough to dine downstairs? MacArthur won't thank me for sending you back to him in a mess.'

Kitto lifted his glass in silent obedience, addressing Crow with rigid politeness. 'By your leave, I'll go and dress, sir.'

Crow raised his eyebrows, watching him go, and then dropped on to the chaise, lying back, managing not to spill any of his champagne. 'Oh dear,' he said, turning his head to look at her. 'I'm still relegated to the doghouse. I'm a dangerous traitor, apparently. He's really not yet learned to see any grey between the black and the white.'

'You must talk to him about Paris. He could even be accused of espionage.' Hester looked down at Morwenna as she suckled; she felt the tingling rush of the milk as it let down. 'You don't think he's been drawn into anything like that, do you? He's so young. What more has he said to you?'

'Nothing,' Crow said. 'It's my guess he escorted a courtesan back to France who no doubt told him she had been most cruelly used. It's one of the oldest tricks there is, but I doubt he told the girl anything her paymasters at the French court found particularly useful. Don't exercise yourself about it.' He closed his eyes again, letting the glass of champagne hang loosely between his fingertips.

'John,' Hester said, unable to quite suppress an odd little shudder of unease. 'John, but you must speak to him about it, all the same.'

'Oh, we began to,' Crow said, his eyes lingering on Morwenna. 'He read me a homily of his own – you would have been proud of my restraint at that moment, let me tell you.'

'But going to Paris? It was an unbelievably foolish thing for him to have done. The outcome might not be so harmless another time.'

He sat up then, and looked at her. 'Do you really believe I don't know it? Trust me, Kitto thinks himself above paying any heed to whatever I might have to say. He isn't and will soon learn as much, but when we have that discussion they'll hear it in Nantewas. He and I are due a reckoning, but it must wait until this place is free of prying eyes.'

'Very well, I suppose that makes sense,' she said carefully. He leaned back against the arm of the chaise and closed his eyes again. She could not help thinking they would all be better served if he and Kitto were simply capable of holding a difficult conversation without shouting at each other or worse, and yet he was her husband and she owed him her obedient acquiescence, or at least the appearance of it. He was the head of this household, and she must deploy her challenges to his authority with care. And before they dined tonight, there was another challenge to mount. *You'll have to choose your battles wisely, with such a one as that,* Catlin had told her, and she'd been right.

'You know very well that despite everything, he would still ride into the heart of an erupting volcano for you.' Hester watched her husband as Morwenna suckled.

'My love, so poetic.' With his eyes closed, Crow didn't move; he was still speaking in Cornish. 'Just a little while more: it'll be such a pleasant change to converse over the supper-table without fear of inadvertently condemning oneself to death on the scaffold by some chance comment.'

'Dorothea came to find me in the stillroom again,' Hester said. Surely there must be a way for them both to navigate this assembled court of vipers? 'She thinks you're a great fool for being rude to Count Lieven. He made you a sensible proposition.'

'I'm never rude,' Crow said. 'But what would you have me do, ally myself to a vast empire with ambitions of which we know nothing? My love, all I can do is pray that Vansittart and the others grow to see Castlereagh for what he is: a fanatic. And then perhaps we'll be left alone.'

Hester sipped her champagne and looked down at her suckling daughter's bee-stung lips, but she could not shake off her certainty that both she and Crow had each played their cards unwisely.

12

They were twenty for supper that night at Nansmornow, and Lord Castlereagh's wife Emily Stewart languorously signalled to Crow's footman for the dish of spiced venison. She had taken more champagne than she could hold with any dignity, and was leaning heavily against Crow's shoulder. If he were to get up to piss, she'd fall off her chair. He breathed in the chopped-onion tang of her underarm sweat, wishing her at Jericho. Hester was at the foot of the table, in cheerful conversation with Admiral Blake, who had been a friend of her father's and was one of the few people in the room who could look her in the eye. All he could do was observe the shape of his wife's smile down the length of the table, her beautiful, generous mouth, and the loose spiral of hair that grazed her naked collar-bone, wishing himself in the place of the heavy embroidered wrap draped around her shoulders.

Emily Stewart leaned close again, and Crow felt the boneless weight of her upper body against his arm. 'It does rather seem as though you might want to keep an eye on your young brother, my lord. Our incorrigible Dorothea has unsheathed her claws. He's so pale after his illness – doubtless that only makes him more fascinating.'

She was right on both counts: the Russian ambassador's wife was sitting to Kitto's left; Dorothea spoke quietly, leaning close to him, letting the tip of one long, elegant finger rest on the rim of his glass.

Crow turned to look down at her, vowing to later advise Dorothea to leave his brother out of her scheming. 'I take it as a compliment, Emily. She's a connoisseur.'

She smirked. 'Enjoying Russian pleasures is something of a family tradition, isn't it? Judging by what I remember of that summer in 1812, which admittedly isn't much, darling Dasha taught you a thing or two as well.' She leaned closer still, creating an illusion of an intimacy between them. 'Do you know, Dorothea and I tossed a coin the night you walked into Sally Jersey's drawing-room with your father, all those years ago. Young Lord Crowlas: you caused quite the stir that season – the prodigal, runaway son of Beau Lamorna, home on leave from the navy and unleashed upon London for the first time. I was quite furious with Dorothea for winning you in our little wager.'

Crow didn't reply: forcing confidences in such a way was so impossibly ill bred that even his father wouldn't have censured him for refusing to listen to them.

Undeterred, Emily went on. 'It's so amusing to think how that wild young Lord Crowlas now has all these many responsibilities. An earldom.' She glanced down the table at Hester. 'A most unusual wife, and a precious child – one can barely tell the dear little thing is coloured, I assure you, and I'm sure it'll be an easy matter to keep her out of the sun. How sad that Captain Wentworth doesn't join us tonight – I must admit I find it perfectly shocking that the criminals who stole all that wrecked cargo have never been brought to justice.'

'Who knows?' Crow said coolly, noticing with grim pleasure that she dared not mention Louisa Burford's child, or not to him, at least. 'Perhaps that's exactly why Wentworth and his young lieutenant refused my wife's invitation this evening.' He was quite unable to suppress a rising need to fight or flee, even though there was no visible enemy, no visible danger. And yet the doors and the windows were all unguarded, he knew. The house was not secure. He was failing in his duty. Battle-ready, a tingling rush soared up and down his lower arms, all the way down to his fingertips and, as he watched, Wentworth's men burst in through the carved wooden double doors, a bright rush of red coats. Crow hauled himself up on to the table and over it, scattering carafes, splashing claret and champagne, silver chargers tumbling. He pushed past Lord Sidmouth and the rector's oldest daughter, who watched him in slack-jawed silence, her shining forehead rippling with a crop of red acne. He swept the books off the shelf and took up the pistol concealed behind the six leather-bound volumes of Livy – it was always kept loaded and primed, and he turned to the door, ready to fire.

'My lord?'

Still in his seat – in reality, he had never moved from it – Crow turned to face Emily again, who was still smiling at him with what she clearly hoped was a coquettish air. He was aware of Kitto and Hester now watching him from the far end of the table, Kitto frowning a little, Hester with the expressionless glance that meant she would ask leading questions when they were alone. They had noticed that particular expression on his face: they knew how he looked when he saw things that were not there, but seemed as real as his own hand held before his face. Sweat seeped down his back, and the room filled once again with competing voices, the clatter of fork against plate. Hester had turned back to Lord Vansittart on her right, but Kitto was still watching him. Crow ignored his brother, draining his glass of claret and wishing it was brandy, wishing he was so drunk that it didn't matter if he saw and did things that were not real. And yet why could he not shake this sense of deep disquiet, an instinct had never failed him in the past?

'My darling boy, do you not attend?' Emily traced a line along the side of his wrist with one finger, and he suppressed a shudder. 'Lord Sidmouth and I were just asking if you think the princess royal will reply to my husband's latest begging letter. It seems so ridiculous that we're still without a king or queen, and she won't take up her birthright. What on earth can she want with that tiny foreign duchy now that her husband is dead, and her son the duke? We'll end as a republic, at this rate. You and Wellington might have rid us of the French, but still we have no king or queen.'

'Neither the duke nor I can take credit for expelling the Occupation. For that you may thank every last British soldier who trained for months in North America only to fight and die at Salisbury.' Crow turned his glass in the candlelight, watching the flames reflected in the carved lead crystal. 'There is no princess royal,' he said. 'Princess Charlotte has been Duchess of Württemberg for more than twenty years. For four of those twenty years, her husband was loyal to Napoleon. Unquestionably, Charlotte has the experience and wisdom we'd all welcome in a monarch – it would be a pleasant change – but whether the people will accept her is another matter.'

'The question on my mind is Russia,' said the rector, flushed with too much claret. 'We took Novgorod and Grezhny from Napoleon and as good as presented them to the damned

Emperor Alexander on a plate, and yet still the man hasn't formally declared his allegiance. What do you say to that, sir?'

The rector was not only talking across the table, which in itself made Crow wish to close his eyes on the whole affair, but to top that he was addressing the Russian Ambassador to the Interim Government of Great Britain.

Count Lieven spoke with all the exhaustion of his forty-four years. 'Naturally, Russia seeks only the most profitable of partnerships with your country. But such things are complicated. Sadly so.'

'It makes a mockery of the efforts of our fine young men, if I may say so,' the rector said, and three seats away his eldest daughter flushed down to her décolletage. He turned to Kitto. 'What do you make of all this, young Helford? You were at Novgorod, Grezhny and Vibetsk, hard won from the French in all cases, and yet still this tin-pot emperor refuses to make his loyalties clear, receiving French diplomats in St Petersburg, so we hear.'

'I'm just a soldier, sir,' Kitto said. 'I only go where I'm told and do what I'm told.' He was learning sense.

But as Crow watched, Lord Castlereagh turned smiling to his brother and Crow found that he could not breathe. 'Enough of Russia. Let's turn back to our own shores. After all, we've been without a monarch for so long. Who would you have as our king or queen, Captain Helford?'

Kitto set down his fork. 'Whoever my brother says should be king or queen, my lord.'

Lord Castlereagh raised his eyebrows, soliciting a ripple of manufactured laughter from those sitting closest to him. 'And are you so obedient to your guardian in all things, Captain Helford?'

'I must be, sir,' Kitto said. 'After all, he holds my purse strings, and the living in Petersburg costs me dearly.'

Another ripple of laughter spread up and down the table. Two seats away from him, Hester held up a single red, translucent grape to the candlelight before eating it, watching Kitto with the extraordinary self-possession that had made Crow desire her with all his soul since the moment he had first laid eyes on her. She glanced at him and looked up at the embossed ceiling. Her bedchamber lay directly above it, and candlelight caught the single diamond she wore on a gossamer-thin gold chain – it rested just above the swell of her velvet-clad breasts. In two days, the house would be entirely their own again. The Season could wait: they would go to London late this year, and enjoy their bed together, and the quiet of a Cornish spring, and their own child, who could now walk unsteadily from between one's knees to a sofa.

Castlereagh signalled to the footman to fill Kitto's glass. 'But I believe your position sets us up with a problem, Captain. What would you do if your brother disagreed with me, and with the rest of the Cabinet? Who would then have the honour of your loyalty and obedience? Me – the government, I should say – or Lord Lamorna?'

All other conversation ended and the table fell silent.

'My brother would do only what was correct,' Crow said, and turned to Kitto. 'Emily is right. You don't look quite well.'

'I'm perfectly well, sir.' Kitto glanced at Crow swiftly, before turning to Castlereagh. 'Surely, when not beneath my brother's roof, I'm answerable only to my colonel?'

'How fortunate we all are that you think so, Captain Helford,' Lord Castlereagh said, and Crow thought of how this man had grasped for himself the power to send anyone around his own table to the gallows: Kitto included, himself included.

In the resulting silence, Hester got to her feet. 'Shall we withdraw for tea?' A fraction of a moment later, she was followed by every other woman present, all obeying her cue to leave the dining-room, abandoning discussion of politics to the men, and ending Kitto's interrogation in a manner even Castlereagh could take no exception to.

13

Hester was pouring tea for Lady Mulgrave in the drawing-room when she heard the dining-room door fly open, crashing into the oak-panelled wall in the hall. Dorothea Lieven stood beside her, setting down the gilded porcelain milk jug with quiet precision. Conversation in the drawing-room came to an immediate end; all ten women fell silent, and there was only the rustle of satin against linen petticoats, the sour smell of gathered bodies in the fire's heat, Dorothea's rose-water cologne, and the crackle of flames behind the grate. Hester knew at last that she had been waiting for this moment all evening. Crow's manner at the dining-table had communicated deep disquiet: the way he'd held himself with that unsettled, excessive awareness of his surroundings. Usually, of course, such things were all in his mind, and he woke up telling her to run from some battlefield that haunted his dreams. But at other times his supernatural apprehension of danger was entirely justified. Hester put down the teapot and stepped out into the hall to find her husband almost at the front door, still dressed for dinner, white linen and pale skin stark against the dark blue jacket, with Kitto not far behind him. Closing the space between them with a few swift strides, Crow held her arms close to her sides with that curious gentle strength.

'Nathaniel Edwards just rode over from Sancreed. Captain Wentworth is to raid Newlyn on Castlereagh's orders – there's a prayer meeting in the chapel. It's said they're plotting sedition, aided and abetted by me. I'm going there now, but only because they will all be cut down like wheat.'

'They're raiding a prayer meeting on your own land?' Hester demanded, knowing it would be useless to argue with him just as she knew this might be the last time she saw him alive. 'Just a prayer meeting? But what possible proof or justification—'

'Ask our guest Lord Castlereagh,' Crow said, pale with incandescent fury. 'He sanctioned the entire manoeuvre. You must take the child and go.' He handed her a heavy leather-wrapped roll of banknotes and the silver pistol that was always kept concealed behind those volumes of Livy on the dining-room bookshelf, along with a ball-bag heavy with shot and cartridges, and turned to face his brother. 'Stay here, Kitto, do you understand? You're commissioned in the British army – you can't be implicated in a Cornish rebellion, however manufactured it might be.'

'No!' Hester cried in Cornish. 'Crow, can't you see what Castlereagh is doing? This is a trap. This is just how he always meant to incriminate you. He wants you out of the way. He'll see you hanged.'

Crow simply kissed her forehead, one hand pressing briefly at the small of her back as he pulled her towards him, then turned and walked out of the wide-open front door, and Kitto followed him, flouting his brother's orders without a word. Even if Crow understood how much Castlereagh hated him, she was sure in that moment that he didn't really know why, and how much Castlereagh had longed for Crow's mother to notice him all those years ago. Hester turned to face Dorothea, who alone had followed her. The dining-room had fallen eerily silent; at a glance through the open doors, she saw the rest of the men still at table, sitting in awkward quiet as though they had witnessed a family argument and not the start of a revolution. After a moment's shocked silence, Hester snatched Dorothea's arm and they ran together to the library, closing the door behind them.

'It was a trap, wasn't it?' Hester demanded. 'Castlereagh never meant to come to terms with my husband. All he ever wanted was an excuse to finish him. Is this for the benefit of Russia, too, or England alone?'

For a moment, Dorothea only stared at her, her face flushed with the heat of the drawing-room and the liberal quantities of champagne before dinner. 'Run,' she said, and Hester knew that she was not speaking as the wife of a diplomat up to her emerald necklace in political scheming, but as one woman to another. Her sudden and unmistakable frankness was terrifying. 'Take your baby, Hester,' she said, 'and run.'

Leaving her, Hester sprinted up the stairs, snatching her velvet skirts out of the way, only to hear the sound of footfalls in the hall below. Turning to glance over her shoulder, she saw soldiers filing in at the front door – men of the 11th Northumbrians who had respectfully bowed to her outside the draper's in Penzance not two days before.

'Lady Lamorna!'

Stifling a terrified scream, Hester reached the landing; she dared not look again but she heard at least two sets of footfalls on the stairs behind her, and darted across the hall into her own bedchamber, where Lizzy had laid out her nightgown.

She reached the door set into the wainscoting and, turning the well-worn brass knob, let herself into the servants' passage, closing it carefully behind her. What would happen to the servants if Wentworth's men raided the house? Tears prickled at her eyes as she stumbled up the whitewashed back stairs, tearing along the narrow corridor that led towards the nursery. The sheer quiet filled her with terror the like of which she hadn't felt since the French Occupation. The servants' door into the nursery was slightly ajar, and stinging bile rose up her throat. The nursery was never quiet. If Morwenna were not crying, or babbling, Beatie never stopped talking to her; even if Morwenna slept, Beatie knitted or sewed, and one heard the soft clacking of the needles, or the creak of the rocking chair, or even the soft sound of their breathing. Now she heard only the sounds of the world outside the house, the call of an owl, and the distant crashing of surf against rocks. She pushed open the door, and the first thing she saw was a pool of dark blood spreading across the ancient waxed oaken floorboards. Vomit surged up her throat and she spat bile and champagne on to the rag rug, forcing herself to step further into the room. Beatie was still in her rocking chair, exactly where she had been sitting as her throat was cut, doubtless from behind as she dozed, her head now lolling to one side.

Sobbing, one hand pressed to her mouth, Hester forced herself to step closer to the silent crib, hearing only the sound of coals shifting in the grate and her own disordered breathing. She reached the carved wooden cradle that had sheltered Crow, and Kitto, and their father before them, and finally Morwenna herself. Now; it must be now. She looked down and saw nothing but the faint indentation where Morwenna had lain with the white lace-trimmed cap, her hands open like a pair of small starfish – and yet there was no Morwenna, there was no blood, only the blanket. It meant nothing. She was only a baby: they might have smothered her, perhaps that had been easier, even for a hardened soldier. Stifling a low, animal moan, Hester cast around the nursery, but saw only the crib itself, the blood around Beatie's rocking chair, old embroidered curtains shifting at a window left ajar, the tidy piles of napkins, blankets and gowns resting beside one another on the linen-chest next to the marble-topped wash-stand – the sheer mundanity of it all was a mockery. Morwenna was not here, dead or alive.

She heard footfalls on the landing outside in the family quarters, muffled by the rug Crow's grandfather had brought home from Rajasthan, long ago. Wentworth's men were coming. They were searching for her, even now. She reached the servants' door and let herself out, pulling it shut behind her, praying that the hinges would not creak. Half sobbing, she paused at the bottom of the next flight of the stairs and ran up towards the servants' attics. It was dark up here, and she stumbled, tripping over a soft, heavy obstacle, rough linen and tightly braided hair beneath her outstretched fingertips.

'Lizzy!' Hester gasped, looking down at her maidservant as her eyes grew used to the moonlit dark. Lizzy was lying on her side, curled up. Hester moved her hand and placed it on the floorboards, touching wet warmth. Not urine but blood. Lizzy's every breath now came in a strangled rattle that Hester knew too well: she was dying of some violent injury concealed by the darkness. Somehow, Hester found her hand and bent over at the frantic, fluttering pressure of Lizzy's work-worn fingers.

'The little maid,' Lizzy said, so quietly that Hester had to lean in close; she could smell the clove pastilles Lizzy habitually chewed. 'Mrs Rescorla took her, but I'm sorry, mistress. They made me tell them where, but I told them the long way round. The soldiers—'

'It's not your fault, Lizzy.' Hester forced out each word. This couldn't be happening. It couldn't be real. 'But where did Mrs Rescorla take Lady Morwenna? Lizzy, please can you—' Hester had to lean even closer to hear what she was struggling to say.

'The old keeper's cottage.' And with one last rattling breath, Lizzy died.

14

After running for half an hour, the keeper's lodge was now no more than a few moments' walk away, and although from this vantage point Hester couldn't see the dark ocean, she could hear it rushing up to meet the rocks far below to the east. Thinking of nothing save the shape of her daughter's hands, plump and strong, and the curve of her cheek, the bed-warm tangle of her curls, Hester pushed on into the trees. Low-hanging branches, gorse and last year's dead bracken caught at the heavy velvet skirts of her evening gown. She ran on, quickly emerging from the sparse woodland, with little choice but to take her chances on the open moorland above Lamorna Cove. Skirts and petticoats alike tangled around her legs as she ran, and the satin boots Lizzy had buttoned her into just hours before were sodden, her stockinged feet sliding around inside them, the skin on her heels quickly rubbed raw. *Lizzy is dead. Lizzy is dead. Beatie is dead.* The words rolled around the inside of her skull like pebbles shaken in a bowl.

Glancing back over her shoulder where Nansmornow lay hidden by trees and the shoulder of the valley, she glimpsed movement and her heart seized. Emerging from the cover of a stand of windblown hawthorn trees came six dark moving shapes. Men: Wentworth's English soldiers. Once, their very presence would have made her feel safe, but now every loyalty had shifted. Now they were surely looking for her as well as Morwenna under Castlereagh's orders. *Don't run,* she told herself, suppressing a sick burst of fear. The walk down the scrubby, sandy path took a lifetime, and all the while she thought of nothing save Morwenna, racked with terror that she would reach the cottage only to find it contained nothing but the trestle table they always used for a shooting supper folded in the corner, the windows cobweb-strewn, whitewash peeling from walls that were always damp when there was not a fire leaping behind the old black grate.

Please God, Hester thought, *please God, still be there. Be safe.* Sheltered by trees, the small stone cottage hove into view as she broached the brow of the hill, skittering and skidding down the root-tangled path towards it. The shuttered windows stared at her like accusing eyes: she had been downstairs drinking champagne and longing to go to bed with her profligate husband even as Wentworth's men quietly infiltrated the servants' quarters, killing her own daughter's nurse where she sat, all of it orchestrated by Lord Castlereagh. And had he done so because she refused him? She had failed her daughter. Hester pushed open the door and found Catlin on her knees, cleaning out the grate with an old brush in the moonlight streaming in through one unshuttered window, and Morwenna sitting fat and unsteady on the hearthstone, passing a pebble from one hand to the other.

'I thought I might as well keep busy.' Catlin stood up, wiping both hands on her apron, and Hester made no reply, lifting Morwenna, her throat sealed tight with agony as she made every effort to recall the precise heft of her child's weight in her arms, the exact softness of her neck, and the wet-sand shade of her curls that would bleach almost white when summer came, even as her skin darkened. Morwenna reached up and grasped a handful of Hester's hair, which was springing loose from pin and satin band alike.

'It's because of what happened in the library!' The words flew from her lips. 'Catlin, you saw – and I refused him. And now this—'

'None of that, my lady!' Catlin said fiercely. 'Do you really believe he wouldn't have done it anyway? Don't be a little fool, Het. Use your brain – *what must we do?*'

'I think it must be Scilly,' Hester said, forcing herself to sound calm, so as not to frighten her child. 'That's where we must go. And then on – on anywhere. I hate to put the Trewarthens in danger, but they keep a skiff by the cottages above the cove.' Like Hester herself, Catlin had been an island girl, and was as adept at the helm of a boat as any fisherman, but hot bile rose up Hester's throat at the thought of her daughter making a thirty-mile crossing over open water. And yet, in Lord Castlereagh's hands Morwenna would be in far greater danger – no more than a pawn moved to ensure Crow's destruction. She closed her eyes and thought of the drowned men lying in the chapel at Nansmornow after the wreck of the *Deliverance*, their bloated and battered features, their swollen fingers. She thought of the corpses in their winding sheets, lying side by side in every cart the estate could spare, and the silent, thin-faced women who had accompanied them home across the moors to St Erth. She, her daughter and Catlin might drown together, but there was no choice.

And then she heard it: the booted foot of a heavy man slipping on the stone-pocked, sandy path that led to the door. With slow, rocking movements, Hester crossed the room and passed her daughter to Catlin, a strange roaring in her ears as she registered the sudden lack of weight in her arms while still breathing in her daughter's nursery scent of milk, urine and mallow soap. Just faintly, she heard what was unmistakably more footfalls, and a sharp intake of breath. Hester drew her pistol. Thank God. Thank God for Crow and his imperious insistence that she carry it. Those men outside were going to come in here, and they would take her prisoner, Catlin and Morwenna, too. They would all three be used against Crow; she knew he would give his life to save them without a second thought, but she could not and would not live in the world without him.

Crossing to the window, Hester prayed that Morwenna would remain quiet. She glanced at Catlin, who met her eyes, pushing her reddened knuckle between Morwenna's questing lips, and then she looked at the window, and Hester prised open the shutters. One-handed, she hoisted herself up on to the windowsill, slapped in the face by iron-cold air. It was hard to balance, but she dared not relinquish the pistol, even for a moment. In wordless agreement Catlin steadied Hester's legs as she made a shuffling, awkward turn on the windowsill. There was no sign of the men on this side of the cottage – they had all gone to the door, assuming that a clutch of women and an infant would present them with none of the difficulties that might warrant surrounding the place.

Hester was just tall enough to haul herself up on to the tiled roof, still white with frost. She couldn't put the pistol down, without allowing it to crash to the heather below, useless. Seized with panic, Hester lifted one foot and felt Catlin's hands beneath the sole of her boot, pushing her up with all of her considerable strength and no warning: she must have set Morwenna down on the flagstones. The pistol slipped from Hester's grasp. With a surge of sour panic, she caught it with one flinging, desperate hand, making a starfish on the roof, hampered by her skirts and heavy petticoats soaked up past the hem. Frozen and half concealed by the pitch of the roof, she watched three soldiers in battered red uniform jackets huddle in conference outside the door, just below her. They'd take her child away. They were going to imprison her. Under orders or not, they must be stopped. One removed his shako to scratch his head, his scalp a teeming mass of sparse, mouse-brown hair and attendant lice, spotted with pus-yellow, infected sores. Hester shot him through the top of his skull and he crumpled like a puppet with the strings cut; she had just murdered an officer of the British army. Like Crow, she was now beyond the law.

At the pistol shot, the dead man's companions looked around wildly, and Hester pressed herself against the tiles, curled up on one side as she reloaded with frantic speed. The shorter of the two soldiers turned towards the encroaching trees, musket cocked. He moved just as Hester fired, and he took the bullet in the back of his neck instead of in the skull; he died anyway, sprawled on his front, and Hester thought of his mother, his wife, his child. The third soldier looked up and in the moment that he fired his musket, Hester rolled to one side, lent speed by her terror for Morwenna. The shot hissed past her ear and she suppressed – just – the need to urinate where she lay, loading her pistol with unconscious speed.

The last soldier fired again and, lent wings by terror, Hester moved just in time; the shot dislodged a tile and she slipped, sliding skittishly down the roof. With all her strength she flung out one arm as she fell. Wrenching her head around to get that red jacket in view, she fired and he dropped like a stone, but even as Hester landed on the heather-rooted path at the side of the cottage, the wind knocked clean from her lungs, she knew he couldn't be dead, not yet – she'd surely only hit him in the shoulder at best.

Gasping for breath, Hester leaned against the weathered stone wall, reloading again. Inside, she could hear Morwenna wailing, and at the sound of the cry her breasts tingled, bursting with milk. Moving sideways, crab-fashion, Hester edged along the wall to the corner of the cottage. Turning her head, she saw the soldier lurch to his feet, one hand pressed to a dark, spreading stain across his belly. He was going to die, but he could still kill her first, and Morwenna and Catlin too. In one swift move, Hester fired, and this time she hit him between the eyes, obliterating the back of his skull, a merciful end. Having killed three British soldiers, she crouched on the sandy path, her face in her hands, shaking with dry, sobbing breaths. Crow couldn't save her now. No one could.

15

From Nansmornow Crow rode hard to the top of the Lamorna Valley, galloping across field and moorland, setting his mare at hedge after hedge, barely registering the leap or landing, the shivering dewdrops clinging to last year's dead bracken and the daffodils growing along the stone Cornish hedges, or the grey, black-faced ewes almost ready to lamb; he was aware only of his white-hot fury. Castlereagh had ordered an attack on his own land, on his own people whilst dining at his table and drinking his claret. Wentworth's men had deliberately stirred up unrest in Newlyn, of that Crow had no doubt. And now this was the result of ignoring his own instinct for danger. Dawn came, the sun rose, and a grey mist settled on the moorland and kale-fields between Kerris and Paul, concealing even the pasterns of his grey mare, but Crow was scarcely aware of that, or the fact that Kitto rode shoulder to shoulder with him. An hour flew past, and then the streets of Newlyn were unpleasantly quiet, and the stone-built cottages of hewn granite with shuttered windows were silent. Crow set the mare hard along the straw-strewn filth of Fore Street, past the well and the jumble of market-stalls where traders gathered to sell salted fish and bread at inflated prices that hardly anyone could afford.

He reined in, turning to Kitto, who had kept pace with him all this time, and who in his fevered condition should not have been setting the gelding at hedge after hedge.

'Where are they all?' Kitto said quickly. Pearls of sweat stood out on his forehead; his hair was sodden with it. 'What shall we do?'

'*Ke dhe dre!*' Crow said in a burst of furious Cornish, all his anger rising like a wave and crashing over Kitto. 'Go *home*. I told you not to come. Do you think I have time now to deal with an insubordinate child?'

'What, you want to be shot down by Wentworth's men in a blaze of glory all your own? Is that what this is all about?'

If they had been standing and not on horseback, Crow would have struck him, and they both knew it. 'You are my heir.' Crow spoke with furious cold enunciation. 'Without you, it like as not all ends today, the entire Lamorna line. Go to Petersburg and back to your regiment. Go now, and you won't be tainted by what happens.'

'I won't leave you,' Kitto said, so headstrong and steering so hard to his own course of action, however thoughtless, that one wanted to shake him.

'If you want to be a hero, protect my wife and child, not me.' And even as Crow spoke, he felt the cobbled streets of Newlyn tumble away beneath his feet, and that he had made the most profound mistake of his life in leaving Hester and Morwenna, because they and the stubborn fool mounted beside him were all that mattered. And yet he held in his hands the lives of so many others who also depended on him. Kitto stared at him with a look of agonised indecision, but even as he did so, the low, pure note of Cornish plainsong rang out – men and women's voices, raised in praise, the sound drifting from the lane that ran parallel to Fore Street. Even though the music was familiar and eerily beautiful, cold fear slicked down Crow's back. Without discussion, they both dismounted, looping the reins around one of the railings outside the Gwyn cottage, Ann Gwyn's neat herb garden spangled with dew-covered spiderwebs. In silence, they walked side by side down the deserted street, past shuttered houses, turning left off Fore Street and on to Barrack Lane until finally they reached the long, low bulk of the meeting house itself. Captain Wentworth's men clustered around the entrance, a shock of red jackets against weatherworn granite and the mud and straw of the narrow street of beaten earth; they were unable to surround the building entirely, because at the back it abutted on to the fish house on Fore Street where the women gutted and salted sardines on long, stone-topped tables. Kitto said nothing, but Crow knew he was trusting in him to act. He could see Wentworth among the Northumbrians, a little behind the men nearest the broad oaken front door of the chapel. They were going to storm it – unwitnessed, or so they thought: it would be easy to say they had been suppressing insurrection on the streets when it had been no such thing, a sure route to that promotion Wentworth so clearly longed for. If Crow had his way it would be a sure route to a court martial, nothing more.

'Ready, men!' Wentworth called out, his voice ragged with anticipation, and Crow watched as if in a waking nightmare as the Northumbrians cocked and raised their bayonets – bayonets in a chapel.

'He's going to charge the meeting house,' Kitto said, his voice cracking in disbelief. And the singing continued, a low, sweet melody rising and falling. The narrow muddy lane now seemed set in aspic, the bright scarlet of Wentworth's men's jackets frozen in time against the granite walls of the meeting house. Wentworth himself turned with animal alertness, shifting in the saddle, his ruddy, good-humoured face spattered with flecks of mud, his eyes empty of emotion.

'Charge!' Wentworth's voice rang out.

Crow hesitated for a bare half-moment; then, and without looking at Kitto, he spoke to him in rapid, quiet Cornish. 'Get around to Fore Street and open the door at the back of the fish house – Wentworth's men won't know it's there, and it's always barred from that side. Get as many of these people out as you can.' Kitto nodded, silent, and Crow went on. 'Halt! Hold your fire.' The men closest to him responded to the habit of command in his voice, lowering their bayonets immediately, turning to stare, and Wentworth turned, too, his face twisted with fury in a way that would have been comical in any other scenario – he looked like a thwarted child denied a paper bag of barley-sugar twists. Crow was just aware of Kitto's absence: he had gone, exactly as ordered.

'Charge!' Wentworth shouted again, and his men ran at the doors, which burst open inwards, and for a sickening moment the singing didn't even falter; and then someone screamed, and the screaming didn't stop. It was all Crow heard as he primed his pistol, raised it, and fired at Captain Wentworth.

16

Market-day was always busy in Hugh-town on St Mary's, the largest island of the scattered archipelago thirty miles across the Cornish sea from Penzance. Baskets of smoked mackerel were piled high alongside rickety stalls displaying glistening, silvery heaps of pilchard, hake and sole, rings of dried apple hung in net bags, and the spicy scent of warm saffron buns mingled with the sharp salt air. With Morwenna heavy in her arms and Catlin at her side Hester edged along the great stone quay, through a crowd that stretched from the cobbled street outside the Dolphin tavern and all the way along to the customs house. Every bone in her body ached after the twelve-hour crossing from Penzance, she and Catlin taking turns at the tiller or clutching a wriggling Morwenna, arguing listlessly about how on earth they would ever arrange recompense for the dinghy taken from the Trewarthens' mooring back in Lamorna Cove without incurring the very real risk of giving themselves away to the English. If Hester never had to leave dry land again, she would be only too happy, but the filthy crossing to Scilly and the heart-stopping wait for a ship was only the start. There was the Channel to face next, and then Saint-Malo. Men and boys she half recognised were still unloading the *Curlew* as she rocked alongside the quay, and it would be half an hour yet at least before they boarded. France was a horrific danger, true, but in Breton quarters they could speak Cornish and blend in, and would be shielded by the Breton, Hester was sure. It was their best chance of safety, however imperfect.

'Lord, don't you wish we could just take the mail-boat to Bryher?' Catlin said, picking up the salt-stained skirts of her gown as she stepped over a straw-filled puddle. 'It's that strange to be so close to home and yet not able to go back.'

'I know, but how can we? It's the first place they'll look for us.' Hester bowed her head, breathing in the scent of Morwenna's lace-trimmed cap, still redolent of the lavender laundry soap they made in the stillroom at Nansmornow. The child shifted, squalling and wriggling, and Hester could see that the *Curlew* was still frustratingly low in the water – her cargo of wool and wine not even half unloaded. She had no notion what had happened to Crow, or to Kitto, and there was no possible way of finding out without giving herself away.

'I think the maid's thirsty,' Catlin said, with her stolid ability to pay heed only to practicalities. 'She does look hot.'

Hester cast a look up and down the crowded quay. 'I can't feed her here.'

Catlin sighed. 'Here, I'll take her if you want to fetch a cup of small-beer from the Dolphin.'

'Small-beer instead of milk?' Hester said, kissing her daughter's rounded cheek. 'My God, Morwenna, your papa would not like that.'

'I shouldn't give her milk,' Catlin said briskly. 'Not from the Dolphin. How should we know that it was kept fresh or what ailments might be festering in it? Small-beer might not be for gently reared children, but at least it won't make the maid sick.'

Hester surrendered Morwenna to her and glanced up at the seagulls buffeted in the wintry sky above, white scraps against angry grey cloud, hoping that the crossing to Saint-Malo wouldn't be too stormy. When she turned back, the crowd on the quay had surged again, and she could only just make out Catlin's pale green cap – she was almost indistinguishable with her red hair braided and tucked away beneath it.

The hum of voices in the Dolphin enveloped her as she walked in: she would have to be both quick and careful. Hester and Catlin had been brought up together here, milk-sisters known by everyone on the islands, but until today, she hadn't set foot on Scilly for nearly two years. Even so, both she and Catlin were so well known there was no telling that people wouldn't talk, even to the English. She pulled the hood of her cloak down low over her face and left the coin for the small-beer lying on the bar, swiftly whisking herself away with the little tin mug of ale splashing over her wrists. If Morwenna was content before the voyage, they stood a chance of a peaceful crossing and perhaps rather than tottering up and down the deck putting everything into her mouth the maid might even sleep, heavy in Hester's lap: there was something about Morwenna's boneless weight when she slept that reminded her irrevocably of Crow on the rare occasions when he slept deeply, untroubled by his dreams. She grieved his loss with the force of a physical blow. Waiting behind a gaggle of Irish seamen in wide-legged striped culottes, Hester sensed what felt like a sudden hush descend, even though the babble of voices continued unabated – it was all the tension of a sudden silence, without the silence itself.

'Fucking English,' one of the Irish sailors said in front of her. 'No more than fucking trouble. When they ask questions it's the gallows rope for someone.'

Hester's breath seized in her chest, her gaze sliding towards the side-door that led out from a side-parlour into the narrow alleyway between the Dolphin and the chandlery shop next door, and from there down to the quay. Quickly, quietly, she moved towards it. Now the entire tavern really did fall silent. Inside the small parlour, she pressed herself against faded flowered wallpaper, listening to what was said in the bar. Everyone else had fallen so quiet that she heard quite easily as an English voice spoke her own name.

'We're looking for Lady Lamorna and her quadroon brat. The bluey bitch shouldn't be that hard to spot, should she, such a fine exotic lady?' There was a pause, a hush, and Hester imagined the English – soldiers or whoever they were – looking around at the gathered crowd, assessing those most susceptible to the promise of blood-money. 'There's a reward offered for her capture. Lord Lamorna and his young brother we already have; it's just the woman we want – it'll be pretty to watch them all swing together.'

In the silent, deserted parlour, Hester pressed both hands to her mouth. Surely Crow was not in prison? Surely, *surely* he could not be blamed for the chaos Lord Castlereagh had stirred up in Newlyn? But of course he would be. That was precisely how Castlereagh operated, how those opposed to reform had always operated, ever since Hester had been old enough to really understand what she read of politics in the *Morning Post*.

'Lord Castlereagh's soldiers, are they now?' some unseen person asked quietly. 'Used to be the king's men, did our army, not the cursed prime minister's.' A bare half-moment later, a pistol shot rang out, followed by depthless silence. Hester closed her eyes. They were looking for her. Englishmen were looking for her and they had just shot a man for questioning the authority of Lord Castlereagh, here in the Dolphin. She had been a fool, a cursed fool to come to Scilly when it was the first place she would be sought out. They would find her, and Morwenna too. Mustering all the nerve she had left, Hester fled through the alley door and ran pell-mell down to the quay, searching for Catlin in a breathless panic so acute that it set up a harsh whining in her ears and she felt as though her heart would burst; her hands shook uncontrollably. Was everyone watching her? Was the crowd wordlessly moving to conceal her as she stumbled across the cobbles, or had she imagined that? She found Catlin at last, crouching on the ground with Morwenna, sorting stray shells into a pile, and Catlin only had to look at her once before scrambling to her feet with Morwenna clutched to her hip, crying and reaching for the shells. Hester snatched up the cockles and passed them to her daughter, holding the half-empty cup of small-beer to her rounded lips. Catlin said nothing at all, letting Hester speak, allowing her to come to the inevitable conclusion by herself.

'They'll find me,' Hester said, knowing one of them would have to say it aloud, 'no matter if people here try to shield us, they'll find us sooner or later. I'm too distinguishable, Catlin – I'll lead them straight to you and Morwenna.'

Morwenna sucked on her shell, content, blissfully unaware. Catlin only nodded.

'Cat, you must take her by yourself. She's light enough that she might be anyone's child, not so obviously mine. But if I'm with you, we'll all be found. You must take her—' Hester broke off as streaming tears slipped between her lips, salty and hot. Without a word, Catlin slipped Morwenna into Hester's arms, allowing her to hold the child one last time, even as the purser aboard the *Curlew* began the call for everyone to board.

'Be a good girl, Morwenna.' It was all Hester could say.

17

At Bodmin gaol, the condemned cell was illuminated only by what daylight penetrated the narrow, barred window. The dank room was crowded; men sat in rows along the walls, heads bowed, waiting as day slipped into day. The air was thick with the stink of unwashed bodies, human waste and a palpable sense of despair that made Crow long to bend the iron bars at the window. Every man in the cell tensed as the sound of approaching footfalls grew louder, the soles of heavy boots scraping against damp, puddled flagstones. It was otherwise quiet. When Crow was a boy, crowds of thousands would gather in the fields beyond the gaol to watch a hanging. No one came any more: hangings had been ten a penny since the French Occupation. Water dripped, somewhere out of sight, and Crow thought of how when the little maid was fretful, her cries shook through his skull and he would silently curse Beatie and Hester for not quietening her, and the silence in the cell crushed his chest. He thought of Kitto, still his ward and his heir, infuriating in his total lack of regard for self-preservation. Kitto would be Lord Lamorna soon, but for how long would he survive without being implicated in this? At least the boy had got well away before Crow himself was surrounded by Wentworth's men. He couldn't bring himself to think of Hester at all.

The cell door opened inwards and there was nothing to breathe. The guards were both English, not local men. No one in Cornwall would work at Bodmin gaol now, and nor would a Cornishman be trusted here. They read out the name on their list with merciful speed.

'Nathaniel Edwards.'

Nathaniel got to his feet, visibly shaking. 'Not me,' he said, 'not me. I've got a woman at home, and my little maids to feed. Not me. Have mercy.'

'It's not our choice, man.' The first guard spoke with a complete lack of expression. 'Should've thought of that before you started a riot.'

'My lord!' Nathaniel dropped to his knees as he passed Crow. 'My lord, don't let them do it, don't let them hang me.'

Crow got up. 'Take me instead, and do it now.'

The guards stared at each other, expressionless. 'Can't do that. We don't choose the name on the list. It's not for us to say.' As one, they both turned back to Nathaniel, who was shaking and silently praying, tears streaking his weatherbeaten face. 'Come on, man.'

'I said, take me,' Crow demanded, forcing himself not to think of the gallows step, the rope.

The taller of the two guards turned on him, suddenly out of control like a baited bull terrier. 'Shut up, or it'll be all of you that gets it, here and now, understand?' Spraying Crow with his own spittle, he gestured furiously at the rows of men in the cell. 'Any heroics and we've orders to string up every last one of you bastards, understand?'

Crow faced him in silence, knowing that this was likely the truth, and shame washed over him because, despite everything, despite who he was, who he had been, he could do nothing to stop this. Instead, he took Nathaniel's hands in his own, speaking in Cornish. '*Na ellam aga stoppya*, I can't stop them, not now. But you go well, do you understand me?' Nathaniel's thin fingers were trembling; it was like holding a moth or a butterfly.

The younger guard glared, disgusted. 'Can't you talk English?' he snapped. 'Fucking savage. That's against the law now, that is, talking in that savage tongue—'

Crow simply looked up and stared at him until the man stopped talking, trailing off into silence, before continuing in Cornish. 'You go well, Nathaniel, and if I can't look after your wife and your daughters then I will make sure that Lady Lamorna does, do you understand? They'll want for nothing.' He didn't know where Hester was, if she was even still alive, but he would give hope to a dead man in his last half-hour. He released Nathaniel's hands, taking in every detail of his starved, underfed face, red-rimmed eyes, overgrown beard, his lined forehead flecked with freckles that would have multiplied in the sun when Nathaniel sat to smoke his pipe on the stump of an oak tree outside the count house at Wheal Boscobel, lifting his cap whenever Crow rode by.

Crow forced himself to watch Nathaniel walk away, stumbling between the two guards; he watched until the door had closed, leaving the men in darkness again. There was quite a long period of tense quiet before the screaming began. Some men went quietly to the gallows; most didn't. Nathaniel had managed to wait until he reached the foot of the stairs that led up to the yard, closer to daylight. When the sun had risen above the rooftops of Bodmin and the hills beyond, he would be dead at the end of a rope. The gallows weren't quite visible from the narrow cell window, but the men had no choice but to listen as Nathaniel shrieked his wife's name, his daughters', and to hear the scrabble of his footsteps as he was dragged up the worn wooden steps, the low mumbling of the priest, and then silence.

It was over now until tomorrow. For the past week, the guards had taken one man every morning, one after the other, as if the waiting should be part of the punishment, part of the deterrent to others. But now he could hear more footsteps, the soles of hobnail boots striking wet flagstone again, again, and again. The surviving men shifted uneasily. No one spoke. The air was too thick with hopelessness and despair for any unnecessary conversation. In here, all conversation was unnecessary. The door swung open again, and the guards stepped in, two different men this time. They looked around the cell, and then one of them spoke with a sneering curl to his lip.

'John Edward Tristan Helford, Earl of Lamorna.'

Crow, he thought. *Just call me Crow.*

18

That afternoon saw Kitto at Nansmornow, sitting with his back against the locked door of his brother's wine cellar. One of his eyes was still swollen shut, but he could see enough to watch dust motes chasing each other through the silver light streaming in at one of the narrow, barred windows that gave on to the gravelled path at the side of the east wing. In truth, he'd lost track of the days since his incarceration, but it was early enough in the morning that dewdrops still clung to the dandelion growing on the path outside the window. He'd been a fool to listen to Dorothea and Count Lieven with all Dorothea's honeyed words as if he might rejoin his regiment as though nothing had happened, were he only to prove his own innocence by coming back to the house. He leaned back against the door as the light changed, an unseen sun moving across the sky, remembering another imprisonment in another cellar, long ago, and the terror and relief he'd felt in equal parts to be retrieved from the French by Crow at his most intimidatingly furious. And so Crow was gone, surely hanged by now. Kitto felt only curious, uncaring emptiness, forcing himself to move when an unfamiliar voice ordered him to shift, and the door swung open, letting in light from the whitewashed passage outside. He followed the cavalryman without a word, ignoring the rough grip on his arm – the man wasn't even of the officer class. Rage kindled again as he was hauled through the deserted servants' quarters of his own home, though the silent kitchen where as a child he'd been given bowls of bread, milk and sugar, or a slice of dark, gelatinous plum-pudding, and where Crow had more recently prised a bullet from his shoulder. Baskets of spring greens were laid out on the table alongside a joint of mutton tied with string and the striped earthenware jug, but there was no sign of anyone, no familiar face. In the family quarters the great hall, too, was empty of servants – two soldiers of the Northumbrian regiment sat slouching on the bottom step of the stairs, watching him pass with insolent curiosity.

By the time the private pushed him through the library door, Kitto was ready to explode with fury, and he did, turning on the man and shoving him so hard that his head struck the doorframe. 'Get your fucking hands off me.'

'You little bastard – you'll soon learn,' the private sneered, revealing brown, tobacco-stained teeth. Kitto rushed him, grabbing the sweat-yellowed fabric of his stock.

'Darling, I think that's quite enough, don't you?'

Shoving the Northumbrian away, Kitto turned around to face Dorothea Lieven sitting alone in his father's old chair by the fire, the fine satin skirts of her gown puddling on the floor at her feet. She flicked her pale fingers at the Northumbrian in an elegant gesture of dismissal.

The soldier hesitated, glancing at the door. 'With respect, milady, it's not safe to leave you alone with him.'

Dorothea raised her eyebrows, managing to convey both astonishment and unspoken anger at his presumption. 'I'll be the judge of that. Wait outside.'

She didn't speak until the private had gone, closing the door behind him. 'Yes, I thought it might go better with you if we met alone, Kitto, without any other man to confuse matters. You're very angry, and I can understand that, but you need to listen now, and you need to listen carefully.'

Kitto forced off a wave of debilitating shame at appearing in the company of a woman of his own class filthy and stinking. 'Where is my brother? Where are Hester and the baby?'

There was no servant in the room with them – what had become of them all? – and Dorothea got up and crossed to the crystal decanter and glasses laid out on the sideboard beneath a portrait of Kitto's mother, whom he had never met. She held out a glass of cognac, but he shook his head – it made him think of Crow. She was going to tell him that Crow was dead; that he had died shamefully, on the gallows. Wentworth had taken that bullet in the side of his skull, it was said, and Crow would have been hanged for murder by now, Lord Lieutenant and Chief Justice of Cornwall or not. Kitto turned away, unable to look at her, walking rapidly to the window. He remembered Crow coming home on leave for the first time in his own living memory, when he was in his fifth summer. Side by side, they had lain in the grass on the muddy bank of the carp pond beneath the beech trees. *Dip your fingers into the water and move them like this, see?* Crow had been a traitor to England, opening fire on British troops – there could be no argument about it. And yet Wentworth had been making ready to fire on innocent people. Kitto thought of his brother with a rope around his neck, heavy around his shoulders, and he turned to face Dorothea, his sight blurred.

'Where are they?' He immediately spun away from her again, staring out of the window at the mist settling on the parkland tumbling away towards the home wood. Beyond that, there was only moorland, cliff-edge and the Atlantic.

'Your brother is not dead,' Dorothea said. And Kitto leaned hard on the windowsill, still unable to breathe, unable to turn and look at her. 'Fortunately, my husband was one of a few who persuaded Lord Castlereagh that his immediate execution would only play into revolutionary hands – Cornish or English. Dissent in Cornwall or not, he's still remembered as the man who freed Wellington from French captivity, and he distinguished himself at Salisbury, which was such a decisive battle when it came to expelling the French from your shores. Ultimately, it would be counterproductive to risk public ire in Cornwall or England by making a martyr of Lord Lamorna – both of which would be entirely likely—'

'Then where is he?' Kitto demanded.

'That's not your concern at the moment; in fact, the less you know, the better.'

'Then where is Hester? And my niece?'

Dorothea frowned a little. 'I'm afraid I can't give you a very precise answer to that question, Kitto, either. Lady Lamorna and her servant Catlin Rescorla were seen on St Mary's, boarding a boat bound for France – the *Curlew*. Naturally, there were several parties who were keen to find them, and so we're quite sure of our witnesses.'

Kitto let out a long, shuddering sigh of relief, no longer caring if he offended her in his foul and unwashed state. 'Oh God,' he said, and he closed his eyes and remembered the wreck of the *Deliverance*, the caravel herself twelve hours at the bottom of the bay and her drowned crew washing up on the beach, and he thought of Hester coming to his bedside no more than a few weeks ago with the child hitched up against her hip and setting the maid down upon the counterpane to grab fistfuls of the quilted faded cotton, and how, long ago, when he had felt quite alone, and desperate, Hester had held him close as if she were his mother. One just had to assume that they would be safe – and so they were, beyond the reach of Lord Castlereagh.

'You haven't asked what's to become of you,' Dorothea said lightly. 'You can't remain indefinitely imprisoned in your brother's wine cellar.'

'What then?' Kitto demanded. Was he to join Crow in gaol?

'Well, you were unquestionably involved at Newlyn,' Dorothea said, watching him with unsettling perspicacity. 'However, it's felt that in light of your youth and the strength of public feeling towards your family, clemency is the least disruptive policy. Believe me, Lord Castlereagh took some convincing, but you're to return immediately to your regiment. The Grand Duchess Maria has been in London, and the royal yacht sails from Plymouth to Petersburg in a week's time. It seems in everyone's best interests if you join her on the voyage, with as little fuss as possible.'

Kitto closed his eyes and thought of the domed, golden Petersburg rooftops, and the ugly statues in the hedge-lined gardens at Tsarskoe Selo, and the ice-choked expanse of the Neva as he had last seen the great river, and hoped that Alexander would decide to finally side with Napoleon or England, and that he could run towards the sound of cannon-fire again, breathing in the stink of smoke, the smell of blood, and that he could forget everything, and that it would all be over.

19

Later that same day, Crow was escorted by English soldiers up the steps at Boscobel Castle, still prison-cell filthy. These Cornish acres fell outside the marches of his own considerable earldom: he was now on duchy land controlled by the English via the social pretensions of Hawkins Boscobel, a lethal combination. The familiar sensation of being found wanting crept through him: long dead, Papa walked at his side. His father was as tall as ever, the Lamorna black hair streaked with grey, his lips still tinged with blood, stark red against pale lips, pale skin. Even in death, he hadn't lost that expression of gelid, unspoken fury, so familiar from mornings in the breakfast-room at Lamorna House in London. Crow wanted to tell him that he knew very well he left so much to be desired, even though he was no longer the young idiot who had scandalised the capital, but the shade of his father faded from sight, leaving him with only the breathless, thirsty anticipation that always came before going into battle, except that this time he had no weapon, not even a knife. It was very lowering, to be sure, to arrive under prison guard at the nouveau riche palace of a man whose grandfather had been lord of all he surveyed in his very own candle-shop in Truro. Crow had scarcely reached the topmost step with his guards when the right-hand door was pulled open just enough to allow him to follow the first soldier inside, swiftly followed by the second. The door was closed behind him with a smart, well-oiled click and Crow turned to face the Boscobels' butler, Williams, who twenty years ago had caught him breaking a window in the orangery and clouted him so hard that his ears still rang the following morning.

Crow was ready to kill if he had to, but here he heard himself speak with measured courtesy. 'Good morning, Williams. How is your wife? Does she still suffer with the lumbago?'

Williams preserved an expression of well-trained indifference and looked through both guards. 'Betty does as well as can be expected, my lord, and I am sure would wish to pass on her fondest respects to you.' Without any indication that he was aware of either the soldiers' presence or Crow's filthy, unshaven appearance, Williams swept up the wide staircase and announced Crow without a flicker of discomfiture, as if he had come for a morning visit. Crow absorbed the elegant proportions of the drawing-room, the faded but respectable brocade curtains, the fantastically ugly oil paintings of various Boscobels along with their overfed spaniels and horses, all so familiar. He'd thought he would never set foot in such a place again, that like Nathaniel Edwards he would die in the squalor of the prison-yard at Bodmin. Two men sat in armchairs by the fire, including Hawkins Boscobel himself, who had the temerity to look uncomfortable at receiving the Earl of Lamorna in such circumstances, when he had not the decency to resist putting the *Deliverance* out to sea when she was unseaworthy, and neither the compassion nor the good sense to relieve the poor on his own estate. The other was Lord Castlereagh.

Castlereagh looked up as if they had just met in the drawing-room again after a day's hunting on Crow's own land, this man who had broken all ancient laws of hospitality, of honour, only to further his political ambition. 'My dear Lamorna. How good of you to join us.'

Crow inclined his head; it was a moment before he could trust himself to speak. 'Are we to bore Hawkins with this discussion?' He failed entirely to conceal his fury. His own people had been murdered at Newlyn on the orders of this worthless person; because of Castlereagh, his wife and child were both far from the reach of his protection.

To Boscobel's credit, he heaved himself to his feet, wheezing with the effort, buttons straining at his buttercup-yellow waistcoat. 'Ring, and Williams can bring you anything you're needful of. I'll away to my library.'

When the door had closed behind him, Crow looked away from the fire and turned back to the prime minister. 'Where in Christ's fucking name are my wife and child? My brother?' It was a grave mistake to lose his temper, but he could do nothing to stop himself.

'My dear boy,' said Castlereagh, making a church steeple with his fingertips, 'would even the Duke of Wellington himself have promised you carte blanche to conduct yourself exactly as you please if he supposed that it was not the greater good of the country that you served? In truth, you serve the interests only of Cornwall and therefore also of yourself, given that you are so rich not only in the spoils of maritime trade but also in the misguided loyalty of the Cornish people. Your duty is to suppress insurrection here and instead you foment it and allow the poison to spread.'

'My duty is to protect my own people. Where are my wife, my child and my brother?' Crow repeated, fighting the intense need to crush Castlereagh's throat with his own hands.

Castlereagh smiled. 'If you value their safety, don't insult me with pretended ignorance about your own intentions. There are so many rumours about a Cornish uprising with which your name always seems so peculiarly connected that it has become quite impossible to ignore them. Your actions at Newlyn have only confirmed everyone's suspicions.'

Crow watched him; he had evaded the question. In that moment, he was almost sure that Castlereagh didn't actually know where Hester was, or the little maid, or Kitto. *Thank God, thank God.* 'What do you want from me?' he said. 'The government under your command controls the Duchy of Cornwall, and therefore all the bits of the county I don't happen to own. Do you want my share, too? Is that it?'

'Don't be obtuse, Lamorna.'

Briefly, Crow closed his eyes and saw himself slamming Castlereagh's head against the hearthstone until his skull cracked and pale, greyish brain matter fell in clots upon the Turkish carpet. He must force himself to speak; he must navigate this battleground. 'Where does all this lead, Castlereagh? Have you not enough to occupy yourself with leading the country? Why do we have no king or queen to relieve you of the responsibility? It's been nearly a year since we forced Napoleon into ordering his troops to leave British soil.'

'Which brings us at long last to my point.' Castlereagh smiled without a trace of mirth. 'If you were me, Lamorna, which of the surviving royals, illegitimate or otherwise, would you choose as our monarch?'

'Oh, don't play games with me. The princess royal,' Crow

said. 'Charlotte might be a woman but she's at least old enough to know her mind, and she knows how to rule. She's had a hand in managing the duchy since long before her husband died, but if you wanted an experienced woman in her middle years with ideas of her own, Charlotte would have been on the throne for months. You want a young and impressionable puppet. Who is it to be?'

Castlereagh poured himself another glass of port, but Crow held one hand over his own glass. 'I suppose you're too young to remember the rumours about the princess royal's sister Sophia? You would have been scarcely more than an infant when all that happened, but I'd wager your father had a hand in covering it up.'

'That? It's true, then? Princess Sophia really did go away to deliver an illegitimate child?'

'In the summer of 1800, yes. And Sophia was a great deal more careful over her child's welfare than the rest of the royal family were about their own offspring, wrong side of the sheets or not. That child has been in Russia since long before Bonaparte escaped Elba in '15.'

Crow knew what was to come. 'Who was the father, then?' he asked. 'And where is this child?'

'Russia,' Castlereagh said, simply. 'The father was Alexander himself.'

Crow suppressed a sensation of incurable weariness. 'Alexander Romanov? The Russian tsar? Where exactly is all this leading, Robert?'

'A youthful peccadillo before Alexander took the imperial crown,' Castlereagh said smoothly. 'The year before he succeeded, the young tsar enjoyed rather more than a state visit to England. It's not generally known – or at least, not here. The Russians are far less exact about such matters. I want you to go to St Petersburg, Lord Lamorna, and find out where that girl is, Alexander's daughter. Princess Sophia's daughter. She is known, I believe, as Nadezhda Sofia Kurakina, and was brought up as the foster-child of a Russian count who had lost a fortune at gaming, and now lives in some out-of-the-way province. A young, malleable queen with ties to Russia – even illegitimate – would be of the utmost use to us at the moment.'

Crow laughed. 'A bastard queen? Castlereagh, I wish you all the very best of good luck in foisting an illegitimate heir on the clergy, even if you can get it around the populace, with all those clever stories you like so much in *The Times* and the *Morning Post*.'

'Oh, don't be so deliberately oafish,' Castlereagh said. 'After all your subterfuge you should know better than anyone how easy it is to make matters appear as they are not. We already have official documents pertaining to a secret marriage that never took place between Sophia and one of the Romanov cousins, now dead. God knows it's easy enough to make the populace believe anything anyone wants – the Kurakina girl can be made respectable enough whether the Russians like it or not. If the tsar doesn't wish his cousin's name to be taken in vain, what can he do about it once our own population have come to fervently believe in the brat's legitimacy?'

'Yes,' Crow said, 'well, you certainly found it easy to firmly convince most of the middling sort and all of the haut ton that the peasantry are a vicious mob who must at all costs be terrified into submission with regular hanging and transportation, and that devout Methodist congregations in

Cornwall, on my own land, are dangerous killers. My days of subterfuge, as you call it, are long gone. Find someone else to snare your bastard princess.'

Castlereagh watching him, unsmiling now, said: 'At this precise moment in time, Lamorna, you are also a danger to the security of the nation. I know you're not afraid of death, but find Nadezhda Sofia and bring her here to me: you won't relish the consequences if you don't. Had you not long enough in prison to consider how it will be for your wife, child and brother to learn what it is to exist as the dependants of an executed traitor? Do you think we don't know exactly which ship your wife and child sailed on, and that we won't eventually find them, that we can't reach your brother the moment he rejoins his regiment?'

Crow closed his eyes and in his mind's eye he saw Hester standing by the window, looking out over the rolling acres of Boscobel parkland with the little maid in her arms, and knew that he was bound to Castlereagh like a mastiff on the end of a leash until they were both safe again, whatever damned fool course of action the man decreed he should follow.

Part 2

ST PETERSBURG

20

At two o'clock in the morning, the ballroom at Countess Tatyana Orlova's St Petersburg townhouse thronged with women and girls in diaphanous silk gowns and men in regimentals – the Russians quite over the top, in Kitto's opinion, the officers of elite and ancient Muscovy regiments older than the Romanov dynasty itself, all dripping with gilding, gorgets and tassels. In couples and knots of three or four, guests gathered near the large windows overlooking the Neva, wide waters glittering in the moonlight. Books with gold-filigree leather spines lined the walls, and between the bookshelves, enormous ornate mirrors reflected the crowd and silver vases of spring flowers breathed out their scent, intensified by the human warmth of so many guests. Tonight, Kitto wasn't dancing but gaming, and he was either about to lose a small fortune, or to win one. Abbotsdale of the 62nd Wiltshires possessed only just enough social *éclat* to be honoured with an invitation to Countess Orlova's soirée. Kitto sat before him at the card-table, his expression inscrutable, the pair of them observed in uneasy quiet by a knot of other fellows from Kitto's regiment and others, as well as the ambassador's son,

George Cathcart. Fresh rumours of Crow's supposed treason seemed to have reached Petersburg even before Kitto himself. Standing by the table, Percy Dangerfield and that officer from the Guards continued to studiously not meet one another's eyes: it had been like this since the moment Kitto had stepped off the royal yacht at the English Embankment and taken a kalasha back to quarters only to find that the drawing-room fell completely silent when he walked in.

'You're crazy, Helford.' George addressed Kitto with a sideways glance. 'My father would have skinned me if I'd run up gaming debts like that before I was twenty-one. He'd have had me back in England and going over turnip yields at Orchardleigh before I knew which way was up.'

'Fuck off, Cathcart. My father's long dead, and who says I'm going to lose, anyhow?' Kitto ignored George's indulgent dismissal of his rudeness: he'd made a concerted effort to sound far more ill at ease than he actually felt, with just the right touch of nervous bravado. He had, after all, been taught by the best.

'If Lord Lamorna were my guardian,' George said calmly, 'I'm not sure I'd be fool enough to antagonise him, in prison or not, even with several thousand miles between us. He's just as devilish high in the instep as he is loose in the haft, is Crow.'

A thick, awkward quiet descended at the mention of Crow's name, and for God's sake he must still be alive. Surely Dorothea Lieven had been telling the truth?

'Are you going to show your hand or not?' Abbotsdale demanded, with all the pink-cheeked, well-fed arrogance of the younger son of an insignificant baronet who had lorded it over the cricket lawn at Harrow and achieved little since. He had a certain air that reminded Kitto of Captain Wentworth, which made him want to crush the man's throat with his own two hands. 'What's the matter, Helford, losing your nerve?' Abbotsdale went on with a slight but unmistakable sneer. It was precisely that smirk that had got Kitto into this. He'd been longing to wipe it off Abbotsdale's face all evening.

'You can fuck off as well,' Kitto advised him with an air of light unconcern.

'Jesus,' George muttered, trying to catch Kitto's eye. 'Helford, you bloody young fool, you'll talk yourself into a duel at this rate.'

Abbotsdale smirked again. 'What's the matter, Helford? Why all the bravado? Are you afraid to lose? Scared that Lord Lamorna will cut the purse strings? He'll find that hard from his prison cell.'

Was Kitto imagining it, or did those other officers from the 51st standing right over near the window now turn to stare? Countess Orlova herself certainly did – she had been talking to them, her small white hands moving so fast, her beringed fingers a blur of bright stones, candlelight from the candelabra finding threads of gold in her delicate sweep of curls. But now she turned to glance at Kitto, a small, inscrutable smile upon her lips, and he inclined his head before looking away as fast as decorum allowed.

'Oh, my God,' George was saying with apathetic and mocking despair. 'Not a duel, anything but a duel. Be quiet, the pair of you. Do you want the tsar to hear of this?'

Kitto turned over his cards, and had the pleasure of seeing all smug satisfaction wiped clean from Abbotsdale's face. Vengeful euphoria coursed through him, and he was scarcely aware of the ballroom clamour and heat – music and the babble of French and Russian, with the occasion burst of guttural English or Prussian, the smell of perspiration and costly hair pomade. Abbotsdale's face was now white and pinched with fury; he was a thousand roubles down – far more than he could afford, Kitto was sure. In fact, he knew quite well that he ought never to have played Abbotsdale in the first place, he with the enormous acreage of the Lamorna fortune at his back, and Abbotsdale with his father's penny-pinched estate in Wiltshire that must somehow be squeezed of dowries for his four sisters.

'I'll wait for your IOU, Abbotsdale,' he said, and got up, pushing back his chair. He suddenly couldn't bear it any longer, simply being here. Kitto could stand no more of this endless round of parties and balls: it felt like that bright and desperate season in Brussels before Waterloo, the damned and the fair dancing together and half the officers blown to smithereens before the month was out. Hardly aware of where he was going, Kitto forced his way through the crowd towards one of the large windows overlooking the river. Johnny and Ned would never have cut him as the others now did, but Johnny had been sliced completely in half by a cannonball fired from the ramparts at Novgorod, and Ned had survived Grezhny only to succumb to typhus on that interminable march back to Petersburg. In truth, one had no friends. Kitto passed Weston and Smyth-Jones, both in his own regiment, and they too each cut him as he approached, turning away as if they had never even heard his name, let alone toasted him with requisitioned champagne in the aftermath of Novgorod, all because he'd volunteered to climb the siege walls, and was the only one to end that particular mission with his life. Kitto had last attended a ball in Petersburg at the beginning of December, the Neva thick with blue-green ice and all the trees dusted with frost, and everywhere he'd looked he'd been met with smiling faces and outstretched hands. Now, because of Crow, men in his own regiment were turning their backs on him. How was it possible to be so entirely furious with Crow for getting himself arrested as a traitor and equally so paralysed with terror, wondering again if Dorothea had been wrong or lying. What if Crow were dead? What then?

'Darling Captain Helford!'

Kitto turned, bowing at the Russian society matron whose name he could not remember, all dark blue silk and ugly diamonds, allowing her to manoeuvre him into a position where he could do nothing but ask her pretty, dark-eyed daughter to dance, not that he cared, and God only knew how many times he went up and down the polonaise with girl after blushing girl, because what else could he do in this godforsaken fucking ballroom when no one save women would talk to him. Kitto was only grateful that he had inherited the Lamorna head for drink, and could take glass after glass of champagne without missing a single step or slurring his words, even as his thoughts became detached from one another and fluttered around his mind like so many moths, leaving him with nothing but an impression of candlelight and bright silk, and the warm, shaking hands of a girl lightly held in his own. At last, he relinquished a raven-haired beauty to her chaperone, with no idea of her name or who she was, not that he cared, and turned to face the widow Countess Tatyana Orlova, standing before him in that lily-fresh gown of silver satin, like a drink of cool water. Everyone said she had just refused an offer of marriage from Prince Volkonsky, who had been her lover for years.

'My dear young Captain,' she said, in her perfect Parisian French, and Kitto glimpsed her pearlescent teeth. 'I declare that Ekaterina Raevskaya's mama is quite ready to scalp you – anyone can see that she is longing for you to favour Katya as you favoured the other girls. You are cruel, honestly.'

'The devil take it,' Kitto said, 'I don't care.' Crow would have skinned him for speaking so to his hostess, or indeed to any woman at all, but Crow was not here, and maybe he was not even still alive, damn his fucking eyes. Countess Orlova was smiling at him. Kitto smiled back.

'You devil,' she said, 'you're far too drunk to be dancing with debutantes – a fact which is quite apparent to me, even if you've managed to conceal it from their mothers. Come and play cards with Alexei Pushkin and Prince Volkonsky before you commit some sort of terrible indiscretion.'

'Volkonsky and Pushkin?' Kitto said, now horribly short of breath.

'Darling boy, I know quite well you're used to moving in the first circles in England, so what difference does it make if you do so in Russia? Your papa was a close friend of the late prince regent, was he not? You can have nothing to fear from Prince Volkonsky.' Countess Orlova held out her beautifully sculpted arm and Kitto took it, allowing her to lead him across the ballroom. No one dared cut him in her company: he wondered if this was why she had done it, and felt a sudden burst of shame that she had so easily identified him as an outcast.

21

Three hours later, at five o'clock in the morning and now more drunk than he had ever been in his life, Kitto tossed his cards on to the table. It would be all right. It would have to be, after all. He couldn't exactly write to Crow and ask for an advance on the next quarter of his allowance. Dimly aware that someone was talking to him, he looked up at the blurred faces around the table. Count Gagarin was staring into the distance, obviously ineffably bored by Kitto's presence. Pushkin exchanged flirtatious nothings with the Georgian princess who stood behind him to watch their play, and Prince Volkonsky himself sighed, with a confidential smile. A hero of Borodino and Austerlitz, the prince was at least forty, with dark, golden-brown skin, deep lines graven into striking features, and an untidy crop of curling autumnal-brown hair. It was said that the ancestor he shared with Pushkin had been an enslaved African prince adopted by Peter the Great. In Kitto's opinion, he didn't look like a man scorned by his lover: he didn't even look drunk.

'And so, remind me, Captain Helford,' Volkonsky said, 'how exactly does Cornwall relate to England and the rest of the United Kingdom? Is it some sort of principality?'

'Yes, we're our own country just as Wales and Scotland are, but no one's allowed to say so.'

'How interesting,' Prince Volkonsky went on, calmly, as if rather than staking treasonous claims to Cornish sovereignty, Kitto had instead made an observation about the weather, or Russian folk customs, or whether it was better to sketch with charcoal or pen and ink. 'Might I take leave to observe that I think your brother, Lord Lamorna, has been most ill used by his own government? And after he played such an important role in British emancipation from French rule – the rescue of Wellington, the sanguinary routing of French forces at Salisbury. Lord Castlereagh and the Cabinet might justly be accused of rank ingratitude.'

Kitto glanced down at his cards and felt sick: he really was hellish in the suds, quite at sea. 'Castlereagh doesn't like my brother because he's so insufferably rich, and the ordinary sort of people like him a deal too much. But actually, between you and me, Crow's just pretty insufferable in general.'

'One's older relatives often do seem so – it's one of life's oddities that at some mysterious point the matter reverses, and one's younger relations begin to seem insufferable,' the prince said, glancing down at his own hand of cards with a reluctant air. 'Oh dear. How unfortunate.' He laid down his cards and Pushkin glanced over, wincing. Kitto felt as though he were falling at vast speed through the floor.

Volkonsky smiled with an almost rueful air. 'A sore loss for you tonight, I'm afraid, Captain Helford. But you know how perfidious is Lady Luck – perhaps next time she'll dance with you.' At his side, Pushkin shrugged and blew out his cheeks with an uneasy glance at Kitto. Perhaps they both thought he'd shy off settling the debt. Count Gagarin had already lost interest in Kitto's disaster and gone to join the cotillion forming at the far end of the room, quite as though no one had just ruined themselves over a game of faro.

Kitto heard himself reply as though someone else were speaking. There was a queer sort of rushing noise in his head, and the slow-moving dancers took on an odd, blurred quality as he reached for the necessary French phraseology, as though he were the only fixed point, and the ballroom itself was spinning. 'I'm afraid I'll have to send you some vowels, Prince.'

'Naturally,' Volkonsky said, employing an amused hauteur that reminded Kitto of his brother with blighting force. 'I would scarcely expect you to carry such a considerable sum about your person, Captain. Pray excuse me, I must have a word with the countess.'

Kitto nodded as though his life were still worth living, watching as the prince got up and walked away across the ballroom, quite resplendent in the tasselled silver jacket of the Semenovksy Guards, soon disappearing into the crowd, and was it wrong to wish that by some childish magic Prince Volkonsky really had simply flickered out of existence, and that the last three hours had never occurred?

'Don't take it as a personal affront, my boy,' Pushkin said, even though he couldn't have been so very much older than Kitto himself: nineteen or twenty at the most. He signalled to one of the countess's liveried footmen, and Kitto watched as his glass was refilled. 'I've known the man all my life, but I'd still as lief not game with him when he's in this sort of mood. Volkonsky should have stopped play long ago – a boy your age – but he's in a terrible temper tonight. It's just a pity that you caught the raw end of it. Woman trouble. Tatyana is a darling but she can be a minx of the first order – she's an unforgivable fool to have refused him. She might be our principal hostess now, but the knives are out for her already, mark my words – and who would want to risk dwindling into an irrelevant widow?'

Kitto gave a mechanical nod, but all he wanted to do was get up and leave, run down the scarlet-carpeted gilded staircase, past the liveried footmen and butler and out of the front door; he wanted to keep running until he crossed the carriage drive running the length of the English Embankment and leap into the cold, unforgiving waters of the Neva where he would drown and be swept out into the Gulf of Finland, gone for ever. Twenty thousand roubles. There was no possible way he could repay it. He looked up to realise that Pushkin was still talking to him; on the one hand, Kitto was grateful for the young poet's presence, but, perversely, in the midst of his loneliness, Kitto also wished very much to be alone, and hadn't the smallest notion what he ought to do if Pushkin continued to bore on about whatever mawkish business had blighted the affairs of Countess Orlova and Prince Volkonsky, who were both even older than Crow, or even asked him about Lord Byron, which he might very easily do.

'The trouble with Volkonsky,' Pushkin was saying, turning an ugly Sèvres ornament over and over with his brown and swiftly mobile fingers, 'the real, irrefutable trouble with Volkonsky is that he ought to have come up to scratch and proposed to the darling countess twenty-five years ago. Only he didn't, and poor Tatyana was married off to Orlov, which was no opera picnic, I can assure you, or at least not while the man lived, and now she and Volkonsky loathe the universe and each other. Therein lies the difficulty. Do you see?' He burst into a surprising peal of laughter. 'Of course you don't. You're far too young to understand blighted love or to be weary of life. And too young to be gaming with the likes of

Sasha Volkonsky, eh? My Tanyushka was a hellcat to have introduced you to him tonight, to be sure.'

Kitto forced himself to stand, managing a clumsy farewell which Pushkin received with an indulgent, throwaway wave before settling back in his chair. Kitto was only too well aware of people watching his unsteady progress towards the enormous gilded double doors. News of his ruin would doubtless spread before he even reached the footmen. Now Gillingham and Peters passed him without a second glance, when just months before Gillingham had been petitioning him with invitations to his quarters for supper and lightskirts. The crowd thickened as Kitto reached the doors, as though there were enemy French troops in formation blocking his way, but really there was just an enormous group of girls all fluttering muslin and long, glittering glances. They switched rapidly from court French into Russian as he passed, breaking out into bright peals of laughter, which was all they dared under the eyes of so many chaperones. There was one girl still in his path, small and plump, in an ill-advised gown of rose-pink crêpe; she turned, and Kitto recognised George's unremarkable sister, Jane Cathcart. She smiled at him in desperation, clearly in the throes of being cut herself by this merciless gathering.

'Oh, Captain Helford, how do you do? I'm sorry to say that we've still had no letter from Lady Lamorna at the embassy.' Jane immediately flushed brick red, and Kitto bowed for want of something else to do other than vomiting on her satin slippers, and what could be taking Hester so long to write? She had boarded a ship bound to Brittany from St Mary's, that's what Dorothea Lieven had told him. Surely she could have written by now? He pushed away a memory of a drowned, wax-white face beneath a glasslike wave in

Lamorna Cove: Hester couldn't be drowned like that, not she and the child and Mrs Rescorla. Jane's face crumpled with mortification, realising she had said exactly the wrong thing, and Kitto saw her tabby cat of a mother move in, steering her firmly away from him, their arms locked together. And as he finally drew near the doors, he heard familiar voices speaking in English above the hubbub of French, Russian and Prussian and looked up to find George standing warily at the side of Abbotsdale, who looked entirely castaway, his lips wine-stained, his thick brown hair in disarray – he'd always had an appalling head for claret.

'You damned little bastard,' Abbotsdale hissed, thrusting a scribbled IOU at him. 'I suppose you'll need all the fortune you can scrounge once sainted Lord Lamorna is hanged for treason. That's what we did to our last crop of traitors, remember? And he's really no better than a Jacobite, is he? The only difference being he's Cornish, not Scots. What's he playing at, setting all the south-west up against the government when we're still at war with France?'

'What?' Kitto spoke without moving, allowing the IOU to flutter to the marble floor between them. 'What did you say, Abbotsdale?'

'Oh, for God's sake, pay no heed,' George said. 'Honestly, Helford, what's the good in letting yourself get riled up by it? Causing a scandal here won't help Lamorna, although I'm certain it'll turn out he's been unfairly smeared by Castlereagh.'

Abbotsdale smirked. 'I think we all know it's a little more than that, don't we?'

He got no further. Lent strength by fury, Kitto felled him with a savage blow to the jaw and silence crashed over the thinning crowd in the ballroom like a vast, cold wave.

Abbotsdale slumped against the gilded door-panels, spitting out a spray of blood and what looked very much like a tooth on to Countess Orlova's cerulean-blue Rajasthani carpet. In a blind, uncomprehending rage, Kitto snatched the older man's jacket, hauling him to his feet.

'Say it again!' he said, quietly, into the booming, appalling moment of silence. 'Say it again, Abbotsdale.' And without waiting for a reply, Kitto hit him once more, in Countess Tatyana Orlova's ballroom, the insult only sharper because he himself had challenged his brother on exactly the same terms.

22

Many hours later, Kitto woke face down, cold stone beneath him. Without moving, he watched light shaft in through a barred, narrow window. Not just a stone floor, but bare stone walls, too. He was locked in and panic shuddered through him: he couldn't breathe. In moments, his eyes grew used to the gloom in his cell, and he saw a pair of shining black leather hessians inches from his face, which was pressed against the filthy stone floor. He sat up, naked without a weapon; beyond the boots, he could see very little.

'Helford, you bloody young fool. What were you thinking? If it's not bad enough to brawl at a godforsaken ball, you could at least have managed not to continue it out in the street just as the damned *politsiya* were passing.'

Kitto got to his feet, determined not to betray his heart-stopping and entirely humiliating fear of confined spaces, glad that it was so dark George likely could not see how much he was shaking.

George sighed. 'God knows I can't even count the number of times I've heartily wished myself at the club the day your brother called on me when I was last in London, you know.

But I wasn't, and I promised him I'd keep an eye out for you, so come on. Let's get you out of this place. *Christ*, so revolting!'

Without a word, knowing there was absolutely nothing he could say to excuse himself, Kitto followed his rescuer along a stinking passageway; the British diplomat's son an incongruous presence in the squalor of the guard-cells, clad in full evening dress and neat as a pin from his black silk pantaloons to the exquisitely cut jacket of superfine. It was odd, though, when one really thought about it: Crow's friends had all died at Waterloo, or in the bloody battles leading up to it. George Cathcart was one of the few of Crow's contemporaries to have survived the Peninsular Wars and Waterloo itself, and yet he never spoke of him. How little faith must Crow have in him, Kitto, to ask George to be his nursemaid in Petersburg, when George had never even been his particular friend?

Outside in the frigid northern night, George had kept the droshky waiting, and the bearded coachman in his voluminous thick blue caftan with the wide Circassian belt and silver buttons that glinted in the moonlight. Kitto got into the open carriage, aching all over and acutely aware of the prison-cell reek of urine-scented stale water and unwashed bodies that clung about him still. Scarcely waiting for George to sit down, the coachman called to the horses and the droshky sprang forward; even now, Kitto marvelled at how the driver used no whip but controlled his horses by voice alone, calling out into the chilly night. George looked at Kitto once, but just shook his head, crossed his booted legs, and addressed his attention to the torchlit streets with an expression of impeccably bred veiled disapproval. Kitto sat in excruciating silence until they reached the aspen-lined boulevard of the English Embankment in all its smoky, fish-scale-spangled chaos, and the Petersburg scents of scorched chestnuts and rotting fish and ancient mud and horseshit, and where the large, elegant townhouses were painted in sugared-almond shades of pastel, like so many iced cakes.

Kitto let out a long breath before he could finally bring himself to speak. 'I really wouldn't presume to put myself in your father's presence.'

George gave him a crushing look. 'Oh, for the Lord's sake. An officer of the Coldstream brawling with a man at a ball? Abbotsdale is a heel of the first order, but there are limits. The pair of you are only bloody lucky Weston and I managed to separate you before either of you tried to call the other out – not that you could call Abbotsdale out, even if you wanted to, given that you're not even close to twenty-one. I was due at Princess Vachekshina's soirée an hour ago, and my father has cancelled his engagements to manage this mess. Save whatever Banbury tale you've concocted for him, I beg you. Dear God, Lamorna was right when he told me that you were born to be hanged.'

Without another word, George turned, striding back to the carriage, and left Kitto to negotiate his way through the crowd, thick and vociferous even at this hour, and as ever pungent with the mingled scents of stale human sweat, smoke, old fish and the reek of church incense that clung to the hair of the faithful. He edged his way through a gathering group of fiercely debating Chinese merchants with their long queues, and was escorted alone by a pair of liveried footmen up the wide, marble steps of the embassy. Pale corridors with scarlet carpets and embossed ceilings passed in a blur of ancestral Cathcart portraits, the footmen both preserved expressions of Russian disapproval, and by the time Kitto found himself waiting outside a handsome pair of mahogany double doors, waxed to such a gleaming shine that he could see his own hollow-eyed, pallid face staring back, he was so light-headed that he had to fight the urge to simply lie down on the rug. This was worse than anything. He swallowed hard, listening to the footman knock and announce him to Lord Cathcart.

The British Ambassador to Russia was sitting behind his desk in a large apartment with green silk wall-coverings lit up by branches of tall white candles. A hundred flames shivered in the sudden breeze as Lord Cathcart's footman closed the double doors behind him. The balding, silver-haired diplomat took what felt like hours to look up from a sheaf of candlelit documents, and when he did at last, he only sighed, but did not invite Kitto to sit in one of the old-fashioned mahogany chairs drawn up to the desk. *You climbed the siege ladders at Novgorod,* Kitto reminded himself, recalling the whine of musket-ball after musket-ball passing him as he climbed hand over hand, and all the while knowing that if that whining hiss of iron through air ever grew quiet, it was because he himself had been hit.

'A fine mess, Helford,' Lord Cathcart said, leaning back in his chair to look Kitto up and down.

'If you'll let me go back to quarters and get my pistol, sir, then I can end it with little more inconvenience to you.' Kitto returned the diplomat's steady gaze. 'I know I've disgraced my regiment, but I also lost twenty thousand roubles to Prince Volkonsky that I've no hope of repaying. I can't possibly trouble my brother—' He broke off, quite unable to discuss Crow's ignominious situation with Lord Cathcart. 'I'm sure that you won't try and stop me taking the only honourable way out.'

Lord Cathcart laid down his pen, the top of his balding head gleamed in the candlelight, but he was no less intimidating for it. 'My dear boy,' he said, with awful, gentle patience. 'How old are you, precisely?'

'I'll be seventeen soon, sir.' This interview was not progressing at all as Kitto had expected; his throat felt thick and dry with thirst.

Lord Cathcart sighed. 'Then I can only assume that you have no notion of the chief reason why Prince Volkonsky ought to have known a great deal better than to play faro with a child.'

Kitto flinched. So he was a killer when they wanted him to be, and a child when it suited them. 'I don't understand you, sir.' Even to his own ears he sounded pompous.

'You are not yet of age, boy. It's Volkonsky who is at fault for playing against you, and I might add that well he knows it. It would be dishonourable of the prince to accept so much as a single kopek from you – which is just as well, since I'm quite sure that I myself would have no choice but to discharge your debt until your brother could relieve me of the responsibility, and I have Jane to bring out this year. As you'll no doubt have noticed, she doesn't do much to help herself.' Lord Cathcart's expression grew pained. 'Gowns, silks, brocades, quantities of champagne – good Lord. Do you think, Christopher, that I would betray your father's memory by allowing you to take your own life in lieu of a gambling debt? Honour is of all importance, but these things can be managed without recourse to opera-hall tragedy.'

Kitto stared at him, suppressing a burst of brandy-fuelled nausea. Even an apology would seem paltry, so he said nothing.

'All the same,' Lord Cathcart went on, 'the debt is only one matter and in fact almost the very least of it, as you well know – you've embroiled yourself in a low-bred scandal, Helford, and that must be dealt with. It's of utmost importance that the British presence in Petersburg is seen by the Russians as a help rather than a burden, and our young officers disgracing themselves in society ballrooms will not gild the lily. I take it that you are not aware that this affair is already talked of everywhere, and that your own family name has even appeared in the news-sheets in connection with it?'

'I'd guessed so, sir,' Kitto said: throwing one's name into the ring for public discussion was the worst of crimes. It was a long time ago now, but he remembered only too well Papa's unspoken, white-faced fury over the breakfast-table whenever Crow's scandalous behaviour saw his name mentioned in *The Times* or the *Morning Post*. Papa himself had scarcely been a saint, but his own dissolute career had at least always been conducted with discretion. Even Crow, to Kitto's knowledge, had never hit a fellow officer of the British army in a ballroom.

'Have you any notion whatsoever, Helford, of the difficult and extremely sensitive nature of current relations between Britain and Russia?' Lord Cathcart went on, consulting another of his papers with only the briefest upwards glance at Kitto.

'We're allied against Napoleon as the greater enemy, but the tsar doesn't trust us and neither do his generals, and neither do the Russian people in general, sir,' Kitto said. 'And the tsar might change allegiance at any given moment, according to what suits him best. Am I to be reduced to the ranks, then, sir?'

Lord Cathcart, who had been studying a map unrolled on the desk-top before him, glanced up at Kitto once more. 'Do you think me quite stupid? A young officer of your courage and ability? No. We must simply be rid of you for a period – your continued presence in town can only fuel such a scandal as this. What, in your estimation, do British forces most lack? And what do the Russian battalions themselves equally lack?'

'Horses, sir,' Kitto replied instantly.

'Very well,' Lord Cathcart replied. 'I understand that the Semenovsky Guards sent several men and a small squadron of Cossacks to requisition new horseflesh in the interior: they were attacked and nearly all killed, leaving only a single newly conscripted young officer to oversee the horses, of which there are several hundred still remaining. You will apprehend the irresistible temptation to thieves and brigands. The officer is, as we speak, taking refuge on the country estate of Countess Orlova, awaiting an escort. You will be that escort, Helford. You will join Lieutenant Rumyantsev in escorting the horses back to Petersburg, although I do hear that the young fool had the temerity to protest by letter to his colonel that he would do better without any assistance at all.' Lord Cathcart glanced down at the map again. 'And I should hope that by the time you return in a blaze of glorious success this unseemly scandal will have quite dissipated, and that your completed mission will only cast a golden light on the helpful nature of Russo-British relations, united in defeating Napoleon, our common enemy. Am I quite understood?' Cathcart didn't wait for a reply. 'I see no reason for any appreciable delay, Helford. Lieutenant Rumyantsev awaits your assistance, and Countess Orlova's estate is quite some considerable distance from Petersburg. You'll need to change horses as often as you can. All necessary documents for travel await you with Colonel MacArthur.' He looked up once more. 'And if you could try to conduct yourself without disgracing the nation or further endangering the diplomatic process, I would be most extraordinarily grateful.'

23

Two nights after young Captain Helford had been so summarily banished from Petersburg, Countess Tatyana Orlova stood at the head of the wide, emerald-carpeted staircase that led down into her Petersburg drawing-room, watching her guests thronging and darting in the vestibule below like fish at the lake's edge. It had been less than a week since that exquisite refusal of a marriage proposal from her lover, and Tatyana felt a pleasurable wave of satisfaction at the prospect of teasing Prince Volkonsky with her continued and doubtless infuriating availability to other men: after Orlov, she would never again be bound in obedience.

Not even to you, Sasha Volkonsky, she thought, and sipped from the glass of champagne handed to her by one of the newer house serfs; she hadn't yet learned his name, he had only recently been purchased from the Rostopchins. The champagne was naturally very good, but she knew full well that society didn't come here only to drink it. They had all been waiting for her to fall, ever since the rumours about Petya began to spread, her dearest little soul. But she mustn't think about Petya. Tatyana assessed the crowd: at half past ten, there was a throng, thank God.

She sensed Sasha's presence before she saw him; a disturbance in the air, a heat. 'Easily enough of a mob,' he said, standing behind her. 'You haven't lost your touch – not yet, anyway.'

Tatyana turned to face him and he smiled, as if in dismissal of his departure at their last meeting: such heat-charged congress of fury and rigidly controlled good manners. 'How acerbic you are tonight, Sasha,' she said, teasing. 'Have you a sore head? Too busy winning fortunes from little British soldiers again?' What gave him the right to goad her? Standing so close to him entirely knocked the breath from her lungs and sent an unbearable spreading warmth between her legs. Sasha raised a finely arched and dismissive copper-brown brow, but Tatyana sensed the rapidity of his pulse: he had by no means forgiven her for refusing him. 'Have you heard any news of the Kurakina girl since that dreadful attack on the Semenovskys with the horses? Were they not supposed to be escorting her to Petersburg? I hear from Dorothea Lieven that the British have a strong interest in the girl. As well they might.'

'Dorothea ought to be more discreet.'

'Oh come now – you know well that she and I tell each other everything, and so does the tsar. To his profit, on more than one occasion. It was a boy from your own regiment who was sent to retrieve her, after all. Does anyone know if the girl is even safe after all those horses were stolen? We can only hope the French didn't get their hands on her as well.'

'Alexander should never have let his damned generals talk him into combining the two missions,' Sasha said, frowning; he was one of the few who called the tsar by his given name.

'In fact, we've heard nothing of Nadezhda Kurakina since the detachment with the horses was attacked. Lieutenant Rumyantsev wrote to say he was the lone survivor, but made no mention of the girl at all, whether she was even retrieved from the Kurakin estate, which makes me wonder if the chit hasn't either been killed or run away.'

Tatyana smiled at him. 'Are you telling me that your regiment has actually lost the most useful girl in Russia? A possible heir to the English throne, and no one knows where she is?'

Sasha merely cocked an eyebrow at her. 'I'm telling you nothing, but the Rumyantsev boy is due to wait for assistance at Yarkaya Polyana, is he not? Why don't you go home and ask him if you're so thirsty for intrigue? I'm afraid I have other irons in the fire, Tanyushka.' He turned to survey the swelling crowd. 'The British are out in force tonight, I see.'

Tatyana followed his gaze, knowing him well enough to be sure he would divulge no further information. 'It's a shame about the Cathcart daughter,' she remarked with a critical eye on the girl, flushed and cringing in yet another gown of pale pink that couldn't possibly have set her off to worse advantage. 'What a waste.'

'You're quite right: Jane Cathcart is entirely unremarkable.' Sasha treated her to one of his more irritating smiles.

'They must be hoping to get rid of her this year, all the same.' He was up to something: Tatyana was quite sure of it. Unbidden, a memory rose up and she was standing, aged eight, with bare feet on the pebbled island where the deep green stream split at the western edge of the farmyard, weeping with rage as Sasha had laughed and shouted from the far bank: *You said you were the better swimmer, now prove it.* Why couldn't she relinquish the certainty that he was about to take cruel enjoyment in punishing her for not accepting his proposal? The English ambassador's wife and her daughter had stopped to talk to one of the Raevsky girls who looked as if she wished herself elsewhere, but Tatyana knew that as hostess she wouldn't escape a tedious conversation about the advance of spring, or the latest Parisian fashion plates.

Sasha laid a hand on her shoulder, and she ignored the bolt of heat that shot down her arm as he leaned down to speak quietly into her ear. 'Who is that?'

The British soldier now talking to Lady Cathcart was tall and pale, with untidy black hair that made him appear almost *en déshabille*. He was surrounded by Ekaterina Raevsky, her rivals, and a crowd of English officers who all seemed to know him rather well. 'It must be Lord Lamorna,' Tatyana said. 'Lady Cathcart sent me a note asking if she might bring him – his ship docked this afternoon. Although, interestingly, he's half French, he rules some kind of irrelevant British principality, and is absolutely dogged by rumours of treachery to England – and on Tuesday you ruined his young brother at faro.' If what Tatyana had heard was true, Sasha had been seeking buyers for all the Volkonsky estates, losses she knew would cause him both shame and pain he would never publicly admit. He made no reply to her confidences, only watching the approach of Lord Lamorna with his usual air of boredom. Tatyana herself was intrigued: rumours of Lamorna's treachery had led to his young brother enduring several excruciating cuts direct here in this very house, but the man himself had attracted a crowd.

Lady Cathcart bore down upon them. With the earl at her side, she held out one limp hand. 'Darling Countess, you're looking so well. And my dear Prince Volkonsky. My daughter Jane you already know, of course,' Lady Cathcart said, 'but do allow me to make Lieutenant Colonel Lord Lamorna known to you.' The diplomat's wife went through the motions of social intercourse with an air of faint exhaustion. Even so, Tatyana detected a hint of panic in her expression of well-worn amiability, and a flicker of interest stirred at the prospect of fresh scandal. Lord Lamorna's mood was inscrutable, but it might well have been he who had induced Lady Cathcart's panic: he really was excessively pretty, with finely sculpted cheekbones, and that black hair and the startling pale grey eyes so clearly handed down the Saint-Maure line. Lord Lamorna lacked his young brother's deep-cut dimples and air of scarcely battened-down mischief which made such a fascinating combination with the watchfulness of a trained young killer, but he did emanate a suppressed animal fury so at odds with his calm exterior that Tatyana couldn't deny a flicker of interest. At a quelling glance from her mother, Jane Cathcart executed a clumsy curtsey, which the entire gathering acknowledged with only cursory attention. Lamorna bowed, conveying the perfect measure of practised good breeding and ennui, together with that intriguing and very thinly veiled menace.

'I don't know if you will have heard the happy news, Countess?' Lady Cathcart gave Tatyana a bland smile. Her daughter was now *in extremis*, the flush spreading from her face and down her neck to her décolletage. 'Dear Prince Volkonsky and my daughter have announced their engagement.'

Adept at concealing any emotion other than smooth congeniality, Tatyana was just able to smile, quite certain that no one – not even Sasha himself – would have detected the strength of her fury and mortification. So this was how he chose to punish her for refusing him: marriage to a squab of an English girl, just to prove that she didn't matter in the least. 'How absolutely charming, my dear Jane, I'm so happy for you. Such a triumph – not even one entire season and you've been snapped up!' Tatyana clasped the idiot girl's pale, slightly sweat-damp fingers, nodding at Sasha even though she wanted to rend her nails down his face.

Abandoning his expression of well-bred boredom, Lord Lamorna gave Tatyana such a beddable smile that, observing it, Jane Cathcart actually flushed again. 'Tell me, Countess Orlova,' he said, 'do you remain in Petersburg for the rest of the season?'

'Actually, I have some business to attend at Yarkaya Polyana – my late husband's estate.' Tatyana stifled a burst of flirtatious fascination that exploded past her rage with the force of a cannonball, just as Dorothea Lieven had archly predicted in her latest letter. *You may very well have some fun with Lord Lamorna, my dear friend.* Tatyana smiled, lying with the smooth grace of long practice. 'Oh, but I've only just realised the connection, Lord Lamorna – you are surely Captain Helford's brother.'

'Oh *goodness*,' Jane Cathcart said, with feeling.

Lord Lamorna ignored her, watching Tatyana with that inscrutable expression. 'Indeed. Which reminds me, Prince Volkonsky, it seems that I owe you twenty thousand roubles.'

Lady Cathcart looked as though someone had just vomited at her feet. Sasha just appeared irritated, and Lord Lamorna continued to smile as though he'd simply remarked on the unseasonably chilly spring. 'It was so good of you not to pursue the boy for payment before he was obliged to leave Petersburg,' he said to Volkonsky. 'I should like to point out that he did not deliberately renege on discharging his debt. Lord Cathcart told him it wasn't eligible because he has not yet attained his majority. In England, you see, it would be quite impossible for a boy his age to be held liable.'

Tatyana would have sworn with one hand on St Agatha's bones that the temperature in the room had dropped by a factor of ten. Jane Cathcart flushed an even deeper shade of puce, casting a furtive but admiring glance at this *enfant terrible* of the English polite world. Tatyana was certain of her conviction that young Jane Cathcart was deep in the throes of a Sapphic affair with her Italian drawing mistress, so surely the girl was immune to Lord Lamorna's fine grey eyes. Apparently, she had wit enough to admire such a devastatingly ill-advised put-down. All the same, Tatyana knew Sasha well enough to detect the briefest flash of shame – a glimpse of the boy he had been, the boy she had known, to whom honour had once mattered more than anything else. Lady Cathcart merely smiled – there was an exchange of curtseys and bows – and she swept the mortified Jane away into the crowd.

'Twenty thousand roubles? I've scarcely given the matter a thought, Lord Lamorna,' Sasha said; beyond the bow and kissing Jane's fingertips, he hadn't acknowledged the departure of his fiancée and her mother, and conversation swept on as if entirely uninterrupted.

'Except, no doubt, to consider the wisdom of dicing with a boy young enough to be your own son,' Lord Lamorna remarked, imparting no more weight to his words than if he were discussing the weather, and not courting a duel. It was another extraordinarily brazen insult and Tatyana froze where she stood, momentarily too shocked to move or to think; Lord Lamorna was really too young for Sasha to consider him a worthy opponent, but he still might very easily risk the tsar's displeasure by demanding satisfaction.

Sasha responded with a slight bow. 'Since we appear to be serving up unasked-for advice in wholly inappropriate company, might I suggest that you cool your temper? Such displays are frowned upon here in Petersburg. Those who cannot pay ought not to play.'

'Wise advice, sir,' Lord Lamorna said, 'if only half the world were able to follow it, so much human misery might be averted. You'll have a draft upon my bank tomorrow morning. I should think that your need must have been urgent indeed to have done such a thing – you won't suffer a wait for your funds, as I'm sure your young fiancée and her parents will be so pleased to hear.' He bowed and walked away, moving with the quick, careless insouciance of a cat.

And even though Tatyana wanted to do nothing but run from the room and weep with astonishing rage because Sasha was going to be married to an English debutante resembling a toad, she laughed, watching Lord Lamorna go.

'Touché, Sasha,' she said, liberating a glass of champagne from a servant and handing it to him, before taking one herself. 'But really – of all the outrageous cheek.'

Sasha had already turned away without even bothering to take his leave of her. How very enjoyable it would be to punish him for this. Lord Lamorna would be the perfect weapon. Oh, she'd summon that English lord with all his barely leashed temper. He would come. They always did.

24

The following morning, Crow sat opposite Lord Cathcart at his desk, watching the manservant pour two glasses of brandy. 'My dear boy,' Cathcart said, 'it was good of you to join us at Countess Orlova's – I dare say it was the last thing you felt like doing after such a long voyage.'

'It was nothing.' The sea-crossing from London to St Petersburg had taken more than a month, a series of jumbled recollections: of the grey seas and the forested, mountainous shorelines of eastern Denmark, a jumble of wooden warehouses lining the waterfront in Copenhagen, and the heart-stopping exuberance of Petersburg itself as they left the Gulf of Finland and sailed down the mouth of the Neva – a shocking mirage of Italianate architecture and the domed majesty of the Smolny Cathedral rising above it all. How much would the little maid have altered in all that time? Did she even have names now for the dogs, for his horse, for that green malachite bowl of shells so precious to her? Crow had to force himself to forget his wife, and his daughter in her embroidered linen cap, and to think only of Cathcart sitting before him, and brandy early in the morning, and the still-incomprehensible calls of the barge-men on the great swathe of the Neva sweeping out before the English Embankment; he'd picked up a little Russian here and there, but not much.

'You'll have your work cut out, Jack,' Cathcart was saying. 'In theory we're allies, but the Russians don't trust us. Alexander admires what he calls our cunning but fears our influence; meanwhile, intelligence tells us that Napoleon's sent Davout with eight regiments into Russia, and no one's sure where any of them are, or where *he* is. At least Napoleon's in Austria – his presence here would make twenty-five thousand men fight like fifty thousand.'

'And so instead of doing something actually useful, such as searching out where Marshal Davout might actually be hiding his regiments, I'm to find this bastard Russian princess?' Crow asked. 'Do you imagine that her people will just allow the girl to ride away with me?'

Cathcart sighed. 'To our knowledge, Nadezhda Kurakina actually has no people – unless you count the tsar himself who has never publicly acknowledged the child, even although her existence is an open secret in Russian society. Both the Count and Countess Kurakin are dead, their sons were killed at Borodino, and the girl has been living at their estate in Kazan with servants and her adoptive grandmother, who died last winter. You'll find that your own difficulties at home with Lord Castlereagh will dissolve if you manage to find us such a malleable young queen after all this time. I must add that I make no doubt you will not be furthering the acquaintance of your French relatives whilst in St Petersburg. I'm sure you understand how it would be viewed as bordering on treachery, if not outright treason – which would I'm sure be the furthest thing from your mind at the moment.'

Crow paused in the act of leaning forwards to light a cigarillo at one of the silver candlesticks foresting Cathcart's desk, fighting an odd, sliding sensation as if the carpeted floor had shot away from beneath his feet. 'My French what? My mother was the only Saint-Maure to survive the Terror. I've no surviving connections in France.'

'Your mother,' Cathcart replied, 'was extremely young when she fled France. No more than sixteen or seventeen, if I remember correctly. About the same age as your brother is now. Ask yourself, does Kitto concern himself with aged relatives on your father's side of the family?'

'Of course he doesn't, but there are scarcely any. A few elderly women – my father's aunts – who were married off out of Cornwall long before our father was born, let alone Kitto or myself. I dare say he never even saw them more than a handful of times. It was my father and then myself who undertook the task of answering their letters.'

'Consider that it might have been so for your mother,' Cathcart said. 'The aristocracy began leaving France in 1789. Your mother was rescued from her convent in Avignon by your father two years later, in 1791, the only one of her family to outlive the terror and confusion – so she thought. Thanks to your father, she survived the executions of her mother, father, brothers, cousins; I understand she herself only escaped imprisonment in the first place because she had been sent to Avignon, and the Republicans had so many others to exterminate that her existence was overlooked.'

'With great respect, my father told me this himself.' Crow exhaled a cloud of smoke, irritated at this recital of his own mother's history. But even as he spoke, he knew quite well that Maman had not liked to think of the past. He'd heard all this from his father, and only then when she was dead, and Papa drunk enough to tell the whole story to a child of eleven: knowing his father, it was entirely possible that he had left out any details that did not immediately concern himself, such as the existence of an *emigrée* aunt living in Russia.

'You understand, then, how a young girl such as your mother was might either forget or simply never speak of the existence of an elderly female relative?'

'I suppose so,' Crow said, 'but what are you saying? That such a woman exists – that she's still alive, and in St Petersburg?'

'That's precisely what I'm saying,' Cathcart replied evenly, 'and I trust that you'll make no attempt to visit her. I speak of this connection only so that you can make every effort not to cross paths with Thérèse de la Saint-Maure.'

Crow heard himself say, 'I didn't even know her name. How can I avoid meeting this woman if I'm to go out in Petersburg society? The Russians still associate as freely with the French as they do with us. The entire court is a crucible of Prussians, Austrians and French, and that's before you even start with the Persians and Turkish.'

'Well, I'll say this – I'm sure you have far too much respect for the Duke of Wellington to seek an introduction to your great-aunt, should you encounter one another.'

'I would do nothing so likely to embarrass my commander,' Crow said, lying with the elegant ease born of long practice as he remembered Wellington watching him across a map-table at the ambassador's house in the Azores: *Really, Jack? Marriage to such a one? You'll permit me to say that you should have shown your own family name more respect.* In truth, he was Wellington's man no more. Crow got up to walk to the door. 'Has there been no letter from my wife? I should like to think that she knows where I am, at least.'

'I'm afraid not, no.' Just as Cathcart's silent footman reached for the polished brass doorknob, the ambassador spoke again, as if with nothing more than an afterthought. 'There is one more thing, Jack.'

There was a queer, light tone in his voice that stopped Crow where he stood.

'I'm afraid there is some news of the *Curlew*, after all.'

'The *Curlew*?' Crow walked over to the tall window overlooking the Neva, watching the pall of wood-smoke rising from the chimneys on Vasilevsky Island, seagulls tossed in the air like cinders above a bonfire. He knew the *Curlew*: a three-masted frigate operating out of St Mary's on Scilly. So Hester had sailed on her, or why else would Cathcart speak of it? Hester and the little maid had sailed aboard the *Curlew*, with bales of wool and barrels of Chambord. He felt poised on the threshold of another world, one he had no desire to enter, and he wished he had never found Hester alone and dripping wet on the beach at Lamorna, years ago now, and that he had never loved her as much as he did.

'Don't tell me,' he said.

'I'm sorry.' Lord Cathcart crossed the room, standing closer to Crow, near to the fireplace. He took up a Venetian glass paperweight from the mantelpiece and passed it from one hand to the other. 'Jack, the *Curlew* was wrecked off Cézembre. She never reached Saint-Malo, where she was bound for. There were no survivors. According to the islanders, she went down in just fourteen minutes.'

And Cathcart carried on talking, but Crow just remembered the day he had gone up to the nursery with Hester a little earlier than usual because the rector and his wife were coming to dinner, and his daughter had still been sitting in her tin bath before the nursery fire, droplets of water clinging to her fine, pale brown curls, Beatie kneeling at her side, looking up with a nervous smile, even though Crow had known the girl all her life. *She likes the water, your little holy child from across the sea,* Hester had said, sliding one arm around his waist, referring to the old tale of the saint their daughter was named after, to St Morwenna, who had crossed the Irish Sea and come into Cornwall from Wales. *Although I believe she was not very holy when it came to the rice pudding, was she, Beatie?*

And so the *Curlew* had sunk and there were no survivors, and in Crow's mind he quite clearly saw Hester running down a streaming, tipping deck with their child in her arms all wrapped in a blanket; she would have tried to get to one of the tenders but, as he well knew, when a ship went down quickly, there was no time to lower any boat into the water. She would have jumped overboard, then, clinging to the guardrail one-handed before that final leap and knowing that to go down with the ship itself was certain death, pulled down into the deep by a roaring sea-maw awakened by the frigate sinking at speed. So she would have jumped, tried to leap free, but it would have all been for nothing, because although Hester, brought up on an island herself, was a strong swimmer, how could one possibly swim with a year-old child, in a storm that had driven a frigate off course, smashing her hull against the rocks that littered the approach to the Breton island of Cézembre? And Crow looked out of the window at the seagulls circling above the glittering Neva, and above the jumbled rooftops of Vasilevsky Island, but all he could see was Hester going down, down in the dark water, pale silver bubbles streaming from her mouth, her nose, those skirts in a billowing cloud around her as she held the bundled, blanketed child close, even as they drowned together, she and the baby.

Now that the maid was dead, he could say her name. It no longer mattered if God heard him speak it and so understood how much he loved Morwenna, his daughter Morwenna, his child, because God saw everything, and God had taken her away forever, as punishment for his many sins.

25

Two weeks later, almost at the close of his journey into the forested hinterland east of St Petersburg, Kitto left the final staging-inn before reaching Yarkaya Polyana, the great Orlov estate, and he could only thank Christ that the countess herself would not be present. He would rather face an entire detachment of French partisan soldiers armed only with his toothbrush after so comprehensively disgracing himself at her ball. To his shame, he had twice lost his way, wasting the better part of three days, and God help him if MacArthur and Cathcart ever heard of that. It was now almost dusk, but if he left now he would reach Yarkaya Polyana before the household retired to bed. Mounting up, Kitto called goodbye to the innkeeper leaning in the lamplit doorway of the kormcha, leaving behind the rows of bottled vodka and the ever-present cauldron of cabbage soup, and the dish of blini attracting flies. Arkady's daughter ran out on to the ridged muddy track to wave goodbye, she of the beautiful eyes and silk-straight black hair of her Kalmyk mother, clutching at the skirts of her long red woollen Russian sarafan. Kitto raised one arm above his head in farewell and spurred the fresh, back-stepping gelding into a hard gallop. Would such a pretty maid have smiled so as she poured sweet medovukha knowing that he'd left Petersburg in disgrace, the shadow of his brother's rumoured treachery following with every step he took? Verst after verst now stretched out between him and the wide European boulevards of Petersburg, leaving all that was known far behind. After riding day after day alongside those seemingly limitless swathes of pine, spruce, fir and cedar shot through with tracts of undulating grassland, Kitto knew he was truly in Russia once more: one never felt quite the same sense of limitless space and distance anywhere else. The maid had said he was now a mere one or two hours' ride from Yarkaya Polyana, and he would soon see a constellation of lit windows even from the road, the great place built as it was on the higher ground, so that the old count might overlook the land and the people that he owned.

Not long before Kitto expected to reach the formal borders of the demesne, when open field, grassland and forest would surely give way to orchard, garden and raked carriage drive, he dismounted, unthinkingly gentling the gelding as he did so, running one hand down the muscled roan neck. Standing on the track, he could not have said exactly what had made him know that he must feel the earth beneath his feet just at that moment, only that something was wrong in this darkening landscape. He waited, letting his gaze travel past the spruce and pine on either side of the rutted, puddle-dotted road. No. It was not anything he had seen, no wrong-shaped clot of shadow just at the furthest limit of his vision that might resolve itself into a crouching French soldier. It was something he could hear: or rather, what he could not hear. The gelding shifted, tossing his great head, back-stepping, and Kitto whispered Cornish endearments into his twitching ear until he came to rest. No, on his right-hand side, there was no birdsong, no song of the lapwing or the bubbling dusk-call of the finch, only silence. In that direction, silence was all he could hear: there were no distant careless voices raised in argument or even song that would have accompanied Countess Orlova's serfs on some errand through the darkening forest. Even an experienced hunter unwittingly made more noise than French partisan troops when they had a mind for waiting, and for killing. Tucking his foot into the stirrup, he mounted up with a quick, silent spring, bearing off into the trees on the left-hand side of the rutted track. Kitto was now riding in the wrong direction, away from Yarkaya Polyana, but his life and the success of this mission, and therefore his own honour, quite depended placing complete trust in his own instinct, praying to cheat with every step the French soldiers he had been waiting to meet for so long.

Night had long since fallen, and in the chandeliered drawing-room at Yarkaya Polyana, Lieutenant Ilya Rumyantsev of the Semenovsky Guards would willingly have offered his own grandmother's soul to be anywhere on earth except sitting on a chaise longue opposite Countess Tatyana Orlova, who had unexpectedly arrived from Petersburg only that morning. Warmed by the flames leaping in the great fireplace, she wore a light muslin gown that clung to every slender curve, and her small, pale breasts rose from a confection of gathered lace. Fair curls were gathered in a careless topknot, encircled by a loosely threaded satin ribbon. Everyone said she was the lover of Prince Volkonsky, and at this time of year, Ilya had expected the mistress of the house to be in town. She smiled and he looked away, tongue-tied. Women couldn't be trusted not to betray him. But he mustn't think about that – about Nadezhda Kurakina: all that blood, and all that unearthly screaming. No, the Kurakina girl would never be seen again, Ilya had made sure of that. It would be perfectly all right: no one would ever know what had happened, and what he had done. He must only pay heed instead to the job at hand.

'You're very wicked, Lieutenant,' Countess Orlova said in her low, musical voice, 'refusing my servants' every invitation to come indoors until tonight.' The drawing-room was vast, walls of a deep ocean blue hung with more portraits and landscapes in heavy frames. Serried ranks of ceiling-height windows were draped with brocade curtains in a delicate shade of cream that made Ilya acutely aware of his filth: he had been sleeping outside for weeks.

He cleared his throat. Her close proximity sent his nerves jangling. 'I'm extremely sorry, ma'am; I dared not risk leaving the horses unattended, even once you returned from Petersburg. As you know, we've already fallen foul of French troops once – they got away with quite a number of good mares and yearlings, and killed my superior officers and all our Cossacks.' He flushed as the countess observed his suppressed agitation with naked appreciation. The truth was, Ilya had done better with the horses alone, and had no need of more arrogant officers heavy-handed with whip and spur; the herd hadn't scattered once since he'd taken sole charge and had backed the herd-mother, a magnificent wild golden Turkoman mare. The other horses followed him on her back because they wanted to, because they felt safe.

'And you alone escaped, Lieutenant.' The countess smiled at him. 'And so what became of Nadezhda Kurakina? I understand that part of your mission was to escort the girl to Petersburg with her maid?'

Ilya pushed away a memory of hot breath, of snow, and appalling silence. 'In truth, we never found her. There was no sign of anyone at the Kurakin estate. We had to leave without her.'

The countess watched him for a little too long, so that beads of sweat traced a greasy slick down Ilya's back beneath his shirt. 'Goodness,' she said. 'How strange, and how concerning. I must say, I wish dear Alexander would simply decide once and for all whether to finally ally himself to Napoleon or the British, and then we can get on with this horrible war if it can't be averted.' She yawned, and Ilya could only pray that she would mistake his discomfiture for shock at her casual reference to the tsar. It was said that she'd been brought up at court by his mother, the elegant and intimidating Grand Duchess Maria Feodorovna, and that the tsar himself was like a brother to her. Ignoring Ilya's hobbledehoy silence, Countess Orlova went on with smooth assurance.

'I'm so glad you managed to receive your letters – and in good time, I trust?'

Ilya swallowed a burst of nausea. 'My letters, madame?'

She leaned forward a little with a confidential air. 'The deliveries here can be disastrously useless, but Simyon tells me your correspondence was all taken care of by special courier.' She smiled. 'No doubt you're plagued with important military matters even as you're forced to linger here! Such a burden for one so young.'

Ilya briefly closed his eyes. If the contents of those letters were ever revealed, he would not live out the summer, he knew. 'I wouldn't dream of boring you with the sort of tedious detail my superiors demand from me, madame. It wouldn't be interesting to a woman.'

'Oh, I dare say. You don't much favour the Rumyantsevs, my dear. Who were your mother's family?'

He battled a sudden, intense thirst, uncomfortably aware of the horses corralled in the countess's pastures with only her serfs to watch over them, sullen and unwilling. As long as the Turkoman mare stayed with them, they would remain. One could trust the horses. Unlike people, they were worthy of affection. 'My mother was a Vashechkin, Countess – her family came from Kazan.'

Tatyana nodded, watching him with close appraisal. 'Kazan? That will be why you don't have that familiar appearance, then, when one knows the family intimately. I must say I don't know *that* branch of the Vashechkins particularly well.'

Ilya swallowed. 'I expect so, ma'am.'

The countess sighed, signalling to a silent, watchful indoor serf to refill his glass of claret. 'How late Captain Helford is. Kuznetsov rode in from Arkady's tavern this afternoon and said he was quite sure the dear boy would be here before nightfall. You must be eager to complete your mission, Lieutenant Rumyantsev. Perhaps there might be a promotion for you, Ilya – if I may – should you be a success. I must say, the cavalry commissariat will be glad to see you when you reach Petersburg with the horses. General Dubretskoy was telling me only last week that if Napoleon orders Marshal Davout to raise any kind of pitched battle, we're unable to mount enough cavalry to meet him in the field. A rather terrifying prospect for those of us who remember Moscow burning in 1812, I can assure you.'

'I'm sure—' He broke off as the panelled door that led to a small music-room flew open, quite unattended by a servant, the polished walnut bulk of the pianoforte just visible in lamplit gloom beyond. Immediately, Ilya got up and moved to the heavy, carved sideboard where he had left his pistol.

Countess Orlova got to her feet. 'What in heaven's name? Simyon!'

The indoor serf went pale, moving towards the door, and the intruder had stepped into the room, tall and dark-haired, but no Frenchman: he was clad in a travel-stained scarlet jacket belonging to one of the elite British regiments, surveying the room with an arrogant ease that quite belied the fact he had just gained entry to the house like a base-born thief.

'Captain Helford!' Countess Orlova cried, getting to her feet. 'What on earth do you think you're doing, coming into my house in such a way? I'm beginning to think you quite lost to civility.'

'Your humble servant, ma'am,' Captain Helford said quickly, and an extraordinary array of emotions chased one another across his features: shock, followed by high-coloured chagrin, and finally a smile of purest devilry, revealing deep-cut dimples that would have been devastating, Ilya was sure, on a girl. 'There might be just the smallest difficulty with some French cavalry outside, but please don't let it trouble you.'

'Just who or what exactly have you brought to Yarkaya Polyana with you, sir?' Ilya demanded in French, *sotto voce*, entirely failing to conceal his anger. Could this young fool really have led French troops directly to the house, with all the horses here for the taking?

'Let's concentrate on the task at hand, no?' Captain Helford's own French pronunciation was noticeably English-accented, slightly guttural and husky, with that strange trace of aristocratic French that laced the speech of the English.

Making no attempt to explain, Helford gestured at them all to follow him: Ilya, the countess and the serf Simyon. His journey to Yarkaya Polyana from the main road east had, by all appearances, been a mess of quite some magnitude. Staring wildly from one to the other, Countess Orlova edged towards Helford like a frightened rabbit. Last to reach the music-room, Ilya shut the door behind them all, the brass doorknob cool beneath his fingertips, enclosing the countess and the serf with two soldiers in the dark, curtained room, a faint line of moonlight striking off the gilded frame of the countess's harp.

Ilya ignored a wave of cold shame. 'The horses,' he said quietly. 'We must reach the horses before the French do.' He couldn't fail in his mission, not now. With exposure, everyone would know what he had done. In the dim lamplight, Captain Helford stared at him for one agonising moment. His eyes were a surprising shade of pale grey, his lashes very dark.

'Never mind your fucking horses, Rumyantsev,' he said, 'first we must get out of this house alive.'

26

Kitto held his pistol with the barrel facing the sky, reassured by the weight of it in his hand. There was a servants' door in the Orlov music-room camouflaged by the same vine-printed silk that covered the walls. It led into the whitewashed passage he had come in by. Silent, he waved the stoop-shouldered Russian soldier and the countess into the passage, even as the serf turned and fled. Tatyana made no move to call her servant back to safety, as though his life was of no more importance than one of the mastiffs roaming the grounds. Kitto had swiftly mastered the dogs with whispered Cornish nothings and a strip of dried beef from his pack, but those French cavalry officers who had trailed him all the way here would not be so easily appeased. Rumyantsev moved surprisingly fast for such a featherweight; as he ran, he primed a Prussian cavalry pistol that had no back sight with unconscious economy of movement, more competent than first appearances allowed. Behind, the countess sobbed with fear as they sprinted towards a scullery she'd doubtless never set foot in before now. Rumyantsev, though, was silent and paltry in his ill-fitting dark-blue Semenovsky jacket, weak moonlight catching the silver lacing at his shoulders as they passed the copper pans, the small keg of soft-soap, the folded heaps of linen that reminded Kitto of Nansmornow with merciless acuity.

Turning when they reached the door, Kitto spoke. 'Wait.'

The countess broke out in whispered Russian, falling silent as Rumyantsev laid one wiry, quick-fingered hand upon her arm as though settling a panicked child or hound. His face was thin and fine-boned; he emanated a queer, dangerous tension. Swiftly, silently, Kitto slid back the bolt, listening. The yard was quiet, but as soon as he stepped outside a heightened sense of awareness pulsed through him even as his boots hit the cobbles. He breathed in the scent of wet laundry on the line stretching away into the blueish darkness of a Russian night and further away, beyond the yard, wet earth, straw and distant horse-sweat.

Now Kitto was outside beneath the rising moon there was no illusion: every outhouse or stable-block might conceal the French troops who had followed him. Kitto could now smell grass and damp earth and, making for the fence and wicket gate that opened out into a rolling sweep of long pasture, he took a halting, zigzagging path across the yard, watching and listening every moment for the slimmest oddity of half-heard sound or glimpsed movement that might betray the presence of an ambush: the French would not let them get away so easily, not with so many precious horses.

Sometimes Kitto moved with slow, agonising precision, or else he was fast, always glancing back to check that Rumyantsev and Countess Orlova were following him, Rumyantsev's arm unexpectedly cradling her narrow shoulders left naked to the night air by that flimsy muslin gown. Crossing the laundry-yard and reaching the fence, Kitto heard the owl's call before he saw it making a silent, ghostly pass above the grassland out to the west. He could see the horses now, too, dim shapes in the moonlight. It was a queer thing: when there were many horses all together, he seemed to sense a single mind, a single driving force. Kitto could hear Tatyana's frightened, panicked breathing, almost sobbing as she picked her way across the cobbles in flimsy satin slippers. It wouldn't be long before she gave them away entirely. There was no other choice: they would just have to run from the shelter of the fence across the open ground, towards the horses, open to pistol-fire from wherever the French were hiding.

He paused and turned to Rumyantsev, speaking in a low voice. 'Will the horses not all panic? They'll scatter.'

The Russian shook his head. 'Let's pray they don't.' He wasn't much older than Kitto himself, his young, narrow face taut with that suppressed tension, the loaded Prussian-issue pistol held at half-cock. He was bare-headed, dusty close-cropped curls shifting in the breeze that had sprung up, bringing the earth-damp scent of rain: he must have left his cockaded hat in the countess's drawing-room, which was just as well. 'Just get us to the horses, Helford, and I'll do the rest.' Rumyantsev glanced at Tatyana as he spoke; she stood silent and still, quite incoherent with terror, and he reached out and took her hand, speaking softly in their own tongue. Please God she wouldn't freeze just when they really had to run.

'So follow me,' Kitto said quietly. 'When I move, move. If I stop, stop.' Knowing quite well that there was no possible way of being more exposed to the enemy, he placed one foot in front of the other, again and again, crossing the wide open space between the meagre shelter offered by the laundry-yard and the nearest of the horses, waiting for a shot to hiss past him. In a moment or two, he forgot the herd, sensing only their vast, breathing warmth before him, listening to the mingled sounds of chewing and hot breath expelled through whiskered nostrils; his vision grew more acute, it seemed, picking out infinitesimal movements of shifting grass on the horizon. He no longer heard the grass-muffled thudding of hundreds of iron-shod horses pummelling wild pastureland, only dimly aware that the horses themselves had now begun to take flight, cantering around the pasture. Instead, he gathered – piecemeal – sounds from further away: the owl calling again, and the coughing scream of a mating fox. And, then, with Tatyana and Rumyantsev still just paces behind him, Kitto saw a clot of shadow away to his left at the edge of his vision – again, he could not have said anything other than that it didn't look right, that the density of the shadow was somehow wrong in that landscape. With only his pistol and no rifle, Kitto knew he didn't have the range to return fire. Instead, he turned and advanced on the enemy, running low to the ground towards the clot of shadow, never stopping, always presenting a moving target. A shot whined so close to his ear that he actually felt the disturbance of air and the darkness resolved itself into two French cavalrymen, using a gentle rise in the land as a firing platform, just yards from the hazel hurdle circling the laundry-yard. They'd got English-issue rifles from somewhere, too – not French Charlesville muskets, which meant they stood half a chance of actually hitting someone.

Kitto fired his pistol, throwing himself on the ground where tufts of longer grass sprouted from boggy earth. Behind him, Rumyantsev fired too, but the shot went just wide. Tatyana screamed. One of the Frenchmen tumbled away from his position and lay still; now Kitto had only one visible enemy, but there might be five more still hidden nearby: perhaps even ten, twenty. Never mind. In the very next breath, he heard the whining hiss of a ball, and then silence. Someone else had been hit – Rumyantsev or the countess, he couldn't tell which. A bolt of pure, instinctive terror shot through him, and Kitto rolled rapidly to the right, splashing in frozen boggy water, avoiding another shot by inches, but failing to hold his pistol up out of the water. For a moment, he stared at the streaming barrel. Surging to his feet and drawing his sword, Kitto charged. The Frenchman was now cursing and fumbling with his rifle, struggling to reload; he glanced up, and Kitto just had time to register the man's stunned realisation as he abandoned reloading and hurled himself into a two-man *mêlée*, armed with the bayonet mounted on his rifle, a full two feet of wicked steel. Kitto had not the reach to strike and so sidestepped, feinting almost as the Frenchman reached him, letting fly with a merciless sideswipe that met solid flesh. The soldier's death-cry filled the air – the sword-blow had struck through his arm and into his belly, almost disembowelling him. And with the well-trained mercy of the hunter, Kitto crouched at the dying man's side and cut his throat, looking away so that he did not have to think of the soldier's wife, his child. Even so, a hot spray of blood splattered across his face. He wiped his sword on the grass and sheathed it before running back to meet the others. Rumyantsev, by some witchery, had managed to catch one of the horses already – not a wild one captured from the steppe but a large, docile gelding doubtless the treasured companion of some provincial farmer's daughter before being requisitioned.

'Mount up,' Rumyantsev said over his shoulder as though Kitto had offered him a cigarillo, not just killed two French soldiers. 'Take the countess with you, and I'll follow.'

Shivering in bloodstained muslin, it was a moment before Tatyana could speak. 'He's been injured,' she gasped at Kitto. 'Someone must help Lieutenant Rumyantsev.'

'Not now,' Rumyantsev said sharply. 'Mount up, will you?'

Breathless with the rush of a kill, Kitto went straight to the gelding's head. 'Good boy,' he said in Cornish, patting his flank. 'You'll humour us a while, won't you, *boya*?' He felt the gelding's hot breath on the back of his neck, and knew that he would tolerate him. Turning to Tatyana, he said, 'Hold on to his mane, and I'll hold on to you.' Without waiting for an answer, he lifted the woman on to the horse, just as he had once seen Crow lift Hester, steadying her as she scrabbled at her skirts and clutched at the gelding's coarse mane; thank Christ she seemed to know to sit forward and that she could ride bareback – evidence of a hoydenish girlhood on some far-distant country estate, perhaps. Glancing sideways, Kitto saw that Rumyantsev was now standing by a magnificent Turkoman mare, pale gold in the moonlight. He'd never be able to mount her. He'd get himself killed trying.

'You fucking fool,' Kitto shouted. 'Hurry up!' Was he going to be left to deal with four hundred horses and a terrified woman? With athletic desperation, he mounted the gelding behind Tatyana, reaching around her shivering, bare-shouldered form to grasp handfuls of mane, thanking Christ for his own misspent youth riding wild ponies bareback on the moor beyond Nansmornow. Kitto urged the gelding into a fast trot and then a gallop, squinting into the wind even as he willed every shred of flesh in his body to keep his seat. And out on the grasslands beyond even the boundaries of the Orlov estate, Kitto rode hard beneath the night with the wind in his hair and Tatyana Orlova all but lying face down on the gelding's neck before him. The gelding cleared the fence, and

Kitto was aware of many, many horses all around them, the world full of drumming hoofbeats. The horses were panicking, he knew, circling each other at thundering speed, swirling like a great school of mackerel, galloping across the path of his own gelding time after time so that he and the countess would be lucky to see morning. But then, at last, Kitto became aware that they were only galloping alongside other horses, not having to weave among them, and that the hot, rising panic of the herd had quite dissipated beneath a clear night all blanketed with stars. Glancing to his right, Kitto saw the Turkoman mare gaining upon them, the small, hunched figure of Rumyantsev clinging to her neck, low down. He passed within an arm's length, small and wiry, with those dusty curls torn back from that pinched face, so alive with concentration, and as Kitto watched them surge ahead, the other horses fanned out around the Turkoman like courtiers stepping back and bowing as before a queen, and Kitto realised that this puny runt of an aristocratic litter whose papa had surely paid a fortune to see him enlisted in the Semenovsky now rode the matriarch of this entire herd of horses, all of them following him, all obeying blood, bone and nerve, accepting Rumyantsev and the Turkoman beauty as their undisputed leader.

The sky had begun to lighten by the time Rumyantsev brought the golden mare to a halt; they were on open grassland now, the forest a dim green shadow on the horizon away to the west, all gilded by the rising sun. As Kitto and Tatyana approached on the gelding, Rumyantsev slid sideways from the mare's back, crashing to the dew-spangled grass. Kitto dismounted, barely stopping to assist Tatyana, who shook where she stood in her bloodstained gown, those satin slippers torn to rags.

'I told you he was injured,' she said, her voice cracking. 'Someone must help him.'

What did she expect, a carriage full of serfs to convey Rumyantsev to the nearest surgeon? There was no sign of human habitation. Exasperated, Kitto turned away, loping over to Rumyantsev's prone form, no more than a dark and seemingly lifeless shape in the grass, and every muscle in his thighs and belly shrieked with agony after so many hours on horseback. The countess followed, halting, limping and shivering. The Turkoman mare bowed her head over the fallen Russian, nosing at him with her pale golden muzzle, stepping away as Kitto approached. Breathless and on his knees, Kitto turned Rumyantsev over – he was so light – and even before he pushed aside the jacket, he smelled hot blood; then he saw it spreading dark over the filthy white linen. Swearing in Cornish, he began unbuttoning Rumyantsev's shirt. He'd either taken a musket-ball, or been grazed by one.

Rumyantsev's eyelashes fluttered, and his thin fingers twitched convulsively. 'No,' he said, pushing ineffectually at Kitto's hand, 'no—'

'I'll do that,' Tatyana said, crouching down at Kitto's side even as he turned to stare at her in astonishment, but he had already peeled back the blood-soaked shirt and, beneath it, instead of naked skin he found the thick, bloodstained bulk of a padded linen corset.

'Christ!' Kitto let the shirt fall as though it were on fire.

'*Oh!*' the countess said, but Kitto ignored her. Now that he knew, it was so obvious. For a moment, they only stared at each other. Rumyantsev's wide-opened eyes were very dark, with such thick lashes.

'Oh, for God's sake,' Kitto demanded. 'Who are you?'

'Nadezhda,' the imposter said, and her eyes flashed with rebellion even in surrender. 'So what will you do with me now, Captain Helford?'

27

Almost a fortnight later, at the Anichkov Palace on Nevsky Prospekt, Crow stood at a window in one of the state rooms overlooking the moonlit expanse of the Fontanka River, with the black armband for his wife and child tied below the elbow of his jacket. He was drunk: quietly but catastrophically so, as he had been for weeks, and to the point that he might appear sober to the uninitiated whilst committing the unforgivable. Lord Cathcart and the quiet, gentle Empress Elizaveta Alexeievna would both have readily excused him from this reception, but retribution was now the single force that drove him to move, to speak, to eat, to not put a bullet through his own skull as he so longed to do, and as he would when this was all over, and he had – somehow – punished Lord Castlereagh.

He caught the scent of warm milk, and the rose-infused oil Hester always rubbed into her own scalp and Morwenna's, and when he turned, Hester herself was sitting in a gilded chair with the child on her lap beneath that large portrait of General Potemkin. She wasn't dressed for a ball; instead, she wore the old muslin gown he knew so well. It was pale green, printed with sprigs of some sort of flower, but cut so low that she always wore a linen fichu tucked into the bodice that he couldn't look at or even think about without wanting to remove the moment they were alone, twisting that fresh linen between his fingers and letting it fall to the floor, revealing the swell of her breasts. Hester watched him with that clear, steady gaze he had fallen in love with, but now there was a strand of rust-brown seaweed in her hair, which had come loose, and floated about her shoulders in that mass of light curls. Without taking her eyes from him, Hester pushed aside the fichu herself and lifted Morwenna so that she could suckle. The little maid grabbed a handful of her mother's hair and Crow had to turn away, knowing that when he looked again, they would both be gone.

'You've been standing here a long time, Lord Lamorna. I'm so sorry to hear of your indescribable loss.' With a rustle of silk against fine linen petticoats, Countess Tatyana Orlova came to stand beside him, looking out across the river. She was formed with the marble flawlessness of a statue, her slim arms perfectly moulded, so pale against the dark blue silk of her evening gown. He had seen her suppressed rage when Lady Cathcart announced the child Jane's engagement to Prince Volkonsky; he had also seen that her fury was concealed from everyone else, except perhaps Volkonsky himself. She turned and surveyed the ballroom with the impassive predatory gaze of a cat. 'I suppose you will have heard about the attack at my late husband's estate? Your young brother conducted himself with great heroism. He escorted me to a staging-inn – I don't think it's any exaggeration to say that I have him to thank for my life.'

Crow couldn't look at her. He would have to tell the boy about Hester, and the maid. He could not make Lord

Castlereagh pay for the loss of his wife and daughter by drinking himself into a mess. But, in truth, he was not sure that he was able to stop.

Countess Orlova went on lightly, her tone sympathetic: 'I don't know if it will be any consolation, but I believe you have another relation present this evening. Thérèse de la Saint-Maure is here – I collect she is a relative of your late mother's? She was my companion when I was a girl. My family took her in after the revolution in France.' She turned to him with that slow, easy smile. So now she had decided that he would take part in whatever game she was playing with Volkonsky. In times long past, it would have pleased him to exact an exquisite punishment upon such a woman with all the pleasure he knew how to deal out, and what to hold in reserve, and for how long. He had already seen enough of Tatyana Orlova to appreciate that she would do anything to avenge herself on Prince Volkonsky for his engagement to Jane Cathcart, and that she quite clearly understood just how badly Crow, still an officer in the British army, would be compromised by paying such public attention to a French great-aunt. Beneath the groundswell of numbing grief, he understood that both pieces of information must be used to advantage. At last, he heard himself reply, 'Then I should be glad to meet Madame de la Saint-Maure.'

And so Crow took the countess's arm, allowing her to lead him back into the throng of the great marble hall, glittering with mirrors and windows, heaving with courtiers clad in silk and superfine, the women in long white gloves drawn up past their elbows, diadems glittering. Heads turned wherever they passed, the combination of his loss and her social standing in Petersburg drew a tide of attention. She kept up a stream of inconsequential one-sided conversation about the tsarina's planting arrangements in the garden at Tsarkoe Selo, steering him to a small knot of elderly women playing hazard for chicken-stakes at a polished chestnut occasional table drawn up close to the marble fireplace. As one, clad in beaded gowns of black and maroon, they all looked up at Crow's approach.

'Well, Tanyushka, and what manner of game is this?' A woman with sparse white hair and a mauve gown festooned with lace addressed Countess Orlova in the old-fashioned, courtly French of the Ancien Régime, in the way that one can at more than eighty, when one no longer cares what people think. 'It is not often you bring pretty young men over to talk to us. To what do we owe the pleasure?'

'Dear Grandmama, I think Madame de la Saint-Maure is best placed to answer that question.' Countess Orlova smiled, showing her small white teeth. 'Dear Thérèse, this is Lieutenant Colonel Lord Lamorna.'

Crow turned to the old woman, wondering how she could breathe with all that lace buttoned up close to her throat. Her hair was wrapped in a turban of pale grey silk, and she was as wreathed in wrinkles as she was with rather dirty diamonds in a setting fashionable half a century ago. Even now he saw the extraordinary shadows of his mother's features arranged with less pleasing symmetry, and he had to fight the sensation that his chest was slowly being crushed by an enormous weight.

Thérèse de la Saint-Maure surveyed him with dispassionate interest as though selecting a fowl for the pot, although he doubted she had ever in her life done anything half so useful. 'My great-nephew, I collect?' she said. 'You won't see too much of your mother in me, if that's what you've come looking for. I suppose you know that Claire was tall as a weed and really quite devastatingly striking – not that it did her any good, in the end, dead in childbed, so I hear, bearing that young hotspur who was so fashionable last winter.' She got to her feet with a surprising degree of agility. 'I suppose you will walk me around this dreadful room – so much gilding! – for we cannot possibly converse here. Unless of course you should prefer to sit and drink tea, and talk commonplaces with my companions.'

Crow had no desire to tell Thérèse de la Saint-Maure that, on the contrary, he saw a great deal of his mother in her. Quite unable to speak, he bowed in acceptance of her invitation, if you could call it that. It was more an order. He relinquished Countess Orlova's arm and took his great-aunt's fragile, lace-clad elbow in a light grasp, steering her away from the group gathered by the fire, well aware that Countess Orlova's grandmother and her acquaintances were watching him with the merciless lack of deference that could only ever be managed by ancient women who had always moved in the first circles. Briefly, he closed his eyes, wishing that he might open them and find that it was his mother he walked with, and not this stranger of an aunt whose face so curiously recalled hers. Looking across the great hall, Thérèse de la Saint-Maure angled a glance over the top of her black lace fan to Lord Cathcart, who stood nearby talking to Kitto's colonel in the Coldstream; both watched him walking with his French great-aunt wearing identical expressions of ill-concealed appalled astonishment. What in God's name did any of it matter?

Thérèse paused before an indifferent portrait of Tsar Alexander's youngest sister, all plump arms and white embroidered linen. 'You're three parts disguised, aren't you? Don't think I haven't realised, just because you appear reasonably adept at hiding it. Montausier was the same

– your French grandfather. Drunk from the moment he got up in the morning, and for the most part, no one knew. But one doesn't forget that sort of thing, and I see it quite clearly in you. Your Creole wife is dead and so is your child, they tell me, and to my mind you're likely a spy, but I can't imagine you'll go on very well about any of it dead drunk.' She flung a disparaging glance across the ballroom. 'Isn't it amusing how this nonsense continues when that Italian upstart's Second Army are raiding from Little Russia and further east every day?'

With all his concentration, Crow suppressed any visible sign of astonishment at her sudden mention of French military strategy, even as he realised that this woman had ruthlessly stripped bare the pointless self-indulgence of his own recent behaviour.

'You think I know nothing about Napoleon or his intentions?' Thérèse continued without looking at him. 'You must know that I am a stateless woman, Lord Lamorna, and have been so since I was forty-two years old. I have lived in Russia since 1790, since the dawn of the Revolution, but do you think any of these people consider me Russian, or will grant me their protection when war breaks out again, as it seems so likely to do? I had to have my manservant barricade the door to my house in 1812 when last the Russians turned against the French, and Moscow burned. Do you have the smallest notion of precisely how dangerous the outbreak of war will be for a woman like me? No? I have lived for a long time, and I don't intend to die an ignoble death, stripped and beaten in the streets. I find it to my benefit to keep abreast of both the military and political situations as they develop.'

Crow stopped walking, bringing her to a halt at his side. 'Will you tell me the purpose of this conversation? I'm quite at a loss. If you're in danger, let me tell you that association with me is more likely to harm you further than to protect you.'

'Perhaps I over-estimate your standing,' Thérèse said, 'for all I've heard about your importance to the Duke of Wellington, and how you were his most treasured intelligence officer before Waterloo, even if your star has fallen now so that this young brother of yours was the hero of the moment one day and cut everywhere he went the next, although I notice that society seems to grant you considerably more leeway.'

Briefly, Crow had to close his eyes.

Thérèse gave him no quarter. 'But look about yourself, Lord Lamorna. English, French and Russian all gathered beneath one roof here at Anichkov, in the very heart of Petersburg. Tsar Alexander could not make his position clearer than if he shouted it from the rooftops. Never mind the skirmishing of last winter in which your young brother so covered himself with glory: in truth Russia has not chosen whom to support, not in the long term, regardless of what the British might assume. So don't you think that someone had better find out what Napoleon's plans are before it's too late?'

Such self-consequence was an impressive thing to retain for the unmarried sister of an executed French duke who had lived most of her life in exile. 'And I suppose you're going to tell me exactly how I ought to find Marshal Davout,' Crow said carefully, 'given that no one knows where he is.'

Thérèse folded her fan with a muted snick of ivory. 'Not here. Even I am not so much of a fool as to discuss such affairs in public. I am the last of your mother's family: it would only be courteous to visit me at home one morning.'

Crow watched her a moment. She looked straight back at him: her eyes were the same grey as his own and Kitto's, as their mother's had been. She didn't look away, but merely let out her fan again, performing the rituals of a courtly language that hardly anyone spoke now, let alone understood. Crow knew it, though, because his mother had taught him, laughing in her bedchamber at Nansmornow long ago as he sat on the windowsill watching Mrs Gwyn dress her for dinner. *If I hold the fan like this,* petit, *it means come closer. But if I hold it so, and look at you, it means seek a private room for us. Heaven knows you might need to know all this when you're grown.* Without even looking at Crow, Thérèse brought the fan down with a flat, sharp stroke, and he instantly recognised the signal: *Listen. There are enemies everywhere.*

'As you wish,' he said. 'I'll call on you.'

'I count myself honoured,' Thérèse said, with an iron-grey stare that suggested she was anything but.

28

Crow escorted his great-aunt back to her seat by the fire, unable to shake off the certainty that Thérèse de la Sainte-Maure was not nearly as senile as she wished people to think, for all her grandiose promises to reveal Napoleon's tactics to him. That surely counted among the most bizarre and incriminating conversations he'd had at a ball, and there had been many of them. Even if she were not just a deluded old woman, it made no sense. She was an *emigrée* – why should she have any sympathy with Napoleon, emperor of a republic born from the Terror that had seen most of her family beheaded? The night had deepened, and as the empress's guests abandoned the torchlit gardens of the Anichkov Palace, leaving their furs with footmen, shoals of willowy Petersburg debutantes flooded the ballroom, all clad in varying shades of white, some with flowers pinned in their hair, others wearing the diadems so fashionable in Russia, candlelight from the chandeliers above setting alight the jewel-crusted branches of silver and gold against shining hair – fair and dark alike. He took a glass of cognac from a tray held by a liveried palace footman and drained it, then took another.

'Oh, Lord Lamorna! What can you be thinking of to walk about with Thérèse de la Saint-Maure? Papa will be so angry!'

He looked down to find Jane Cathcart perspiring through yet more unwisely chosen pink muslin, mouse-brown hair escaping from the unflattering confines of tong-singed ringlets.

'Will he?' Crow said, finishing the other glass of brandy. 'And is it really your place to tell me so, Miss Cathcart?'

She flushed again, and he immediately regretted the put-down, and held out his arm in invitation. Jane accepted it, with a look so pathetically grateful that he took two glasses from another footman. Champagne. He handed one to Jane and drained his own, beneath her shocked gaze. She was alone in a ballroom, exactly the type to be deposited by an exasperated mother with a crowd of far more fashionable girls who would then lose her at the first possible opportunity. Once, he'd been just exactly what her mother ought to fear, but how could he harm such a girl now? He was married, and one never publicly humiliated one's wife, even though there might be indiscretions and opera girls. Either way, he'd never wanted another woman since the day he'd set eyes on Hester, soaked to her skin on the beach at Lamorna Cove. And the truth of his bastard child's existence had wounded Hester just as surely as any affair: the blameless chronology of her conception wouldn't matter to those who whispered about Hester wherever she went. But Hester was gone, in point of fact he wasn't married any more, and he had hurt her by siring a child that would have been a thorn in her side, just because it had been so very easy to tup his own stepmother. He felt as though he were falling. Jane was talking to him; he forced himself to listen. It was so damnably hard to continue with the mechanical operation of living.

'My goodness, thank you, Lord Lamorna,' Jane was saying. 'I was on the verge of being lost for good. Mama said that I ought to mix with Princess Dubretskaya and Alina Kutusova, but in truth they don't like me at all, and they have so much influence amongst the girls of my own age, and their mamas are so fashionable, that their ignoring me in that horrid way would have put a sure end to every other invitation for the rest of the season.'

Crow steered her towards the edge of the room where the crowd thinned as dancing began again. 'Forgive me then, Miss Cathcart, for bringing you away. I'm not at all sure that you wouldn't delight at being cast out into a social Siberia.'

She looked up at him with a surprising and very warm smile. The girl might be blessed with luminous dark eyes, but she was not in Volkonsky's style; that much was already clear. The betrothal made little sense: Volkonsky played for high stakes, true, but the Cathcarts couldn't offer the sort of dowry required by an inveterate gamester. Why, then? Did Alexander want an ear to the ground within the embassy?

Jane surveyed him with an edge of pity he could hardly bear. 'Well, it can't be helped – now I've been singled out by you, I'm the envy of half the room. You're notorious, my lord.'

'Take care, Miss Cathcart. I'm the very last person who ought to be advising others on their conduct, but unless I'm much mistaken, in time you'll be welcomed by anyone who enjoys rational discussion. Only lose the affected arch manner – it doesn't suit you. Now where would you like me to take you? To your mother?'

Jane flushed again. 'No, please take me to Miss Paolozzi. You know – my drawing mistress. I was quite happy with her until Mama insisted on leading me about the room like a prize sheep at the harvest fair. We were in one of those anterooms, having a beautifully quiet evening.'

Jane let her arm rest upon Crow's again as he steered her through the gathering; she spoke with sensitivity about the row of portraits and landscapes they passed, and he felt a flicker of honest pity for her. She would have flourished in bluestocking circles in London, or leading a country life with knowledgeable friends to write to and visit, but marriage to Volkonsky doomed to the girl to a lonely life in the Russian provinces. There was no way on God's earth he'd keep her in Petersburg.

'Just here, my lord,' Jane said and, as Crow took her into the candlelit salon set off the main ballroom, she broke away from him, calling out, 'Ana-Maria!' He watched as she ran to Miss Paolozzi, a slight, dark-haired woman perching on the end of the crimson brocade chaise arranged beneath a vast window giving out to the darkness; Miss Paolozzi had been looking through a book of watercolour plates, but pushed this aside as though caught slipping silver spoons into her reticule. At the sight of Jane she half rose, abruptly sitting down again as she registered Crow's appearance. Jane flew back to him, clasping his hand with hers in a childlike gesture that reminded him with disastrous force of Kitto as a young boy. He would never see Morwenna grow to be so; she would never now take him by the hands and enthusiastically bore him with intricate details of what the kittens in the barn had done. 'Thank you, Lord Lamorna,' Jane said. 'I really am grateful to you, even though I expect I made an awful job of showing it.'

'It was nothing at all.' Crow bowed and turned for the open door; he had no desire to end this dreamlike hellscape of an evening making polite conversation with a drawing-mistress chaperone, even one with the intriguing habit of looking at the child of an English diplomat precisely how the third daughter of a provincial clergyman might eye a half-pay officer at a country ball, resplendent among so many farmers' sons. He left, pausing on the threshold, watching the elite of Petersburg throng in the empress's overheated ballroom, the chandeliers glittering with crystal and shivering candle-flame above it all. How was he to put one foot before the other? How was he to continue? He was so drunk, and very far from home, both of which lent an edge of vivid unreality to this limitless sense of loss. When all this was over, what was there then to do? He would go home to Nansmornow but find the morning-parlour empty; Hester would not be sitting before the fire, watching their infant daughter pulling shells and bright silk ribbons from a pasteboard box. And Hester would never again be waiting in his bed, that beautiful hair loose in a cloud of tiny spirals, the fine lawn nightgown slipping from her shoulder, ready for him to take such pleasure in giving pleasure to her, his heart's delight. She was gone. He had to be alone; he'd been a fool to come here at all.

He stepped from the library out into the sweaty heat of the main ballroom and a chaos of fluttering silk, only to immediately take refuge in the salon next door. The room was surprisingly small for a palace of Anichkov's proportions, and the walls were half clad in panels of vivid green malachite. Pale lace curtains draped the tall window, and landscapes in heavy gilded frames hung on the walls amongst oval portraits more than a hundred years old, from the years when Catherine the Great had ruled all Russia and loved Potemkin. Crow walked to a writing desk set beneath the window, leaning on it as he looked out at the dark, lamplit waters of the Fontanka, the marble cold beneath his touch, and he sensed Tatyana

Orlova's presence before she even spoke. If she knew what was good for her she would not stand so close.

'I'm so sorry, Lord Lamorna – I do believe I might have inadvertently caused a little awkwardness between you and Lord Cathcart. I tried to smooth it all over, but I'm afraid he wishes to speak to you.'

Breathe. 'You knew precisely what you were doing drawing so much public attention to my relationship with Thérèse de la Saint-Maure,' Crow said, looking down at the pattern within the marble, swirls of palest grey against white. 'I don't in the slightest bit care why you chose to make such an example of me, but you will not do so again.'

She moved closer still. The dark silk gown clung to her hips; her petticoats were of silk, too, not linen, rendering every wanton curve of her body entirely visible from the waist down. She smiled. 'I merely wanted you to notice me, Lord Lamorna, and something told me you would be unable to resist the possibility of coming face to face with one of your mother's relatives. There is something I particularly wish you to do.'

'I don't doubt it. You mean to place me at a disadvantage, which I'll admit you've done. Tell me why, Countess.'

'Oh, do call me Tatyana. We need not be so formal with one another. Please – everyone knows you're as much of a Saint-Maure as you are anything else, but as with so many things in life patriotic loyalty is all too often about appearances only. I do understand that such a public meeting with your great-aunt might have further eroded your superiors' trust in you. Allow me to make reparation. Would it be idiotic of me to surmise that the British would like to learn the whereabouts of a particular royal bastard?'

Crow knew his expression didn't change at all. 'If the British had any interest at all in such a person, what would induce you to tell me about it? Surely you must know that putting me in possession of any such information places the English at a likely advantage over Russia. Even having this conversation with me amounts to treason against your own tsar.'

'That's my affair,' Tatyana said. 'But I know how you might re-establish your credit. Just imagine if you were the one to find this royal offshoot.'

'Imagine indeed,' Crow said. 'It's almost as if you knew I am supposed to be looking for her. Are you going to enlighten me any further?' Dorothea Lieven had warned him that Tatyana Orlova had links to the Green Lamp, who sought to undermine the tsar. He had no idea if her motives were political, or more personal, relating only to Prince Volkonsky, and neither did he care.

'That depends,' Tatyana said. 'There is something I'd like you to do for me first: Jane Cathcart. As a guest in her parents' home, you know the girl. A most unsuitable match for Sasha Volkonsky, as I'm sure you'll agree. I'd like you to make sure that he doesn't marry her.'

Crow watched her. 'Oh, believe me, there is one way I would very much like to do that, but I doubt my putting a bullet through your own Volkonsky would do much for Russo-British relations. What interest can you have in that affair? If you're his mistress, why should his marriage stand in your way?'

'Because I don't wish him beholden to anyone else except me, that's why. For God's sake, anyone can tell that marriage into Petersburg society will be as much of a mortification to Jane Cathcart as it's likely to be to her husband. You do realise people noticed when you rescued her from those mean-spirited debutantes? It would take very little more for you to go a step further, and to ruin her.'

'It's not the effort involved that prevents me from accepting your proposal,' Crow said, yawning. 'What if I find the notion abhorrent as well as extraordinary? You must consider this royal bastard very important indeed to think that finding her would be worth ruining a young girl of my own nation, of my own class.'

Countess Orlova stepped closer; unbidden, he turned to face her. She reached up, gently brushing a stray lock of hair from his forehead. 'At least listen to my offer.'

'And what is this offer, exactly?'

'I will tell you the assumed name and the whereabouts of this bastard child. The British need her so very badly – even I can see that. There is not another heir in Europe untainted by alliance at some stage with Napoleon, and your Lord Castlereagh's clumsy handling of the poor has brought Britain to the brink of revolution. You need a queen, and you shall have one. But when – and only when – you have so severely compromised Jane Cathcart that Prince Volkonsky will never marry her.' Tatyana smiled. 'I trust you know how to do it?'

Crow looked down at her. 'Oh, I do know how to do that,' he said, almost gently. 'You're forgetting one thing – the necessary consent of Miss Cathcart.'

'I'm sure a man like you won't have to work too hard to obtain her full capitulation, Lord Lamorna.' Tatyana raised herself up on to her tiptoes and brushed his lips with her own, letting out a gasp of surrender when Crow kissed her back, hard. He took her by the hand and kissed the delicate skin at the inside of her wrist. Then, in his destructive misery, he pulled away and looked her in the eye, trailing the tip of one finger across the curve of her breast where it rose from the smooth confines of her short stays, running the edge of his thumb over the satin trim of her bodice, knowing that it would just graze her nipple. Her body melted against his, both lithe and smoothly curved, and with his other hand he cupped one of her rounded buttocks as though she had been one of the whores he had kept, long ago. If Tatyana Orlova wanted to play games with him, he would not stop her. She might be his opponent, but this was her weakness: he knew precisely how to leave her in his power and wanting more.

29

In the damp wilds of North Somerset, Hester stepped into the muddy courtyard of the inn, treading on cobbles strewn with cabbage leaves and stinking heaps of manure. Every shred of flesh in her body ached after so many weeks on foot, and she kept the rain-soaked woollen hood tugged low over her face: that postillion stepping down from his place on the London to Falmouth stagecoach might be the very one to whisper in a soldier's ear: *Wasn't that Countess of Lamorna, the murderess they're all looking for, the one who sailed to France?* She was quite sure that there were now more troops stationed throughout the countryside than during the Occupation, except that now they were English, not French. If she was caught, here and now, she would have a rope around her neck by morning. Leaving the sketchy safety of lane, field and woodland for a coaching inn was unsafe to say the least, but Hester knew she could go no further without replenishing her supply of small-beer. She'd tried to drink water drawn from village pumps as the oxen did, but one couldn't walk twenty miles a day with a griping belly. Her breast milk had dried up on the long, painful journey north, and she was awash with the feverish grief left behind by her missing child, the absence of Morwenna's warm, damp weight in her arms. What right did she have to even think of her baby, a mother who had abandoned her own child? Had it been a mistake to let Catlin and Morwenna set sail from St Mary's without her? Would Morwenna not have been safer at her side? She had not dared even ask for news of the *Curlew*, and pushed away a memory of handing Morwenna to a silent Catlin on the quayside in all that rotten-seaweed and salt-air confusion of the harbour at Hugh-town: a sickeningly dangerous double bluff. Pray God they were now safe in France, in Brittany, where Catlin, with her Cornish, could at least speak the local Breton tongue.

'What are you waiting for, bluey, the bloody footman?' The ill-shaven driver climbed down from the box of the stagecoach, trailed by another grinning postillion. Each shoved past her, barging her with their shoulders so that she nearly stumbled. She stepped into a puddle, soaking the skirts of her gown, and felt the ghost of Crow's presence with acute agony; old Mr Trewarthen had once told her that at night he was plagued by the need to scratch between the toes of his right foot, even though it had been close to sixty years since he'd lost that leg. She could only console herself with the fact that Crow was so notorious that his execution would surely have been all over the news-sheets, gossiped about in every marketplace between London and Truro, and yet she'd heard nothing. Squaring her shoulders and sweeping her stained and faded silk-velvet skirts out of the straw-splattered filth, Hester went into the inn. It took a moment for her eyes to adjust to the gloom within. She breathed in the roast-mutton stink of insufficient tallow lamps, forcing herself not to instinctively reach for the weight of the pistol holstered in the makeshift ammunition belt around her waist, concealed between her petticoats and the skirt of her gown. She already clutched a penny in one hand, but the pouch resting against her other hip held a handful of coinage and the thick roll of banknotes Crow had insisted she take, still only slightly diminished. It was safer to sleep outside, curled up between the thick, cradling roots of a moss-covered oak than it was to risk being recognised for the sake of a louse-ridden bed in an inn, and damp sheets shared with a stranger. Every banknote was doubly precious – there was no possible way of replacing a single one. Without Crow it was impossible to withdraw funds from Coutts, even if doing so wouldn't entirely give her away. *One day at a time, one step at a time,* she repeated to herself, investing each word with the weight of the Hail Mary. Each table in the gloomy inn was occupied. Respectable, starch-aproned farmers' wives and their maids stared at her with insolent superiority, and now a group of sailors in filthy striped culottes and stained jackets leered at her from a table in the corner.

'Here, love, come and sit with us – Hardacre likes a black beauty, don't you, mate?'

Hester ignored them all and walked straight up to the bar, her way blocked by an unshaven, louse-bitten and dissolute gathering who looked as if they spent most of their time draining local supplies of blue ruin. Although Papa had also been black, and in fact much darker than Hester with her white mother, his fortune and reputation had largely shielded her childhood from this sort of blatant contempt whenever they left the safety of Bryher, her childhood island home. No sailor would have dared speak so to the daughter of Captain John Harewood. Never before had she travelled without the protection of Papa or later Crow, sheltered then not only by a fortune but also an ancient name which was a blessing on the road and a curse in the salons of London where since her marriage she'd had little choice but to frequent and endure the staring and impertinent questions of the beau monde.

Oh, how beautifully exotic you are, Lady Lamorna: Hester recalled standing in a blue-painted morning room as Lady Jersey reached out to touch her hair, quite uninvited, even as she fought back tears of anger, and then the heat of Crow's presence at her side. *My wife is not a circus exhibit, Sally,* Crow had said with smiling fury. When they got home, she had burst into his dressing-room, dismissing his alarmed valet, and drummed her fists against his naked chest. *How dare you make it worse? How dare you?* He'd looked down at her with astonished anger and chagrin, just letting her strike him. *Het, it's my duty to protect you, and the woman was behaving like an insufferable idiot. Who does she think she is?*

It had taken her and Crow a long time to begin to forge an understanding of each other that would underpin their love, and now he was gone. She longed for his presence with the desperation of a priest questioning his faith in God, but she had to learn to be without him again, for now at least, here in this filthy inn that stank of old tallow and fried rancid bacon.

'Are you deaf, or what?'

Hester looked up; she still hadn't got over being addressed in such a shocking fashion on this interminable journey north. The tavern-keeper's wife leaned on the bar, a thin-faced woman with a greasy bonnet crammed on to a coiffure tinted a brassy shade of gold that could never have been natural.

'Two pints of small-ale, if you please,' Hester said, rummaging in her sackcloth bag for the flattened leather drinking flasks. She'd quickly learned to modify the way in which she spoke to such people – in their eyes, she was no lady and never could be, which was just as well considering that the Countess of Lamorna had shot and killed three men of the 11th Northumbrian regiment.

The tavern-keeper's wife sneered. 'Daft as well as deaf, then? I said, we don't serve your sort in here. No blacks, all right?'

Hester froze, enduring a rush of silent fury and humiliation. 'I have no desire to stay. Please fill my flasks, and then I will go.'

The brassy-haired woman raised both sparse eyebrows in insolent astonishment.

'Hoity-toity, aren't you, bluey?' one of the sailors called out from the table at the back. 'Don't spoil the fun, Margery. Let's have her over here and we'll take it in turns to teach her some manners.'

'You heard,' the woman said. 'Get out.'

Hester turned and walked out of the tavern, tears springing to her eyes the moment she reached the courtyard. In the taproom behind her, she heard the screech of wooden chair legs on sawdust-covered tiles. One of the sailors getting to his feet, making ready to follow her. Picking up her pace, she crossed the courtyard, loading the pistol as she went with swift, thoughtless skill. She couldn't just keep killing men who wanted to harm her, tempting though it was. Sooner or later she'd be caught and hanged for it. Once out on the muddy, tree-lined lane, Hester scrambled over a mossy drystone wall. The field was sown with green wheat not yet tall enough to hide her, and so she crouched in the mass of cow parsley lining the hedgerow, and there among the tall green stalks tears started to her eyes again because the creamy abundance of nodding flower heads reminded her so much of ocean spray, and she was alone without child or friend, and so very far from home. All she could do was clutch Crow's pistol with shaking fingers as she prayed to God that no one would find her.

30

Tatyana closed her eyes, leaning back against the cushions on the chaise in the morning-parlour that looked out over Nevsky Prospekt. Hot-house peonies in silver vases on the sideboard dropped silken, pale-yellow petals on to the wax-polished wood. The rustle of silk shift against her skin made her think of Lord Lamorna running his hand with excruciating slowness up her inner thigh in that quiet anteroom at the Anichkov Palace, with the violin-tuning, chattering clamour of the ball just yards away. Would he take the bait she had offered? It was treason, after all, promising to tell an English lord where to find the tsar's own daughter, worse even than attending those naïve little Green Lamp salons with Alexei Pushkin. It was just so painful to wait like this, day after endless day, going to soirées to find Lord Lamorna still missing. It had been a week since that night, and still she had not seen him. No one had – or not in respectable society, at least. He had simply exploded across the Petersburg social scene like a grenade in one extraordinarily volatile and beautiful mess – a disastrous combination of all-too-visible grief, scandalous whispers about the reputation of Jane

Cathcart, and rumours of high treason – and then had simply disappeared. Jane's unsatisfactory brother was going to be a poor substitute. She sighed, gazing out of the window and watching George Cathcart arrive on foot, the well-cut jacket not quite managing to conceal the weakness of his shoulders, that thick fair hair brushed with too much precision. But needs must. Tatyana summoned up an expression of eager feminine concern as he was announced, flushing already at the prospect of being alone with her, even as her butler retreated, leaving a tray of glasses by the steaming samovar, and closing the double doors behind him.

'Darling George, won't you sit down? I'm so grateful to you for coming. It's a matter of such delicacy that I'm afraid to trouble your mother with it.'

'I'm afraid Lady Cathcart is already sorely troubled.' George sat in one of the armchairs, crossing one leg over the other. He frowned like a thwarted child, and really, how could the foolish boy not see why despite being elevated to the Duke of Wellington's staff at Waterloo because of his father's connections, and despite being the son of a diplomat, he'd never been trusted with a position of real responsibility, much less given a part to play on the grand stage of world affairs? Every sulky emotion lit up his face like a beacon. Tatyana could read him like a volume of fairy tales: his jealousy of Lord Lamorna was both profound and completely obvious.

Standing by the samovar, and allowing his anticipation at being so close to her to build, Tatyana poured two steaming glasses of tea. She added shavings of sugar from the silver bowl before passing one to him, standing so near that she sensed his unpleasant dog-like eagerness. It was time for her opening gambit. 'Well, one does feel so sorry for Lord Lamorna, but after the way he behaved at the Anichkov affair last week, parading your sister around the empress's own ballroom, one's sympathy is certainly challenged.'

George set down his tea. 'My sister is merely naive, Countess, and has no real interest in Lamorna – as I hope you'll say to whoever asks. I have too little faith in the impertinence of most people in society to hope that no one will be crass enough to pry into my family's affairs. You hold in your own hands the power to rescue Jane's reputation – everyone listens to you. It's a damnably awkward situation.'

'I can see that.' Tatyana sipped her tea. 'Except one can't help but feel almost sorry for the poor boy – it's just so tragic about his wife and child.'

'It was a terrible *mésalliance* in the first place,' George said. 'Who else would even think they could get away with doing such a thing? I don't care who Lady Lamorna's mother's people were. She was black, for God's sake. You must know that Wellington was furious. Lamorna threw himself away on her, he said.' He broke off, setting down his teacup. 'Well, she's gone now and so is the child. I dare say it's just as well.'

Tatyana smiled. 'Really? I've always felt you've been unfairly sidelined in Lord Lamorna's favour, George. It just seems wrong. It's a shame Wellington didn't recognise that there isn't much use in real talent unless it comes with a sense of responsibility.'

'Yes, well, Lamorna will soon no longer be of much consideration to anyone, I dare say.'

'Oh?' Tatyana asked carelessly, almost unable to believe how easy it had been to tease out this critical piece of information about just what the scheming British intended for their own favourite aristocratic delinquent.

George flushed. It was embarrassing. Cathcart ought to just send the boy home to manage an estate. He was less cut out for playing the great game than his sister was for entrancing a ballroom. 'Well, after the scandal Lamorna's kicked up here I dare say he'll not be welcome in any respectable part of Petersburg. I should think my father will advise him to go home to Cornwall and have done with it. My mother said the sooner he marries again, the better.'

'I'm so relieved,' Tatyana said, as the truth of the situation dawned upon her. Honestly, the English deserved to fail in all their dealings. 'And so where is his lordship now? I heard that after disgracing himself at the Anichkov in such a way, no one saw him for days.'

George shifted in his seat. 'Unfortunately, no one has a very precise notion where he is. He's rioting all over the worst parts of town, from what we heard.'

'Which will only make gossip about him and dear Jane spread with far greater ferocity – to a mean-spirited observer, it might even look as if your father had turned Lord Lamorna out of the embassy, lending even more substance to all those rumours, even though you and I know not a word of any of it is true, of course. All he really did is walk darling Jane across a ballroom, and poor old Thérèse de la Saint-Maure too – people can be so uncharitable.'

George sipped his tea, obviously warming to his subject. 'The fact is, Lamorna's a loose cannon and always has been. The sooner that marriage between Jane and Prince Volkonsky takes place, the better. It's the only real way to stop this scandal spreading.'

'Oh, I quite agree,' Tatyana said, even though she had no intention of allowing Sasha to marry this foolish boy's sister. He was clearly overjoyed at being entrusted with the task in hand – to ensure that Lord Lamorna never returned to England – but Tatyana couldn't allow that to happen until

Lamorna had played his part in her own game. It was quite simple: she must just ensure that her players now moved with speed and precision.

31

'Wait here, Jacques, do you understand?'

Tatyana's coachman stared at her, gripping the reins in cold-reddened fingers. For a May evening with cherry trees blossoming up and down the Fontanka, the streets of Petersburg were unexpectedly cold. 'My lady,' Jacques said, 'I know it's not my place to say, but this isn't the sort of establishment your ladyship ought to visit alone. I'm sure I ought to come in with you, or perhaps we should go home and fetch one of the footmen.'

Tatyana sighed. There was no time for this sort of impudent halting-at-fences from one's servants. 'I know very well that we're outside a bordello, Jacques, let's not beat about the bush. Your orders are to wait precisely here, ready to leave quickly, do you understand?'

By the time Tatyana had been admitted into the black-and-white-tiled vestibule of a smart townhouse by a footman who openly leered at her with the most disgusting impertinence, she was starting to regret leaving Jacques outside. There was a difference between sharing a couple of the season's prettiest young officers with one's adventurous cousin, and walking into a room of partially clothed strangers. And why had she not thought of the fact that she would in all likelihood recognise some of the men? She was a stranger in this world, but they were not. Sitting at a marble-topped table by the window, Pushkin and young Sergei Gagarin were playing cards with two fleshy young trollops clad only in diaphanous silk shifts. Tatyana tugged her ermine-trimmed hood forward, aware that heads were turning.

One of the girls sitting with Pushkin looked up, laughing. 'Don't be shy, sweetheart.'

Tatyana surged on through the crowd. It was a good thing darling Petya couldn't see her here – whatever would he have thought of his mama in such a place? She suppressed a frightening rush of emotion, taking a glass of champagne from a tray held by a pox-scarred footman. Now wasn't the time to think about her son, her only child – the single constant light in the long, miserable years of her marriage. Her footman had been following Lord Lamorna for days. For the love of Mother Mary, surely he had to be here now? Tatyana edged past a group of young lancers surrounding two entirely naked young women, glimpsing a flash of downy underarm hair as one of the girls raised her arm to embrace a soldier as he grasped her pale backside, allowing his fingers to linger between her legs before he touched them to his lips and then hers, laughing. There was absolutely nothing, Tatyana realised, to stop any of the men in this establishment from treating her with exactly the same level of disregard. The champagne rushed to her head, and then, at last, she saw Lord Lamorna lying on a chaise at the back of the room, his long legs crossed one over the other, his boots all over the scarlet brocade. He was stripped to the waist, and a brassy-haired creature in a silk toga sat astride him, trying and failing to wake him up.

'Off,' Tatyana said in such a commanding tone that the girl fled, disappearing into the insufficiently dressed crowd. Lord Lamorna lay with his head turned to one side, his black hair in a dishevelled mess, and she saw that his naked torso was covered in an extraordinary pattern of swirling blue-black tattoos. Tatyana sighed and with one hand on the arm of the chaise she leaned over him and tipped the remains of her glass of champagne into his face. His eyes opened immediately, grey and shockingly devoid of emotion, his pupils the size of pinheads. She felt the pressure of cold metal at her wrist and looked down to see that he was holding a knife to the delicate skin, precisely where he'd kissed her with such gentle savagery at their last encounter.

'What do you want?' He didn't question her presence; she realised he could not have cared less about what happened to her in this place, and that it was simply usual practice for him to draw a knife immediately upon waking.

She forced herself to sound calm, as if she were dealing cards to a debutante, not risking her life countermanding the efforts of a man with nothing to lose. 'Where can we be more private?'

He got to his feet and walked away without waiting for her to follow. The tattoos went all over his pale, muscled back, too. He held open the door to a gloomy side-room with mocking chivalry, closing it behind her. Stained crimson velvet curtains shut out most of the light. Wrinkled sheets lay heaped on an empty bed, and the air was thick with cheap scent and the stale perspiration of strangers. He leaned back against the bedpost, waiting for her to speak. It was light enough to see that his pupils were still constricted – he had been taking opium, then, in one form or another.

'How deep does the addiction run?' Tatyana asked conversationally. 'I'm surprised you don't place more value on your brother's life and reputation. Surely you realise both will be at risk if you fail in the task set for you by Lord Castlereagh? Have you even started looking for the girl yet? But how can you, when you don't know where she is?'

Lord Lamorna's only reply was to reach into the pocket of a waistcoat hanging over the end of the bed for a cigarillo, lighting it, as was his habit, from a candle guttering on a dressing table littered with an array of silk scarves, the recent use of which she preferred not to contemplate.

Tatyana sighed. 'The marriage of Jane Cathcart and Prince Volkonsky is to take place in less than three weeks, I'm given to understand. Do you wish to learn the whereabouts of Nadezhda Kurakina or not? It's quite simple, Lord Lamorna. Ensure that Jane is so thoroughly compromised that no man would marry her, much less a man of Sasha's standing, or I won't tell you where to find your malleable little heir to the English throne, and your handsome brother's life will be as good as finished. We are running so short of time.'

Lord Lamorna exhaled a bloom of smoke. 'Do you think I really care, Tatyana?'

She stepped closer, shrugging back the ermine-trimmed hood of her velvet cloak. 'I wonder if your young brother knows yet that you're in Russia? I'm quite sure that even now you won't allow Captain Helford to suffer for your own failings, however lost you might be. Think of his life, his reputation, if you continue to drink yourself into an early grave instead of carrying out the mission you were entrusted with.'

Saying nothing, he walked out, stepping past her, leaving her alone, and Tatyana pulled up the hood of her cloak, wishing that she had never come to this place: she had underestimated him, or overestimated the strength of any fraternal affection – risking her own reputation in this place all for nothing. The large salon was now thick with the sickly scent of opium smoke, and Tatyana felt as though the walls and the ceiling were sliding closer to her. She was almost at the door when long, strong fingers closed about her upper arm in a bruising grip, with such sudden speed that she couldn't breathe. She dared not turn around, prolonging the moment of exposure.

'What in the name of Christ are you doing here?' It was Sasha himself, leaning so close that his breath was warm against her neck. A stunning combination of relief and fury shot through her, as well as a living terror at the prospect of her machinations being revealed to him. How maliciously he would smile if he knew what she was doing. And how dared he address her so? 'Don't look around,' he went on, 'just keep walking.' He loosened his grip on her arm but placed one hand on the small of her back, his fingers spread wide. Outside in the street, he handed her up into the carriage, Jacques staring directly ahead with leaden stoicism.

Without asking, Sasha climbed up on to the box beside him, as though he had any kind of right over her, and she sat in impotent fury on the velvet upholstered cushions, remembering how Lake Ilmen had shone like a mirror on the day she had fallen in love with Sasha Volkonsky for the first time at her father's estate, when as a fifteen-year-old orphan he had been forbidden to go on the wolf hunt for speaking out of turn to her papa, his own godfather and guardian. Herself corralled indoors on a wooden chaise spread with wolfskins, there had been nothing for Tatyana to do but ply her needle, drawing crimson thread through white linen; in less than a month, she would be married. She'd thought of Count Orlov touching the rose-patterned nightgown with his thick, bristled fingers and had swallowed a surge of nausea, tossing her embroidery to one side, unable to continue with it a moment longer, as if every stitch brought her closer to the marriage she so dreaded. Running to the window, she'd gazed with painful longing at the dark green canopy of the forest and the silver vastness of the great lake, only to see that Sasha was now swimming in the mirror-bright water. He lay on his back, zigzagging like a long-legged water beetle. Tatyana had imagined the silken feel of that water on his naked skin, and what it would be like to look up and see nothing but the sky and the forest. She could have watched him for hours – water streaming down the golden brown skin of his back, the dark reddish golden brown of his hair. Hitching up the long woollen skirts of her sarafan, she'd climbed out of the window, taking great gasps of the fresh air as though she were parched and it was water. One of the chickens pecked the grass just an arm's length away.

'What are you doing, Tanyushka?'

Tatyana had looked up, flushing, to see Sasha himself silhouetted against the sun, and she scrambled to her feet, facing him. He'd thrown on his shirt and breeches but his hair was wet and dark, so much so that she could not see the bronze in it; it sent runnels of lake-water down his sun-browned neck. He was a cousin of Pushkin; in summer, his skin darkened quickly.

'Nothing.'

Sasha shrugged. 'You climb out of windows for nothing?'

Tatyana had closed her eyes, sensing the warmth of his presence, his closeness. What would it be like when Count

Orlov mounted her like a farmyard beast? She succumbed to a wave of stark terror. 'Sasha, never mind the window, I want to climb out of my life.'

He smiled. She'd never been able to resist that. 'Come swimming with me. All of the servants are arguing with Orlov's coachman in the yard – no one will see.'

Standing right there in front of her, he'd untied the ribbon at the neck of her sarafan, slipping the long robe over her shoulders, right to the ground, and Tatyana had known even then that for the rest of her life she would never forget walking to the water's edge with him, clad only in her shift, their fingers outstretched towards each other yet barely touching.

But when the kalasha drew up outside the Orlov mansion on Nevsky Prospekt, Sasha didn't look at her at all. He just waited in domineering silence for Jacques to hand her down, and walked up the steps beside her, saying nothing until they had passed the gathered servants without seeing any of them, up the wide staircase and into the morning-parlour, even though there was no sun, and not all of the candles had been lit.

'What in the name of God were you thinking?' Sasha demanded, closing the door behind him with an imperious snap. 'Believe me, you're lucky at this moment that you did refuse my offer – if you were promised to me, you'd sorely regret this adventure by now.'

She had always known how to defuse his temper. 'Sasha—' She didn't reach to touch him, but the air between them grew hot; he had never been able to resist that certain expression, that look, and indeed now he did not, but leaned into her angry kiss, letting her fingers tangle in the curls of his hair. Why had he not spoken to Papa, that summer when they were both fifteen? Why had he not begged for three or four years to prove his worth as a man? Instead she had endured marriage to Orlov, and all that had come with it.

'I honestly fail,' Sasha replied, stepping away, 'to see how you can go on for much longer without entirely destroying yourself, Tatyana.'

She knew it was too late now, for both of them. It had been too late for twenty-five years. One was no longer the idealistic girl who could simply love him.

'Oh, why don't you go and play dice?' she asked. 'I'm sure you'll find someone young and foolish enough that you haven't ruined yet.'

Sasha turned and left without another word, and Tatyana sat down on the chaise, very straight, not moving even long after he had gone. One had standards. One had pride, if nothing else.

32

Hester sat side-saddle on one of the blossoming cherry tree's spreading branches, leaning back against the trunk like a child playing hide-and-seek, a grown married woman of nearly twenty-five. From her vantage point in one of the walkways leading off Rotten Row, the crowd in Hyde Park was noticeably thinner than it would have been at five o'clock in the afternoon in March, at the height of the Season. Hester could only pray that Dorothea Lieven's affair with Lord Vansittart had kept her in London. She'd waited here all the previous day, inadvertently witnessing an entire range of secret assignations, some of which were between people she had played piquet or conversed with at one of the many balls and salons endured as Crow's wife during the Little Season the previous November. There was no sign of Dorothea in her usual haunt. There was nothing to do but wait – it was hardly as if she could seek admission to the Lievens' house in Berkeley Square. Her belly twisted with hunger, but the single warm currant bun she'd clutched in her hands outside the pie-shop near Piccadilly in the hour after dawn was now long gone. She'd entered Hyde Park as soon as the watchmen opened the gates at seven o'clock in the morning and had concealed herself there ever since, quite unable to take the risk of being moved on as an unwanted presence, or – worse – actually recognised. At last, a slight, dark-haired figure clad in an ermine-trimmed pelisse emerged from Rotten Row on to the walkway where primroses blanketed the moss-covered roots of the cherry trees. Flakes of blossom littered the path like snowfall and, hardly daring to breathe, Hester swung one leg over the branch and dropped quietly to the ground.

'Dorothea!' Her own voice sounded odd, strangely ragged. It had been so long since she'd exchanged more than a few necessary words with a street vendor or with the hackney-carriage drivers who snatched the penny fare from her hands in contemptuous silence. Absorbed in her own thoughts, Dorothea didn't look up from the drift of blossom at her feet until Hester whispered her name again, in increasing frustrated desperation.

Looking up, Dorothea stared with mingled terror and affront at being so addressed by a lone black woman in a grass-stained velvet gown and muddy worsted cloak. She stood completely still, her lips slightly parted as understanding dawned, and Hester realised that Dorothea really was profoundly shocked, horrified even, as if she'd crawled from the earth at her feet clad in a grave-shroud. '*Hester!* My God, what are you doing? I thought you'd fled the country, or worse.'

'Not without Crow.' She didn't trust Dorothea enough to even mention Morwenna and Catlin, and where they had gone. 'Where is he, Dorothea – what happened to him after he was arrested?'

'He's not dead,' Dorothea said swiftly, and hot tears slipped down Hester's cheeks because Crow was still in the world, somewhere, with his permanently untidy hair, and his elusive smile that was so devastating when it appeared, and his habit of kissing her behind the ear before he led her in to dinner, so that she would spend the entire evening in anticipation of being alone with him. Taking one long, steadying breath, Hester put her hands up to her face, wiping away the tears. Convulsively, Dorothea grasped Hester's dirty hands in her own.

'Where is he?' Hester forced herself to sound steady and reasonable. 'If you know where he is, please tell me, I beg you.'

'He's gone to Russia. Castlereagh sent him to retrieve an heir for your throne, Nadezhda Kurakina – Princess Sophia's bastard daughter with our tsar. She's been an open secret in Petersburg for years, but even in Russia scarcely anyone knows who her mother was.'

'Princess Sophia?' Hester repeated, astonishment seeping through the sheer relief at knowing Crow was alive, even if he was hundreds of miles away and lost to her in a strange country. 'But even if that's true, the child would be illegitimate.'

Dorothea shook her head. 'Trust me, there are ways around the girl's birth which will appease both the Church and the general population – not least the element of desperation. Castlereagh has turned your country into a powder keg ready to explode at any moment. You need an heir to the throne – at this point, even the Church understands the necessity. And so Crow was sent to Russia to bring the girl home.'

Hester closed her eyes in relief. 'Well, if anyone is likely to manage that, it's my husband.'

'Listen, we have so little time – Vansittart is due to meet me here at any moment, and God only knows you mustn't be seen. *You don't understand,*' Dorothea said, fixing Hester with the unwavering attention of her steady, intelligent brown eyes. 'Castlereagh sent Crow to Russia, but he doesn't want him to succeed. Castlereagh expects Crow to fail, and has indeed taken measures to ensure that he does.'

'What measures?' Hester's mouth was dry with terror. 'Dorothea, what on earth are you talking about?'

'Please just listen,' Dorothea went on urgently. 'You know as well as I that Crow was a folk hero even before Newlyn, and not just in Cornwall or even the south-west. He freed Wellington from captivity. He fought at Salisbury. Can you imagine how the common people feel about him now? Castlereagh knows quite well that if your husband returns to Britain alive, he's powerful enough to become a threat to Castlereagh's own position. All that rubbish about your peasants calling him the King of Cornwall is just that, rubbish – complete fustian. But there's a very real chance Lord Lamorna might be elected to the Cabinet. Even with his reputation, he could easily be recast as a far more popular prime minister than Castlereagh ever was, even as a stabilising influence precisely because of his popularity among the general population. Possibly even with you as his wife.'

Hester stared at her, too humiliated and enraged to speak. Dorothea had articulated the quiet, persistent doubt that dogged the long watches of her own sleepless nights for so long. *We should never have married. I am a burden to him, and I should never have subjected myself to this.* There was no point in reminding Dorothea that she had married Crow only to save her life and her honour – long ago, it seemed. She had never wanted to live among these people.

'Don't look like that,' Dorothea went on swiftly. 'You're an intelligent woman, Hester. You must know that this is the reason Crow no longer corresponds with Wellington – the duke was furious with him over your marriage.'

'Let us concentrate,' Hester said, mustering all her self-control, 'on the task at hand.'

'Very well,' Dorothea said. 'It was thought not safe to execute your husband – the public feeling would be too strong; it's too dangerous a ploy, even for Castlereagh. Crow is to die quietly in Russia, Hester – he and this heir together.'

Hester's head swam. Dorothea listened and whispered everywhere: she had the ear of every great man, from the Duke of Wellington to Tsar Alexander of Russia. Hester might loathe her at this moment with every fibre of her being, but she was telling the truth about the danger Crow stood in. 'But who could even do it?' Hester demanded. 'You must know that assassinating my husband would be no easy matter, and nor would it be the first time that such a thing has been attempted.'

Dorothea glanced down the walkway back towards Rotten Row, as if impatient to move on. 'I'm afraid both my husband and I heard the same thing, from an all-too-reliable source. As you know, Emily Stewart becomes very talkative after several glasses of claret. And Castlereagh discusses everything with his wife, for all that she is afraid of him. Emily knows, Hester. This is incontrovertible.'

'I'm going to Russia,' Hester heard herself say; it took a moment to swallow enough of her anger that she could even speak. Castlereagh had been a guest in their home and had ordered Crow's death; on Castlereagh's word, Hester's own servants had been slaughtered like hoggets. On his word again, Crow's death had been engineered with cowardly attention to detail. Dorothea, too, had accepted the hospitality of Crow's ancient name and house and yet had made no effort to save his life, content to watch this bloody game play out as if it had been laid on for her entertainment. Hester looked at her, shaking with anger and disgust. 'I suppose I should count myself grateful that you told me.'

'I know you're angry,' Dorothea said calmly. 'But you must understand that neither my husband or I could be seen to intervene in this affair without giving the impression we were acting for Russia. I place my own national interest at risk even by having this conversation with you – were it not for our friendship, and the high regard in which I hold you, I'd say nothing. If Crow had showed an interest in allying himself – and Cornwall – with Russia, perhaps matters would stand differently and my husband would have acted to save your husband's life at an earlier point, and you would now be with your daughter.'

Hester let out a long, shuddering breath and turned to walk away.

'Wait,' Dorothea said with such a steel-edged tone that Hester stopped where she stood, still listening. 'I haven't told you everything you need to know, Hester. Your husband is half French. Obviously he has good reason to despise the current regime in France, but consider how much his loathing and distrust of England has now grown. Some might say there was a possibility it might match his hatred of France, and of Napoleon. I can't be certain of this, but I've heard there is a risk the French might attempt to persuade Lord Lamorna to act as a double agent, this time in their own interests. After all, it wouldn't be the first time he's been involved in such ambiguity, would it?'

Hester froze. Of course. Dorothea Lieven knew and controlled everything, like a spider at the centre of a web.

Naturally, she also knew that during the French Occupation, Crow had acted for Wellington as a double agent, liaising directly with Napoleon's ex-wife, Joséphine Bonaparte.

Hester forced a tone of light dismissal into her voice. 'My husband is not an easily persuadable man – you know him well enough to realise that.'

'No,' Dorothea said, 'but he loves his brother very much, does he not? And he's also an extremely dangerous man, and viewed as such by French and English alike, much as both sides will use him if they can. Make no mistake, the French high command know enough of Crow to be certain that if they have Kitto in their power, they'll lure Lord Lamorna to his complete destruction whether he does as they wish or not. If they don't assassinate him themselves, associating with the French will ensure the British people come to loathe Crow as much as Castlereagh does himself. It'll be enough for the English to publicly crucify him without risk of stirring up unrest – and that's if Castlereagh's assassin doesn't reach him first. However one looks at it, your husband has walked into a trap, Hester.'

There was nothing else to be done or said. Hester inclined her head in the slightest of curtseys and walked away through the fallen cherry blossom, praying that she would be able to reach the Port of London alone and unprotected as she left Dorothea to wait for her lover.

33

A fortnight – no, more – had slipped past in a blur of grassland and pine-scented forest since the moment Nadezhda had so unceremoniously given up her secret, and still neither made a single further mention of the fact she was not Ilya Rumyantsev. Each day was nothing but flying mane in one's face and aching limbs, and waiting for another ambush that never came. They might even yet succeed, and deliver all four hundred horses to the commissariat, except that Nadezhda shook and ached with lingering fever, and she dared not look at the deep graze ploughed below her ribcage by the musket-ball at Yarkaya Polyana. Now, as the sun sank above the plains half a day's ride from the town of Chudovo, she sat astride the golden Turkoman mare, the herd-mother, watching wild peonies bleed streaks of crimson across the grasslands. Bees and insects hovered above the grass and a hawk circled, keening into the wind. Just a few yards away, the River Kerest snaked with green, reed-edged persistence through gathering dusk, and the horses were restless as they gathered at the riverside; sunlight glimmered off haunches and the mares patrolling the outer reaches of the herd tossed their manes below a cloud of lazy flies, all because Captain Helford had ridden out on patrol. What if he did not come back?

Who will you tell? Nadezhda had demanded on the night of the ambush, the night he learned her secret, bleeding into her corset on the open plain beyond Yarkaya Polyana, his only reply a blasphemous assurance that he didn't care who she was.

I just need to get back to Petersburg with what's left of my reputation intact. Which, I might add, has been thoroughly fucked up the arse by my brother. Captain Helford had broken off at the combined silent astonishment of Countess Orlova and Nadezhda, herself no stranger to soldiers' invective. *Oh, Christ,* he'd said. *I'm sorry.*

The countess was kinder, if less socially catastrophic and handsome. *I was once a young girl, too,* she'd said, sponging Nadezhda's fevered forehead with a frill torn from the hem of her gown and soaked in water. *You have no idea how often and how sorely I regret not having the courage to flout my father's wishes and live the life I chose for myself, with the man I really loved.* And yet what did that mean, really? It was certainly no guarantee that Countess Orlova could keep a secret. The news that Lieutenant Ilya Rumyantsev was actually a young girl might easily be all over Petersburg, and Nadezhda watched the mare's gold-dipped ears flick forwards: her own fear was infectious as she pushed away frozen memories of snow soaking through the back of her gown, and the meaty scent of Ilya Rumyantsev's hot breath in her face. At any cost, the truth must be concealed.

At last, she saw Captain Helford approach from the west at a flat gallop, leaning hard over the neck of his own gelding, making free and expert of the whip. His horse had run with the rest of the herd as they fled Yarkaya Polyana, tack and saddlebags intact. He had a beautiful seat and rode as if he was part of the gelding's back, but he was no different to anyone else, treating his horse no better than a slave. If he carried on like that, the gelding's fear would spread like ripples chasing each other away from a pebble tossed into the river, and the horses would scatter. Nadezhda longed to snatch that whip from his grasp and serve him the same: how would he like a taste of it? Riding up close, Helford urged the gelding down to a witchy, nervous trot, circling Nadezhda and her mare as he grasped reins and whip one-handed.

'There are other ways to make a horse do what you want, you know – especially one like that,' Nadezhda snapped, her anger lent wings by a feverish ache rippling from the wound festering beneath those dirty wrappings, and she watched the gelding shift, his sensitive, fine-cut nostrils flaring. Long narrow welts glistened on his shoulder; his flank was dark and foaming with sweat. 'They'll scatter if they're frightened,' she went on, 'and he trusted you. Have you never been betrayed and hurt by someone you looked upon as your protector? How would you like it?'

Captain Helford's eyes widened, and an expression of sheer fury chased away a trace of shocked chagrin. His dusty hair was in disarray, his black lashes dark against the pale hollow of his eye socket, the rising cheekbone. The predatory awareness of his surroundings that had characterised his every move since the French attack at Yarkaya Polyana was momentarily stilled as he subjected her to a ruthless appraisal, just as he had ignored her question. 'It's got worse, has it not?' he said. 'You do realise you're little use to this mission dead? For reasons known only to yourself, you've been riding around the country in breeches for Christ only knows how long. It's not as if the proprieties could be any more outraged, is it? Let me see the wound.'

Nadezhda just looked at the horses, wishing herself one of them.

He failed to suppress his irritation. 'Oh, for God's sake, do hoydenish girls in disguise not fall victim to the mortal complaints of gangrene and infection? Do you ever plan to tell me at least why you did it? I suppose you realise what my reputation will be if anyone finds out you're a girl – and a Kurakin, too.'

'Oh, naturally all this concerns only yourself,' Nadezhda snapped. 'I see like all men you assume control, even when no one has invited your concern – if that's what you can call it.'

'Forgive me if I'd rather not fail to carry out my own corporal's orders because of a stubborn fool of a headstrong girl,' Helford said. 'You're sick and I'll be damned if you continue to ride that mare bareback. You can bloody well dismount and take the gelding instead. Don't think I won't make you.'

'You touch either of us and I'll have a knife in your ribs.' Furious, Nadezhda leaned forwards over the Turkoman's neck and squeezed gently with her thighs, asking the great golden matriarch to canter. How could he not understand that she and the mare were one and the same, a single soul? The pain intensified at the mare's rolling gait, the makeshift bandage beneath Nadezhda's corset chafing the skin, and when she dismounted at the riverside, shaking and nauseous, she leaned her forehead on the mare's gleaming gilded flank, praying for strength and for courage, and for Captain Helford to go to the devil.

Stepping into the dappled shade, she passed the horses taking their turn to drink, breathing in their warm scent along with the dank, greenish smell of the trampled wet mud, taking comfort in their gentle awareness of her presence. Sitting on a lichen-covered fallen branch, she pulled off her boots, gasping aloud with the pain, setting one beside the other, and the rush of memories struck her like floodwater surging in the spring thaw: the baby wood pigeons Cook had let her rear in a straw-stuffed wooden crate by the old iron oven, the sharp smell of garlic and herbs mingled with the bloody scent of minced pork as the kitchen-girl rolled out dough to make *pelmeni* dumplings when snow fell outside, and how, as Grandmama lay dying, Nadezhda used to help old Grisha the head serf dig the virgin snow, ready to bury a cloth-wrapped bundle of *pelmeni* for winter. They would all be gone by now, long since rotted in the tall grass or eaten by foxes and rats. Nadezhda knew she must forget about home, and the taste of those hot meat dumplings with a spoonful of melted butter when the snow outside was neck-deep, and Ilya Rumyantsev's familiar, arrogant smile as he had walked towards her across the snow-deep yard. *What, no kiss for me, Tasha?* She must close a door on the past. It hurt even to unbutton her shirt, her every move sent blood-stiffened fabric dragging across the shallow cut that French musket-ball had carved just beneath her ribcage. It could have been worse. She should be grateful it wasn't. With a muttered, furious prayer, Nadezhda balled up her filthy shirt and threw it to the pebbled riverbank, reaching around to tug at the corset lacing. Pain pulsed with astonishing strength: she pictured the wound as a gaping mouth and felt sick again at the thought of it.

'I'm sorry.' Captain Helford was standing right behind her. Nadezhda stood in the river, completely exposed in only her breeches and blood-blackened corset. He moved so quietly, even for a soldier. What did he want? What might he do to her? She was unable to move or to run, just like that morning when Ilya Rumyantsev would not stop walking towards her, his gleaming new boots crunching in the new-fallen snow. But, unlike Ilya, Captain Helford didn't touch her. She sensed precisely how close he was – more or less a foot behind her – and yet he remained there, and her terror fluttered wildly, like a bird in a trap.

'I'm sorry that I'm even standing here when you're without your – your shirt,' he said, 'and I'm sorry that it hurts. I'm sorry for behaving like a godawful high-handed bastard, too. I won't pry into your affairs, and if we've got this far I'm sure we'll find a way to deliver these horses to the commissariat without anyone finding out who you really are, and if riding that mare bareback hasn't killed you yet I should think it won't now. God only knows I've been in some awkward fixes myself.' He paused, leaving her free to walk away, and only continuing when she did not. 'It's just that it looks like you can't take your clothes off. Or at least it's taken you nearly half an hour to unlace your corset. And you can't very well clean the wound like this.'

Nadezhda felt a rising breeze tease the curls at the nape of her neck, and folded both arms across her chest without turning to look at him. She was unarmed, but she must continue to breathe, to not panic.

'Listen, I swear I know how horrifically improper this is,' he went on, 'but if you want, I'll help you undress. Without looking, as much as I can. Do you understand?'

Still facing away from him, Nadezhda didn't know how to answer. She only knew that she had seen a kitchen-maid die just three days after suffering the smallest of cuts to the side of her thumb. More than anything she could not shake away the sensation that to Ilya Rumyantsev she had been no more than a wooden bucket, a leather saddle, or anything else one might use in the farmyard. If she didn't clean this seeping wound, she'd be even less than that – indeed she would be nothing at all – and she couldn't clean it alone.

'A graze like that might easily kill you if it's gone bad,' Captain Helford said, still behind her, still not touching her. 'I don't want to frighten you, but it's true.'

Nadezhda had so much to lose, as she knew to her cost, but there was something in his light, low voice that she could trust, something that convinced her he was not the same as Ilya, the boy she had known her entire life, that younger son of a great family who felt himself so entitled to take whatever he wanted from the world that he'd taken her. She heard the slight scrunching of pebbles beneath Captain Helford's feet as he moved closer, the river now lazily enveloping their legs, and the breath caught in her throat as he tucked one of his long, sun-browned fingers into the infuriating lacing of her corset, pulling it free, loosening the ribbon through one eyelet at a time until the corset slipped down to her narrow hips; she had never been a very satisfactory girl, anyhow – small and scrawny and always nut-brown from the sun. She reached down to pull the corset up over her head, gasping at the pain as the wound yawned, not daring to look down at it to see how far the crimson swelling of infected tissue had spread –up towards her ribs, perhaps? Down her belly towards her groin?

'I'll do it,' Helford said, and a wild heat grew deep in Nadezhda's belly as he lifted the corset over her head, his fingertips grazing her naked skin chilled by the cool air rising from the water. 'I've a spare shirt,' he said. 'You could wear that, if you want.'

'Don't go. Not yet.' Nadezhda heard the words slip from between her lips, unbidden. She drew in a deep, shuddering breath and turned to face him, her thin arms crossed over the meagre rise of her breasts. He was taller by quite some way; the canopy of beech leaves cast shadows across his face. He'd thrown her corset on to the riverbank and stood with his hands loose at his sides, looking down at the wound, his lips forming a sympathetic moue, his black brows drawn together. He wasn't at all disconcerted by her nakedness: she wondered how many concubines had smiled for him, although he was so young, and forced herself to speak. 'The ridiculous thing is I can't make myself look at it. It's absurd, but I can't.'

'I know,' Helford said, sympathetic. 'I once crossed my – someone. All right, if we're exposing all our deepest vulnerabilities, when I crossed my brother a few years ago he gave me the most godawful beating, and afterwards I felt sick whenever I looked at any of it. It wasn't a whipping or anything like that but, Christ, he clouted me so hard that I bled everywhere. I wept like a waterspout. My ears rang for nearly a year afterwards. Sometimes they still do. I can't even begin to tell you how bad it was.' He half laughed. 'In fact, I've never told anyone about that before. It makes me feel queerly ashamed even to think of it – to be put in my place just like a child or a servant when I thought I was grown. And see, if I can tell you that, then this isn't so bad, is it, to be standing here in this fix we find ourselves in?'

'You *bled*? Surely it was something worse than a punishment for a child.' Nadezhda stood with the greenish river water swirling past her bare legs, looking up at him. 'And anyway, that's dreadful – a shocking thing to do to anyone. In Russia, such treatment is only for peasants and serfs.'

He frowned, but then he looked down. 'Well, we are more egalitarian on that front in Britain. And I'm afraid I was that sort of child. Look. If you stand like that, with your arms across your, across there, then I'll clean it for you.' He drew a reasonably clean muslin cravat from the breast pocket of his jacket and let it hang into the cool green water. Then he wrung the cloth, folding it. She couldn't look down, but that meant she could only look at him, in his filthy scarlet regimental jacket, with those dark lashes, and the bronze sheen of his skin. Sunlight caught the gold campaign medal pinned at his breast.

'Where did you get that?' she asked, just for something to say as the cool wet cloth touched the graze beneath her ribcage. With a light touch, he steadied her, just his fingertips grazing her naked skin once more, and again that queer heat pulsed through her. She gasped, and he looked up, his grey eyes suddenly dark with emotion. 'One so rarely sees an English officer with a medal for gallantry,' she went on. 'They say Wellington is not generous with them.'

'I got it at Novgorod,' he said, looking down again, now kneeling in the river to get a better look at the wound, so that all she could see was the top of his dark head; he was soaked. 'It sounds all right, except when you think that everyone else who went up those siege ladders is dead. One's friends. Anyway, what do your orders say about Chudovo?'

She stifled another gasp at his touch, so gentle but somehow reassuringly deft and commanding at the same time, so different in every conceivable way to the manner in which Ilya had pawed at her in the farmyard at home with his thick, moist fingers. She steadied herself before speaking. 'There's a Polish cavalry unit stationed there with Cossacks, and the pastureland is rich. We're to requisition the Cossacks as well as all the horses we can find. The farmers aren't going to like having their horses taken at this time of year, so close to harvest, but we've no choice. We're supposed to rendezvous with a lot of Polish cavalry on the way there.'

He looked up sharply at the mention of a rendezvous, of relinquishing control of this mission. 'Rendezvous with the Poles? But I suppose you remember what Tatyana Orlova said?'

'Which bit in particular? *Why is there no serf to deal with this mess; how long do you expect me to ride with no saddle;* or *I have a ball to arrange, you know?*'

'When she told us that your best chance of getting away with this is to arrive in Petersburg with four hundred horses, as a resounding success,' Helford said, rinsing out the cloth, cleaning the wound with surprisingly expert panache. 'I think you ought to leave the corset off and wear my shirt. It looks as if it needs the air more than a bandage. But you're lucky: it's not gangrenous.'

'Have you ever tried,' Nadezhda asked as he stood once more, now soaked from the waist down, breeches clinging to the lean length of his legs, 'to ride without wearing a corset? And anyway, that wasn't what I asked you.' She flushed again, knowing she wasn't making any sense: his very nearness had rendered her incoherent.

'Well, obviously, yes. But that wasn't really my point,' Helford said, and even though he was no longer touching her, they were standing much closer together, there in the river, just bare inches apart.

'And your actual point was? We seem a little lost.' Nadezhda turned towards the wide pebbled bank, battling an extraordinary combination of latent terror and the desire for him not to move away.

In unspoken acquiescence, they walked side by side to the water's edge, her arms still folded across her chest, and Kitto tossed her a shirt of fine white lawn from his pack. 'It's clean,' he said. 'Well, I only wore it once. I thought we'd have time to wash our things at Yarkaya Polyana.'

He turned away as she struggled into it, breathing in a combination of fresh laundry soap and a faint and intoxicating warm salty scent which must be his own. At last, she dared glance down at the deep graze: an ugly, blackened line reaching from her navel to her lowest rib. Looking back at him, she saw him smile at her again, with that ever-present promise of rising devilry.

'I'm going to piss.' It was a strange relief just how often he seemed to disregard the fact that she was a girl, and spoke to her as though she were truly another soldier, his comrade in arms: she had never been more sorry about all the things she had not told him, and must never tell him. And in that same moment Nadezhda saw that queer air of resty stillness transform him, even as she herself realised that they were not alone.

34

On the riverbank, Kitto turned, knowing he wasn't going to be quick enough, and heard the whine of a shot passing within a quarter of an inch of his left cheekbone. 'Down!' he yelled, but Nadezhda had already flattened herself behind a tall hazel, her cutlass drawn. He dropped into a crouch and loaded his pistol, but when he aimed at the advancing figure, the trigger jammed. Alive with panic, Kitto squinted through the darkness. He was going to die, here and now, out in the godforsaken Russian wasteland, with this odd, half-silent Russian girl who obviously preferred horses to people, with her head full of lies, and whose bare dusty neck he longed to kiss. In a succession of flashing, dreamlike images, he watched the French assassin emerge from the shadows and move to reload his own pistol. Head down, Kitto charged him, slamming his bowed head and shoulders into the Frenchman's solar plexus so fast that his opponent dropped to his knees, winded. Not trusting the pistol, Kitto drew his Mameluk cutlass but the Frenchman snatched him around the knees with one crooked arm, and he crashed to the ground. Dodging a punishing close-fisted blow, he found himself in a choke-hold, the cutlass bouncing away through muddy, trampled grass.

'Come on, you little bastard,' the Frenchman hissed, flecking Kitto's earlobe with hot spittle. 'You're coming with me. You're going to be sorry you were ever born, *quoi*?'

Kitto hung his head as if defeated, alive with panic because he couldn't see Nadezhda: she had simply vanished into the night. Moonlight glanced off the polished steel at his throat. *You're coming with me.* So he wasn't meant to die here, not yet. He was meant to be a prisoner. Why? With one swift, entirely reckless movement, he reached for the dagger at his belt and forced it hard into the Frenchman's upper thigh. *Hit a big vein if you can,* Crow always said. He'd had to guess at the site of the femoral artery, but blood spurted through his fingers even as the Frenchman let out a shriek, cut off with startling immediacy. Kitto felt a line of heat draw across the fine skin at the base of his throat, and knew he'd been cut, and then wet warmth spread over his lower back as the Frenchman died pissing all over him and crashed to the grass, arms sliding limp from around his neck. Kitto spun around to face the corpse, and Nadezhda crouching as she casually wiped her own knife on the grass.

'I stabbed him in the kidney.' She got up, resheathing as though she'd done no more than gut a trout.

Without another word, they ran low and hard back to the horses cropping the grass just paces away. 'There'll be more,' Kitto said, 'trust me, there are always more of them.' It was only when Nadezhda stared at him in incomprehension that he realised he'd spoken in Cornish instead of French. He was losing control; he had to push away an intrusive memory of her naked back, her slim legs in breeches, those curls at the nape of her neck. Christ. Kitto grasped the gelding's mane and leaped up into the saddle. Nadezhda, too, mounted like a Cossack, with a wild, nimble swing across the Turkoman mare's back. Had either of them been a lesser horseman or in need of a mounting block, Kitto knew they'd both be dead or captured, and this was what you got for letting your guard down. Still in wordless agreement, moving as one, they leaned forwards over the necks of their horses, presenting as little of a silhouette as possible, and Kitto followed as Nadezhda spurred the mare into a gallop, peeling around the far reaches of the herd, past all the young stallions and the older mares who habitually protected the younger and more vulnerable horses, all gathered in the middle. The entire herd was moving now, four hundred horses, and all Kitto could feel was the smooth gait of the gelding beneath him building in speed and intensity until they became one, with the wind in his face, as they flew from death itself.

They rode until dawn, the rising smoke of Chudovo's chimneys now a blue blur on the horizon, the canopy of beech and ash alive with birdsong as they blinked away dust pounded from the steppe by hammering hooves. They dismounted, surrounded by hot, sweating horses, and lay down side by side in the grass; neither noticed, but they had long since begun to operate as one, to unwittingly mimic each other's movements. Kitto closed his eyes, still sensing the warmth of Nadezhda's silent presence at his side, still seeing the outline of cloud against the flesh-toned shadow of the darkness. He'd had a knife to his throat: he'd nearly died, leaving this girl beside him quite unprotected. The memory returned, as he had known it would, as it always did following moments of extreme helplessness, creeping forward like a little rill of shining seawater snaking up the beach as the tide rose. He surrendered to it, unable not to live that agonising half-hour again, all pressed into a series of images that flashed before his eyes: facing Crow in the black-and-white-tiled hall at Lamorna House in London, his own white-hot rage at Crow's affair with their stepmother swiftly punctured by the hard-handed slap Crow had dealt him before all the servants. Some of them had nodded in approval, because he'd been quite ungovernable, because he'd been caught buying gunpowder and plotting rebellion against the French. But then the blows had fallen one after another and shame had brought tears to his eyes long before the pain became unbearable. Even now, lying beside Nadezhda, Kitto could feel the overpowering strength in Crow's fingers taking his arm in a sickening grip, Crow hauling him up the stairs so fast that he tripped and his shins smashed into the steps with a burst of agony, brass stair-rods glimmering in the morning light. He remembered the taste of blood, too, lying face down on the carpet in his bedchamber, battling the relentless pain of a burst eardrum, and the tears that would not stop, and the shivering nausea at being afterwards locked in that room. He'd been a child then; he was not a child now. And he had told Nadezhda of it as they stood in the river as green, reed-streaked water rushed past their legs.

'You needn't torture yourself,' she said now, still lying at his side in the grass, looking up at the scudding clouds, and Kitto jumped as though startled from sleep. She turned over to watch him, leaning on her elbow. 'I know what you're thinking: you wish you hadn't told me about the time you were beaten and couldn't bear to look afterwards. Well, doesn't it feel just a little better to have spoken of it? Men are all the same – concealing grievances for decades and then doing something ridiculous and destructive, like fighting a duel.'

Kitto stared up at the racing clouds once more, reaching in vain for a reply. She read his mind just as easily as his long-dead half-sister Roza had always done, as Hester did. He turned to face her, leaning on his elbow as she had done, and the wind-driven clouds above sent fleeting shadows across her sun-browned, high-boned features. 'Why are girls so knowing? You would have given yourself away, had I still believed you were Rumyantsev.'

'It would have been confusing,' she said lightly, 'to have remained Rumyantsev in your presence for long.'

Silence boomed between them, and it took every ounce of Kitto's self-control not to kiss her. The Kurakins were one of the old families. One couldn't simply kiss girls like that, regardless of whether or not they rode the steppe dressed as a boy.

Nadezhda looked away first. 'Just please don't make me tell you why I did it.'

'I wouldn't dream of doing anything so prying.' Kitto knew quite well that he was stronger than her, more powerful, just as Crow had once been stronger than him, but he was not Crow. He would compel no one to give up their secrets in a shameful mess of blood and tears. 'Look, I was in so much hot water when I left Petersburg that if I fail to get these horses to the cavalry commissariat my own honour is at stake. I don't doubt your secret is an honourable one: keep it. I'm not about to force confidences.'

Nadezhda's voice trembled as she spoke again. 'God knows what I'm to do if it *can't* be kept.' A note of panic crept into her voice. 'If Countess Orlova gives me away, what then? She easily could. I can't go back. I can't go home. You do realise that I can't be a girl again?' She let out a short, humourless laugh. 'I've ridden unchaperoned with eight Cossacks and four remarkably stupid Semenovsky Guards, until they were all killed by the French. I'm here with you now. My father was penniless when he died – the estate is mortgaged to the ends of creation. If Tatyana Orlova tells the world what I've done, there is only one way I might make my living—' She broke off, sitting up, and Kitto saw that she was shaking just as he had shaken on the morning Crow had hit him until he could no longer stand and then ordered him to be locked in. Nadezhda hugged her knees to her chest.

'The oldest profession in the world?' he said, thinking of the concubines he himself had visited in Petersburg and in Paris: their scented limbs, their satin small-clothes, and the sheer lack of expression in their eyes. 'It won't come to that, I swear. We'll think of something.' Again, some animal urge warned him not to touch her – not even for reassurance; instead he sat at her side, staying with her as he breathed in her faint, fresh scent of green river water. In the same instant, they turned their heads to look at one another, her earth-brown eyes dark with emotion.

'You know my given name, but you still haven't given me yours in return. You know who I really am, but who are you?'

He could do nothing but let her steer the conversation into safer waters. 'My name is Christopher, but no one ever calls me that save my brother when he's furious enough to talk to me in French.' Even as Kitto spoke, he recalled a dim awareness of Crow's constant presence at his bedside at Nansmornow after he'd been shot, when the fever had seemed never to end. *Est-ce que ça te fait mal, Christophe?*

'Khristofyor,' Nadezhda said, turning her head to smile at him. 'It's nice. But what do your friends call you?'

Kitto pushed away a memory of dissolving into helpless laughter with Ned when Johnny threw a grenado into a cache of gunpowder, blowing it to the sky, even as they were all terrified of being hanged for it. 'Helford,' he said, at last. 'But that won't do for you. When I was a boy, just a child, I had friends who were girls. They called me Kitto, just as my family do now.'

She smiled at him. 'Kitto.' They lay in silence for a long time, turned towards one another; their faces were less than a handspan apart as they sprawled in the scrubby grass and the dust. As he watched, her eyes grew shadowed, as if she had thought of something she would rather forget. Her lips parted as if she were about to speak, but then she looked away, up at the vaulting sky, and he wondered if he would ever find out what she'd just decided not to tell him.

'We're too young,' he said quickly. 'You know that, don't you? If we meet up with this cavalry detachment before we reach Chudovo, they'll take all the credit for getting the horses from Yarkaya Polyana to Petersburg, however much of a nonsense that might be. You have your reasons for this deception but the countess was right: if you want to keep it alive, we go back to Petersburg without help or hindrance from anyone else.'

'I suppose by that you mean without the assistance of any ham-fisted cavalry officer who will doubtless scatter the entire herd?' Nadezhda asked with a slow and entirely surprising smile.

'I mean exactly that. I mean we do this without help. We've come this far. We can do it.'

She smiled. 'And what cause have you to rage and rail against the world in such a way? What have you to prove, Captain Helford?'

'That no one can stop me.' He closed his eyes. Crow would one day come never to forget that.

As one, they turned to face one another again, each lying curled towards the other, their knees touching, and for a long time they said nothing, but were consoled by their closeness.

'Why did he say, *You're coming with me*, that Frenchman?' Nadezhda asked at last.

'I don't even want to know.' In truth, Kitto had no idea. What use was he to anyone, an English officer of the most insignificant breed?

'Is there any reason,' Nadezhda asked as their fingertips touched, 'why the French might be hunting us not for the horses any more, but for you?'

Part 3

COUP DE GRÂCE

35

Hester stood at the end of the great hall at Nansmornow, cradling Morwenna. They were both cast into shadow by low evening light streaming in through the arched window behind her. She wore a light muslin gown that hung from her hips in loose, Grecian folds, and in her arms Morwenna held on to her necklace of coral beads. Crow longed to pull her towards him, Morwenna safe between them. He tried to walk to his wife and child but he couldn't move; he called to Hester and she came closer, his desperation rising with her every step, but when she was close enough to emerge from the shadows, she turned her face to the light and he saw that it was no longer her own, but the bloated, ruined mask of a drowned corpse, a penny-sized crab crawling out of a dark fissure in her cheek.

Several days before Kitto and Nadezhda neared Chudovo, Crow woke to a room ringing with the echo of his own scream, and a headache of sickening ferocity. Every day when he woke up, it was to the same unbending truth: he was never going to see Hester and Morwenna again. He closed his eyes and instead saw Tatyana's face, her mocking smile as she spoke: *I'm quite sure that even now you won't allow Captain Helford to suffer for your own failings.* In truth, he had indulged in such destructive grief that he'd squandered his brother's future as well as his own. Only when he found this bastard Russian princess would his name be worth passing on to Kitto, only then could he hold a pistol to his own jaw and end this relentless nightmare. Coloured lights swam before his eyes, and there was no warm, perfumed body in the bed beside him, no scent of unfamiliar stale breath on his creased pillow, and so where was he? Somewhere, someone was knocking on a door. Leaning over the side of the bed, he reached for the chamber pot and spewed. Recognising the willow-leaf pattern on the top edge of the pot, he saw he was back at the embassy. Swearing quietly in Cornish, he lay back on the laundered pillows, breathing in the incongruous scents of starch and the ambassadorial lemon-balm barrel-soap. The door-knocking intensified.

'What?' he demanded, still in Cornish, and then switched to French. '*Quoi?*'

Cathcart's valet, Varley, edged his way into the room. 'As your lordship doesn't have your own man, my lord, Mr Brooks suggested that I might perhaps assist you with dressing for dinner. It's six o'clock already, sir.'

'Good luck, Varley,' Crow said, and closed his eyes, missing Hoby, whose chief virtue had always been judging when to preserve a diplomatic silence. He had no way of knowing if his own valet was even still alive. How was it possible that he must dress for dinner, that such a thing could be considered of even the vaguest importance? He was still drunk, and there was very little anyone could do about it.

At last rendered outwardly respectable with hot water, soap, clean linen and Varley's steady hand with a razor, Crow went into the library to smoke and found both George and Jane Cathcart standing before the fireplace engaged in bitter argument, both speaking in rapid French so that the brace of bored liveried footmen were given no really detailed fodder for servant-hall gossip. He suppressed a moment's hunger for Nansmornow: there, any person found enacting melodramas when one wanted a cigarillo could be summarily sent to the devil. He made for the door, but not quickly enough – both Jane and George had seen him.

'I'll say no more, George,' Jane said, 'but I think you are grossly unfair to Miss Paolozzi – and to Signor Paolozzi – as well as vastly uncaring about the unhappiness of your own sister!'

'Oh, for God's sake, that's quite enough. Do you really think Lord Lamorna wishes to hear of your embarrassing schemes? For the last time, I haven't the smallest intention of speaking to Papa on your behalf – as if I should do anything to encourage so foolish an idea.'

Jane flushed and sat down, pretending to leaf through a book of watercolour plates even as her rounded young hand shook with suppressed emotion.

George turned to Crow with that slightly supercilious edge to his smile that had always made one look straight through him wherever possible. 'My lord. I trust you feel more rested?'

Crow just looked at him; doubtless it was George who had known where to find him, which bordellos to search in. The better ones were always much closer to palaces and embassies than the uninitiated supposed. Out of all who could have survived Waterloo, why had it been George Cathcart? Crow pushed away a memory of long, convivial suppers in Brussels, faces that he would never see again. Hester had stepped into the chasm left by his long-dead friends, and now she too was gone. He found himself standing at the sideboard, his hand steady as he poured cognac from a decanter into one glass, then another. He drained his own, passing the other roughly to George so that brandy slopped over the idiot's milk-white hands.

'Run along, George,' said Crow idly. 'Your papa will be waiting to know that I'm coming in to dine – he's had a good few days to prepare the reprimand, and I'm sure he'll want an audience for it.'

George opened his mouth to speak, but said nothing.

'And don't worry,' Crow went on with malicious tenacity, 'I'm in no condition to ravish your sister.'

George walked out of the room past Crow, expressionless, still holding his untouched glass of brandy as though he did not know quite what to do with it. Crow poured himself another: he needed to maintain this queer sense of unreality; without it, he knew he couldn't force himself not to walk straight into the Neva and drown.

'Lord Lamorna, please don't go.' Jane spoke with a surprising degree of steady calm.

He stopped where he stood. 'Miss Cathcart?'

'Please, just come and sit with me.' Her voice shook now, and Crow gave in, not least because it was so hard to stand up. He sank on to the sofa opposite her, desperate for a cigarillo. He should have had fifteen years in which to brace himself for Morwenna to enact him the tragedies girls this age were so fond of, but Morwenna would never now have the chance. He pictured his child's corpse washed up on a silent, pebbled beach, pitifully small. Crow had seen enough shipwreck victims to know that from far away she would look like no more than a bundle of cloth. Closer still, she would appear to be sleeping.

'I suppose you know what's happened.' Jane's chest heaved with passion and her eyes were bright with tears, and Crow fought the urge to simply walk out of here and down two flights of stairs to the gunroom.

'You're going to marry Prince Volkonsky: a match to be congratulated upon.' What did any of it matter?

'I'm supposed to be grateful.' Jane pressed a sodden handkerchief to her face. 'And you loathe Volkonsky anyway – I know you do. He ruined your brother at cards. As if I was planning on spending my entire life as a lumping unmarried sister getting in the way of my parents' social engagements. But everything I really wanted is just, just – *ashes* now.'

He decided she was enough of a child still that he could smoke in her presence, and lit a cigarillo from the silver candelabrum on the sideboard. He'd failed to manage Kitto with the remotest degree of either kindness or compassion whenever the boy had got himself into a similarly foolish adolescent mess. Listening to her was small atonement. 'Was there someone you preferred?' He'd already compromised her reputation just a little – enough that people would believe a scandal more readily. But he was also experienced enough to sense that he would never have the pull over this plump, sensible young girl that was so easy to exert over Tatyana Orlova.

'Oh, not in the sordid way you all think. My drawing mistress's brother is a very respectable person. He's just got a position as a court musician; he's left the employ of Count Gagarin's brother in Moscow and will be in Petersburg tomorrow—'

'Wait,' Crow said, even though he was supposed to be destroying her reputation so that she could never marry

Volkonsky: he hoped he would never have been the sort of father to push a daughter into an unwanted marriage, but he'd never know now. 'Your drawing mistress's brother might be a musician in the court of the Shah of Persia for all anyone cares,' he said, 'but that doesn't make him a suitable husband for you.'

She laughed, entirely unexpectedly. 'Oh, you're just the same as all the rest. Of all people, I thought you might be different, Lord Lamorna, considering you're so *spectacularly* badly behaved.' She looked up with a guilty flash of conscience. 'According to my mama, of course. I'm sure I've never seen you conduct yourself with anything other than the strictest propriety and good manners. I don't know why my mama is so furious with me for walking with you across the ballroom at the Anichkov Palace. I'm sure I don't give two straws if the empress herself *did* remark on it.'

She had almost made him smile. 'I'm glad to hear it. But what's so different about this? You're not the first young woman to fall in love with someone unsuited to her station in life, and you won't be the last.'

'That's it,' Jane said, impatient, screwing the handkerchief up in one hand. 'That's what none of you understand. I don't want to be married. Not to anyone. I just want to live in Venice with Miss Paolozzi as my – my companion. All we want is to play music all day, and to sketch, and visit churches; we each have a small independence and would want for nothing more, I can assure you – neither of us dice, or have a taste for extravagant gowns, and we both hate parties. Her brother will escort us there on his way to Madrid. He arrives in Petersburg tomorrow, and what could be more exceptional than his taking us to Venice?'

'Nothing,' said Crow, 'only that your parents have forbidden it, which makes the thing entirely ineligible, doesn't it? Lord and Lady Cathcart won't allow you to cry off and you'd better believe that Volkonsky can't – I'm not going to insult your intelligence by pretending that there is anything other than a diplomatic motive behind his proposal, and the tsar will have his reasons.'

'Unless I do something so dreadful,' Jane said, 'that everyone would have to let me release Prince Volkonsky from the engagement, because the tsar wouldn't want him to marry me then, anyway. But look at me. You just think I'm the least likely person to get swept away in a scandal, and you're right. Men simply don't commit indiscretions with girls like me.'

'Men don't commit indiscretions with sensible girls,' Crow said, getting up to leave her, 'and I'm persuaded that you're one of the most sensible girls of my acquaintance.'

'Wait.' Jane stood, too, facing him across an ottoman scattered with fashion plates and a grandiose, half-finished sketch of the palace of Tsarkoe Selo. 'I don't care what everyone says, and I'm most dreadfully sorry about your wife and your little girl, even though no one ever seems to mention it, as if the fact that they drowned is some kind of awful unspeakable secret, quite as though you'd actually ravished a debutante instead of everyone just pretending that you walking with me across a ballroom was as bad as you, you – kissing me behind a fountain, or something. You're a kind man, Lord Lamorna, and you probably think I don't notice but I can tell you're still extraordinarily drunk, or you wouldn't have listened to me for so long. Surely you don't want me to be married to Prince Volkonsky? Can't we be just mildly indiscreet again – you and I – at another ball or something?'

'Miss Cathcart, trust me, you would not wish that to happen.' So there was steel within this quivering mass of weeping social disaster, after all. Crow had to credit her courage, even if on some deep-buried level he was appalled that she had it within her to suggest such a thing. He left Jane by the fireplace before the girl bore witness to the devastation she'd unwittingly rendered him incapable of hiding, with her bald, brutal honesty.

A short while later, Crow leaned back in his seat at the Cathcarts' table. Thanks to four granules of opium taken with a glass of champagne before leading Lady Cathcart in to dine, he was watching the candle-flames pulsate and change colour – green one moment, cerulean blue the next: reality was best endured in a state of semi-dreaming.

'Are you quite well, Lord Lamorna?' Lady Cathcart said, repressively watching the footman spoon beef olives on to her plate beside a gelatinous slice of creamed spinach tart. 'I'm sure you haven't eaten a single mouthful.'

'Don't fuss the boy, Elizabeth,' Cathcart said with false joviality. Crow knew quite well that he still must face complete excoriation for walking across a ballroom with not only Jane, but his own French great-aunt, not that he cared about any of it. Surely on one level it was quite impressive to have attained the sort of reputation that would ruin a girl just because you'd spoken to her about oil paintings?

'Doubtless he's wondering what Papa has to say to him,' George said, slipping a forkful of sliced veal between his pale pink lips. 'I know I should be quaking in my boots.'

'That,' Crow said, 'is because you're a coward and an idiot, George, and you always have been.' He set down his glass, signalling to the footman to fill it again. Across the table, Jane sat wide-eyed and silent, fork halfway to her mouth.

'It's so wonderful how the cherry blossom is out at last,' Lady Cathcart said, 'it's been such a lingering winter.'

'How dare you,' George said, setting down his fork. 'If you were not so appallingly drunk, I'd call you out for that.'

Crow laughed.

'Don't be ridiculous, boy,' Lord Cathcart said. 'You can't call Lamorna out, or anyone else. Jack, in the absence of anyone else who might have the slightest chance of being listened to by you, I really must call you to order. I simply won't have this sort of behaviour.'

Crow just smiled at him, letting the half-full glass swing from between his fingertips, claret splashing wildly.

'It's the outside of enough,' George said. 'Look at the state of him. Is there nothing he can't get away with? Wellington's golden boy – I ask you.'

'What's wrong?' Crow replied – unwisely. 'Do you object to me talking to an old woman at a ball, George? Almost the last of my family. Surely you don't begrudge a sentimental soldier such a thing?'

'Thérèse de la Saint-Maure is French,' George said. 'In case you haven't noticed, we're at war with France. Although perhaps a French alliance suits your much-rumoured purposes in Cornwall, Lamorna?'

'Oh for goodness' sake, be quiet, George,' Lord Cathcart said. 'Jack, you've had far too much to drink. Have a care for my wife and daughter, at least.'

Crow just smiled at him again and, lifting the glass, tipped the last of his claret on to his untouched plate of food, and the starched white tablecloth, and he watched the wine spread like blood.

36

On the following morning, Crow left the embassy when only the servants were up, after breakfasting alone on cold beef, ale and coffee with a sickening headache that sent his stomach into spasms. Leaving behind the maritime chaos and architectural splendour of the English Embankment, he walked alone to the Assignation Bank. A rotting stink of primordial mud rose from the Griboyedev Canal as he crossed the bridge, and a north-eastern wind chilled him even through his greatcoat. Reaching the bank, a vast, semi-circular neoclassical riot of elegant windows and Doric columns, he went up the front steps at a run, walking straight to the nearest available desk, letting the letter from Coutts fall on to polished walnut.

'Four hundred in silver and notes.'

Bowing, the clerk disappeared. He was gone so long that Crow had to suppress rising annoyance. Reaching for his tinderbox, he struck the flint and lit a cigarillo, but even the throat-raking smoke was little comfort.

'My lord?' The clerk returned from the bowels of the bank, appearing through a heavy mahogany door behind the counter, and removed his spectacles, polishing them with the tip of his handkerchief. 'I'm extremely sorry, but that account is embargoed.'

'What in the devil is that supposed to mean?' Crow already knew, but even so he felt a bolt of fury, and the sheer, half-forgotten thrill of the hunt. So England was his enemy: navy, army, aide-de-camp to Wellington himself and now outlaw.

The clerk replaced his spectacles, putting up one hand to adjust his old-fashioned wig. 'It means that I can't give you four hundred roubles, my lord.' He coughed. 'Or anything at all.'

Without thinking about it, Crow shortened the distance between them, stepping closer to the desk, forcing his features into an expression of polite enquiry, and speaking so quietly that the clerk was forced to lean forwards to listen. 'By whose order?' Unable to afford a moment's hesitation, Crow was already holding his unsheathed hunting knife to the clerk's quivering throat, and was reminded inexplicably of the time he'd found a fledgling starling beside a dusty hedgerow one summer at Nansmornow, and held quivering, terrified life in the palm of his hand. To an outside observer, he knew it would look as though he and the clerk were in head-to-head combat over a ream of paper – not unusual, even within the hallowed halls of the Assignation.

'I cannot say who gave the order, my lord, all I can say is that the account is embargoed until such time as we—' A thick, dark drop of blood landed on the polished surface of the desk. 'The order was signed by Lord Castlereagh himself,' the clerk went on in a hoarse, terrified whisper. Crow turned and walked out without looking back. Who knew what arrangements Castlereagh might have made with the Russian court? England was now his opponent, but who else? Russia too, perhaps. It would be more than possible.

Running down the steps, Crow hailed a kalasha, demanding in his limited but still entirely imperious Russian to be taken to the one address he had faithfully promised Lord Cathcart never to visit. Half an hour later, Crow sank into an ancient chaise longue in a dim, shuttered drawing-room, and looked up at his great-aunt Thérèse de la Saint-Maure, who was standing over him with an amused expression, pouring tea from a steaming silver samovar resting on the side-table.

'You do realise I'll stand trial for treason if I'm seen here today? Not that it matters – it seems very likely to happen regardless of what I might do.' Crow accepted a glass of tea and closed his eyes. In Castlereagh's eyes, he was already a dead man.

'Oh, don't enact tragedies for me,' Thérèse said. 'It was really extraordinarily stupid of you not to anticipate that Castlereagh had only really one motive for sending you to Russia, Lord Lamorna. Fortunately for you, with age comes foresight, and so given that you're no use to me dead, and you've been too busy disporting yourself in drunken misery across Petersburg to do anything either of use or sense, I took action myself. There's someone here I particularly wish you to see.'

Crow let his head tip back on to the heap of cushions. He heard a side-door open and close, the soft creak of a floorboard. Whoever it was, the visitor was unannounced, ensconced in the house before he arrived. He felt all the out-of-control rush of galloping full tilt on a horse he knew might refuse the hedge, leaving him with a broken neck. It was one thing for England to act against him, quite another to deliberately play the traitor himself. Was he really going to do this?

'In my day,' Thérèse went on conversationally, 'a well-bred man would stand in the presence of a lady, and particularly one so very much his superior.'

'Good morning, Lord Lamorna.'

Crow opened his eyes and sheer force of habit drove him to his feet. He stood up to face a diminutive vision in plain grey muslin, grey-streaked chestnut curls cropped short and arranged with simple éclat, an Indian shawl draped around the narrow shoulders. For a moment he could not speak; even had he been able to find his voice he would not have known what to say. Again, habit alone propelled him into a curt bow as he ignored the slow, considering smile of the woman standing before him – Joséphine Bonaparte, divorced former wife and now the mistress of Napoleon.

'Forgive my impertinence,' he said at last, 'but I haven't the smallest notion how to address you these days.'

'Oh, Jack,' she said, casting a quick glance at Thérèse, who was watching without comment, and Crow flinched at the use of his name. 'Don't put yourself into such a passion – you needn't worry. We're such old friends, are we not? Just call me Joséphine, as you always have. I'm here to help you.'

'And how precisely do you mean to do that?'

'I suppose it might be of assistance to a man in your unenviable position to know where Napoleon is?' Joséphine asked, quite gently, and Crow almost choked on his tea.

'Austria?' he said with acerbic impatience. 'Tell me what manner of game I'm supposed to play for you this time, Joséphine. Truth be told, anyone with any sense would be vastly more interested in the whereabouts of Davout and his eight fucking regiments of French cavalry.'

She picked up her own glass of tea, cast an appreciative glance over the spice biscuits arrayed on a gilded plate beside the samovar and took one, taking a small, neat bite. Her teeth were as bad as ever. By rights, she ought to be two years in her grave, killed by a London mob. And here she was, yet again.

'Unfortunately for both Russia and Britain, you've been a little outmanoeuvred.' Joséphine smiled at him. 'Don't be angry. Thérèse and I are trying to help you, Jack. Now listen, I'm perfectly willing to tell you where Napoleon actually is – in Russia – which means you'd know more than Tsar Alexander and all of England's spies combined, and with a word to Wellington and a word to Westminster, you might swiftly despatch Lord Castlereagh and his apparent vendetta against you directly into the realm of irrelevance. A place which, I assure you, is usually fatal.'

'*In Russia?*' Crow stared at her, trying to ignore creeping horror. 'Napoleon is here in Russia?' Wellington and most of the British army were waiting for Napoleon and the First Army in Austria: one almost – *almost* – had to admire the man's genius for manoeuvre. After two years of extracting information from Joséphine during the French Occupation of England, Crow knew her well enough to be reasonably sure she was telling the truth, but didn't presume to even guess at her motivation for doing so. If Napoleon was truly in Russia, England and Russia each faced an all-out rout: French soldiers fought for Napoleon in a way they had fought for no one since Charlemagne. Crow had weathered enough battles in the Peninsula before Waterloo to know only too well that Napoleon's presence alone was easily enough to double the effectiveness of his men. There was every chance he would take Petersburg, and from there the North Sea. 'And so?' Crow went on, determined to conceal a maelstrom of nauseating emotion, knowing that if he looked up, he would see crows circling as they had waited for him to die in the mud after Waterloo, regardless of the fact he was sitting in his great-aunt's drawing-room. 'Why on earth would you compromise your own loyalty to Napoleon by telling me where he is? I hear you're living together again even though he's still married, like a pair of damned down-at-heel poets.'

Joséphine sipped her tea, watching him. 'Listen, my darling, judgemental, so-conventional boy. I love Napoleon dearly, and the poor man must have someone to comfort him now that his cold-blooded Austrian tartar of a wife has taken herself off back to Vienna with her brat, but all the same he won't listen to reason. He simply won't be content to go back to Paris and get on with the job of ruling the French nation. He spreads himself too thinly – I think he can and he will win in Russia, but at what cost? What next?'

'And what has this got to do with me?' Crow said. He got up and walked over to the tall window; leaning his forehead on the glass he looked down at the painted mansions, and the rag-clad girl traversing the straw-strewn walkway with a basket of barley-sugar twists for sale.

Joséphine smiled, reaching up to tidy his hair with a gesture at once disturbingly motherly and erotic, with that verbena-oil scent rising from the delicate skin at the inside of her wrist. 'You're going to tell Napoleon that Alexander plans to secretly swear his final and unshakeable allegiance to the British, that Wellington will cross the Alps and march on Paris with Russian troops behind him, trapping the French First Army between them. It makes no difference whether or not this is actually true,' Joséphine went on with placid calm. 'Because if Napoleon becomes convinced that the Russo-British alliance is truly impregnable, he will know there's no choice except retreat. The vast majority of the British army is with Wellington, and now in Austria. Lord Lamorna, think how many lives might be saved by averting this conquering of Russia, and perhaps then England once more, too.'

Crow leaned back in the chaise, watching her and wondering how much if any of what she had just said was true.

'It's not treachery to England exactly, even if you would be consorting with the French without Wellington's consent,' Thérèse said. 'It's just going to look like it, regardless of whether or not the end result will be to England's benefit. Joséphine?'

'You're both making the mistake of thinking that I care about any of this,' Crow said. 'I don't care if Napoleon takes the imperial throne of Russia for himself. I don't even care if he does rampage across the North Sea straight from the Gulf of Finland and invades England again.'

'Oh, we're quite sure that you've lost all interest in the world stage,' Thérèse said, opening her fan. 'Aren't we, Joséphine? But I take it you do have an interest in your brother's welfare.'

He smiled, savage. Tatyana had tried just the same move. 'I do wonder when people will tire of appealing to a better nature that I don't possess.' Crow ignored Thérèse and directly addressed Joséphine, Joséphine who knew that long ago he had once stayed up all night playing dice for the child's life. And if he were killed in this city then what would happen to Kitto?

'Young Captain Helford has been rather conspicuous on his latest mission,' Thérèse said gently. 'All those horses, and he's with only one other soldier – a boy little older than he is. If you think that French scouts haven't been tracking their every movement since they left Tatyana Orlova's estate, you're dearly mistaken. I understand that there have been one or two skirmishes already – your brother has become quite the expert young killer. But if he isn't in French hands already,

Lord Lamorna, he soon will be. What would you do to ensure his safety?'

'I have some business to attend to this evening, but I'll meet you on the Tsarkoe Selo road tomorrow morning,' Crow said, sparing them both the details: everyone would know soon enough that he had ruined poor, innocent Jane Cathcart, but no one would ever learn that he'd done it to make Tatyana Orlova sing like a bird about the whereabouts of his quarry Nadezhda Kurakina. And for now, Thérèse de la Saint-Maure and Joséphine both thought they had won, that he was their instrument. He would act for France, or seem to: he had little choice. Smiling as she adjusted the shawl around her shoulders, Joséphine crossed the room to a small braided travelling chest resting on the end of a chaise longue beneath the window. She raised the lid, and Crow caught a glimpse of red wool and jet-black feathers. Joséphine lifted out the scarlet, gold-braided jacket of a French aide-de-camp. 'I think I've a reasonable eye for what will fit you, Lord Lamorna. Or perhaps now we should just call you Duc de Montausier? You might even get your title back, after all.'

Crow walked over to the sideboard, raised the carafe of 1805 brandy to the light, and poured an ample dose into one of the crystal glasses resting on a japanned tray. He drank the entire measure.

37

Many hours later, Crow returned to the embassy in a kalasha hired in a respectable but unfashionable district of Petersburg, where fur merchants lived cheek by jowl with icon-painters and musicians in a confusing jumble of tall wooden houses, and the air smelled of woodsmoke, spices and cabbage simmering in vinegar, and the boiled gold used to paint the halos of saints. Speaking in rapid Italian, Crow told his nervous companion to wait, and stepped down from the kalasha into the evening quiet of the English Embankment, burning torchlight glittering across the moonlit waters of the Neva. Concealed beneath his jacket and greatcoat he wore two flintlock pistols, each ready loaded and primed. The dagger at his waist and the smaller knife sheathed in his boot didn't lend him much more confidence. He was a dead man. It was only a question of when. Night had fallen, and the tall windows of the ambassadorial dining-room glowed candlelit yellow. He wondered who were the guests, and how Lord Cathcart had chosen to explain his absence: his own erratic reputation would doubtless have laid the foundations for all manner of fabrication. At any rate, he was about to exceed the wildest expectations of the many people who had devoted their time to gossiping about him since the day he'd joined the navy at the age of twelve, entirely without his father's permission or knowledge.

Instead of allowing the butler to announce him midway through dinner, Crow ran down the cellar steps and crossed a succession of stable-mews and laundry-yards hung with wet sheets before letting himself into the house through a servants' entrance. In an acerbic fug of lye soap, he passed a scullery and a laundry-room; all was quiet. The servants were dining in their hall next to the kitchen: this was as close as he would get to being unobserved. Running up two flights of stairs, he let himself into the ambassadorial family quarters, and polished parquet spread away into the warm glow of an amber lamp set on a marble-topped side-table. Most of the bedchamber doors were ajar, revealing darkness within, but there was a light still lit in Jane's room. Crow let himself in without knocking and found Jane and her nervous Italian drawing mistress sharing the same velvet armchair beneath the window, embracing as they kissed.

'Having no appetite for supper, you retired early with the headache?' he asked.

Jane and Miss Paolozzi broke apart and stared, and then Jane let out a disbelieving burst of laughter. Crow reached for a gaberdine travelling cloak hanging over the chest at the end of the four-poster bed, tossing it towards them. 'Do you want to go to Venice, Miss Cathcart, or not?'

Much later, in that liminal time close to dawn, Tatyana lay alone between sheets and eiderdown, a glass of brandy at her bedside. The room was lamplit, and a fire glowed behind the brass grate, but the brandy wasn't helping. She closed her eyes and saw deep green lawn leading away from the orchard at Yarkaya Polyana and Petya running towards her barefoot, holding a branch of pear blossom, his face glistening with tears. *Mama, Mama, but there won't be any pears.* She remembered his scent – the camomile soap they used in the nursery – and the softness of his fair hair as she gathered him close, just four summers old. *It doesn't matter, my darling love.*

She heard the faint snick of the window-catch and opened her eyes; Petya was gone. A cold draught snaked through a gap in the damask bed-curtains, and she sat up, afraid. Was the window open? Was he trying to come in out of the cold, her Petya? A shadow loomed, the curtains were drawn abruptly back and a cry died in Tatyana's throat as she saw Lord Lamorna, the shoulders of his greatcoat glistening with raindrops that clung in his black hair like so many tiny pearls.

'Good God. Do you enjoy frightening women alone at night?' Tatyana got out of bed without bothering to reach for her wrap; she had no reason not to allow him to appreciate the gossamer froth of silk she wore.

He shrugged, without taking his eyes off her. 'I've done what you wanted. Jane Cathcart has departed for Venice with her Italians and, just to make it really difficult for Lord and Lady Cathcart to dress the affair in clean linen, quite a decent handful of servants saw me leave with her, in the end. So there you have your scandal and Volkonsky is yours for the taking, for what it's worth.'

Tatyana crossed the room to her dressing-table; the carafe of brandy still stood there and she poured him a glass, holding it out. He shook his head. 'I'm waiting, Countess. You have your own end of this bargain to keep. Where is Nadezhda Kurakina?'

And, in the back of her mind, Tatyana was standing once more at the shore of Lake Ilmen, barefoot in the mud, Sasha at her side, before she was married to a man she'd never loved, before she had lost everything, and then she thought of Nadezhda herself, riding that Turkoman mare as though they were one and the same creature. If she must sell the freedom and the future of a young girl just as hers had once been, Lord Lamorna would pay a fair price.

She turned to him, speaking before she had really fully considered the weight of what she had to say. 'No.'

'What?' His fury crackled towards her; she felt the heat of it, like the invisible flames stirred up by a conjuror at a midsummer party at the Anichkov Palace.

The room spun around her, and nothing mattered any more. 'I've just decided: there's another price to pay,' she said, laughing, and how could Lord Lamorna believe that there was any mirth behind that laughter? She was so tired.

He didn't move, but the coiled strength of his rage frightened and aroused her in equal measure as he enunciated each word with cold fury: 'And what price do you ask now?'

'This.' Tatyana stepped towards him and slid her fingers beneath the lapels of his greatcoat; he neither flinched nor looked away as she slid the coat from his shoulders, letting it fall to the floor: after all, he had little choice but to allow her to use him. His usual expression of suppressed grief and animal ferocity flared into something more vivid and frightening, and without taking his eyes from hers he stripped off his jacket. Stepping forwards, he cupped the back of her head in his hands and kissed her, tugging his fingers through the arrangement of her curls. Breathless, before Tatyana knew what he was about, both of his hard hands slid down her back, all the way down, and he tasted of salt, of brandy, of something sweet and wholly his own, with just a fine layer of silk between her naked skin and those hands. She let out a gasp.

'What?' he said, his voice harsh with checked emotion. 'Is this not what you wanted? Do you want me to stop?'

'Don't stop,' she said, unbearable warmth spreading in her lower belly as she reached up to begin the work of unknotting his cravat: she wanted to strip him, but as she loosened the snow-white muslin from around his throat, drawing it free, letting it fall to the floor, he leaned closer again, whispering into her ear.

'Whore. But you know that, don't you?' He pulled her close and eased the nightgown up around her waist, and his touch snatched the breath from her lungs. 'Were you so sure I would obey?' he asked, mocking her quite obvious readiness, but his eyes put her in mind of a snow-blasted winter landscape, stunningly empty and cold, and just as she began to surrender to warm waves of pleasure at his fingertips, he kissed her neck and grazed her naked shoulder with his teeth, and then let her go. 'Turn around,' he said, and such was the note of command that she obeyed without question. 'If I were you, I'd hold on to something.' There was an edge of savage laughter in his voice and the room spun in a blur before her eyes. 'Come now,' he said, guiding her hands to the nearest bed-post as she leaned forwards, grasping smooth varnished walnut, so extraordinarily vulnerable and so aroused that she felt faint, her sight darkened and for a moment it was hard to breathe. Heat rushed to her cheeks as he slipped the nightgown up around her waist once more, easing her legs apart with his knee so that she was entirely revealed to him, and then, thank

God, those long, hard fingers again, so firm and teasing and so relentless, with one hand on her narrow hip in a firm grasp, until she could do nothing but rise on to her tiptoes, letting out another involuntary cry as he ceased his attentions almost at the height of this incontinent pleasure.

'You really are the most wanton little bitch,' he said, 'and God knows someone has to teach you a lesson.'

She writhed, looking over her shoulder, completely exposed to him, entirely bent to his will, which seemed to be to reduce her to an incoherent mess, and she saw that he was kneeling, his dark head bowed low, and then she felt the warm touch of his lips between her legs, his tongue, and it was all she could do to hold on to the bed-post. At first, she buried her face in the crook of her own arm: she would not have the servants smirking at her cries; but that intention was swiftly derailed. Only when she was quite inchoate did he turn her around, lifting her on to the tumbled sheets of the bed, where she lay as he stripped off his shirt, revealing those extraordinary Otaheitan tattoos all over the lean, smooth, muscled expanse of his chest and torso. She watched, too, as he unbuttoned his breeches; she wanted to take him in her hands, but there was clearly no need, and he was obviously in no temper to allow her to lead so much of a step of this dance. Holding both hands above her head, he filled her entirely, and she breathed in the warm scent of his hair as they moved together, she and this furious boy who would not kiss her again, but turned his face away from hers, just as she had seen concubines do. Even so, dawn light filled the room before he had finished with her, and for a few moments he lay at her side with his boots on, and his unbuttoned breeches, and as he sat up, she sat up beside him, tilting his face towards her with her cooling fingertips.

'No,' he said, and she could not be sure whether he was refusing another kiss or whether he simply didn't want her to see the tears now coursing down his face. 'I've betrayed her,' he said, with simple and quite unexpected honesty.

'No, my dear,' Tatyana said, and now he submitted to her embrace, his dishevelled head against her breast as she smoothed his unruly hair. 'I'm afraid it sounds as if your wife is quite gone where you cannot harm her in any way.'

Whispering now, Tatyana gave up Nadezhda Kurakina's secret. She held him for a long time afterwards.

38

A week earlier, Hester stood on deck in the moonlight, adjusting her balance to the heaving swell as the *Wellington* traversed the darkness of the Kattegat, heading south for the rock-strewn Danish Passage and on to the Baltic. Beside her, the ship's boat swung gently on its davits and she suppressed a flicker of memory – bare feet swaying, three figures hanging from the chestnut tree at Nansmornow, long ago. She was a wanted woman herself. She might yet meet that same fate – the noose around her neck. Forcing herself to forget the possibility, she leaned on the guardrail, listening to the rhythmic rolling of the mast stowed inside the little boat along with the oars, watching the sprinkled lights of Aarhus beyond the water. The shipboard scents of hot tar and rum peeled away the years like so many flakes of onion skin; as a little girl she would have climbed on to the poop and spent hours afterwards drawing Norsemen and porpoises, but those days were long gone – she was a woman alone, with no indulgent father in the captain's cabin to protect her. She thought of Crow, too, as the young midshipman Papa had so often spoken of, but she'd never for a moment expected to marry. The immensity of sea and lost time and sky overwhelmed her; she pictured Morwenna safe with Catlin in some far-off Breton fisherman's cottage, but Crow was lost in all the vastness of the world. He was not meant to come home. What if the English assassin had already reached him? What if the French had Kitto? She closed her fingers tight around the guardrail. Crow had served his country for more than ten years, offering up his life time and again at sea and on the battlefield, and he was repaid with treachery. Sometimes she thought that anger was all that pushed her onwards, away from her child in search of her husband. She sensed the sailor's presence before she saw him – the harsh, irregular rhythm of his breathing – and stared with steadfast terror at the lights of Aarhus slipping past as the *Wellington* gathered way; coming up on deck had been a mistake.

'Haven't seen much of you, darling,' the sailor said, behind her. 'Keep yourself to yourself, don't you? Down below deck in that little cabin of yours. Everyone's been talking about you, wondering who you are, what you're doing, a bluey with cash to spend – a private cabin, like – and all on your own, too. Paying young Nicholls to bring you pudding from the galley. Is that all he gives you, we're wondering?'

Hester ignored him and the insulting reference to the colour of her skin. She clung to the guardrail, wishing that she'd dared spare enough banknotes to hire a maid as chaperone, wishing she'd never stepped outside her cabin, because freedom from stale air and boredom wasn't worth this. Speaking to a man would be seen as an invitation. The best she could hope for was that he would simply go away.

The sailor went on a conversational tone. 'Most of the men are thinking you're probably some high-class whore, but what none of us can make out is why you're going to Russia. Seems curious, somehow, doesn't it?'

Hester watched the lights of Aarhus disappearing aft, listening to the calling of the men as they let out more sail; there wasn't much wind. He'd go away. Surely he would just go away. She'd issued no invitation of any kind; she hadn't even looked at him. She sensed him lean closer, as if her disinterest only piqued his interest. She could smell his breath now, foetid, tobacco-tinged.

'I've been afraid for you, lass. That's it: afraid. You see, some of the lads have been thinking you've got something to hide. What you need is a protector. Someone to look after you.'

For a price, Hester thought, willing him to grow bored, to leave her alone.

'So what's your problem, whore?' The wheedling tone had left his voice, hardened now with aggression. 'Not very friendly, are you? Think you're better than us, do you?'

And Hester saw that there was nothing she could do: to speak would be an invitation; to ignore him an insult. He laid his hands upon her hips, letting one hand drag down her thigh. Moving with slow deliberation, she drew the pistol from beneath her cloak and turned around; she held it to the sailor's jaw, right beneath his chin; she was tall enough to look him in the eye. He might have been handsome once, his features marred by age and the regular consumption of liquor, his nose swollen and reddish.

'I suggest,' Hester said calmly, 'that you don't make the mistake of touching me again.'

He stepped away, his dissipated features twisting into the most extraordinary expression of simultaneous disgust and alarm. He called out, and in a moment Hester was surrounded by crewmen. She wondered if all this had been planned, they appeared so quickly. No one said a word. There were ten or fifteen men, at least, all stepping closer with unspoken, sickening menace.

'What in the devil's name is going on?' An aristocratic midshipman elbowed his way through the mass of men, most of them twice his age at least. His mouth fell open as he saw Hester's pistol. Her hands were shaking, and moonlight glinted off the filigreed silver stock.

Escorted by the young midshipman at her side, his face a mask of frozen indignation, Hester climbed down the stairs to the lower deck and she closed her eyes, longing to open them and find her father sitting in the captain's cabin, charts and books littering the desk before him. Instead, it was only Captain Wythenshawe of the *Wellington*, examining a chart of the Denmark Passage. He had a narrow, intelligent face and a shock of fox-like reddish hair, and Hester ignored the odd sense of having seen him somewhere before she'd ever so much as set foot on the *Wellington* at the West India Dock in London. When he spoke, even the northern inflection to his voice was familiar.

'What is it now, Milton?' he said to the young midshipman. 'Why don't you make yourself useful and show me how you'd plot our course south?'

'She'd pulled a pistol on the men.' Milton's Adam's apple bobbed furiously. 'She's a danger, sir. What kind of madwoman pulls a loaded firearm out right on deck? Oughtn't we to have her locked up?'

Terror lurched in Hester's belly, but in the very next moment she wondered if she wouldn't be safer imprisoned.

Captain Wythenshawe looked up. 'I think that's for me to

decide, not you, isn't it? Leave us now if you can't be useful. Put the pistol on my desk.'

Hester swallowed, watching Milton walk out, casting a resentful glance at her: he'd brought her in expecting praise, and received only a reprimand for his trouble. Her throat felt tight; it was hard to breathe.

Wythenshawe smiled, reassuring. 'Come here, Miss – Miss? I'm afraid your name escapes me. Sit down.' He gestured at a chair. Hester sank into it with half an eye on her pistol.

'My name is Mrs Pengelly.' Hester forced herself to sound confident, as though there was nothing at all unusual in an unchaperoned woman with brown skin travelling alone to St Petersburg in a private cabin secured with a roll of banknotes. At that moment, Captain Wythenshawe leaned back a little, steepling his fingertips on the desktop.

'Mrs Pengelly?'

And then Hester knew where she'd seen him before, steepling his fingertips together in precisely that way – sitting opposite her at the long table in the great hall at Castle Bryher, her childhood home. A guest of Papa's, he'd played draughts with her when she was no more than fifteen. She'd won – or he'd let her win, little more than a child at the time; she'd never been sure which. Their eyes met across the table, and Hester couldn't breathe. He knew who she was. He remembered, too. There was absolutely no point in continuing with the lie.

'No,' she heard herself say. 'My name is Hester Helford.'

'Countess of Lamorna and fugitive from justice?' Captain Wythenshawe picked up his brass sextant, turning the instrument over with pale, freckled fingers. 'You've been hunted all over Cornwall – it's been in *The Times*, the *Morning Post* – everywhere. You realise, don't you, that, rightfully speaking, I must apprehend you?'

Hester said nothing and only looked at her pistol; it lay just inches from her grasp, but Captain Wythenshawe would never allow her to reach it. She couldn't kill every man on the *Wellington*. Her only protection was now as good as a hundred miles distant. They were so very far from land: she wondered if this was why he had waited before confronting her – now, when they wouldn't make landfall again until the *Wellington* docked in St Petersburg.

'Goodness, my lady, you needn't look so worried.' Captain Wythenshawe smiled: she was entirely in his power. 'Please, sit down. I'm not a monster. I've been concerned about you, hiding away in that cabin, all alone. Do listen – I have a proposition.'

'A – proposition?' Hester repeated, trying not to imagine exactly the expression on Crow's face if he were ever to hear a man say such a thing to her.

Wythenshawe smiled again. He'd been a friend of Papa's: it would be all right. Papa had been necessarily cautious about whom he chose as his friends. He didn't invite just anyone to Castle Bryher, and she'd played parlour games with this man as a young girl at the long, scrubbed table in the great hall, with her mother's portrait looking down upon them. 'I'd like to ask you to dine with me, Lady Lamorna. Your current habit of paying Nicholls to bring you mugfuls of slop from the galley would, I'm sure, be most unsatisfactory to your husband. And I hate to think of what Captain John Harewood would have thought if he'd known I'd had his daughter under my protection, and had allowed her to continue in such conditions of shocking penury.'

Hester moulded her expression into one of obedient acquiescence – it was usually the fastest and surest way to divert a man's attention to the sound of his own voice. Her gaze was drawn to Captain Wythenshawe's desk, and the array of charts spread out. She saw St Petersburg marked on one at the mouth of a vast river, the Neva. Beside the charts an array of nautical instruments had been laid out – sextants, dividers, a telescope in a brass case. She closed her eyes and saw Papa's tower-top library at Castle Bryher with a window at each point of the compass, those faded red curtains shifting in the breeze, and the acrid smell of the seaweed pits making potash for gunpowder. There, Papa had shown her how to use a sextant, how to read a compass and trace one's progress on a chart. Knowledge was freedom, but she was not in charge of the *Wellington*, sailing her up the Neva and into harbour. Instead, she was entirely at the mercy of Captain Wythenshawe.

'Lady Lamorna?' he said with the barely disguised impatience of a man who had already repeated himself once. 'Will you do me the honour of dining with me tonight?'

Hester looked up. He was smiling, but she didn't miss the sense of entitled impatience. She ought to be grateful. He was her protector, her saviour. She was not the mistress of this ship, or any other, and never would be. All the same, she wondered how long it would be before Captain Wythenshawe noticed if one of those dusty sextants disappeared from the varnished oak shelves above his desk, and how many charts of the Baltic approaches to Russia there actually were, and how obvious it would be if one went missing.

Hester forced a smile. 'I would be honoured, Captain.'

'Good. I think you'll find that the – distinction offered may protect you against unwanted attention in future. In the meantime, I'll escort you back to your cabin.'

Hester curtseyed to him, knowing that there was absolutely nothing else that she could do. Not yet, at any rate.

39

Tatyana woke to find Masha drawing back the bed-curtains. The maid's professional smile froze as she set the lamp down on the bedside table.

'Mistress, are you quite well?'

The aching pulse of the bruising at Tatyana's wrists told its own story: Masha wasn't referring only to the fact that she had slept all day, and that a summer's night was now drawing in again over Petersburg, late and slow, a vast pale grey sky that even so early in the year was never quite dark. Last night, Lord Lamorna had held her wrists above her head, pinning her down, giving to her what she had demanded of him with that merciless, devastated passion.

'Quite well, thank you. You may bring some tea.' Tatyana smiled as she spoke, her victory complete. Sasha would not now be marrying Jane Cathcart – how could he? – and aside from that, she had taught darling, spoiled Prince Volkonsky a long overdue lesson. He was not the only man to please her, and she could please herself elsewhere, wherever and whenever she chose.

Masha stared, swallowing hard. 'But your shoulder, mistress—'

'Never mind that.' Tatyana nursed a memory of Lord Lamorna grazing her skin with his teeth, with barely restrained animal fury; God, his rage at being so manipulated, combined with his clear and obvious need for relief. Her nightgown lay in ruins by the foot of the bed. Masha swallowed, smoothing down her starched white apron, and went to the armoire, bringing out a dressing gown of silver-shot Rajasthani muslin.

'Is there any post today?' Tatyana asked, carelessly, as Masha tied the wide ribbon across the front of the dressing gown. No, she had got what she wanted. For now, it was enough to know that Lord Lamorna had submitted to her power even as he had mastered her completely. What was wrong with Masha, standing there with her fingers clasped together as though praying? With the ball so soon, the silver tray in the hall ought to have been overflowing with acceptances: there was work to do.

'Mistress, there is only this one letter.' Masha turned to the tray she had carried in with her, passing Tatyana the cheap, folded paper.

'You may go.' Battling a rising and horribly fluttering sensation of panic, Tatyana was sure what she was going to see even before she broke the seal, but no one else must witness this, not even Masha. The maid withdrew; even with years of training she didn't manage to disguise a frightened frown as she closed the door quietly behind her. Tatyana took a steadying breath, reaching for the half-empty glass of brandy that had sat on the table since Lord Lamorna's arrival the night before. Dusty cognac seared her throat as she broke open the clumsy seal, unfolding thin, cheap paper that felt almost greasy to the touch. It was not a letter, but worse than that. She'd seen certificates like this before – printed and sold as a cruel joke to mock cuckolds or simply to spread malicious rumours. She'd even deigned to smile at one, every now and then, if it was laughingly drawn from a beaded reticule and shown to her at a salon. Light-headed, she looked down at the one that had been sent to her, and read it. *This certificate is presented to Countess Tatyana Orlova on the occasion of her being a Prize Slut. How can we also fail to credit her for being the Mother of a Coward?*

Tatyana folded the certificate and leaned back against her heaped up pillows. How many other people had received it?

Crow closed his eyes, leaning his head back against the upholstered cushions of the kibitka. Joséphine and Thérèse sat in the forward-facing seat, wrapped in Kashmiri blankets, reminiscing about Versailles before the Terror. He should have foreseen that they would know each other, that he couldn't cross swords with Thérèse de la Saint-Maure in a Petersburg ballroom without Napoleon himself and his consort eventually hearing of it, and that they would find a way to use him. Beneath his shirt, he felt the scratches left by Tatyana's nails, but there had been no sense of release when he took her as she had demanded, only of sickening betrayal, as though Hester were still alive, even though she was not, and he would never see her again, and she would never slap him as hard as he deserved for what he had done to insult her memory, and that of their daughter.

'Darling Thérèse,' Joséphine said lightly, 'give your nephew something to drink; he looks as if he's about to cast himself beneath the carriage wheels, and he's all that stands between three armies. We can't possibly waste him.'

'I find this depression quite insupportable, Lord Lamorna,' Thérèse said. 'If you must conduct wild affairs in the public eye, you could at least not inflict a tragedy upon us about it afterwards. It shows a lamentable want of style, which your Saint-Maure grandfather would have looked upon with the most profound disgust.' She dug into her bandbox, drawing out a flask smelling strongly of Benedictine, but Crow shook his head, addressing her with iced courtesy.

'I thank you, madame, but I'm quite well and in need of nothing.' He didn't care if Napoleon positioned his troops for a dog-fight that would crush England and Russia together; he didn't care if Petersburg burned to the ground or if George Cathcart put a bullet between his eyes for England. But he must have an heir of honourable reputation to safeguard his lands and his people. There was no choice but to spring Kitto from this French trap, and to find this Nadezhda Kurakina, so indecorously disguised as a boy, and in his own brother's company.

Joséphine smiled. 'Darling Jack, but Thérèse is quite right: you mustn't throw yourself into the blue megrims simply because Tatyana Orlova has worn you to death and you've ruined the reputation of a young English girl scarcely out of the schoolroom. No, don't look like that – obviously the whole of Petersburg is talking about it already. You were hardly cautious. Your dear aunt is right: it only takes one servant with a loose tongue, darling.'

'You need not lecture me,' he said.

Thérèse frowned. 'I'm fond of Tatyana, but she really is a fool, especially if she thinks this little scandal is the worst that will ever happen to her. There is already a vast quantity of gossip about her son – there were so many unpleasant rumours of cowardice after he died it's a wonder she survived another season in such an elevated position. The last thing she needed was a scandal of this magnitude. There is only so much one can get away with.'

'Well, she and everyone in Petersburg can expect worse than complete social ruin if our little gambit here does not succeed,' Joséphine said. 'I know you don't care about the fate of nations, Jack, but if you do as we ask there is still just a little time to save your brother.'

Crow said nothing at all until long after the kibitka had pulled up outside a dacha reached along a winding carriage drive through woodland, pine branches and aspen leaves shivering in a twilit breeze. With a queer sense of disconnection, he considered the possibility that he might very easily be dead within the hour – that rather than accepting him as a double agent acting against England, Napoleon simply intended to have him shot – and that Joséphine had been despatched to bait a trap. Killing women was never easy, but there was the pistol. There was the knife. Joséphine's lackeys might cut his throat as many times over as they chose, but not until he had run Kitto to earth; he would not leave the boy and generations of the Lamorna name to the tender mercies of French hostage-takers. Crow felt a queer sense of breathlessness, as if the still air within the upholstered interior of the kibitka were too thin, or not quite fresh. Thérèse had long since dozed off, quantities of black lace at her throat bobbing with the gentle, well-sprung movement of the carriage.

Joséphine looked up from the book in her hands, smiling at him, lashes lowered. 'You needn't be so suspicious, you know.

If my dear Bonaparte wanted you dead, my lord, you would scarcely be sitting here now, would you?'

Crow could find no words to answer her, but every time he closed his eyes he saw Tatyana's powdered curves, which only made the lack of Hester more acute, and he felt yet more breathless, and that now familiar sensation of his chest being slowly crushed. As if prompted by an unseen puppeteer, he was first to alight from the kibitka when at last it drew to a halt outside a house, taking in scattered impressions of white stucco, long windows alight with spreading sunset, the metallic curve of a stream overhung with willows. A silent groom appeared at Crow's side, and Crow handed first Thérèse and then Joséphine down from the carriage and walked into the house, conscious only of odd details: evening sunlight slanting across dark floorboards waxed to a gleam, the smooth dark hair of a Kalmyk maidservant, the rounded, creamy dull-silk heads of half-opened peonies in a blue and white china vase on a sideboard. Mechanically following a liveried manservant up a flight of stairs, Crow began to smell gunpowder smoke where he knew there was none, that cloying, so-familiar scent that caught in one's hair, in the very fabric of one's clothes. The shape of the shadow cast by an occasional table sent him reaching for the pistol holstered at his belt; he was quite unable to breathe until he had closed his fingers around it, but even that would not be enough; he knew it would not, because he could already see blood spreading across the floor, and although he could hear Joséphine and Thérèse in conversation beside him, and in fact Joséphine's fingers rested lightly upon his arm, it sounded as though they were underwater, or that he could only hear them from some far-distant part of the house. The young Belgian soldier slumped in a far corner of the long, galleried room, sitting in a pool of his own blood. The gold lacing on his blue jacket caught the light, and even from this distance it was clear that the boy was dead, because Crow himself had cut his throat at Waterloo, but also that his clear grey eyes were quite open. Crow looked down: Joséphine had tightened her grip on his arm.

'Don't worry,' she was saying, 'of course all the servants here are very discreet. We remain overnight and will be near Chudovo by late afternoon tomorrow. But with Thérèse and me in your train I'm afraid you must travel in more civilised order than I expect you're used to, darling. There can be no riding all night, I'm afraid! We'll have a new team of horses, too. Jack? You do look tired. Are you quite well?'

He made some reply; he couldn't look away from the young Belgian. When the boy spoke, his voice was thin and rattling, the thin edges of the wide wound at his throat fluttering as he spoke: *Maman, Maman, Maman*— The choking smell of musket-smoke now filled the room with yellowish, sulphuric clouds that Crow could actually see, clear as day, and he reached to take Thérèse's thin elbow, because how could she tell where she was going with all that smoke? And how could Joséphine not notice that her buttoned-up jean boots were now splashed with blood as they walked through dark, glossy puddles of it? The butcher's-shop reek of it turned his stomach and made him want to puke, even as he was dimly aware that they had all stopped walking, and that someone was talking to him.

'Sir?' The manservant spoke in Russian, gesturing at the panelled door they had halted at, and Crow had enough of the language to understand most of what he said. 'Sir, your chamber?' The man was staring as though one had just pissed all over the floor, and with every shred of self-control Crow managed not to drive a fist into his face. 'Sir, the madame?'

Crow turned his head and saw that Joséphine and Thérèse were staring up at him, horrified, Thérèse's one lace-gloved hand over his as he gripped her old, thin arm, those fragile bones held far too tight in his grasp. 'When you have quite finished?' She spoke with her usual hauteur, but this time with an undeniable edge of alarm: his grip was hard enough to bruise. He released her as though she were composed of fire, and indeed he'd left long red marks around her forearm, just visible beneath the lace sleeve of her gown, and she said nothing, only turning to study a still life of a bowl of fruit, which was worse than if she had descended into hysterics, and Joséphine was still openly staring at him, her lips slightly parted.

Crow turned to the lackey, speaking again in Russian; it was this facility with languages that had led him to such a life – the ease with which he absorbed foreign tongues had paved a road to damnation. 'Bring me some brandy. Madame, Aunt – I bid you goodnight.'

'Jack?' Joséphine said; then she turned to Thérèse. 'Whatever—'

But Crow could not reply to her; it was all he could do to walk into the bedchamber and close the door behind him, and why were they taking so long with the brandy when the floor was awash with blood? He leaned on the door, fighting for breath; the candles were already lit, and white linen arrayed the bed, embroidered with red flowers, and dark wood panelled the walls, which seemed to push closer with every moment. There must be relief, or he would start screaming and not be able to stop. They must bring brandy, port, anything. Forcing one foot before the other, Crow made himself walk across a faded carpet to the bed, but before he reached it, his foot struck a yielding object, and he looked down to see his brother on the floor, curled up on his side in a filthy shirt and breeches, both hands held to his bloodied face. Crow knelt at once at Kitto's side.

'Child, what have they done?' he asked, in Cornish, but all this was wrong, and he still saw what was no longer there – this Kitto was only a boy: younger, more slight, with no shadow of beard at his jaw, and one of his eyes swollen shut with plum-dark bruising even as he shook like a leaf in the wind. When at last Kitto turned his head to face Crow, the eye he could actually open was stretched wide, his pupils dilated with liquid terror, his teeth set hard together, and Crow knew that he himself was the one who had reduced the boy to this state, striking him again and again: the past now leaked into his present with all the white, foaming ferocity of the ocean breaching a ship's hull stove in against rock, and to make this stop he must watch himself bleed. Crow unsheathed the knife concealed in his boot and by the time he had done so, Kitto was no longer there, and there was only the faded Turkey rug, and God only knew where the child might be, really, in all this vast and unforgiving country, hunted with every step by the French. Sitting down, Crow tried again to breathe, but the air felt hot in his lungs, bringing no relief, and the room spun around him in a whirl of oak panelling, pressed white linen and candle-flames leaving trails of light upon the darkness. He closed his eyes and saw a succession of faces, those he'd killed: the Belgian child at Waterloo, French soldier after French soldier from the Peninsula and afterwards – names he'd never know. Kitto, too, nearly dead at his own hands. Crow peeled off his jacket and rolled up the sleeve of his shirt, revealing the pale skin of his inner forearm. If he did not open himself up to let this out, it would consume him before his job was done. Light caught the blade as Crow made his incision. Dark blood welled.

'Jack—'

He looked up to find Joséphine standing over him in her gown of white muslin, holding two glasses of brandy as his blood dripped on to the carpet, where just moments ago he'd seen his brother lying, as real as Joséphine herself now was. Try as he might, he could not speak.

'I know, my dear,' Joséphine said, regardless. Handing him one of the glasses, she crossed the room to the copper bath pushed into a corner near the fireplace, taking up one of the folded wraps lying on the stool beside it. Sitting down beside him as he drank, she held the cloth beneath his bleeding arm, and they both watched in silence as dark red stains spread across white linen.

40

Hester stood on the aft-deck leading directly off Captain Wythenshawe's cabin, watching heaving grey seas. Ahead, Kotlin Island rose up from the Baltic, forested and fortified, a string of smaller islands on either side, guarding the as-yet-invisible St Petersburg like a row of teeth. Gulls keened and swept through the air as green-clad hills reared on either side of the vast grey outer estuary of the Neva, and without looking around she knew that Captain Wythenshawe had come to stand beside her. It was odd how Crow's tobacco smoke always seemed to mingle with the other, more indefinable scents of the heat of his body and fresh laundry soap in a manner so intoxicating that she felt a sudden spreading warmth just to think of it – and yet the smell of Captain Wythenshawe's pipe turned her stomach. He was standing very close, almost touching her. She looked down at the yellowed linen cuff of his shirtsleeve emerging from the well-tailored but equally well-worn blue jacket. He had returned her pistol, at least, with some leering remark about how she would have to guard her own virtue when he was engaged with nautical affairs.

'St Petersburg is extraordinarily well guarded,' she said, for the want of anything else. He had come to tell her that the covers were laid for dinner and she didn't want to sit alone in that cabin with Captain Wythenshawe again, watching him slice pickled veal and chew so slowly with those flecks of pastry on his lips, never looking away from her for a moment, so that she did not know where to look herself. Her eyes were drawn to the cold, forested shore on the far side of the estuary: Crow might be anywhere in all that hinterland which spread to China. How was she ever to find him? The light was fading, and it would soon be dark.

'Well, Petersburg is Russia's most important seaport,' Captain Wythenshawe said, 'her only notable port at all, in fact – otherwise there's only Archangelsk in the north, but that's entirely frozen for months at a time.'

'And so here is the Russian gateway to Europe.' Hester watched a sprinkling of lights appear on Kotlin Island, ahead. She imagined unknown servants lighting lamps in the fortress, in merchants' houses. 'For trade as well as warfare? If the French were to attack from the sea, St Petersburg will be lost, surely.'

'Our own navy is extremely unlikely to allow that to happen,' Wythenshawe said. He moved his smallest finger infinitesimally, so that it just touched Hester's, and she swallowed a surge of bile. 'When an attack takes place, it will certainly be on land. It's simply not in our interest to allow France to gain control of Russian territories again, and Lord knows what will happen with French troops manoeuvring all over the Russian countryside, but at sea we still have dominion – unless Napoleon takes Petersburg, of course, but that is surely impossible.' On speaking the word dominion, Wythenshawe drew away his hand, and Hester forced herself to suppress a visible sigh of relief, of release. 'Now then, Lady Lamorna,' he went on, and she detected the sour scent of bad port on his breath. Port before dining to lend himself courage? 'Our repast grows cold inside my cabin. Come and eat with me, my lady. It's late, and you must be hungry.'

His quarters were empty. Two lamps glowed on the bare oaken table laid with covered pewter dishes, and lamplight glanced from a cut-glass decanter filled with dark red wine. Had he instructed Milton to ensure they were left alone? There was something appallingly intimate about a man spooning sliced veal on to her plate with no servant present: it was so improper that he might just as well have touched her, and she crushed a sickening surge of panic.

Captain Wythenshawe smiled at her across the table. 'Have you no appetite, Lady Lamorna?'

'It would seem not.'

He got up, walking around the table, moving naturally with the rolling of the ship. He was in his element and she was not, and vulnerable. Standing behind her, he leaned over, reaching for a dish of spiced peas, so close that his lower belly pressed against her back. He let a spoonful of the dark, gelatinous mixture slide on to her plate, and then ran one finger down the back of her neck.

'Your hair,' he breathed. 'Your hair is so beautiful, Lady Lamorna. Excuse me, but I can't help myself. I want to touch you.'

Hester froze, cold terror flooding through her. If she moved to get up out of her seat, she would only force her body closer to his. If she turned around, he would kiss her. He leaned closer, speaking into her ear in a gentle tone that throbbed with thick intensity. 'I have such a weakness for dark girls.

Exotic, dark girls like you are just so much more willing than your milksop European sisters.'

Hester scanned the table. The only knife within reach wasn't sharp enough to do him any harm. She turned to face him; standing now. She had always known that, sooner or later, he would demand recompense for his protection of her, that those nights of careful, polite conversation over the pewter serving dishes would not be enough. He moved to kiss her, but she leaned away. 'Wait.' She forced herself to rest a hand on his shoulder. His sun-lined, freckled face loomed before her, reddish bristles quivering on his damp upper lip. 'Captain,' she said, 'let me make myself ready for you. It's been a long voyage, and it will be a long night. I should like to be fresh, to make the night more pleasurable for you.'

'Are you teasing me?' Wythenshawe was so close that the tip of his nose now brushed hers, and she crushed a shudder of revulsion.

'Surely not, sir.' Hester looked at him from beneath lowered eyelashes. 'I promise you the wait will be worth it. Don't you find that a little anticipation lends savour to a dish?' She dropped into a curtsey, praying that such a well-worn mark of respect, the habit ingrained in them both, would force a little distance between them.

'Very well.' Captain Wythenshawe watched her as though she were a plate of meat laid out for his delectation. 'But don't make me wait too long, Lady Lamorna. There is, after all, nowhere else for you to go.' He smiled again as he spoke her title with barely veiled mockery. Hester dropped into a deeper curtsey, giving a coquettish sideways smile as she bowed her head and left, allowing her hips to sway in a manner she hoped would whet his appetite for a dish that, God willing, he would never sample.

41

Head down, Hester walked around the side of the poop deck, praying that no one would see her. The wind was steady and light, and she passed a crewman gazing idly up at the flock of moonlit sails above. She heard the creaking of lines pulled tight, sails thrumming, and the hum of men's voices from the deck below. The davit ropes were creaking, too, as the little tender swung between them. Hester's mouth was dry, and tears of blind fear snaked hot down her cheeks. There was so little chance of success, but she had to try. Moving with swift, sure steps now, she reached the nearest davit. Her fingers weak with terror, she uncleated the rope at the tender's stern and let it off until the little boat hung at a drunken angle. Glancing up, she glimpsed the lights of Kotlin Island between rising masts and taut sails. This was her only chance of escape. She would have to lower the tender into the water in excruciating stages, tilting it first at the stern and then at the bow. In silence, she ran to the second set of tackle and, suspended over the guardrail, the tender now plunged bow-first towards the surging ocean below: if she did not take care, she'd risk sinking the boat. She flew to the other davit and let it off once more. The tender's stern plunged into the water, and the little boat was instantly twitched hard away, its forward line pulled taut. Immediately Hester heard a male voice. 'What's that? Something's dragging.'

Sweeping her skirts and petticoats out of the way, Hester climbed over the guardrail, frozen as she watched a figure approaching, backlit by the moon. Knowing there was no choice, she caught handfuls of her skirts, looped her arm around the bundle of ropes leading down into the tender and slid into the boat as the sea rushed up to meet her. She crashed with bruising force into the bottom of the tender, which bucked and swayed beneath her. Indistinct shouting drifted down from the deck of the *Wellington*, and she reached into the bodice of her gown for the little knife sheathed between her corset and her shift and sawed with savage desperation until the last rope parted, whipping up away into the spray-filled night even as the small boat plunged bow-first into the waves. The vast, rising hull of the *Wellington* filled her world, the coppered wood rimed with barnacles, and the ship surged on. She thought she heard a shot from above, but couldn't be certain, and there was no time to concern herself with dying.

With a lurch, she stepped the mast as Papa had taught her, long ago, and unrolled the sail, hauling it up until it was tight to the mast. Hester scrambled to the stern of the boat, sail flapping, and picked frantically at the knot on the rudder-board until the rudder plunged down into the sea. Her face wet with spray, she took hold of the tiller, hauled in the mainsheet, and instantly felt a soaring rush of joy as the sail filled and the little boat came to life. Then, gasping for breath, she steered away from the wind, cutting across the Gulf of Finland towards Kotlin Island and, beyond it, to the city of St Petersburg itself. She knew better than anyone that, on board ship, time was money, and all she could do was hope that Captain Wythenshawe was too much in thrall to the owners of his cargo of wool and pig-iron to risk chasing her up and down the Baltic, even if she had stolen his tender. But even as she felt rising joy at the sensation of cold air soaring past her left cheekbone, watching wind fill the little sail, Hester realised that in her dank cabin aboard the *Wellington* she had left behind her much diminished roll of banknotes, and that for her own survival she was entirely reliant on finding Crow still alive in a country that stretched from the northern reaches of Europe to the very furthest east.

42

The guard at the gates of Chudovo subjected Nadezhda and Kitto to a moment of heart-stopping scrutiny, then yawned again, shook his head, and scratched himself. 'Leave your mounts with me. General Krakowski's orders – he's in charge here. Our Cossacks will see none of the horseflesh falls into French hands. Krakowski's requisitioned the mayor's house. Third street on your left – you can't miss it.' His gaze flickered with complete disinterest over both of them, and Nadezhda knew he hadn't seen past her cropped hair, her jacket and breeches. Lounging at her side, Kitto thought he knew everything about her, but he was wrong. She pushed the thought away: she had her duty. She had been as honest with him as was wise, perhaps more so.

'I don't like this,' Kitto said in French. 'I haven't a clue what he just told you, but I don't like it all the same. There's something not right in this place.'

Forcing herself to concentrate on the present moment and not on her imminent betrayal of him, Nadezhda eyed the quiet, dusty streets – a jumble of wooden buildings and straw-strewn alleyways snaking off into sunlit quiet. The guard just watched them both with the impassive boredom of a man with his orders. Kitto couldn't have looked less receptive to explanation, his fine black brows drawn into a frown.

'There should be at least a hundred head of horses around here,' Nadezhda said, playing her part, saying what Kitto would expect her to. 'If we get to Petersburg without them, and I've disobeyed my orders—'

'Ilya's orders, not yours. Anyway, your promotion won't be valid in hell,' he interrupted with laconic arrogance. He looked down at her now with his eyebrows raised, and she walked off down the street. He might have the hunting instincts of a young Amur leopard, but he was also the cosseted second son of some English noble house, and it was quite clear that as a result he possessed no concept of failure's true cost – isolation, shame and poverty. And yet Nadezhda didn't have to look to know that he'd followed her, catching up with a handful of loping strides.

'You must see that it's too quiet in this town,' he said conversationally. 'Why are the houses here all shuttered in the middle of the day? The French have been here.'

Nadezhda stopped where she stood. 'Well, what can we do about it? The town gate is guarded, and if they don't want us to leave it's a safe bet we'd both of us take a bullet before we were even halfway over the wall. Whatever's amiss here, I don't see what else we can do but play along for now.' He was right: the entire town seemed almost to pulsate before her eyes with concealed danger. She suppressed a moment's wild panic, knowing just how much they would have to trust each other, and how much she was keeping from him about her true intentions. Still oblivious to the extent of her deception, Kitto shrugged, but as they fell into step beside one another, she knew he'd slipped into that almost otherworldly state of awareness, silently assessing every clot of shadow, every shuttered window.

'This must be the turning.' She forced herself to sound unconcerned for the benefit of anyone else who might be listening. A narrow, shaded alleyway led away from the dirt-rutted main street, shaded by cherry trees blossoming with incongruous cheer. Here, at last, were signs of life. They passed three shaven-headed Cossack horsemen sitting outside one shuttered house, stirring a pot of wheatgerm kasha on a fire belching gobbets of smoke that raked the back of Nadezhda's throat. Children burst from one of the houses and ran across their path. Little girls in white embroidered blouses and long bright skirts now splashed with mud stopped to stare at their stained and dusty uniforms before disappearing into a shadowy back door, herded inside by a watchful Kalmyk woman wearing a long white apron that almost glowed in the dark doorway where she stood. The alleyway opened out into a neat square with a fountain playing in the middle, and Nadezhda saw the mayor's house immediately – a gabled wooden mansion with carvings of wolves and pine trees above the wide front door.

Krakowski's manservant led them into a light, elegant drawing-room; the wooden walls had been painted a pale shade of grey, and lace curtains danced at the windows. Nadezhda suppressed another wave of hideous unease and turned to the Uhlan general advancing upon her, one meaty hand held out to shake.

'You must be Lieutenant Rumyantsev.' Heavily built, General Krakowski was still clad in a padded dressing gown over his drab grey uniform, and Nadezhda held her breath through the usual heart-stopping moment of uncertainty, but his gaze swept over her with disinterest. He turned to Kitto, so tall, silent and ever watchful in his scarlet jacket, dusty black hair disrespectfully untidy. 'And this, I take it, is Captain Helford of the Coldstream Regiment, no less? Won't you join us to break your fast? I believe we've a certain matter to discuss. The need of the cavalry commissariat in Petersburg is quite understandable, I assure you, with Marshal Davout's intentions as well as Alexander's still so confoundedly unclear, not to mention Napoleon's. My wife and daughters will be quite delighted with your company at breakfast – we have none of that by-your-lady lounging about drinking chocolate in bed here, you'll see.'

Kitto nodded, the barest minimum demanded by courtesy, and Nadezhda pulled the roll of orders out of her bag, thrusting the sheaves of paper at Krakowski. 'I've orders to requisition all horses in Chudovo, General,' she said firmly. 'Any in the town not for the immediate use of your men are to come with us. I'm grateful for the assistance of your Cossacks, but I'm entirely responsible for the herd, as you'll see from my orders, and can leave the horses no longer.'

'Can you not, sir?' General Krakowski was clearly not used to being so addressed by subordinate officers, even if they were commissioned into the Semenovsky Guards. He took the orders from her, glancing through them. 'What's this? *Meet with troops stationed along the Chudovo road for assistance if this is felt to be expedient.* I see you dispensed with that piece of advice. How unwise.' The hollow expression in Krakowski's pale brown eyes was completely at odds with the mundanity of his tone, and Nadezhda felt another cold slick of fear down her back. Beside her, Kitto stood in tense silence, one hand resting on the hilt of the Mameluk cutlass sheathed at his belt. Krakowski glanced over to the double doors which at that moment flew open, admitting a bright, fluttering explosion of feminine voices and laughter, and a woman of high colour and fading fair hair drawn into a low knot at the nape of her neck advanced on them both in a flurry of greetings, without appearing to notice the Siberian atmosphere. Madam Krakowski was flanked by daughters, one who looked just out of the schoolroom and the other younger still; they both stared at Kitto, who contrived to be so infuriatingly breathtaking in his filthy scarlet jacket.

'Now then, Lieutenant Rumyantsev,' Madam Krakowski said, taking both Nadezhda's hands in her own, which were damp with sweat, 'I can tell you're a well-brought-up young man – you won't refuse us. Do join us for something to eat before you get on your way. When I think of my own sons off at war, I like to think of other people's mamas taking care of them!' Her eyes lingered on Nadezhda's face with that familiar air of faint puzzlement. Women so often sensed that something here was awry, even if not precisely what.

Nadezhda bowed. 'I'm afraid we really must get on, ma'am. The farms with horses are surely spread over quite a distance, and Captain Helford and I have been long expected at the cavalry commissariat in Petersburg with the horses.'

'Of course they'll join us. Lads your age are always hungry.' General Krakowski cleared his throat and sat down at the scrubbed wooden table, shaking out his napkin with an air of finality: there was no choice but to sit down. 'Don't trouble yourself about the horseflesh, Rumyantsev. Your attention to duty is admirable, but I've dispatched a detachment of my Cossacks to guard the horses you already have, so what harm can possibly be done?' He reached for a dish of fresh butter, obviously considering the matter closed.

Sitting, Nadezhda accepted a basket of bread rolls from the now silent Krakowski daughter at her side. Every instinct screamed at her to walk out of the door, find the horses and ride away from this godforsaken town as if the unquiet dead were at her heels. They must leave this place, she and Kitto. She tried and failed to catch his eye, but he had taken a seat on the bench and his gaze was fixed with a predator's intensity on the window facing the street.

Madam Krakowski smiled brightly down the length of the table. 'Well, how odd it is, to be sure, that you're on the way to Petersburg, Lieutenant. That's exactly where my elder daughter and I have just come from.'

'Spending far too much on silks and furs, as usual, and going to endless routs and balls.' Krakowski spoke with such false indulgence: it was as if he wore a grotesque mask that kept slipping. Nadezhda felt as though she were watching characters act out roles in a play. What was she missing? Kitto might sense the presence of a French soldier from thirty feet away, in the dark, but he seemed not to notice the unspoken current of unease between all of the people in this room, or share her unpleasant certainty that the Krakowskis were not all they seemed. Still looking out of the window, Kitto passed a dish of spiced pears to a freckled Krakowski daughter with mechanical courtesy. The girl at his other side fidgeted with wild curls bursting from the end of one long red braid, stealing glances at him, and then flushing as she stared at her plate of pickled turnip and sliced beef.

The elder daughter glanced up from her bowl of kasha and preserved pears. 'We heard the most extraordinary story in town, didn't we, Mama?' A thicker, even more uncomfortable silence fell, and the Krakowski girl flushed purple, but instead of conceding her error, she persisted. 'Only think of it,' she went on with brittle and disingenuous good humour, speaking much too quickly, 'they say that an English officer has dishonoured Countess Tatyana Orlova as well as the English diplomat's daughter.'

'Really, darling, we don't discuss such stories,' Madam Krakowski said, unconvincingly, in Nadezhda's estimation, because there was no other way her daughter could have learned such a thing. What were they trying to hide beneath this second-rate society gossip?

Apparently oblivious to his daughter's merchant-trader's manners, Krakowski genially asked Kitto to pass him the dish of cream. There was no reply. Nadezhda glanced at him; Kitto had put down his knife and fork.

'What,' he said with sudden and succinct menace, every shred of his attention now focused entirely on the girl, 'was the English soldier's name?'

'Oh, surely that's not important, Captain Helford?' Krakowski replied, dismissive. 'There are so many of you milling about all over Petersburg, this fellow is very unlikely to be an acquaintance of yours – or I should hope not, anyway.'

Kitto ignored him with breathtaking rudeness, turning to the talkative daughter. 'Who was it?'

She flushed up to the roots of her hair and glanced uncertainly at her mother. 'Lord Lamorna. Apparently he's a famous rake.'

Nadezhda watched Kitto tip a spoonful of sugar into hot coffee and stir it.

'And now Lamorna's a traitor, apparently.' Krakowski shook his head. 'A traitor to his own nation, making up to the French, so they say. Disgraceful. No doubt they'll catch up with the man before long, and he'll get his just reward. Never mind, my dear. You go off with your sister to practise your music – we've business to discuss here.'

Kitto had gone white. Nadezhda had never seen him look

truly angry before; he said nothing but his air of suppressed fury silenced the room, even as sunlight glanced in through the window illuminating the dish of yellow butter and the silver bowl of damson preserve. The meal concluded in silence, and the girls and their mother dutifully pushed back their chairs and filed from the room, each pausing to kiss the general on the cheek as she passed, the picture of such feminine obedience and duty that Nadezhda felt sick to observe it; if they died here she would never go back to that, at least. Kitto was silent still, his long fingers now turning a silver salt cellar over and over.

'The horses, sir—' Nadezhda began, but Krakowski held up one hand.

'There's something far more important to attend to. As I've said, my Cossacks will take care of your herd. Listen, Rumyantsev, there's a French force of very significant size just twenty versts from here, and I want you to get into their camp.' Krakowski smiled as though he had just suggested they join him on a picnic with his daughters.

'Twenty versts away?' Nadezhda heard herself say. '*Twenty versts?*' Another day, and she and Kitto would have herded four hundred horses directly into enemy hands. Kitto glanced up then, as if the prospect of annihilation was a mere irritation compared to Petersburg gossip about this sibling of his.

Krakowski smiled again. 'It seems Marshal Davout has managed to move his men with rather more circumspection than anyone suspected. One never knows what one might hear, and I'm sure your superiors would agree that any failure to investigate would border on treason.'

'*Our* superiors? Mine and Captain Helford's?' Nadezhda stared at him. 'Sir, I understand the need for reconnaissance, but why can't you order your uhlans to do it? Captain Helford and I have our own mission. We must take these horses to Petersburg – the commissariat's need is surely even greater if the French are so close—'

Krakowski shook his head. 'The only people in this town who speak French are me, my wife and our daughters. None of my men have enough of the language to learn anything useful. I can hardly abandon my post or send my daughters in lieu of myself.'

Kitto looked up with a smile that made Nadezhda instantly uneasy. 'Petersburg can wait a little while longer for the horses, surely? This is far more important.'

'No, this is suicide,' Nadezhda heard herself say. 'It's sheer foolishness. I have my orders, General. Without horses, the army is hobbled – our own cavalry is useless, and the French are clearly manoeuvring.' She turned to Kitto. 'If we don't arrive in Petersburg by the end of next week, we could be shot for disobeying orders—' She fell silent, aware of Krakowski watching, his face slack with disgust. She'd broken an unspoken code: Krakowski now suspected her of cowardice, of not conducting herself as a real man should. Kitto had led her into a position from which there was no other course of action but to accept this idiotic mission or risk exposure – all because he had lost his temper. If Nadezhda ever had the misfortune to meet Lord Lamorna, she would have something to say to him.

43

Chudovo reeked of death. Kitto sensed the stink of it in every narrow street of this Russian hellhole, behind every shuttered window. Even in the smiling face of Krakowski's faded wife, he'd seen the bared teeth of a corpse from a two-week-old battlefield. He walked at Krakowski's side to the north gate, listening to the heavy crunch of the general's boots in dried mud and small, scattered stones, wondering if Nadezhda too had realised that there was no birdsong here. She and Krakowski had been exchanging Russian small-talk, but when she fell back to walk side by side with Kitto instead, he sensed her equally constant appraisal of the dusty streets along with her barely concealed fury, and felt a moment's relief that they were quite unable to talk freely with Krakowski as their escort.

Regardless, she turned to him. 'I suppose you're pleased with yourself. What have you just talked us into? For what?'

He ignored her, angrily hooking one forefinger into his grimy white leather ammunition belt.

'All this is because of some ridiculous second-hand Petersburg gossip about your brother, isn't it?' Nadezhda hissed.

'If you knew him, you wouldn't say so.' Kitto knew only too well that he was almost incoherent with anger. 'If you understood what we'd suffered in the Occupation – and then he just switches allegiance to France because it suits him. *France.* If Castlereagh doesn't hang him for this, I'll kill the traitorous bastard myself.'

'Oh, how ridiculous,' Nadezhda said in a furious undertone. 'We have our own task to do here, in case you'd forgotten—'

'Oh, believe me, I haven't,' Kitto replied. Was the world not a difficult enough place for Hester already, without the humiliation of being married to a man who couldn't be bothered to keep his indiscretions from the rumour mill in every capital city between London and the Urals?

'Well, that's just as well,' Nadezhda said, 'because something tells me we've got more to deal with here than your godforsaken family.'

He knew she was right. A bucket lay on its side outside the front door of a tall, narrow wooden house with a pattern of flowers carved on the gable. The dusty earth was stained with a trickle of dark liquid, and Kitto detected the faintest scent of sour goats' milk. Spilled milk that no one cared about. A bucket not picked up. Nadezhda had moved on ahead, talking to Krakowski again, her shoulders defensively hunched in that guard's jacket, with all the silver embroidery on the epaulettes. They'd nearly reached the north gate, silent wooden houses with strawberry beds and tidy rows of fresh young cabbage leaves giving way now to scrubby grassland, the fence nothing more than a ring of hazel hurdles enclosing the town in a lazy embrace, the wooden gate bleached pale silver by years of northern winter and elusive summer sun. Krakowski nodded to the silent gate guards and, led by some deep-rooted urge, Kitto felt his gaze drawn to a patch of wilting dandelions and scrubby grass that had attracted a cloud of flies hovering low to the ground. Half hidden beneath diseased yellow dandelion leaves, he glimpsed embroidered leather, a shoe small enough to fit a child of no more than three or four. Beneath a mat of shifting, glistening bluebottles, the leather was stained almost black with old blood.

He and Nadezhda would be allowed to leave the town alive, Kitto knew that immediately – why else would they not already be bayoneted in the dirt, flies hovering over the mess – but what was next? He watched in silence as Nadezhda saluted farewell to Krakowski, and one of the guards opened the gate. Krakowski turned to him, nodding and smiling, and Kitto raised his own right fist in a salute, bringing it up to his forehead. The guard averted his gaze as they walked past, which in itself would have told Kitto that he and Nadezhda were now the walking dead.

Leaving Krakowski, the gate guards and Chudovo itself behind, he and Nadezhda walked in silence across a meadow incongruously streaked with bright swathes of wild flowers. Bees hung in the air at knee-level. A thick line of forest blanketed the horizon with faint trails of smoke just visible above the treeline, the only visible sign of the twenty thousand French soldiers that lay between Kitto, Nadezhda and St Petersburg. He couldn't shake a bone-deep sense of loss without the horses – of their warm breath, that awareness of the herd intelligence.

Nadezhda spoke without looking at him, fixing her gaze on the forested horizon. 'Chudovo's already been taken by the French, hasn't it? It's not just that they've passed through. Krakowski's actually acting on French orders. But what do the French want with us?'

'I've no idea,' Kitto said. 'But I'd wager he wishes his wife and daughters were still in Petersburg.'

'If we don't get to the camp, those girls of his are going to die, aren't they? Raped, most likely, and then killed.' Nadezhda spoke still without looking at Kitto.

The Krakowski family were likely already dead, but what was the use in saying so? 'Oh, let's go into the camp all the same,' Kitto said, doing his best to sound unconcerned. He'd twice faced a dishonourable death at the end of a rope. At least here he would die fighting.

'Well, we've lost the horses,' Nadezhda said firmly. 'The least we can do is get back to Petersburg with some intelligence. What I don't understand is why the French are manoeuvring around Petersburg like this if Napoleon's in Austria. Surely that's where his real business is, not here? If he means to take Petersburg, would he really leave that to Davout?'

Kitto shrugged, eyeing the grassland for any signs of sabotage or ambush, fighting a queer sense of inevitability. They were going to die beyond that forest, he and Nadezhda, of that he was quite certain. It was only a question of when. At his side, she stopped where she stood, and in that moment they reached for each other, his hands lightly gripping her waist.

'Are you sure?' he said, and she looked up at him, tanned golden by the sun, her eyes like dark earth.

'Yes. It's my decision,' she replied, and so he kissed her then, with the sun on his back as he leaned over her; she was swiftly responsive, and her light, strong fingers touched his face, one thumb grazing the smooth, secret hollow of skin behind his ear, and she tasted him until they broke apart, the kiss lent heat by sheer unthinkable danger of being seen: to all appearances two boys kissing. She laughed. 'Whatever happens in that camp, I'm ruined – completely ruined.'

'You need not be,' Kitto said, trying to appear careless. 'You might marry me, if you like, and then you won't be ruined at all. Will you?'

Nadezhda replied with another kiss. 'Yes,' she said, so quietly that he could scarcely hear, and he wondered if her eyes only shone with tears because they would be killed before ever she had the chance to be his. 'Yes, Kitto, I will do that, and gladly.'

The French Second Army's campfires lit up the plain like stars fallen to earth. The night air smelled of pine sap and Kitto was restless, eager to move after waiting so many hours in the forest for darkness to fall. He wanted only for this all to be over, wanted really to kiss Nadezhda again, to slide the worn-out jacket from her shoulders. None of it could happen, not now. Side by side, they walked in silence down the French side of the reverse slope, and Kitto heard his brother's voice in the back of his mind. *Always conduct yourself as if you have every right to be exactly where you are*. Why must Crow forever be such an eternal disappointment?

The moon slid behind a bank of cloud and, as they approached the camp, Kitto began to pick out the voices of individual French soldiers, men gathered around guttering fires, the smell of frying bacon. He doubted they'd hear anything useful, about French intentions or the deployment of other troops, but one never knew – not that it made any difference, considering the sheer unlikelihood of getting out of here alive. They were, after all, expected. He heard nothing except snatches of irrelevant conversation about who had contraband to sell, and which of the camp whores had the pox. Then, without a word, Nadezhda took hold of Kitto's wrist, immediately releasing him as if scorched. They turned to look at each other, and she nodded towards the pale shape of a field tent now just visible as a large group of French infantrymen moved past, drinking from hip flasks and exchanging crude jokes about a Polish woman. The tent was lit from within, shadowy figures clearly visible sitting at a camp table; one got up and walked across to adjust a lamp where it hung.

Despite everything, Kitto felt a high, wild surge of excitement: whoever commanded this rabble would be in that tent and, to judge by the quantity of staff officers in cockaded hats going in and coming out, there was someone important inside. Even then, the night air was punctuated by a thin, desperate scream that made his insides clench. The girl screamed again, louder this time. Perhaps she was from Chudovo. The wife or daughter of some town merchant. They were in the middle of a camp of soldiers: no one else was listening. Nadezhda stood quite still, a muscle twitching in her jaw. A further shriek. It was the same in any English camp: disgraceful. Rape for men who couldn't get a willing woman. Without a word, Nadezhda began walking towards the source of the screaming.

'What in hell's name are you doing? Kitto said quietly, following her. He reached out but Nadezhda shook his hand away and carried on walking. They were closer now. Side by side, they passed a cache of stores – piled-up barrels, sacks of grain still loaded on a wagon. Another scream rang out and Nadezhda moved faster, with swift, purposeful intensity. She was talking to herself very quietly, in Russian. Repeating the same words over and over again. *Nyet, nyet, nyet*: no. Dark, long-suppressed memories rose up in the back of Kitto's mind: riding home across the moor to Nansmornow with Crow, Hester and a servant, long ago now, miserable in the certainty that he was in for a hiding, all that eclipsed by the sight of three bodies hanging from the chestnut tree. He remembered his half-sister Roza's pale, naked legs, her inner thighs stained with dark blood. Roza would have screamed like this as those French soldiers raped her, right up until the moment they hanged her. Kitto grasped the handle of the cutlass sheathed at his belt and glanced across again at Nadezhda, who walked on towards the covered commissariat wagon with an unsettling, hungry expression. Reaching it, Kitto swept aside a curtain of burlap. In the wagon, a bald-headed soldier was on top of the girl, facing towards them but intent on his task as he thrust with brutal force, a knife held to the girl's throat; her cap had fallen off and her meagre, mouse-brown braids spilled into the sawdust she lay in. Perhaps the knife made it impossible to go on screaming. Two more cavalrymen stood idly by, as though waiting their turn for water at the village pump.

'What the fuck do you want?' one of them said, looking up – a tall, moustachioed officer in an unknown French regiment. The rapist just continued with his rapid, dog-like thrusting, letting out an animal grunt.

'*Nyet,*' Nadezhda said and Kitto realised that he was the only one to notice that she had drawn her pistol, holding it loose at her side, her hand shaking so much that she hadn't a hope of hitting anyone. Thinking only of Roza hanging from the chestnut tree at Nansmornow, Kitto snatched the cutlass from his belt, but by that time Nadezhda had gathered her wits and fired at the rapist's forehead in the very moment he looked up, blowing his brains out through the back of his skull. He dropped like a sack of wheat, with lifeless force, and the girl scrambled from beneath him, her mouth stretched wide in a silent shriek, blood-splattered.

'What the fuck? You mad little fuckers.' Snarling like a dog, the moustachioed officer stepped towards them, but Kitto just raised his own pistol and shot him between the eyes. The second dead man dropped into a motionless heap where he stood. The other French soldier raised both hands above his head and fled into the night, and the girl crawled as far from Kitto and Nadezhda as she could manage, tugging ragged woollen skirts back down to cover her pale, dirt-streaked legs.

'Run,' Nadezhda advised her, even as Kitto saw French soldiers closing ranks around them.

Part 4

THE ART OF WAR

44

Kitto and Nadezhda were dragged by silent and furious soldiers around the edge of a trampled rose parterre and a kitchen garden now containing only a single row of onions. Kitto knew there was a bruise forming along his jaw, and he ignored the pain with a dizzy sense of unreality: rapists or not, the men they'd shot had been as brothers to their captors and a camp girl was nothing to them. Shaking, Nadezhda whispered a quiet prayer in Russian, and Kitto saw a post jutting up before a crumbling garden wall; the old, worn bricks and the post itself were both marred with dark stains. They were going to be tied up and summarily shot here, their brains blown out – he'd seen it happen on more than one occasion, the white-faced forced march, the strangled shouting, the loud report of the guns followed by a silence that always seemed too short before the usual chatter and kettle-rattling of the camp rose up again. Now he was the wretched fellow marched to the post he could hardly breathe; he supposed it was better than being hanged.

'Oh, God,' Nadezhda said quietly, and he sensed her reach for his hand; he snatched his own away, much as it hurt him to do so, knowing how desperate she must have been for comfort: she was as leery of touch as a yearling broken harsh to the bridle, but what did she think these men would do, these disinterested soldiers milling about with tin mugs of gruel and flasks of wine, all moving away from the firing post? They were no different to English soldiers: so well acquainted with death that an execution was an unpleasant bore rather than an attraction. But two young men holding hands would warrant special punishment. Silent, Nadezhda cast a look up at him, and yet her expression was now resolute: she had more courage even than he.

Kitto's guard hissed into his ear, flecks of spittle speckling his cheek, the inside of the ear. 'This way, you sneaking murderous little shits. Time for a taste of your own quack-cure.'

Kitto stumbled as they were dragged to the post, and he breathed in the familiar stink of campfire smoke, and burning bacon, and stale wine, and the sweaty fug of so many gathered men, even as he felt the rough rope around his wrists, pulled so tight that he suppressed the urge to cry out. Soon it wouldn't matter, anyway. 'I'm sorry,' he said to Nadezhda, unable to believe that this was actually happening, 'I'm so sorry.'

'It's my fault.'

'I'm the one who listened to Krakowski.' They should have been halfway back to Petersburg by now, but he'd lost his temper over second-rate drawing-room gossip about his brother.

'It wouldn't have made any difference if you hadn't,' Nadezhda said. 'The French meant to have us, and now we're here.'

The French soldiers were arguing about a missing lot of ammunition, and Kitto saw them line up ready to fire, ramming shot and cartridge down the barrels of their Charlesvilles; in under a minute this would be over. But then, as he watched, all seven men stopped what they were doing to salute a pair of passing women with their long cloaks sweeping the muddy grass, and why in Christ's name could this not just be done with?

'What on earth is going on here?' The smaller of the two women's voice rang out with imperious clarity.

He heard muffled voices of explanation, and then the woman's voice rising up again. 'Well, then, for goodness' sake, where are they from?'

Whoever you are, shut up, he thought, *and let this be over*.

'They're not French, that much we're pretty sure of, ma'am.'

'*Then take them to your emperor.* What on earth can you be thinking – if they are spies, who knows how useful they might be?'

'But they—' The woman must have silenced the protestor with just a look, because he fell silent even as Kitto realised they were not to die, not quite yet, and he leaned back with his head against the post, listening to Nadezhda's disordered, sobbing breathing as one of the soldiers advanced to unleash them.

The air was thick with smoke and the usual army-camp miasma of rum, bacon and the biscuity tang of burning gruel, overlaid by the piquant edge of Crow's own cigarillo smoke. He hadn't slept or eaten in far too long. His entire body was suffused with the nervous heat that always used to keep him awake the night before a battle; as a younger man, he'd always needed a woman at times like this. He would never lie with Hester again, and no one else would be enough, but he could not think about that. Not now. The black feathered hat was heavy, pressing into his forehead, but wearing it made him instantly identifiable as a French staff officer, marking him out as beyond reproach. Joséphine had briefed him closely on the regiments assembled here, and who in this guise he would have been commanding, and which regiment he was to say he had been drafted in from, should anyone ask. Castlereagh and the entire English government had been looking the wrong way all this time, down to Cornwall when they should have had their eyes on Russia. Never mind insurrection at home, Napoleon had made his move, and any question of an heir to the English throne was soon going to be irrelevant.

Crow lit another cigarillo from the end of the one he had just finished, tossing the glowing stub of it away into the darkness. Having washed, shaved and changed his shirt and cravat after the final leg of their journey, he was due to rendezvous with Joséphine and Thérèse in the presence of Napoleon himself, but it was becoming increasingly hard to distinguish his own imaginings from the world of flesh and blood and consequences. The sky wheeled with tossing crows, starlings and gulls that he was certain no one else saw: such close proximity to gathered soldiers brought the carrion birds of Waterloo, and only the familiar operation of smoking pinned him to the world everyone else knew, where the past did not leak into the present. He could see the opulent field tent from here, and as he grew closer a staff officer leaving the tent stared at him with an insolent lack of curiosity. It wasn't hard to summon up the brisk, harassed air of the aide-de-camp; he had, after all, been the Duke of Wellington's. Crow stepped over Turkish carpets laid out on the bare turf, and he went into Napoleon Bonaparte's field headquarters, little more than ten miles from Chudovo, and a hard day's ride from Petersburg, knowing he was acting completely without permission or precedent, and that he could reasonably face either a French or an English firing squad for what he was about to do.

Inhabited by silent orderlies, the interior of the tent was thick with stale smoke and the fatty reek of boiled mutton, hung with swags of linen printed with a pattern of the imperial *abeille*: there was no sign of Joséphine or Thérèse, and in the distance, somewhere in the camp, Crow heard pistol shots ring out, followed by bursts of shouting. An ensign emerged from Napoleon's curtained-off inner quarters bearing a covered tray. He glanced at Crow without interest; Crow guessed that, to him, he was just another ambitious aide-de-camp come to beg for the reinstatement of ancestral aristocratic titles stripped from his family in the revolution: it happened so often. He lit yet another cigarillo, savouring the harsh, raking smoke. The sentries murmured quietly about a bet they had on with a lancer, taking little notice of Crow, who could do nothing but wait. Just as he was about to light yet another cigarillo, in the absence of food, sleep, or any semblance of peace of mind, a sentry emerged, holding back a swag of fabric, and Crow ducked under the bolt of printed linen into Napoleon's private quarters. Freezing sweat slid down his back. A man with the bilious complexion of a long-standing martyr to a liver complaint sat at the writing desk. He wore a padded vermilion dressing gown over a gold-braided blue jacket; his pen travelled effortlessly over several sheets of foolscap. So here was Napoleon, this architect of nations, this arch manipulator who had fooled everyone into thinking that he meant to hold ground in Austria, not attack Europe from her northern back door, just as a hunting dog might pounce on a hare to crush tender bones with her long teeth. He didn't once look up and Crow thought how easy it would be to kill him, without even a guard to intervene. He had two loaded pistols; he could change everything. With Napoleon dead, France would be plunged into all the chaos of a messy succession, and Europe ripe for England's plucking: England who longed above all else for mastery over trade – which indeed meant over everything. Crow need only reach into his greatcoat and pull out his cavalry pistol, and it would all be over. But he remembered the cell at Bodmin gaol, and Nathaniel Edwards's hands shaking as Crow held them in his own, tears standing in the man's eyes as he was led away to the gallows. England had drowned Hester and Morwenna. England deserved mastery over nothing.

'What is it that you have to tell me, Lord Lamorna?' Napoleon Bonaparte spoke, still without looking up, and Crow was surprised at the strength of his Italian accent – he hadn't expected that. It was so strange to hear this man say his name, this man of all men. A plate of congealing mutton and potatoes lay on the desk beside him, almost untouched. 'And, more to the point, why in God's name do you have anything to tell me at all?' Napoleon went on, with a dry, almost humorous edge to his voice. 'In truth, you're still a lieutenant colonel in an elite British regiment, Lord Lamorna – Wellington's hero. Indeed, two years ago you snatched the man from my grasp, enabling him to defeat my brother's forces in England. What possible proposition can you have for me? Surely we are the most bitter of sworn enemies, you and I?'

Crow allowed his gaze to wander to the linen-slung tent doorway. Somewhere out there in this camp there would be a bloodstained post, six feet high. He imagined the feel of the bonds at his wrists, and wondered whether they would blindfold him before the shot was fired. He was never going to get away with this. 'Castlereagh took me prisoner and massacred innocent people on my own lands, your excellency,' he said. 'Because of him, my wife and daughter fled Cornwall, and drowned. I'm a Cornishman; as I am quite sure you know, my mother was French. I once swore loyalty to England, and gave all I had to that country, and this is how I am repaid. Any loyalty I once had is entirely extinguished.'

At last Napoleon looked up. His cheeks were hollow, the candlelight accentuating the sallow, dyspeptic tone of his complexion. 'Well?' He gestured at an ornately carved folding camp chair. 'Tell me what it is you have come to say and let's have done with it. I've made the mistake of underestimating Joséphine in the past, but swore I would not make that error again. In many ways, she is a little fool, but no one can deny she has perfected the art of eliciting important information from pretty young men. If she thinks you are worth my while, perhaps she's right.'

Crow obeyed and sat down, stretching out his legs. 'Tsar Alexander has struck a deal with Lord Castlereagh and the Cabinet: in exchange for open trade routes across the Black Sea, Britain will assist the tsar in the expulsion of French troops from Russia. You'll be cut off, your excellency. It's now nearly the end of May. If you move now, Davout and his men can return safely to France long before winter sets in.' Crow stared at Napoleon steadily. Everyone said he would never again return to Russia, the scene of his greatest and most shameful defeat. And yet here he was, in Russia. It was said that after Waterloo Napoleon had recovered his faith in manoeuvre, and not least a degree of confidence in his own ability as a war leader. England had been lost because of his brother Jérôme's failings, not Napoleon's own.

'Well, that's extremely interesting, if it's true. It's entirely believable, but you must understand that Alexander has, of course, made his own overtures to me. How can I be sure which of you is lying: you or he?' Napoleon stared, unsmiling. 'Castlereagh has always been an idiot, entirely unable to judge the mood of first the Irish people, and then the English. He really has eroded any loyalty you felt for England, Lord Lamorna, has he not?'

'Yes, your excellency. I have no loyalty to England.' And Crow looked back at him – at this ill-made and wholly unremarkable-looking man whose ambition had altered the very face of the world, bringing order out of the chaos of revolution, but always led by the need to conquer, never to simply rule those whose lives and wellbeing he had taken responsibility for.

'No one can deny you're the sort of man who makes things happen. Your loyalty, Lord Lamorna, is a prize indeed. Might it indeed really now lie with France?' Napoleon asked with a curious lightness of tone.

There was something so frank and so shockingly confiding in his expression now, in his slightly protuberant blue eyes, that Crow simply told him the truth. 'Your excellency,' he said, 'in truth, I just want to die.'

'That seems somewhat wasteful.' Napoleon watched him carefully. 'But in the meantime, I think we must test your loyalty, Lord Lamorna. You'll forgive me if I don't trust it. This news of Britain and Russia maintaining their alliance is alarming, to be sure, but I wish for more precise information. You must return to Petersburg and bring it to me.'

Crow had envisaged such an outcome, but the devil if he knew yet what he must do about it. He longed for another cigarillo, and let his gaze slide towards the tent-flap. Outside, the damp trudge of footfalls grew louder, men tramping across trodden-down muddy grass, and a young ADC came in, ducking beneath a swag of gathered linen in his feathered hat. He glanced uneasily at Crow and saluted to Napoleon, bearing the look of a man who wasn't at all sure if he was not about to talk himself before a firing squad.

'Prisoners, your excellency. Madame says you'll want to see them yourself.'

'Very well. What madame wants, madame must have, is that not so?' With frozen sarcasm, Napoleon leaned back in his camp chair, resting both hands on his rounded belly. 'Do bring them in.'

And, as Crow watched, his young brother Kitto came in with a Russian soldier no older than he, each guarded by two men. Joséphine and Thérèse swept in after them all, twitching their skirts away from the muddied grass. A shivering tingle spread from Crow's fingertips throughout his entire body: this was just another trick played on him by his shattered mind.

Tall, shambolic and disgracefully ill shaven, Kitto looked him up and down, taking in his French uniform with an expression of such kindling rage that Crew knew he was no illusion. '*Che vastard*,' Kitto said in furious Cornish. 'It's really true what everyone says. You bastard fucking traitor.'

He was there, clearly as real to everyone else as he was to Crow, but Kitto could wait to be cut down to size: his companion was the real prize. Entirely ignoring his brother, Crow turned his attention to the undersized Russian soldier at Kitto's side, recalling the portrait Lord Castlereagh had shown him so long ago at Boscobel Castle, and he saw immediately that Tatyana Orlova had been telling him the truth: Kitto's companion was no young soldier at all, but a thin, dishevelled hoyden of a girl with cropped curls and the liquid dark eyes of her mother, Princess Sophia of England.

Kitto surged towards him, held back by the guards, King George's granddaughter scowled, and Napoleon looked on.

'My word,' Crow said to his brother in Cornish, 'you do seem to find yourself in some compromising situations, don't you?'

45

In a field tent rich with cloth-of-gold drapes and hangings, Kitto barely registered the presence of the escort guards and the two old women who had saved his life. He half noticed the man who could only be Napoleon Bonaparte, with his rich red cloak, gold-braided tricorn hat and liverish features, watching everything with a hard, agate-blue gaze. For Kitto, there was only Crow, tall and commanding as ever, and dressed in the red braided jacket of a French aide-de-camp, behind French lines, still daring to look as though Kitto was the one who had better swiftly find an explanation for all this the moment they were alone together.

'Kitto, don't,' Nadezhda said quickly, but anger completely scorched away his relief at being led away from the firing squad, and he lunged forwards at his brother, breaking free of the guard, who froze in the presence of Napoleon, unable to move or act.

'Don't you know what everyone's saying about you in Petersburg?' Kitto heard his own voice rise up to the cloth-of-gold upper reaches of the tent, furiously uncontrolled. 'That you're a turncoat working for the French? The rumours have been spreading for months. *Why are you here?*'

'Are you finished with your so-well-bred greeting, Christophe?' Crow asked in ice-tinged French, and Kitto noticed with creeping horror that his brother's eyes had that detached, lightless quality he remembered from the aftermath of Waterloo, as if he'd just witnessed cannon-fire at close quarters.

'No!' Kitto snapped. 'No I am not! It's bad enough that you dishonour the family name all over Petersburg, but how you can think you deserve Hester if you're going to shame her by screwing diplomat's daughters and bloody fucking Russian countesses right out in the open so that everyone knows – the gossip is all over Russia—'

'That's enough,' Crow said with reined-in calm. 'You will not mention her name again. Recover just a little breeding.'

'How could you do it, even you?' Kitto shoved him hard in the chest with a moment of breathless gratification because Crow had to take two quick steps backwards to regain his balance, a victory swiftly extinguished by the fact that he only smiled with an appalling air of self-control.

'What's the meaning of this absurd display?' Napoleon turned to the younger of the two old women like a city merchant complaining to his wife about the quality of the beef vermicelli at supper. 'Joséphine, what do your prisoners mean by brawling in my presence? Explain what has happened: who are they?'

'Sergeant Villefranche was about to have them shot – not without reason, my love.'

'Shot,' Napoleon said. 'Oh?'

Joséphine produced a brittle smile, and Kitto found himself feeling almost sorry for her – and even for Villefranche. 'They have trespassed into the camp,' she went on. 'One seems to be English, one Russian. Further to that, they've shot and killed two of your own men. The tall and ill-bred one is Lord Lamorna's brother. I thought it rather a shame they should be executed when they might be useful first, if Lord Lamorna should need any encouragement to seek more information about English intentions.'

'They were rapists,' Nadezhda said quietly, and Kitto shook his head. No one cared about that in here. So his life was to be used to abet Crow's treachery. He thought of hanged bodies swaying beneath the chestnut tree at Nansmornow; he would find a way to kill himself before he was party to this.

Paying Kitto no heed at all, Crow executed a slight bow at Joséphine Bonaparte and her black-clad companion. 'Oh, my compliments to you, *mesdames*. Aunt Thérèse, I must congratulate you most particularly. A most masterly and theatrical piece of manipulation. How extraordinary that these disastrously ill-mannered children just so happened to be here as I myself am here.'

'*Aunt* Thérèse?' Kitto demanded.

'*Be quiet*,' Crow said with such suppressed violence that for a moment no one spoke, not even Napoleon himself.

Joséphine shrugged. 'Well, what did you expect, Jack, really? You're here to help us, after all.'

Thérèse de la Saint-Maure just ignored them all, regal in black-beaded bombazine, which for a moment made Kitto almost admire her. He'd seen her in Petersburg, he realised, just some tedious and extremely elderly relation of a mother he'd never known, and after all one could hardly fraternise with the French, even if half the blood in one's veins was French and everyone knew it. How did Crow dare to call her Aunt Thérèse, with such disgusting familiarity? He was a traitor to England, a puppet for this crimson-clad French emperor who sat observing them all as though a hound had got in and befouled the floor.

'You can go to hell,' Kitto told his brother with succinct fury.

'A little more, and you'll begin to make me really rather angry,' Crow said.

'You traitorous, lying bastard,' Kitto shouted, completely unable to control himself. The guard at his side visibly winced.

'My God, get them out of here,' Joséphine said to the guards, placing both hands on Napoleon's scarlet-clad shoulders. 'Darling, they shan't trouble you any longer.'

It was queer how it was Crow who held the room: how all eyes were on him, rather than Napoleon. Unmoving, he just gave a lazy and entirely humourless smile. 'Christophe, at the risk of becoming a bore on the subject, I do think we can save what remains of this temper tantrum until we have the luxury of indulging without inflicting it on an unwilling audience.' Turning aside, he bowed to the emperor. 'I shall consider your offer, your excellency.'

'The devil take his fucking offer,' Kitto said, in Cornish, as the guards escorted Nadezhda towards the tent-flap. He couldn't stand the sight of them touching her, but Crow at once took his arm, his long fingers digging right between muscle and bone.

'I won't tell you again,' he said, sounding so bored that Kitto felt another surge of nauseous rage, at Crow and at himself for the mistake he'd so nearly made. He'd almost shouted at Napoleon's men not to touch Nadezhda – the words *get your hands off her* actually on his lips – when by all appearances no one else had yet noticed she was even a girl. One could bet Crow knew it, though, just as he always knew everything. Kitto was so shocked at the sight of him and so angry that he now lost almost all sense of his own surroundings, which became nothing but a wild, scattered series of impressions: a blast of fresh air in his face as the guards escorted them outside, the scent of wet earth, the crushing pressure of Crow's fingers on the spare flesh of his upper arm, Nadezhda's silence, the musty smell of rice and bacon boiled in a camp kettle, the cool interior of a requisitioned farmhouse kitchen, a dark and cobwebbed flight of stairs and finally the metallic click of a key turning in a lock. They were in an upstairs parlour – he, Crow and Nadezhda – the windows shuttered and barred, the room lit by stinking tallow lamps arrayed upon a table laid with a grease-spotted cloth. Crow released him with a contemptuous jerk, and Kitto turned on him, but Crow moved as fast as ever and Kitto's fist only glanced off his shoulder. Crow was now only a matter of a few scant inches taller, but he still had the advantages of weight and experience, and Kitto found himself slammed against the silk-papered wall with such force that the back of his skull cracked against it. Crow gripped his forearms with punitive force, those fingers digging in once more.

'Good God, what a display.' Crow's eyes were hard and grey as knapped flint. 'I can tell you now that I've seen quite enough of it.'

'How dare you?' Kitto battled to keep his voice level, determined not to show how much it hurt, both his head and Crow's sickening, pinching grip, pinning his arms to his sides. The calm ferocity of Crow's retaliation momentarily punctured Kitto's anger, and his eyes burned with a wild urge to weep. 'Everyone said you were a traitor, and I *fought* to clear your name, and got myself thrown out of Petersburg for it, and in the end it's all true. I wish I'd died at Novgorod. I wish I'd died by that firing squad just now.'

'Oh for God's sake, spare me the melodrama,' Crow said, releasing him, a good lot of his own anger now spent. 'Be quiet. I'm not here to sell English or Russian secrets to the French, despite what it may look like. Did I ever do anything so obvious in my life?'

'Why should I believe you?' Kitto demanded.

'Why indeed?' Crow walked away across the room, drawing a cigarillo from the tin in his waistcoat pocket and lighting it at the stinking, roast-mutton tallow lamp. In that moment, he looked momentarily so much like his usual self that it was hard to breathe. 'Incidentally, what in Christ's name were you thinking, killing people on reconnaissance? If you'd undertaken this mission under my command I'd have had you both flogged.'

'If you dare so much as lay a finger on her,' Kitto said, 'I'll kill you. I swear to God.' Nadezhda stared at him in purest furious terror, and Kitto fought the urge to kick the table. 'Oh, there's no use pretending to him. He knows, sure as anything.'

'Quite,' Crow said. 'This really wouldn't be Shakespearean enough without girls dressed as boys. Now, how are we going to get you out of this ridiculous mess?'

Nadezhda waited with her arms folded across her stained blue jacket, the silver at her epaulettes a little afire in the candlelight. 'I beg your pardon, but you don't know anything at all about it,' she said rapidly, looking Crow up and down. 'I haven't the honour of being formally acquainted with you, sir, but it's clear enough who you are, and although you might claim jurisdiction over Captain Helford, you have none whatsoever over me, and so I take leave to beg you to keep your opinions to yourself, whatever you're doing here.'

'He has no jurisdiction over me, either,' Kitto snapped.

'Don't I?' Crow said gently, tapping ash into the fireplace. He ignored Nadezhda, who was watching them both in wary, hostile silence. 'Has she told you who she really is yet? Show me that look again and you'll regret it. I find your manners despicable.'

'As I find your conduct, sir,' Kitto spat each word.

Crow stepped closer again, but Kitto didn't move; blood pounded in his ears.

'Oh for goodness' sake, do stop it,' Nadezhda said, turning to Crow. 'I don't see what any of this has to do with you, or why you're here. Unless of course you really have sold yourself to the French as an informer – which does seem the most likely probability from where we stand, I can assure you.'

Crow spoke as if he hadn't heard her; they had not, after all, been introduced. 'I said, has she told you who she really is?'

Kitto suppressed the urge to throw the bowl of wizened apples on the table hard across the room. 'Lord Lamorna,' he said, 'might I introduce Nadezhda Sofia Kurakina, late of Kazan.'

Lord Lamorna only smiled.

Nadezhda stared at them both; being caught in an argument between her own Captain Helford and his alarming brother was akin to imprisonment in a carriage behind a pair of bolting horses. She now felt as if she'd been hurled from the carriage into a breathless heap, certain that in the space of less than half an hour's acquaintance, Lord Lamorna had seen through every last layer of her deception with the expertise of one who could only be as accomplished a liar as she was herself. Clearly furious, Kitto took a step closer to him, which seemed to her extremely unwise.

'My dear child,' Lord Lamorna said with that chilling lack of emotion. 'My very dear boy, I'm sorry, but she's no more a Kurakin than you are.'

'Jack, what are you talking about?' Kitto demanded, and was met with only a laconic shrug. Rising bile scorched up Nadezhda's throat; he didn't know anything about her, this Lord Lamorna – how could he? And yet she was sure he did: she could see it in his wry, almost amused appraisal of her. Unlike Kitto, he knew everything. Kitto was now standing at his side, watching her with a queer, hostile expression she hadn't seen since the night he'd discovered her secret at Yarkaya Polyana. Lord Lamorna merely looked empty, and unsmiling. How could brothers be any more different? In his presence, Kitto had quite lost his usual air of suppressed laughter, which made him appear almost forbidding.

'What's he talking about, Nadezhda?' Kitto said crisply.

'I don't know,' she said. 'I really don't.'

Lord Lamorna smiled again. 'Oh, come now.'

Nadezhda walked right up to him. He had no right to demand answers, but she couldn't bear the way Kitto was looking at her. Lord Lamorna just watched with an air of grim amusement she found infuriating.

'All right then, I haven't the smallest notion what my history has to do with you, but if you must know I had always wondered if Mama and Papa weren't my real parents. I looked nothing like either of them, and my brothers were so much older, even though they died at Borodino so that now I have no one but myself to rely on—' She took a long, shuddering breath. There were ways to give away as little of the truth as she possibly could. Hadn't she always meant to tell Kitto who she really was, one day? It was frighteningly easy to convince herself.

'Nadia—' Kitto said with such gentleness of manner that tears came to her eyes. No one had used the pet form of her name since the day Grandmama had died in that narrow bed, clutching her hand, leaving her quite alone in the world.

'Do go on,' Lord Lamorna said, sounding bored.

'*No one* but myself,' Nadezhda said, and now she had begun, she could not stop, and the words spilled from her lips, uncontrollable as hot vomit. 'And maybe I was the last to know that the Kurakins weren't my real parents, but what of it? No one ever tells anything to a young girl. Which is why Ilya Rumyantsev thought he could just use me like one of those camp whores out there, because I haven't a name of my own, and it's why I'm glad he died doing it, and even though I didn't kill him I wish I had, I wish I'd been brave enough, but I wasn't. I just let him do it and he died – he just died. And so I was happy to shoot that damned fucking soldier.'

Lord Lamorna raised his eyebrows infinitesimally, and despite everything Nadezhda found herself feeling ashamed of the soldiers' language she'd employed in his presence, and could not go on.

Kitto turned to his brother. 'I know what you're doing,' he snapped. '*Stop it.*'

Lord Lamorna ignored him and pulled out one of the carved wooden chairs. Nadezhda sat in it, pressing her hands to her face, which was wet with tears.

She found that she wanted to keep talking. One felt, perversely, as though it was in Lord Lamorna's power to do something about this entire mess. 'Have you any idea,' she went on, 'how many times I've asked myself why I didn't fight back?' Tears streamed down her face; her nose was running; it hurt to speak the truth, to remember what she had been forced to live through, and she wished beyond anything that this was a lie, too, that it hadn't really happened. Lord Lamorna passed her a handkerchief, and she took it, breathing in the oddly reassuring scent of fresh soap. 'Ilya Rumyantsev died as he forced himself upon me. He just died. I don't know why, or how. Perhaps it was his heart. Perhaps it was a punishment from God, I don't know, but he just died. One minute he was alive, the next he was dead. That's all. And I'm glad of it. I'm truly, honestly glad he's dead and I wish I'd shot his brains out.' There was nothing else to say, and ordered speech was now quite beyond her power. She had spoken the truth about something, at least.

'Are you happy now?' Kitto demanded of his brother. She sensed that he was reining in his rage at Ilya Rumyantsev in order not to frighten her with it, and he seemed to know that she would want no one to touch her, so only came to stand close to her chair. 'I'm sorry,' he said to her, 'I'm so sorry that happened to you. If he wasn't already dead, I would kill him, I swear to God.'

Lord Lamorna made no reply – he had an unsettling habit of listening to other people only when they interested him – but he went to the sideboard and took up a dusty cut-glass carafe from a sideboard laid with a grubby lace cloth, removed the stopper and poured a glass, holding it for one moment beneath his nose before passing it to her.

'Abysmal,' he said, 'but it won't kill you, child.'

She wasn't sure if he was talking about Ilya Rumyantsev's violation of her or the brandy, but it didn't occur to her to refuse it, and the cognac lit a trail of fire down her throat.

Lord Lamorna pulled out another chair and sat down beside her, and again she felt entirely safe in his presence. 'You've no idea who your natural parents may have been?'

Kitto watched with ill-suppressed rage. 'Don't answer him,' he said. 'He's manipulating you.'

Weakened but still strong enough to keep some of the truth to herself, Nadezhda felt the lie leave her lips as though tugged on a string. 'No,' she said. 'No, I haven't the smallest idea.'

46

Crow finished his cigarillo and lit another immediately as the girl blew her nose into his handkerchief. She might well weep.

'No one's going to hurt you again,' Kitto said to her, just as fierce and hot-headed as he was wrong. 'Do you understand? I don't care who your father was, or even your mother – no one will touch you.' He went to stand behind her chair; she leaned her head back, not quite touching him, but as though his nearness brought her comfort and, really, this was all Crow needed.

'Have you been fucking her?' he asked in Cornish, breathing out coils of smoke.

Kitto went quite still, and gave Crow a look that was unsettlingly reminiscent of their father. 'What did you say?'

'Well?' Crow disregarded the urge to soundly slap him.

Nadezhda herself looked up. 'It's really extremely rude to converse in a language I can't understand.'

They both ignored her. 'What do you take me for?' Kitto demanded, also in swift, furious Cornish. 'She was raped.

And even when she wants to, it's not going to happen until we marry.'

Crow put out his cigarillo, and the entire room seemed to move into sharper focus, from the grubby floorboards to the disordered cushions on the chaise longue beneath the window. 'Say that again.'

'Well, what else can I do?' Kitto demanded. 'We've been riding alone together for weeks – you of all people ought to understand that. It's exactly why Hester married you.'

Crow laughed, knowing exactly the effect it would have. 'I've never heard anything so entirely ridiculous in my life. Dear God. If you live long enough to marry anyone, you'll do so with my consent or not at all, and if indeed we leave this place still alive, which seems unlikely from where I stand, you'll return to Cornwall to recall a degree of conduct.'

'I'll return to my regiment, in fact, sir,' Kitto said, briefly summoning a measure of frigid calm.

'As of this moment, you no longer have a regiment.' Crow let Kitto shove him again. He was much too angry to get the better of anyone, least of all Crow.

'You can't take me out of the army,' Kitto shouted, all pretence at self-control now quite abandoned.

'I can and I will, as you well know.' Crow contented himself with watching Kitto step away, and the boy gave a hard-edged laugh. Crow turned on him before Kitto had time to regain his poise, pushing him against the wall once more, so that a three-legged stool shrieked across the floorboards. Kitto glared at him, their faces just inches apart, his chest heaving.

'I really don't think,' Crow said, 'that it would be wise to test me, do you?'

'Stop it!' Nadezhda cried out. 'You're both abominable.' Even as she spoke, the door swung open and Joséphine and Thérèse de la Saint-Maure stepped into the room, Joséphine issuing a swift command to the guards outside to leave them all locked in together.

Thérèse swept the room with her gaze. 'I do prefer not to have the name sullied by public brawling. We heard you all the way from the bottom of the stairs: extraordinary.'

As Kitto watched, now too angry to speak, Crow let him go with a little shake, as though he were some cur or street urchin, and bowed to their so-called great-aunt, lighting yet another cigarillo. 'You must tell me, ma'am, how I may serve you,' he said with a sarcastic gesture of welcome at the chained and padlocked shutters, the squalid crumb-littered tablecloth and the grease-smeared glasses arrayed on the japanned tray.

The woman Joséphine cast a curious glance in Kitto's direction, ignoring Nadezhda completely. 'Come, Jack – you could hardly suppose Napoleon wouldn't want to test your loyalty. You only need ride to Petersburg and return with at least one piece of significant intelligence that we don't already know.'

Kitto laughed again, but only with contempt. 'So you're not working with the French after all, *Jack*?' He was now long past the point he had arrived at once before to such catastrophic effect, so furious with Crow that he no longer cared what he might do or say. 'Oh God, you're such a worthless bastard. Do you think I'm an idiot? You just lied straight to my face not ten minutes ago.'

Nadezhda winced, but Thérèse de la Saint-Maure, Joséphine

and Crow barely seemed to notice this fresh outburst, only glancing in his direction as though he were a starling that had got in by an unshuttered window.

'I'm so sorry, ma'am,' Crow said, 'but given that I'm now considered a turncoat by everyone from Petersburg to Southampton, how easy do you think it would actually be to glean any useful intelligence from England, beyond what I've already given up to Napoleon? I came here on your invitation, to do one specific task. How must I manage this expansion of my brief?'

'By doing what you apparently do best, my dear,' Thérèse de la Saint-Maure said, 'lying and cheating.'

Crow smiled, humourless. 'Well, I'm afraid that I have no more cards to play, so then we find ourselves at an impasse.'

'No,' Nadezhda said, 'no, we don't.' She was standing right beside Joséphine, who held herself curiously rigid.

'Your Russian soldier is holding a knife against my back,' Joséphine said with surprising calm. 'Obviously Napoleon's guards made a poor job of stripping you all of your weapons.'

Nadezhda only smiled, her fine-boned face vivid in the lamplight, and Kitto remembered the knife sheathed in her corset. She must have reached around to quietly tug it free. Crow was just watching them all thoughtfully: dangerously quiet, in Kitto's opinion. They would never be able to get down the stairs and out of the door, even with Joséphine as a hostage. Still holding her prisoner, Nadezhda glanced up at the dim, cobwebbed ceiling, and Kitto followed her gaze to a loft hatch. He moved a chair beneath it, climbed up and moved the hatch, revealing a yawning black maw above. Without a word, Crow walked to the door and bolted it from the inside with one liquid movement.

'What on earth is the meaning of this?' Thérèse demanded, watching as though they were drunken villagers chasing a pig.

Crow just shook his head, tossing off another glass of brandy. 'Madame,' he said, 'it takes in the region of five minutes to die from a well-placed knife wound to the kidney. If I were you, I wouldn't risk finding out just how accurate the Russian boy's aim is. I'm extremely sorry for the inconvenience, but we're leaving, and I'm afraid you'll have to come with us, for part of the way at least. We can't possibly let you stay here to sing like a bird, my dear.'

'A pair of old women,' Thérèse said, scornfully. 'Do you really think any of them care what happens to us? If they see us, you'll be shot down before you so much as reach the garden wall, and we alongside you.'

Crow gave her the sort of smile that Kitto always thought of as his brother at his simultaneous worst and best, equally as charming as he was life-threatening. 'Well, since we don't appear to have any other choice, we'll just have to put your theory to the test, won't we?'

'You can't even begin to be serious,' Joséphine said, 'you can't—' She broke off, gasping, and Nadezhda shrugged, obviously more than happy to allow Joséphine to feel the edge of cold steel right through the scant protection of linen and muslin.

'I'm sorry, madame,' Nadezhda said.

Dispensing with further discussion, Crow sprang on to the stool and hauled himself up into the gloom of the loft space above. 'Here,' he said lightly, reaching down with both arms. 'The stool will slip. Use a chair, boy, or better still the table, and do it quietly.'

Kitto ignored the fact he'd decided Crow was dead to him and followed his brother's commands to the last breath; he moved the table, edging it cautiously across the filthy waxed floorboards beneath the critical gaze of Nadezhda and the two old women, and then went to Thérèse de la Saint-Maure, who was watching him with such a look of awful disdain that it was hard to speak.

'I'm sorry,' Kitto said and, standing behind his great-aunt, he put his hands around her waist and lifted her on to the table; she was light as a bird: nothing but tea, toast, whalebone and venom. Crow reached down and with a whisk of bombazine gown and cedar-scented petticoats she was gone, up into the loft space, and it was such a profoundly terrible thing to do to an old woman that Kitto wasn't at all sure whether he wouldn't rather have been shot, his brains blown out against that bloodied post, but Crow appeared again, head and shoulders, black hair hanging in his eyes, and said, 'The devil! Move.'

Nadezhda and Joséphine came to the table, somewhere between an undignified dance and a shuffle, and Kitto lifted Joséphine, too – Joséphine Bonaparte, consort to the Emperor of France – and Crow twitched her up into the loft as well, and Kitto only just managed to turn his head from the swirl of damp, mud-spattered linen. He was left with only Nadezhda, so pale and resolute in her worn and stained uniform that he wanted to kiss her even more than he wanted answers from his brother: nothing else seemed to really matter. He would happily have spent the rest of his life living in the look that passed between them, her clear brown eyes holding his gaze.

'You're holding the knife, may I remind you,' Crow said from above with studied calm.

'Are you so worried about being overpowered by two old women?' Nadezhda demanded, jutting her finely moulded chin up at the roof space, and Kitto shook his head. Now that his own anger had cooled, even just a little, he saw that of course she didn't understand that quite empty expression in Crow's eyes; she didn't know that in such a frame of mind Crow might continue apparently as normal for weeks, if not months, and then suddenly snap with such bloody-fisted destruction that nothing was ever the same again. God only knew what had happened to him, but it was just a matter of time before he made everyone in his close vicinity pay for it. Heedless of all this, Nadezhda climbed with wiry competence, shaking off Crow's steadying arm, and Kitto followed her and, with all the strength and silent speed he could muster, he twisted around to sit on the vast, rough beam where Joséphine and Thérèse perched, emanating silent outrage. There was something almost sacrilegious about seeing two women of that age sitting with their legs swinging over a yawning gap, like a pair of little girls perched on a beam in the hayloft. The dark space disappeared off into a deeper blackness on either side of the hatch: the loft ran the entire length of the farmhouse. Between the beams, only a relatively small area at the far end of the loft had been boarded out, with heaps of last winter's straw and apples laid out on old news-sheets emitting that faint rotting scent; the rest was only plaster and lath, and Kitto knew if he didn't take care he'd put a foot through the ceiling of either this bedchamber or some other upstairs room in the house.

'When you're quite ready,' Crow said, at his most insufferable, stepping with swift precision from one beam to the next until he'd crossed the length of the loft, balancing with all the natural grace of a cat, even though in just the last half-hour he'd drunk enough brandy to fell most reasonable people. At the far end, at what must be the northernmost end of the house, where the apples and hay were heaped up, the faint grey outline of a door showed. 'This way,' Crow said. 'We can get out here. *Now.*'

Kitto felt sweat break out all over his back beneath his shirt, and turned to his forbidding great-aunt, who looked at him as though he had just vomited in the middle of her drawing-room. 'If you'll allow me, madame,' he said, helping her to her feet, stepping with her from one beam to the next as Crow had done. Crow passed them again, entirely focused on going back to assist Nadezhda and Joséphine.

'And what do you propose to do now?' Thérèse de la Saint-Maure said with an acerbic precision that reminded Kitto acutely of Crow. 'It's going to be rather a long way down.' Steadying her, Kitto sidestepped a large wooden tray of wrinkled apples. The two loft doors were vast, towering up to the narrow space at the very top of the roof. Peering through the half-inch gap between them, he breathed in the scent of woodsmoke, frying onions and horseshit. They must be above the kitchens, and somewhere near the farm stables. The loft doors were held shut from the outside by a narrow wooden latch, and Nadezhda appeared again with Crow, Joséphine and her knife, and pushed the flat of the blade into the crack between the two doors. With one frenzied movement, she brought up the blade with enough force to lift the latch outside. The doors swung open so fast that each one crashed into the wall behind it, and light flooded in.

'Quickly,' Crow said and, turning, he climbed out of the door, clinging on briefly before dropping four or five feet to the farmyard of beaten earth below, immediately reaching up his arms with a single commanding gesture.

'I'm sorry,' Kitto said, uselessly, and helped Thérèse and then Joséphine climb down into Crow's arms. Nadezhda followed, scrabbling down of her own accord, holding the knife to Joséphine's back once more; Kitto jumped in a hurtling rush and cast one last look up at the shouldering bulk of the farmhouse as a fine spray of raindrops spattered his face.

'This way.' Crow jerked his head towards the dark line of beech and pine just visible beyond the farmyard and hurdle-fenced kale patches. French campfires glowed and, beyond them, the dark mass of thick, ancient forest spread out for miles. How many men sat between them and the relative safety of those trees?

'Don't look at anyone, do you understand?' Crow said quietly. 'Just walk as if you're supposed to be here – start when I start, and don't stop until we reach the trees.' He stared at Joséphine and Thérèse. 'If either of you screams, it will be the last sound you make.' He turned back to Kitto and Nadezhda. 'We reach those trees and we then leave them, understand?'

'Wait for me there,' Kitto said and, without waiting for an answer, he moved away from his brother and from Nadezhda and their two enraged prisoners, because if they left this place without weapons, they might as well not bother leaving it at all. He could deal with Crow's attitude to disregarding orders when his own mission was complete.

47

Leaving them all behind, Kitto ran fast and low towards the nearest cluster of campfires, listening all the time. It was still early, and few of the soldiers would be dead drunk yet, which meant he would have to be all the more careful. Every sound swelled in significance: the crackle of campfire-flame, the low, rumbling talk of the men gathered around the nearest fire cleaning their muskets and whitening their belts with vinegar and chalk, one voice singing of the lavender fields and apricot orchards and the dark-eyed girls of his faraway Avignon homeland. Kitto could hear his own breathing, too, and the floral scent of his great-aunt Thérèse's hair pomade clung about him still. If Crow was going to comprehensively delimb him this unsanctioned mission might as well be worthwhile. He stepped closer to the campfire, half listening to the ebb and flow of conversation: the men were waiting for orders to march on Petersburg, but Napoleon was wavering, so it was said, cautious about being trapped with his army once more in the grip of another murdering northern winter if Russia's alliance with Britain proved unshakeable.

There were seven soldiers sitting around the fire, all from the same regiment, and all with the emaciated and blistered look of men who had in recent weeks marched a very, very long way. They were boiling a kettle of rice, the youngest of them crouching on his haunches near the camp kettle, sawing the end of a dried sausage into it. Their muskets and packs were ranged a yard or two behind them, and Kitto knew that if he were seen here he'd be dead within minutes: perhaps he was destined to die in this camp after all, perhaps Death had been waiting for him at that firing post and refused to be cheated. Moving quietly forward, he lifted one discarded Charlesville musket, slinging it over his shoulder by the grubby canvas strap, instantly reassured at feeling the weight of a weapon again. He snatched up a pack with a ball-canister still strapped to it, weighty with lead and cartridges, and then reached for another Charlesville, hanging it from his other shoulder. He heard the men's chatter, and the rise and fall of the late evening birdsong, and then he simply walked away, step by agonising step, knowing that every moment brought him closer to being shot in the back of the head with a pistol, but equally that to run would be to attract fatal attention. Looking ahead towards the looming woodland, he could just see Crow, Nadezhda and the women disappearing into the trees, no more than a hundred yards away: what had taken them so long? They must have stopped for some reason. He walked on until he saw them waiting for him in tense silence in the darkness of the beech and pine; he had reached them, he was alive, and they were no longer unarmed, even if it was only muskets that were near impossible to aim at a target. Joséphine watched him approach with both hands pressed to her mouth, but Nadezhda only turned away as Kitto reached out to hand her one of the Charlesvilles.

'All right, they're not rifles or pistols,' Kitto said, 'but it's better than nothing.'

'What an absurdly suicidal thing to do,' Joséphine said, and at last Crow turned to him, and Kitto found that he couldn't stop shaking.

Crow took the musket Nadezhda had refused and cast a critical eye over it. 'French piece of shit,' he said, squinting down the barrel and then hooking it over his shoulder by the strap. Kitto was quite sure that Crow was going to hit him, but instead Crow just gave him a very slight nod, and he felt exactly the same sense of sickened disbelief as he had after surviving Novgorod when all his friends had died at the ramparts.

'You complete and utter young idiot,' Crow said mildly, and unslung a coil of rope from over his shoulder that he must have stopped to liberate from one of the wagons. Nadezhda wouldn't look at either of them, and Kitto realised that his brother was about to tie two elderly women to a tree.

'Jack, you can't,' he said.

'What, do you want them to run for help before we've got away?'

Silently, prompted by Nadezhda and the angled blade of her knife, Joséphine and Thérèse stood side by side at the pine tree, and Crow roped them to it with all the swift, unconscious expertise one would expect in a man who'd spent his formative years before the mast. 'I'm extremely sorry, Josa,' he said, 'but you really shouldn't have made me quite so angry. You can scream when we're gone.'

Without a word, and leaving the two speechless women quite behind, Kitto, his brother and Nadezhda all started running at the same moment. Every step felt like Kitto's last, as the three of them ran as hard and as fast as they could, and every time one stopped, leaning against a tree, the others stumbled to a halt, too, kicking up sprays of pine needles before they ran again, together, as one.

48

Dawn hadn't yet broken, and exhaustion shuddered through Crow as he sat up. Running, sprinting and walking in turn for hours through the night, they had finally all slept on last winter's dead leaves among the birch and pine. He sat and waited, flicking dead leaves off his jacket, breathing in the scent of leaf mould, but heard only the wind in the trees and the faint crackle of the campfire. There was no sign of any pursuit, and he idly hoped that Napoleon had been in a protective mood towards Joséphine: only then might Joséphine in turn take care of Thérèse, not that he should care a damn what happened to either of them. Every shred of flesh in his body ached and even though in part at least Crow knew he had succeeded in his mission, he only remembered waking beside Hester in her wide, fresh bed at Nansmornow, and Beatie Simmens bringing the little maid in, and Hester settling back among the creased linen and lace of her pillows to let the child suckle. Last night's victory meant nothing at all. Now that the boy was with him, and safe, Crow was only even more acutely aware of all that he'd lost. Moving with accustomed silence, he sat back, leaning against a thick birch trunk, looking across at Kitto and Nadezhda Kurakina. They were curled up together like young dogs, she with her chestnut curls close-cropped, in her breeches still instead of the seemly dress she would soon have to wear, Kitto's arm draped protectively across her waist, in possession of the prize Crow had been hunting for so long, dishonouring himself with such spectacular results, all just to find this girl. As he watched, Nadezhda shifted a little in Kitto's arms. She got to her feet and tugged the French camp blanket over Kitto, slipping away into the trees to relieve herself in the dark, Crow presumed. When she returned, he was smoking again and she froze, her eyes fixed on the glowing end of his cigarillo.

'Come here,' he said in a tone that brooked no disagreement.

After a moment's hesitation she sat before him, cross-legged and wary.

He smiled, knowing that even as he did so he still looked a little cruel. 'I remember your mother,' he said. 'I met her at St James's Palace when I was only a boy – a long time ago. It was just before Christmas, and she gave me a candied orange. You're extremely like her, you know.'

'I never knew her,' Nadezhda said. 'I never even saw her.'

Even Crow couldn't be quite sure just how much of the quaver in her voice was manufactured, but pressed home his advantage all the same. 'I do think she pined for you, just a little. She always used to look at us children with such a queer starveling expression that we were rather afraid of her: you could not have been much more than an infant then, thousands of miles away. My mother used to say it was a shame the princesses were kept at home by the queen, never allowed to marry, never allowed to taste the joys of life beyond that prison of a palace. One has to admire Sophia for that delicious affair with her father's young Russian guest all that time ago, no?'

'I suppose so,' Nadezhda said. Her caution in the face of his confidences was laughably obvious to him.

'Now listen to me,' Crow said, playing on her uncertainty, 'if I hear another word about marriage to my brother, I'll do something that we'll all regret.'

She frowned, pettish, hugging her arms about herself; now the fire had died down it was cold so far from the embers. 'You're very fond of making pronouncements about what you don't at all understand, Lord Lamorna,' she said. 'For all that, you're not my brother – you're not my guardian – and you have no right to give me instruction.'

'Oh no,' Crow said gently. 'If you were my sister, I would have taken you across my lap and quite comprehensively schooled you long ago, you manipulative little witch. Christ knows I'm tempted to do it anyway, and hang the resultant threepenny opera.'

She gasped, furious, unable to help herself.

'But then again,' Crow went on, merciless, 'if you were my sister, you would never have found yourself in this unenviable position to begin with. You would have been at home, stitching your sampler and playing the harp and staying up all night at dances.' He ignored the fate of his actual sister, Roza, which had been a long way from this idyllic picture, and levelled his gaze at Nadezhda, gauging the effect of his words, which had produced in her an expression of horrified revulsion.

'I would rather die,' she said, 'than ever live like that again.'

'Would you?' he asked. 'Who are you working for? The tsar himself or the Green Lamp? Are you loyal to your father, or has someone persuaded you to work against him because he left you in the wilds of Kazan for eighteen years to be raped by some entitled young bastard?' He knew quite well that was likely the only thing she had told the truth about, and he pitied her for it despite himself.

'I don't know what you're talking about,' Nadezhda said, and Crow laughed.

'You won't beat me at this game. I've played it far longer than you. You know exactly who your parents were and I'm willing to bet you always have. I'm only curious to know exactly what I'm about to unleash upon England – a Russian queen loyal to her tsar or working against him. No? You'd rather not say?'

Stiff and shaking, Nadezhda got to her feet. 'Leave me alone. You don't know what it's been like, being used as a chess piece.'

'Oh, yes I do,' he said, breathing out a trail of smoke. 'But one day I'll make you very sorry for my brother's part in it. Remember that.'

With frozen dignity, Nadezhda got to her feet and stalked back to the fire, nestling once more above Kitto's crooked knees, twitching the grey woollen blanket over them both, and Crow knew that anyone else who had met the elder Sophia would also see the resemblance immediately, irrefutable evidence of a holy sense of humour somewhere. As he waited, the sky began to lighten, thin streams of sunlight lancing down between the branches above heavy with fresh green leaves. Unable to rest, he gathered brushwood and woke up the fire with rag and kindling from the stolen French pack while Kitto and Nadezhda lay fathoms deep in the clear sleep of the very young. He went to piss, and when he returned, Kitto had woken and was methodically disembowelling the French pack, taking out a small kettle and a twisted newspaper wrap of coffee. Neither said a word, and Kitto got up and went to the stream to fill the kettle as Nadezhda slept on, the air thick with unasked questions, and when he came back, he set the kettle near the edge of the licking, leaping flames and crouched down to watch steam curling away from the water.

He spoke without looking at Crow. 'Jack, why are you here?'

Crow sat down, stretching out his legs. 'Much as I understand how ironic it is for me to deliver any kind of homily, you'll be well served if you learn to control your temper from now on. And since you now seem able to ask with a degree of civility, you may have your answer: I've come for her.'

Kitto turned abruptly, responding exactly as Crow had known he would do to such provocation. 'What? Is this why you said I can't marry her? You must at least consider it – what else can we do? She's completely and utterly ruined. You heard what she said about that Rumyantsev bastard who died, and she's been alone with me for weeks. What on earth do you want with Nadezhda?'

Crow knew quite well that it would do him no favours to say that it felt like only five years had passed since Kitto had been born, and that even if that were not so, any question of marriage was impossible. 'I'm afraid you can't marry her. Even if you were twenty-one and need care nothing for my consent, you still could not.'

'Why? Why can't you just give me permission? It's the right thing to do. It's what you did.' Turning away, Kitto jabbed at the kettle with a stick, sending up a spray of tiny sparks like flecks of amber. 'Hester would say you should allow it.'

'I can't.' Crow tossed the end of his cigarillo into the lengthening flames, steadying himself. He would soon have to tell him the truth about Hester: it would be the first time he'd said it aloud: *She is dead. We will never see her again, or my child.* 'You can't marry Nadezhda, and it's not because you're absurdly underage and I won't grant permission, but because she's the Russian royal bastard everyone's gossiping about from here to London, that's why. She's Princess Sophia's daughter by Alexander. Castlereagh wants her as heir.'

Kitto turned to look at him, dirty and unshaven, that irrepressible urge to laugh rising in him even as his eyes darkened with emotion. '*Nadezhda?* They want her as Queen of England, and they sent you to fetch her? Why does that not surprise me in the slightest?' He frowned, as if all this were an irrelevance to be brushed aside. 'Crow, why are you drinking brandy at first light? It's not as if it's ale, or even wine.'

Crow was saved from answering that question by Nadezhda herself, who sat up with dead leaves in her hair. 'Have you finished discussing my future with no reference to my wishes?'

'Nadia—' Kitto said, reaching out to her as if he were gentling a frightened horse, and despite Crow's white-hot fury with her, he saw that her own anger died a little as she looked at his brother. She came to sit beside Kitto then, cross-legged once more, her hand beside his so that their little fingers brushed close together.

'Is it true,' she said to Crow, 'or were you lying to him?' Oh, she was good: very good. One had to hand it to her.

'I very rarely lie to him,' Crow said, watching her steadily, hating himself for allowing her this deception, for letting her continue to convince his brother of this romantic fiction between them when really she was in the employ either of the tsar or the Green Lamp, and in either case Kitto was for her merely a means of obtaining Russian leverage over England. But the lie must hold for a little while longer. 'They want an heir untainted by association with Napoleon.'

'A young manoeuvrable heir that Castlereagh can do what he wants with, more like,' Kitto said, watching him. 'What a great lot of colossal nonsense.'

'Castlereagh will not live long after I return to England,' Crow said, well aware that Kitto was now looking at him with increasing alarm, almost as if he knew there were now only two inches of brandy slopping in the bottom of the flask.

Nadezhda smiled. 'I'm not doing it.' The expression on her face changed from incredulous amusement to shocked anger. 'Do you think you can drag me to England against my will? I don't care who my parents were, or what happens in your country. Why should I? I've never even been to England. I'm Russian.' It was a truly magnificent performance, Crow had to admit.

'All the same,' he said, 'you'll come there with me now.'

She got to her feet. 'The devil I will not.'

Crow sighed and stood up, too, just close enough to remind the pair of them that he could quite easily overpower her. 'Rail against it all you want, it makes no difference.' In his time, he had lied and cheated his way around Europe and beyond, but Kitto's serious expression and his fingers grazing Nadezhda's knee rendered it all tawdry, and all Crow wanted was for this to be over. He closed his eyes a moment and saw Hester slipping down a sodden, tilting deck with the child in her arms. He reached across with another cigarillo and lit it from the embers of the campfire, but the smoke only made him feel nauseous, and as though he must shake until he spewed, and that there could be no relief. 'I'm going to shave,' he said. He fought the queerest desire to peel away his own skin and step out of it; he couldn't stand up a moment longer without moving.

49

Kitto watched Crow walk away into the trees in the direction of the stream, and Nadezhda stood at his side as they both stared after him. For what seemed a long while, neither spoke.

'Is he always like this?' Nadezhda managed eventually. 'He's really rather a lot, your brother, don't you think?'

'He's out of his mind drunk and he looks as if he hasn't slept for weeks.' Kitto let out a long, shuddering breath. 'You can put the knife down. You won't be needing it.'

Nadezhda glanced at him, her fingers white with tension around the leather-bound handle of her knife. 'Who says I won't? Have you forgotten that he was in the French camp, in French uniform? If he's working for them, how do you know you can trust him?' She shook her head, apparently bemused.

'I need to talk to him alone. God, this is just unbelievable. *He's* just unbelievable. Wait here.'

Nadezhda frowned, and Kitto left her, following the path Crow had taken through the trees. He found his brother stripped to the waist, revealing the swirling blue-black tattoos that covered his torso and back as he knelt by the stream.

Crow didn't turn, wet hair dripping between his shoulder blades as he plied the razor, calmly shaving in the middle of chaos – it was all just so entirely like him.

'Jack, all this about Nadezhda being an heiress to the throne, I mean it's ridiculous – she doesn't want that,' Kitto said, the words tipping out in a rush. 'I mean, she so obviously wants no part in it. This is – it's medieval. You can't force her, you really can't.'

Still without turning, Crow dipped his razor into the stream, shaking away bright drops of water; the tattoos across his shoulder blades shifted as he moved. 'Surely you know me better than that,' he said, without elaboration.

'What do you mean?'

With a flick of his wrist, Crow swept the razor up his throat in one long stroke and rinsed it, speaking without bothering to turn and face him. 'I told you. She's coming back to England with me to satisfy the whim of Lord Castlereagh. As are you. To learn some damned fucking manners, if nothing else.'

Kitto couldn't even begin to comprehend it. 'No,' he said. 'I do mean no.'

Still facing the stream, Crow put down his razor in the pebbles lining the edge of the rushing stream.

'I don't even care about any of the rest of it – who Nadezhda's parents are. That's her business,' Kitto said, fighting to keep his voice steady. 'But, Jack, what's wrong? You're in pieces. I can see how drunk you are, even if she can't. Never mind all that stuff about the French, about Nadezhda. What have you done?'

Crow leaned forwards, the muscles in his back rippling beneath the tattoos as he splashed his face with handfuls of water bright in the morning light. 'Come on then and say what you want to say, why don't you?'

Kitto hated him then with a fierce, bright intensity. 'All right. We both know what you're trying to forget. How could you do that to Hester – those rumours about Countess Orlova? Isn't it difficult enough with the things people say about Hester already – even *to* her? And then you do this, shaming her before all society.'

'You actually believe I would have done that to my wife, if she still lived?' At last, Crow turned to face him, standing up with that same wholly unsettling calm as Kitto tried to grasp the enormity of what he'd just been told. 'I did it because she's dead,' Crow said, and Kitto felt as though he'd been kicked in the stomach by a horse. 'Because Hester and Morwenna drowned when the *Curlew* went down off Cézembre, escaping the English you are so loyal to.'

Crow turned away, taking up his razor and continuing to shave, and Kitto walked back to the fire; it took all his composure not to break into a sprint. He found Nadezhda crouching before the flames, stirring coffee.

When Kitto spoke, he said only one word. 'Run.'

Crow knew his brother well enough to be sure that he and Nadezhda would both be gone by the time he returned to the guttering campfire. They had pulled the kettle from the embers, leaving him an inch of coffee, a childish act of courtesy that made him want to laugh. He pulled his shirt back over his head and drank the remains of the coffee: it was very nearly cold, but he knew he couldn't go on without it. Streams of sunlight glanced down through the mass of leaves above, glancing off a flash of gold in the leaf mould. He reached down and picked up a fine chain threaded through the flat gold coin of a pendant: the St Christopher charm Hester had given to Kitto for his Twelfth Night gift when they had drunk champagne in the nursery as Hester fed Morwenna, and the boy had been so infuriatingly up on his high ropes. Only half aware of his surroundings, Crow turned the medal over and read the initials carved on the reverse. *May God keep CMH, with love, HGMH, JETH.* Christopher Meryon Helford; Hester Georgiana Maria Helford; John Edward Tristan Helford. His brother's name, his dead wife's, his own. It was done now. Expressionless, his vision shamefully blurred, Crow let the charm fall into the breast pocket of his waistcoat.

50

Nadezhda walked a few steps ahead of Kitto, swinging a birch twig at the undergrowth, trying to ignore his silence. Every verst between this stretch of forest and any town or village reached before her, seemingly endless and impassable. At last, she stopped, turning to face him.

'It's hopeless,' she said. 'At this rate, the French will take Petersburg before anyone can be warned.' She hacked angrily at bracken with the birch branch, tiny green leaves smashed and shivering. 'We'll get the blame for it, too, you and I – everyone knows our orders were to make for Chudovo. We should have gone straight back to Petersburg as soon as we got there.' She turned to Kitto, infuriated by his silence, and by the knowledge that their capture had been just as much her fault as his. 'Are you even listening? We took Sevastopol and the Black Sea off the Ottomans, but if Napoleon takes Petersburg, it'll be his navy all over the North Sea and not ours or yours. Maybe this is what he's been planning ever since you chased the French out of England. All those people—' She broke off: why did Kitto only watch her with that entirely emotionless look, as though none of this even mattered? 'What's wrong?' she said, gripped by blind panic: what had his brother told him?

He only shook his head, walking on straight past her, still with that stunned, disbelieving expression he'd worn since leaving Lord Lamorna by the stream and bidding her quietly to run. Nadezhda ran after him, catching him by the arm, and a bolt of heat travelled through her entire body, right from her fingertips. Her first instinct was to draw back, but she did not, and they both stood looking at her hand on his arm.

'I told you the worst that has happened to me.' She let him go, but did not look away. 'You know everything now – you even know what I never before knew myself.' Helpless in the face of his misery, she grasped for words. 'The tsar came to my father's estate once, all the way out near Kazan,' she went on, looking up at Kitto's devastated, irresolute face. 'He came and stood in the kitchen with my father, and I showed him the turtle doves I used to keep in a crate by the stove without even knowing who he was, and when he'd gone our kitchen serf boxed my ears and cried into her hands.' Nadezhda could not forget how that tall man in his magnificent and glittering uniform had crouched down before her, so much younger than Papa – Count Kurakin – who had looked so old and so vulnerable by comparison in his long Russian robes, almost as though he were wearing his dressing gown; she remembered such painful embarrassment.

And so this is your young daughter, Sergei Grigorovich? Tsar Alexander had said, tilting her chin with one crooked finger so that she had no choice but to meet his clear, blue gaze. *She is a good child, I make no doubt of that.*

Always, Papa had said nervously, and it wasn't even true, not by the fairest estimation.

Shoving birds in a crate at the tsar? Cook had said, once

Papa had left the room with the tsar himself. *Oh, you'll be sent to the Solovetsky Monastery!* The slaps had rained down on either side of her face: one, two, three, four; and Nadezhda had stood in the kitchen with tears streaming down her stinging cheeks, wondering why the world seemed to have shifted in this queer way.

And there in the forest, she took Kitto's warm, dry hands in her own, feeling the strength in his long fingers. 'My Khristofyor,' she said, 'what did your brother tell you?'

'I won't let him make you go to England just to be used by damned fucking politicians,' he said. 'I won't let him catch up with us. We'll go wherever you wish, do whatever you wish.'

'We can't go back to our regiments,' she said, knowing that this was not the reason he looked so devastated. 'We could join the Cossacks, or the Circassians – or, I don't know, anything. I only want to ride with you, forever. But you're not telling me everything. I know you're not. Please, I'm not a child. I don't need to be shielded from the truth, whatever it is he told you.'

For a moment he only looked at her, as if he couldn't bear to speak. Finally, he took a long breath, as though he were about to swim beneath the surface of a lake, right down to the bottom. 'You don't know them,' he said, still almost grey with shock beneath the dark growth of stubble. 'It won't mean anything to you.'

She stepped closer. 'Tell me. Don't endure this alone.'

'Hester,' he said at last, 'Hester and Morwenna. My brother's wife and his child. They are both dead. They drowned escaping persecution in England. In the country whose army in which I am enlisted, in whose name I've killed more men than I can count, Nadezhda. And you may not understand this, but without them Crow is gone as well, because now he'll only ever be the very worst of himself.'

She let him turn and walk on ahead then, knowing it was because he couldn't let anyone witness the shocked and hopeless grief that one only saw when those so dearly loved were mourned. Beyond Kitto's despair all she could think of was the wider tragedy; of the bustle and clamour of Petersburg, a distant memory from the single visit she had made there as a child, with the calling of the droshky drivers ringing out in every wide boulevard, and all those many hurrying, jostling people riding in gleaming kalashas or selling charred sweet chestnuts, who would surely not escape in time if Napoleon led Marshal Davout's regiments into an attack on the city. In her mind's eye, she imagined women and children screaming, running. Even walking, she felt trapped in one place, watching a chain of events that she could do nothing to prevent. By the time Kitto stopped at last, waiting for her in silence, the quality and the angle of sunlight streaming down through the tangle of branches had changed. He turned to look down at her as she came to stand at his side, and she saw that he had wept for a long time.

'Nadia,' he said, and again the pet form of her name was like a caress, conveying his heartfelt thanks for leaving him alone with his grief, 'someone's following us. I'm sure of it.'

She stopped, became still. Had they endured this state of constant alertness so long that they'd become just like those shambolic old soldiers one saw sitting outside taverns in worn-out uniforms, throwing knives at rats in the corner and twitching every time a door slammed? But in Nadezhda's heart, she knew that Kitto's instinct was still true. Wordless, they each reached for the other and stood hand in hand, and she too sensed the presence of another intelligence, close by and observing them. They stood in silence, watching as a pale, shining horse stepped from between the gathered trees, her coat reflecting the light like liquid gold, and now Nadezhda's eyes filled with sudden and quite uncontrollable tears. Kitto broke into a smile with such a total lack of affectation that for half a moment Nadezhda's entire awareness encompassed only him, and not the Turkoman mare at all; then came the full force of her relief, and she stepped closer, clicking her tongue as she held out one hand to the mare, seeing only her pale fingers ingrained with mud and filth against the green and russet backdrop of the forest, and the mare watching her.

'Well then, my beauty,' she said, 'did you come to find us?'

The mare backed up, tossing her head a little, and Nadezhda stopped where she stood, glad that Kitto had the sense to do the same. The mare's narrow ears flattened. She was afraid: it was in her nature to be so, but at the same time she hadn't fled. She remembered who they were. Standing still, she turned her elegant head to one side – the same rebuke she would have given to a pushy young horse.

'It's you, is it, my brave soul? You escaped from Chudovo – you didn't wish a French cavalry officer for your master?' Nadezhda spoke quietly, still holding out her hand, knowing she must show reassurance, not fear. It was a risk, but she took another step forwards, softly clicking her tongue behind her teeth, and the mare only flicked her tail, her ears still flattened back. Nadezhda dared not breathe. At last, the mare stepped closer, pushing at Nadezhda's shoulder with her muzzle as though she were a yearling colt that had to be scolded, but was welcomed back into the herd. Letting out a long breath, Nadezhda leaned her forehead on the muscled, golden expanse of the mare's flank, breathing in her warm horse-scent. Testing the bond between them, she stepped backwards and the mare followed her; she turned away and the mare came closer still, resting her muzzle on Nadezhda's shoulder once more so that Nadezhda could feel warm horse-breath tickling her ear even as Kitto watched in silence.

She turned to look up at him, aware of the distance now gulfing between them even though he stood just an arm's length away. 'You ride well enough bareback, if my memory serves me, Captain Helford.'

Kitto looked at her, filthy and tear-streaked, and unbearably handsome with it, and she wished that she had not had to lie to him for so long. 'I don't see that we've anything to lose.'

She turned, walking a few paces away from the mare, testing the bond between them once more. Understanding, the mare went to her, her great hooves stirring up the dark, rotten earth of the forest; the odd fresh beech leaf shone from the grime like so many fallen shards of bright green glass, her pale golden tail was tangled with mud and dead leaves, and Nadezhda walked around her, talking still; and let out a long breath as she went to the mare's head, holding out her hand once more, and all the while the only sound was the soft crunch of her boots sinking into the mess of dry leaf mould. Then, at last, she went to stand at the mare's side, and stood for a moment with one hand resting on her neck. The Turkoman's ears pricked up, and Nadezhda twisted handfuls of coarse mane and swung herself high up on to her back. She looked down to see Kitto reaching out with one hand held towards her.

'Well, Lieutenant Kurakin?' he said, and mounted himself behind Nadezhda, steadying her as he did so, and she felt the restrained strength in his fingertips resting lightly at her waist, higher now, at the waistband of her breeches.

It frightened her – in allowing him to extend her even the smallest protection, she was vulnerable. Breathless, Nadezhda grasped handfuls of the mare's mane, and Kitto released her for a moment even as she turned to look at him. He wore an expression of apologetic chagrin, and his eyes were dark with unspoken desire, and so, she guessed, were her own.

Nadezhda cleared her throat. 'You'd better hold on, Captain Helford, unless you want to find yourself face down in the mud.' She dug her heels into the mare's flank, and the breath caught in her chest when she felt the warmth and strength of his arms around her waist as he held on behind her, and together they rode, the three of them, Kitto, Nadezhda and the mare.

51

In St Petersburg, Hester gathered the salt-stained cloak around her shoulders with one hand and the wide boulevard spread out before her, lined with the spreading expanse of the River Neva on one side and tall, elegant houses on the other, all painted in pale shades of yellow, blue and green. Above the rooftops, the domes of a Russian church stood bright against a clear blue sky, alien and extraordinary, a riot of gold and bright stripes of wild colour – green, red and turquoise. She had managed to find her way to the British Embassy from the wharf using only French, finally eliciting a reluctant reply from a well-dressed Russian woman in a fur-lined green cloak who had looked her up and down with a combination of open fascination and disgust. What if she was too late and Crow was already dead, lying with his throat cut down some alley? It was entirely possible that she'd got this far only to learn that she was already a widow, and one now separated from her own child by oceans. Thinking about Morwenna and Catlin even for a moment made her stand still, fighting to breathe, her chest squeezing in panic, but surely it could not have been a mistake to leave them? Surely they were safer and less distinguishable without her? She couldn't think about that now; only of the danger Crow was in. Hester edged her way through the crowd on the embankment, passing bearded Bokhari traders in long caftans, an American sailor arguing with a tall, fair-haired Swedish midshipman about a gambling debt, and haughty white debutantes flanked by older duennas who stared at Hester with open curiosity and hostility. There were more sailors of every nationality, and wrinkled old women in bright headscarves selling baked sugared chestnuts from glowing braziers that spewed woodsmoke: Hester felt adrift among all this humanity after so long alone at sea with only gulls wheeling overhead as she tacked and sailed into the wind, her face raw with spray.

Reaching the embassy at last, Hester trod wide front steps scrubbed gleaming, cold with apprehension, knowing she was entirely dependent on the goodwill of an ambassador who might even be complicit in her husband's assassination, if it was true what Dorothea Lieven had said about Lord Castlereagh's intentions for Crow. The footman standing by the front door held out one liveried arm to bar her way, demanding something of her in Russian. Hester had not survived for so long in Crow's world that she didn't immediately understand that he was directing her to the servants' entrance. Steadying herself, she drew the salt-stiffened cloak around her throat and addressed the footman in her rapid aristocratic French.

'You will have received my husband here in the last month. His name is Lord Lamorna. I must see Lord Cathcart immediately.'

The footman stared at Hester for a moment with an expression she at first found incomprehensible. It was almost pity, and yet followed by an unmistakable smirk, and she felt a flutter of dread, along with a sickening certainty that the bedrock of her entire existence was shaking and about to crumble.

'Lord Lamorna? Certainly he has been here, madame.' The footman schooled his features back into an expression of rigid professional emotional detachment, and Hester found herself swept into a tiled foyer, handed over to a silent butler and borne by this man up a wide flight of crimson-carpeted stairs. The scent of beeswax polish and stale air wasn't quite disguised by the bowls of freesias and peonies set out on a marble-topped table in the middle of the hall. The hum of many voices rose up as they drew closer to a large pair of double doors at the end of the hallway, and Hester turned to protest to the Cathcarts' butler that of course she would wait to see Lord Cathcart if his wife was receiving visitors; it was one thing to demand an immediate audience with the ambassador concerning the official business of finding her husband, but she could not be expected to intrude on a private party.

'Wait—' she began, on the verge of requesting him to escort her to Lord Cathcart's quarters, but with a malicious smile the butler had already flung open the double doors into a loud drawing-room crammed with women in long gloves and muslin gowns and men in close-fitting jackets of superfine, boots gleaming with polish. Before Hester even had the chance to protest, the butler had announced her by title, flinging her name like a stone into the sudden, spreading silence even as she stood there in her salt-stained, filthy dress and her torn cloak – the same clothes she had worn to supper at Nansmornow, all that time ago.

A hush now blanketed the entire drawing-room, and she found herself an object of undisguised curiosity, stared at in complete silence which was eventually broken by a ripple of quickly stifled laughter from a group of young girls gathered at a harp in the corner. Hester was so tired, and the muscles in her arms still screamed with the effort of rowing when there had been no wind, and her face was stiff and raw with salt water. All she wanted to do was to know that Crow was still alive, that she was not too late, and here were all these people, watching her and smirking, as though they were all thoroughly enjoying a joke she wasn't party to. She wished they would all just go away, and her eyes blurred momentarily with horror-struck tears as the room moved into sharper focus. Her gaze was drawn to a woman standing nearby, somewhat apart from the crowd, as though no one would quite go near her. Slim and fairy-like, this other outcast wore her fair ringlets piled into an elegant arrangement *à la grecque*, and a gown of palest green silk. She looked so much the very height of fashion that Hester, in the midst of her own disaster, couldn't help wondering why the poor woman was apparently being shunned by everyone else in the room. She turned to Hester with a courteous smile, as though they had just been introduced, even though they had not; surely she was not about speak, Hester thought, because to do so before an introduction, stared at by all these people, was such a very disarming and strange thing to do.

'Lady Lamorna? But how extraordinary to see you here in Petersburg.'

Hester had nothing to say; everyone was watching them standing together with expressions of horror, of amusement, of mortification, and she found herself casting around the vast room, longing to see the tall, louche figure of her husband. 'I don't think, ma'am, that I have the pleasure of your acquaintance?' she managed at last, in a low voice, for perhaps the customs were different here in Russia: if this fashionable woman could address her without being introduced, maybe it was not such a terrible faux pas in Petersburg as it was at home.

The fair-haired woman smiled; she was so sylph-like that even though she was surely nearing forty, she had retained all the enviable grace of a young girl in the glory of her first season. 'Oh! Of course. How stupid of me. I am Countess Orlova. But this is almost too unbelievable, to see you here.' Even as Countess Orlova spoke, Hester realised with a surge of horrified pity that she was drunk, her eyes bright, her speech slightly slurred, just like a gentleman who had taken too much claret at supper, or one of those unfortunate pauper women who drank gin when they could get nothing to eat. Countess Orlova smiled again, her pretty features queerly lopsided, just as another woman swept through the staring crowd towards them. Beneath her elaborate faded-blond coiffure her face was a mask of amiability, yet the look in her eyes was cold and aggressive – she could be none other than the hostess of this salon, Lady Cathcart herself, surely.

'Thank you, Tatyana, dear,' Lady Cathcart said, and turned her back on the woman, such a savage cut that Hester almost gasped aloud as she became aware of a small, wiry, dark-skinned man approaching, edging with expert grace through the crowd. With a shock of light curls just like her own, and blue-grey eyes, he was clearly of African ancestry, but no one seemed to stare at him as they did at Hester herself.

'Tatyana?' he said to Countess Orlova, with a quick smile and a bow to Hester. 'Perhaps it's best you come away, my diamond.'

'Oh no, Alexei, darling, I wouldn't miss this for all the world – it's just perfection.' Countess Orlova turned to Hester again. 'So new to Petersburg, Lady Lamorna, I trust you haven't met Alexander Pushkin – our most promising young poet, I can assure you. And so well beloved of all our women, who long to witness a display of one of his famous African rages. Do you have those, too, darling?'

'I think you've said enough, my angel,' Pushkin said, and in that moment his gaze held Hester's in a moment of shared and weary understanding, even as he steered the poor woman away.

Lady Cathcart reluctantly held out one hand, so obviously unwilling that Hester had to fight off a wave of furious nausea. 'My dear Lady Lamorna.' Lady Cathcart turned to the bald, imposing man who approached with an expression of well-practised calm, as though he were poised to begin negotiations at the Congress of Vienna, and to him she spoke in English, with false lightness of tone. 'My lord, Lady Lamorna has been so good as to visit us. Dear, this is such a surprise – we all thought you had sailed on the *Curlew*.' Abruptly switching to French, she went on to address her husband, 'And, my love, what we must tell her about Jack's indiscretions with Tatyana, or the drownings? Does she even know that the ship went down weeks ago? How very like Lamorna to leave one with such an appalling mess on one's hands.'

Morwenna. Catlin. The room spun about Hester in a whirl of light, of gilding and bright colour, and she saw Catlin passing her a handful of shells on the town beach on Bryher twenty years ago, long red hair whipping around her face as she smiled into the easterly wind, and she saw Crow holding their linen-wrapped newborn daughter in the Azores sunlight, tears streaming down his face. *My God, I'm sorry,* he had said, in half-laughing, rueful amazement at his own tears. Hester found that her legs would not support her, and the young poet Alexei Pushkin stepped forwards again, steadying her, cupping her elbow in one hand, murmuring something soothing but indistinguishable. An indiscretion? Crow had been having an affair with that fair-haired Countess Tatyana Orlova, who now stood but a few paces away with that strained, desperate look on her face, her eyes too bright?

'*My child—*' Hester said; unable to breathe, her sight darkened. She had left Morwenna behind. She had walked away from her own child on the quay at Hugh-town, leaving her with Catlin, condemning them both to death, to drown. 'Where is my child?'

'Find her somewhere to sit down – somewhere quiet,' Pushkin was saying, and Hester heard him toss an angry remark over his shoulder at Lady Cathcart, who stood still, both hands pressed to her mouth: 'Good God, whatever made you suppose she could not understand French?'

And Hester heard a burst of unstifled laughter, just as Lady Cathcart reached her.

Stumbling towards the gilded double doors, almost tripping over the skirts of her gown, Tatyana knew there could now be no going back. Even as she had opened the invitation from Lady Cathcart for this afternoon's soirée, she'd known it must have been sent before the rumours began to spread in earnest. How queer it was, she thought, that just like everyone else one might have affair after affair for decades, really, but then it took only a single night to end everything. Even Pushkin was not coming to help her now; all his attention was on Lord Lamorna's Creole wife, who had not decorously fainted at learning of her child's death at sea and her husband's unorthodox manner of mourning, but rather vomited bile into her hands; one could not help but pity the woman. Even the footman would scarcely look at Tatyana and she had to ask him three times to fetch her wrap. These people had all been waiting for her downfall since those awful rumours about Petya began to spread, just like so many vultures out on the steppe, circling over a weak and stumbling horse.

'Tanyushka!' Pushkin caught up with her then, his familiar face bright with emotion. 'You fool, darling – did I not tell you to go back to Yarkaya Polyana until the entire pack of scavengers had found something else to gossip about? Oh, why did you come here today?'

'How could I not, you silly boy? How should I go to Yarkaya Polyana when the last time I was there, I barely escaped with my life?' She forced herself to smile. They might say that Petya had died a coward at Grezhny, but she herself would face the darkness with such fortitude that perhaps those rumours might at last go away, and her only child could rest in peace, the shattered remains of the boy she had once cradled in her arms now rotting in some distant, unmarked battlefield grave that she could not even visit to mourn over.

'At least let me walk you to your carriage,' he said. 'Good God, why is Volkonsky always somewhere else when one most needs him?'

'Oh, I don't need Sasha,' Tatyana said. 'Not at all. Or anyone. I'll just go home. Alexei, dear, you should go back inside. You do realise what will happen if you follow me, don't you? You have your brother and sisters to think of, their reputations.' She smiled at him. 'Quick, before too many people remark on your absence, darling.'

Without turning to look back at him, Tatyana walked alone to the head of the stairs.

52

Kitto counted out a handful of tarnished kopeks for the tattooed woman selling curd cheeses wrapped in leaves from a basket set out by her campfire. Night was falling over the Nogai trading camp, and the warm, lavender-like scent of flowering Russian sage rose from the grassy plains north of Petersburg, drifting across the sprawling temporary city of goatskin tents and scattered campfires, mingling with the warm fug of gathered people and animals, and the scents of woodsmoke, and of kasha boiled with chopped lamb, butter and spices. A trail of windblown children ran past, boys in wide trousers and the girls with bright jackets buttoned over their gowns, long braids flying out behind them. Campfires glowed across the plain like so many stars, but Kitto knew that even here among the Nogai traders he and Nadezhda wouldn't be safe for long. She was too valuable a chess piece to be allowed to play her own game, and yet so many days after leaving Crow behind, there was no sign of him.

Nadezhda sat alone by their own campfire, cross-legged in her usual way, head bent to the work of polishing the Charlesville's stock with a cloth dipped in linseed. Kitto went and sat beside her; without looking at him, she passed the leather flask of kumiss. Steeling himself for the alcoholic fizz of mare's milk against his tongue, Kitto drank, passing her one of the leaf-wrapped cheeses as he assessed their surroundings, and wondered if he'd ever shrug off this habit of waiting for attack, watching the landscape for a storm of starlings bursting up from the furze, or an unexplained knot of shadow. Bats flew low, and the children ran from one campfire to another. A youth in wide trousers and an embroidered jacket tossed a much younger boy on to the back of a yearling mare with no saddle, standing aside with watchful care as the mare tossed her head, soon brought under control by the young boy, who now had her cantering in a figure of eight between the nearest campfires. Kitto turned away, unable to look at them.

He must think about anything other than Crow. 'Nadia,' he said, looking at her from the tail of his eye, 'how did you really suppose you'd keep all this up once we got to Petersburg? Any one of a hundred Rumyantsevs could have disowned you. They're such a well-known family.' He suppressed a murderous urge to crush Ilya Rumyantsev's rotting bones, if only they could be found.

Nadezhda held the flask of kumiss up to the light, and sparks danced above their campfire. 'I supposed I'd have to transfer out of the Semenovksys to a less well-known regiment as soon as we'd reported to the commissariat with the horses. Look here, I'm sorry. You probably just think I'm the most appalling liar in Christendom, but you're the only person I've actually cared about deceiving. For my sake, you've sold your own brother up the river and you're absent without leave from your regiment – how will we get you out of this mess, Captain Helford?'

'Perhaps I don't wish to be anywhere other than here.' They sat side by side, so close that their knees were touching, and she didn't pull away: he wanted so much to kiss her as they had done beyond the gates of Chudovo, but here the risk was too great. He smiled, unable to help himself. 'It's hardly as if I could return to my regiment. We were absent without leave the moment we walked out of Krakowski's front parlour.' He did look at her then, hardly daring to give a voice to his fear. 'Am I a coward not to go back and face up to my colonel?'

'Don't be a fool.' Nadezhda took the flask of kumiss, drinking it without so much as a shudder, this tsar's daughter who fought to kill, who preferred horses to people and who could drink fermented mare's milk like any Nogai warrior. 'You might get shot without being lily-livered about it, but surely the English would just use you against Lord Lamorna, wouldn't they? It would have been so dishonourable if you'd refused Krakowski at Chudovo. We had no choice.'

Kitto stood up, unable to sit for a moment longer and bear her rewriting of the past, which she seemed to do with alarming alacrity: the truth was, they had gone into the French camp because he'd been so angry about Crow's treachery. His name hung between them, putting an end to all discussion.

'You should eat something,' Nadezhda said to him at last. Unwrapping the dock leaves, she bit into the cheese with her usual economy of movement. Kitto tossed a stick into the fire. She did look up, then, and for the first time in all their extraordinary weeks together he saw pale tracks left by tears coursing down her filthy face.

He crouched down before her, with one hand on her knee – that was safe enough, surely, here among all these people? 'Nadia,' he said. 'What is it? Listen, you're safe. No one is going to compel you to do anything you don't wish to. We can trade horses all the way to Persia, you and I.'

She smiled up at him, tearstained. 'It's not that, but I only wish we'd not had to sell the Turkoman.' She could kill a man without hesitation, but it was the loss of a golden mare that had made her cry like a child.

'We had to sell her,' he said, desperate. 'Fugitives don't get far with no money, and you got a good price for her. We just have to pray that everyone here doesn't know exactly how much coin we're carrying now. We need to leave at first light.'

Nadezhda wiped a smear of oil from the barrel of the Charlesville and the silence between them beat like a drum as she glanced across at the stolid mare hobbled a few yards away. 'It's going to be like riding a barrel downstream,' she said, shaking her head. 'It's a good thing your brother wasn't mounted when we left him.'

She passed him the flask and Kitto swallowed another mouthful of kumiss, wincing at the taste, and he could no longer sit still; he got to his feet, pacing around the fire.

'Where is he? It's been days, and there's been no sign of him. Just nothing at all. It makes no sense.'

Nadezhda shrugged, her expression shielded. 'We were on horseback before long. We outpaced him: perhaps it's as simple as that.'

'If you knew him as I do you wouldn't say so.' The truth was, Crow had been tasked by Lord Castlereagh with bringing Nadezhda to England. What price would he pay for failure?

53

When Crow reached Petersburg, the weather had changed, and the bright neoclassical buildings and gilded domes were stark against a drizzling sky. Rain pockmarked the Neva, but the English Embankment was as busy as it ever was: the promenading beau monde mingled with girls selling round loaves of black bread from baskets balanced on their heads, and sailors in wide white breeches walking in groups down to the more workmanlike end of the embankment where caravels, trading vessels and the tsar's warships were moored. It was to the fashionable part of the embankment that Crow rode his stolen and exhausted horse at eleven o'clock in the morning, so hard and so fast that well-dressed pedestrians, English doctors, poets, opera dancers and Russian Guardsmen in feathered, gold-braided jackets all had to rush to the side of the embankment, and voices speaking in many languages rose up with a crackle and pop, threatening to call the tsar's police and arguing with loud vehemence about who would get their neck broken first. Once outside the British Embassy, Crow swung himself out of the saddle, and an English naval engineer from Southampton stepped out of the way, turned to his outraged wife and said he was perfectly well ashamed of one's own countrymen. Ignoring them all, Crow tossed the reins to a little Bokhari girl holding a basket of smoked eels packed in straw and sprinted up the wide front steps to the British Embassy. Ignoring the footmen, Crow ran inside and up the stairs. The Cathcarts' butler approached wearing an expression of incredulous yet battened-down servant's disapproval that Crow supposed was inevitable: he'd spirited Jane away from the care of her parents as well as an unwanted marriage. Without waiting to be challenged, he pushed immediately past the man.

'How dare you set foot in this house?'

Crow stopped then at the sound of a familiar voice and looked up to find George Cathcart standing at the far end of the corridor, fine as a pin as always, his thick, fair-brown hair brushed to a gleam; he was clad in a well-cut jacket that did not quite disguise the imperfections of his personality, and he stood with all the unsettling stillness of a wolf spider found behind the gun rack at Nansmornow. In all his filth and mud, Crow waited for George to approach, which he did, and the hubbub of many voices from the drawing-room behind him seemed somehow to fade away until Crow heard only the heels of George's highly polished boots striking percussive tap after tap against parquet waxed to a honeyed shine.

'Sir?' The Cathcarts' butler glanced nervously from George to Crow and then back again. 'Will I show the gentleman out, sir?'

'You need not.' Crow replied in his limited Russian, never taking his eyes from George's face. The pale skin at his temples glistened with sweat. 'Mr Cathcart is just about to show me into the drawing-room, where I must urgently speak with his father.'

George sneered. 'You'll be lucky not to be taken out and shot in the yard at the Coldstream barracks. Do you not realise you were seen leaving Petersburg with Thérèse de la Saint-Maure? That your connections with France are so widely known as to brand you a traitor, sir? And your brother, too, absent without leave, having completely failed in the task he was assigned, leaving both our own cavalry and the Russians' without enough horses to mount them? In the end, it all comes down to bad blood, does it not?'

'Oh, George, when will you ever learn to stop being so damnably irrelevant?' Reining in his temper, Crow pushed past him and walked straight to the double doors leading into the drawing-room; he didn't deign to look back as the two footmen let him in unannounced. As was usual at this hour, Lady Cathcart's drawing-room thronged with the beau monde of the Polar Venice; as one, they all turned to look at Crow, familiar faces and strangers all united in assorted expressions of horror, amusement or shock, like so many Greek theatrical masks.

A silence fell that was so profound for a moment Crow heard only his own breathing. For days, he hadn't slept or eaten, only walked and then ridden hard until he reached the wet-mud and woodsmoke stink of Petersburg itself. Exhaustion rolled over him like the wheels of a fully laden ammunition cart. Cathcart stood very near the door, in close conversation with Kitto's colonel, MacArthur – that was an encounter that would have to wait – and they both looked up and stared at Crow with disgusted shock.

'A word, my lord, if you please,' Crow said to Lord Cathcart. This was going to be no better than Waterloo.

'I scarcely think so, Lamorna,' Cathcart said. 'Whatever you think you may have to discuss of such importance, I can assure you there are other matters which more swiftly merit your attendance.'

'There are not,' Crow said, in a low voice calculated not to alarm the women, 'and if you won't receive me officially then I take leave to tell you now that Davout's regiments have amassed near Chudovo, with Napoleon himself in their company, only a few days' march from this city.'

MacArthur stared at him and, having turned away, Cathcart looked at Crow once more, in the act of having his glass of wine filled by a footman. 'What?' Cathcart said. 'What did you say?'

'You heard me,' Crow said, aware that he would have excoriated his brother for such a lack of address. 'So tell Alexander, and let him decide whether to evacuate Petersburg before it burns, or afterwards.'

MacArthur immediately turned and walked away, crossing the room towards a knot of generals from the Guards and a couple of the cavalry regiments, their heads all immediately bent together in hurried conference.

'Jack—' Cathcart began, and then just stopped talking, a diplomat of thirty years' standing entirely lost for words, and Crow became aware of just how closely he was now observed by the Cathcarts' usual slew of morning guests, fashionable Petersburg's full complement of morning dress: muslins, silks, hessians, and he in all his unshaven filth, splattered in mud up to his shoulders, and the crowd parted before him to reveal Hester, sitting with rigid poise on a chair of pale gold brocade, just beneath the window, wearing a gown he recognised as belonging to Lady Cathcart's personal maid, and he felt a rush of fury, because even in such a small way, someone had sought the means to insult his wife, who was still alive, who was actually here in this room.

She couldn't be. He had seen her so many times, as real as his own hand held out before him, but in truth no more than a trick played by his mind. Mirage or not, Hester simply sat watching him with that devastating calm which had destroyed his every defence since the first moment he'd laid eyes on her on the beach at Lamorna Cove, all those fine, light curls gathered in a topknot, some trailing down her shoulders, just watching him with those dark, discerning eyes. She was not real. She could not be alive; she could not be here, and yet this time the Cathcarts and all their guests were staring at her, too. She was alive. She was here now. What had they told her? Crow felt as though he were falling at great speed and could do nothing to stop himself.

Hester gave no sign of noticing that every last one of the Cathcarts' guests and all their assembled servants were watching her. Tall and straight as a queen she walked towards him, saying nothing. She wore a curiously distant expression, as though the greater part of her being were really somewhere else. *Morwenna.*

She stood before him now, studying his face with the intensity of a scholar translating an ancient text; she would never believe how much he loved her. No one with any sense would believe that, not after all she must have heard, and after all he'd done. He sensed the heat of her body, so close after all this time, and she was real, she was here, she was alive. He longed to reach out and touch her but knew he had no right. He'd betrayed her, however unwillingly, but had done it all the same. And yet if Hester was really here, standing before him, then where was the little maid: *where was Morwenna?*

The first piece of communication between them was entirely unspoken, and Crow was rendered speechless because everything in Hester's expression told him that even if she had not been on the *Curlew*, Morwenna had, and he realised that of course she would have sent the child with Catlin, to be safe away from her, because she herself was too easily identifiable as his wife. Without a word, she walked past him, twitching her skirts out of his way. He felt a sudden, uncontrollable spurt of anger curdling with relief that she still lived, and with such fresh, unbearable grief that tears sprang to his eyes. He was overpowered by a tidal wave of excoriating emotion as he followed her out of the room, and yet was unable to stop himself, despite knowing that the reason his own brother had betrayed him was because his greatest fault had been to show terrible, destructive anger when in fact he was afraid.

54

The moment they left the drawing-room, doors slamming unheeded behind them, Crow caught Hester by the arm, turning her to face him. 'What in the name of Christ are you doing here?' He was so furious, so unshaven and entirely covered with mud that he looked quite wild. How dared he be so angry with her? 'Did you come here alone? Tell me!'

'Don't touch me.' Hester walked away from him, fighting waves of building rage. If she let loose her anger in this house people here would say she was uncivilised, that she was a savage, and unlike him she had not the luxury of not caring what was said about her. Morwenna was dead, the *Curlew* wrecked, down in fourteen minutes, her child lost. Hester had seen too many shipwrecks to hold on to a scrap of hope. Morwenna and Catlin had both drowned without her, sucked down into a cold, unforgiving sea. Since arriving at the embassy, she'd had a day and a night to absorb the truth of it but could not, even pressing the corner of a pillow into her mouth in last night's fourth-best guest-chamber and letting out an unending silent scream had not really made it seem true. She let out a gasp as Crow caught up, taking her arm again.

'*Hester—*'

'It's true, isn't it?' she demanded, twitching away from his grasp, and she could not bear the sight of him, and the loss of her baby, so acutely painful that she had vomited green bile into her own hands before an entire drawing-room of people. 'It's true what they're all saying? That you came here and couldn't keep your hands off some countess and a young girl, for God's sake, a debutante, your host's own daughter?'

'It's true about the countess, but not about the girl,' he flung back, almost defiant, and how dared he? There had been too many amused, pitying looks flung her way since her arrival at the embassy to seriously doubt the story, but to hear him actually admit it was as hard to bear as the all-encompassing pain of childbirth, and that had all been for nothing, too, and so had this marriage. She could no longer look at him, at the man she never would have chosen for herself but who had been thrown into her life in the middle of a war, so long ago now, it seemed, and who had made her love him with such acute and devastating intensity, the man she had followed across half the earth to warn that he had been sent here to die, not to bring home an heir. All she wanted was never to see him again. She turned and ran for a servants' door in the grey-painted, wainscoted hallway. Letting it slam shut behind her, she found herself stumbling in her long skirts along a windowless, whitewashed corridor lit at intervals by tallow lamps guttering on assorted mismatching tables and stools, knowing that soon she would find her way outside.

'Hester, for God's sake, come *here*.' Crow had followed her. Of course, she was his property and he must control her, he must forever have the last word. She stopped. He was standing behind her, his hair wild and stiff with dirt, his coat and jacket unbuttoned, still heartstopping even in this unshaven mess; how dared he have the temerity to still look so angry? Hester turned and snatched a lamp off the nearest table and hurled it at him, china dish, flames and hot tallow, everything. She didn't wait to enjoy his reaction but ran so hard that her chest seared with pain, and still he caught up with her, slipping past with infuriating physical prowess and then blocking her path. Even the white linen of his cravat was splashed with mud.

'I don't care if this place burns to the ground,' Crow said, 'but I swear to God I will not leave you here.'

'It's you they want to kill, not me,' Hester said, measuring out each word with fury. She had come here to warn him of this and so she must. She turned but he was so close that she couldn't get away, now having to stand with her back against the wall.

'And so now what do you propose to do?' Crow said, ignoring the question of his own assassination, as though it were irrelevant to him. He leaned with one arm on the wall above her head, all soot-black lashes and grey eyes so pale against his skin, and the faint but intoxicating scent that even now made her want to lean against him and rest her head in the place beneath his collarbone.

'What do I *propose*? Never to see you again. And to divorce you as soon as I get back to England. After all, we no longer have a child that you might keep from me if I tried it.' Hester looked up at her husband and, hating him with as much passion as she had once loved him, she slapped him with all of her strength, and in response he took firm hold of each of her wrists, holding them gently at her sides.

'Hit me all you like, because God knows I deserve it. But you're still married to me now, and the marriage holds until we reach England and a lawyer, regardless of your feelings for me, do you understand? It's still my duty to protect you, whether you like it or not.'

With blistering rage, Hester snatched her hand from his grasp once more. 'You'll forgive me if I don't hold up my own end of our so-called sacred vow and obey you. I have no desire to travel anywhere in your company, so let's take it in turns to destroy the sanctity of marriage, one oath at a time. You began, now it's my turn.' At that moment, Crow turned away, and she instinctively followed his gaze. Three serving-maids stood at the end of the corridor, staring at them open-mouthed over the piles of folded embroidered tablecloths they were each carrying.

'Well,' Crow said in Cornish, 'for now, we're still married and I'll either carry or drag you out of this godforsaken city beneath the gaze of a full audience, or you'll come with me now and leave your dignity intact.'

'Dignity?' Hester said with cold fury. 'You took that from me when you couldn't stop yourself bedding half of St Petersburg – a widower so *very* devoted to the memory of his wife. I wish that I had died with my child. Why did I not die with her?' The expression on his face reminded her to put nothing past him, not least the rank hypocrisy of all men when it came to the sanctity of marriage vows. She turned and walked ahead of him, tears burning her eyes and streaming down her face, already trying to forget the acute grief and the unbearable joy being part of this man's life had brought to her.

Part 5

BY WEEPING CROSS

55

Side by side, Hester and Crow walked in silence over filthy cobbles slippery with algae, she tearstained and he still liberally mud-splashed. Gulls wheeled overhead, flashes of white against a bright, mocking sky; they had left the embassy with nothing other than the clothes they stood up in. Why did her grief feel so much sharper and more acute now that he was here at her side? No matter how much Hester now loathed her husband, it was clear to her that he too was quite undone; as they walked to the wharf, he lit one cigarillo directly from another. She dreaded the moment the last cigarillo was gone. They passed a wagon loaded with crates and barrels, observed by a little boy smoking a pipe in a patched blue caftan with the padded sleeves rolled up to his elbows, and Hester couldn't escape a sudden certainty that they were being watched – not by the child, but by someone else. Just a few moments ago, a harassed-looking ship's purser had hurried past with a sheaf of foolscap papers, heading for the forest of masts waiting at the wharf. She stopped and Crow turned to her, so expressionless that she felt a deep sense of unease.

'What?' he said. 'We'll lose the tide.'

'There's someone watching us.' It sounded foolish even to her, but was it so foolish, given all she knew? As one, they glanced up and down the alleyway, listening to the clamour of the wharf hundreds of yards away, the wide spread of the Neva still concealed by the bulk of wooden warehouses, seagulls overhead. Hester heard only the crash of wood against cobbles as someone carelessly lowered a crate from a davit on to the wharf, the resultant burst of furious shouting and, somewhere, the incessant barking of a dog. Even so, she still felt watched – an odd, cold sensation on the back of her neck, and then she heard the sharp report of a pistol shot, and breathed in the harsh smoke. At her side, Crow dropped to his knees, head bowed; even as the pool of blood spread, he was half laughing. Hester opened her mouth to scream but as if in a nightmare she could make no sound. She turned and saw George Cathcart hurrying towards them, breaking into a lopsided jogging motion – he must have followed them from the embassy, so earnest and shambling; they could get help after all. But then she saw what George was actually doing with his hands – he was fumbling to reload his pistol, tipping powder on the wet cobbles instead of down the barrel.

'For God's sake, stop making a fucking mull of it, George,' Crow said, leaning over as he knelt in the filth of the seaweed-strewn cobbles, blood spewing from between his fingers as he clutched at the wound. He'd already drawn his own pistol but George was now upon them and with surprising agility kicked it out of Crow's hand, his unremarkable face twisted into a ratlike expression of concentration. Crow reached out for it, but George kicked him again, hard in the belly this time, close to where the shot had struck, and Crow lurched forwards.

'Always the golden boy, weren't you?' George said conversationally, ramming a ball down the barrel of his pistol. 'Always Wellington's favourite, like a son to him, everyone said, no matter what you did. Even losing us Waterloo because of your ineptitude wasn't enough to make him see you for what you really are, was it?'

On his knees, Crow looked up at Hester with such an extraordinarily desperate expression that she opened her mouth to call out to him, but couldn't speak; before she could move, his shoulders heaved and he vomited blood on to the cobbles. Purged, he swore in an inventive patois of French, English and Cornish and got to his feet, dark blood still seeping from between his fingers. 'Hester, run!' he ordered, still as much of an autocrat as ever, even now. Head down, spitting blood on to the cobbles, he charged with a lopsided lack of grace, but George kicked him between the legs so hard that he went down again, falling with the sudden, swift finality of a stone dropped into a river from a bridge.

'Even marrying your blackamoor slut wasn't enough to make Wellington see the truth about you, was it, Jack?' George sneered as Crow lay on the cobbles, arching and twisting like a dying mackerel. 'Although the gossips tell me he wasn't precisely delighted with your choice.'

Crow forced himself up on to his knees and George strode over, slowly, enjoying himself, his pistol ready at last. High above the warehouses surrounding them, gulls wheeled in the blue sky, and Hester saw Crow glance across the cobbles at his own firearm, knowing that if he went to reach for it George would shoot him.

'It's about time you learned that you can't have everything your own way, you entitled whoreson bastard,' George said, and so Hester pulled out the pistol she had carried for hundreds of miles and shot George Cathcart directly through his right ear, so that he fell sideways into a heap of his own fragmented skull and shattered brain matter, releasing a rising stench of human ordure. Crow waited on his knees, bleeding through his fingers still, until she dropped into a crouch, and then he forced himself to his feet and held back Hester's hair as it escaped from pins and from ribbons, and she retched on to the cobbles.

56

The droshky driver was sanguine about the condition of his passengers, one a filthy and near hysterical woman and the other bleeding with alarming profusion from an abdominal pistol-shot wound that hurt like the very devil. At his laconic call, the horses stopped at the end of a boulevard far less fashionable than the environs of the British Embassy and the Admiralty, drawing up outside a tall but down-at-heel mansion painted the dirty peach-pink of last year's smoked fish.

'What is this place?' Hester demanded of Crow through shut teeth, pressing wadded folds of linen against the bleeding mess; she had undone his cravat with shaking fingers, and he could not forget other times when she had done so, only looking at him then with a quite different expression in her eyes. Crow had no strength to answer her now but, summoning all his willpower, he climbed down from the open carriage and handed Hester out of it, noticing odd details as shock, pain and fever began to overwhelm him – the crimson of the droshky driver's padded caftan against the grey, muted boulevard, and how Hester's curls sprang free of the wide binding ribbon she wore and all those wretched pins, and how much he wanted to leave a kiss curls behind her ear as he had done so often before. Now, she could not let go of his hand fast enough, as though even the thought of his touch repelled her, and amid rolling, endless waves of pain he could not forget the soldiers' prayer he had repeated every morning and evening for so many years of his life: *God keep me from the surgeon's knife.*

'Never mind where we're going,' he managed. 'There're a few kopeks in my waistcoat pocket – if you would pay the driver, please.'

Hester's eyes blazed as she dug in his pocket, passing a careless fistful of coins to the droshky driver, who smiled grimly as he took them, and Crow had not the heart to tell his heiress wife that Castlereagh had long since embargoed his bank accounts as though he were already in a cell awaiting the gallows, and now they had no money at all. He glanced up at the house and saw that all the windows were shuttered, quite dark, and fought an urge to call back the droshky even as the little open carriage whisked to the end of the boulevard. Penniless and hunted by his own government, there was nowhere else to go but here.

'If you please,' he said to Hester, and leaned on her arm, leaving a glossy trail of blood as she helped him to the door, silent and resolute, and how could he have failed her so comprehensively? Everything that had been wonderful and good he had destroyed, and could never have again. With what little remained of his strength, he hammered on the door, and the same lantern-jawed butler admitted him as the last time he had come here, so long ago now, it seemed.

'Oh, but Madame is surely at home,' he said, in answer to Crow's incoherent enquiry for his great-aunt even as blood seeped from between his fingers, quite as though he had come to call for an ordinary morning visit, and was not falling over his own feet because everything had grown so dark, and the pain was now nearly unbearable. At his side, Hester maintained a dignified, shattered silence as they were led up the stairs – indeed he would have fallen if were not for the strength of her grip at his elbow – and it was not until they were admitted into the familiar gloomy drawing-room and Thérèse de la Saint-Maure and Joséphine herself got up from painting watercolours at a marble table by the fire that tears began to stream down Hester's face.

'I'm not at all sure who either of you are,' she said, 'but my husband seems to know you and, if you please, he has been shot.'

Crow was just conscious of being led to a chaise below the window; Joséphine and Thérèse were too old to be much shocked by anything, it seemed, even being manhandled through the loft of a noisome barn and left tied to a tree, and he heard his great-aunt call for a servant. 'You really do have the most extraordinary quantity of impertinence,' she said with caustic ire, leaning over him to hold a burning feather beneath his nose.

'I know,' Crow managed. 'Truly I'm sorry. It's only that I don't wish my wife to be left quite alone. I'm so very happy you're here after all, and indeed I do thank you.'

'I think we should let him suffer, just a little,' Joséphine said, and the last thing Crow saw before darkness claimed him entirely was Napoleon's mistress unbuttoning his shirt.

Hours later, Hester stood by the window, looking out at the moonlit, aspen-lined boulevard, peaceful shards of lamplight glimpsed between the shutters of the other houses: there must be so many ordinary Russian families sitting down to their supper, perhaps a daughter of the house standing by the pianoforte to sing, or accompanying a sister at the harp, children not yet sent up to the nursery playing at spillikins by the fire. She couldn't bear to turn and look at Crow lying sprawled on the chaise before the hearth, his wound dressed by Thérèse de la Saint-Maure's household servants. *Don't worry yourself, girl,* Madame de la Saint-Maure had said. *My people all know how to keep their mouths shut. You'll get away from here as quietly as you like.* And Hester could not be quite sure if the old Frenchwoman had only meant to be kind, or whether she called her girl as one heard that slaves were called girl, or boy, and denied the distinction of a name. Hester was aware of a disturbance in the air and the faint scent of rose oil as Joséphine Bonaparte came to stand beside her with only the faint shushing of starched petticoats beneath the fresh muslin of her gown: a woman, Hester thought, who had survived for so long by learning how to move in near silence.

'I suppose this is a very odd thing to say, Lady Lamorna, but you do remind me of my sister.' Joséphine smiled as she stood at Hester's side, joining her in this vigil. 'Her name was Euphémie, her mother a slave on our plantation. She came to France with me from Martinique when I was first married – which was a most miserable affair, I can assure you, long before ever I met Napoleon, you know. I rather think I would have put period to my existence without Euphémie.'

Hester did not know what she was meant to say, how on earth she was supposed to respond to such confidences: there was more to unravel here than she had the strength to even begin to unpick.

'Will my husband live?' The words poured swiftly forth, and surely Hester was the greatest sinner alive to be overwhelmed with fury at the thought of Crow's death.

'I do think it's likely, yes, as much as one can be certain about these things,' Joséphine said with genuine pity in her expressive hazel eyes. 'Madame de la Saint-Maure's butler served as an army surgeon for many years, and he says the ball only left a deep nick without embedding in any vital organ, perhaps grazing the stomach itself. Had the shot penetrated where it struck, Lord Lamorna would be facing an unpleasant and protracted end. Nevertheless, I'm sure you'd like nothing more than to box his ears. Can there be anything more infuriating than someone one is entirely enraged with then getting himself shot, so that one must feel sorry for him, and so horribly afraid?'

'Very little, no,' Hester said. 'And it sounds as if he treated you with an amazing lack of consideration, too, so I wouldn't be at all surprised if you felt the same.'

'Indeed I do,' Joséphine said. 'You absorbed the entire story with such a lack of hysteria that it only goes to show you're precisely the right sort of wife for Lord Lamorna, and never mind all those stories one hears.'

Hester burned then with shame, and with anger, and felt tears start to her eyes, hand in hand with scorching mortification. Everyone in this city knew just how long Crow had mourned her supposed death. Soon the gossip would reach London, Vienna and Paris, just as it had done after they were married, scurrilous little notes crossing Europe in double-lined hot-pressed paper. They would say she had received no more than was due to her, and that of course she'd deserved nothing else. Against the loss of Morwenna, none of it even mattered. She herself did not matter, and neither did Crow, now so deeply asleep on the chaise drawn close to the fire by the servants, his black hair disordered against a crisp white linen pillowcase. Joséphine passed her a handkerchief in silence and then, to Hester's surprise, this small and vivacious Frenchwoman led her to the chaise opposite the one occupied by her unconscious husband, and made Hester sit down upon it.

'It's so very hard about the little child, is it not?' Joséphine said, and when Hester could not reply, and could not even breathe, the older woman sat beside her, and held her as she sobbed and shook, and it was the first time anyone had done so since Morwenna had died: at the embassy Lady Cathcart had only looked mortified, and half-heartedly offered her smelling salts, until there was nothing one could do but seek solace in the confines of that fourth-best bedchamber shared with an indigent English governess who had fled a master with groping hands in some distant Russian province. After some time, Joséphine poured Hester a glass of brandy, which she drank although she would have preferred a strong cup of tea, with thick Cornish milk. 'Now,' Joséphine said, 'when your husband wakes, you may tell him that his gamble paid off.'

Hester stared at her. 'Madame, I can only begin to guess.'

'Darling, we're in retreat. Among others, your husband sowed seeds of doubt in Napoleon's mind. Marshal Davout has been sent west, and out of Russia. You'll remember the retreat of 1812 when France lost so many sons. We cannot risk losses of such a magnitude again, and it's already nearly June. Five months between now and the first snows is too little time when one can't even be sure who is an ally and who is an enemy.'

Hester felt the brandy scorch down her throat; she didn't care about the fate of nations, she knew only that Catlin and Morwenna had drowned as they fled Lord Castlereagh and the English government, and if buried at all they'd have been committed to the earth with no name, and no one to remember who they even were, and perhaps not even together, although one heard stories about drowned women and sometimes men washed up with a child still in their arms. Try as she might, she had no answer for Joséphine, who sat watching her, expectant of seeing her counsel give rise to comfort.

'My dear Lady Lamorna,' Joséphine said with the air of one making a last-ditch attempt. 'Believe me, you would find your grief easier to bear if you would consent to share the burden of it with your husband.'

Hester could only sit in helpless silence, even as Joséphine took her hand in her own.

'Child,' she said, smiling, 'at the least, you must take it from me that there are few things more attractive than a repentant man. And, trust me, your husband is very sorry indeed. Why not let him beg?'

Numb and unfeeling, Hester sat with Crow long after Joséphine had followed Thérèse to bed. He stirred towards morning, and she turned to look at him, realising that he had been watching her for some time.

'My love,' he said. 'Oh, my love.'

Hester ignored that, her sight darkening and uncertain for want of sleep. 'I've accepted Joséphine and your aunt's offer of safe passage tomorrow morning, although God only knows why either of them still wish to help you in any way, after the turn you served them. You scarcely deserve it, but Thérèse has also given us a sum of money: she says it is no more than you're due, as the heir to Saint-Maure, but indeed I think she's a fool to indulge you.'

'So do I,' Crow said, and she saw how thirsty he was, and held a glass of cold fennel tisane to his lips. 'Never mind it, I promise you can be released from my protection as soon as it's safe.'

'As if you're in any condition to protect me,' Hester said, briefly enjoying her own cruelty, and still far too angry with him to accept Joséphine's counsel. 'What happened to Kitto, then, and this Russian princess you were supposed to bring home?'

She watched in uneasy confusion as Crow managed to laugh, closing his eyes. 'The boy has her. And God only knows, he betrayed me with quite royal magnificence, my dear.'

57

Three weeks later, at the western reaches of the Danish sea, mountains rose up on either side of the fjord in the choppy grey waters of the Skaggerak, and in the pearlescent, stretched-out twilight of a northern summer Hester tacked the tender, edging tentatively closer to the dark bulk of shoreline. Deposited under French protection at a tumbledown wharf in St Petersburg, she had sailed single-handedly from a reed-choked mooring to the mouth of the Neva and into the Gulf of Finland, skirting the Baltic, through the island-strewn waters of the Kattegat, finally reaching Skaggerak, this ocean gateway to the North Sea.

One hand on the tiller, shifting it in response to the touch of the wind on her cheekbone, she glanced overboard and saw drifting green seaweed and rock-strewn sand. Sprawled in the narrow space between the mast and the prow Crow was mercifully unconscious with his sailor's ability to sleep in the most damp and uncomfortable of places. Part of her longed to shake him awake in fury at his utter uselessness. At least the fever had abated enough to allow him to truly rest, thanks to the vials of foul-smelling pastes and liquids she'd bartered for valuable ammunition in some windswept Danish fishing village stinking of smoking green wood and dried cod.

'Damn you, John Helford, for that's who you really are, despite all your godforsaken titles,' Hester said succinctly, but her only answer was the crash of surf against rocks and sand. Blaspheming quietly to herself, she dragged up the centreboard and hauled the rudder out of the water, securing it with the tiller-line. She was shivering already, but that was only going to get worse. 'I hate you,' she told her sleeping husband. 'I hate you with every breath in my body.' And then she gathered up her skirts and slid into the water, gasping at the shock of the all-encompassing cold as she plunged in past her waist, wading ashore with the painter in her hand. Tears seeped as she dragged the tender as far up the beach as she was able with Crow a dead weight inside it.

Blaspheming quietly, she reached into the tender and hauled out a coil of rope, tying one end to the anchor chain before staggering up the beach holding the anchor, the chain running along beside her. Calculating the distance with shrewd, exhausted expertise, she let the anchor drop on to a heap of seaweed and allowed the line fall beside it. There hardly seemed to be any tide here at all but, as she slept, the tender would stay afloat. Her eyes burned with exhausted tears as she struggled out of her gown and petticoats; wringing the ruined fabric and then spreading her garments over rocks to dry, she lay down in her short shift, shivering and exhausted, wishing that she was dead. Later, she ignored the splash as Crow stepped out into the shallows, even when moments later she felt the damp, warm weight of his greatcoat spread over her. Even with her eyes shut, she still saw the beach in the never-quite dark of a northern summer night, and the small outcrop of seaweed-covered rock that, at this distance and from this angle, might have been a very young child sleeping on her front. Not sleeping, but drowned and washed up on a beach. She couldn't look. She must not look. That way madness waited.

'You should have woken me,' Crow said. She opened her eyes at the timbre of his voice, watching as he walked up and down beyond the tideline, collecting driftwood. He moved with slow deliberation, as if drunk, even if for once he wasn't. At last, he crouched down so close that she could have reached out and touched his salt-stained jacket. He cursed softly at the pain, at the cost of moving, tipping sparks from his strike-a-light into a heap of dried seaweed, coaxing tiny flames from thick white stinking smoke. The dressing on his wound ought to be changed, she knew. The gouge was healing well enough, so the pipe-smoking Danish bone-setter had assured her with sign language, or she would by now be a widow. It was little consolation.

She closed her eyes and when she opened them again he'd walked down to the waterline, now so much closer; the sea a dull silver edged with fiery northern twilight, the sky above deep blue, the tender now afloat but thankfully still securely anchored. She felt that hours had passed, even though the sky was still light, and Crow was stripped to the waist, and she could just hear him repeatedly swearing to himself in French as he pulled away the blood-soaked bandage. Without a word, she forced herself to sit up, to walk down the stone-strewn beach to where sea met the land, shivering in her shift. There was nothing to say, but without looking up at her husband she pulled away the bandage and let it fall into the water at their feet. The wound was still angry, skin and flesh not knitting together. She took from him the vial of herbs pounded in oil, pouring it in a slick on the fresh crumpled strip of linen. He let her smooth the bandage over the wound, circling the taut, muscled expanse of his belly, the faint strip of dark hair that led down from his navel. She tied it as best she could, knowing that they could risk bartering no more ammunition, and had little else to sell.

'Why did you fail to find this Russian princess?' she asked, again voicing the question that still lingered between them, unanswered, for so many weeks. 'You never fail at this kind of thing. I was quite capable of spiriting myself out of Russia just as I spirited myself into it. Don't tell me you abandoned the mission for my sake – Kitto's reputation depended on you succeeding, so why would you risk that?'

Crow looked away out to sea; she couldn't help looking at the unshaven and distractingly beautiful line of his jaw. 'Just keep me alive,' he said, 'until you are safe in England. That's all I ask.'

'He really did betray you,' she said, wanting him to suffer, 'is that it?'

He made no reply and, unable to help herself, Hester glanced up the beach, and Crow followed her gaze to the rocky outcrop that from here looked so much like a child asleep on the sand. The drowned so often looked to be sleeping when one found them. Crow turned away from her, expressionless, which was just as well because she could never allow him to hold her again; she could never admit even the most distant possibility of another child to lie between them in the night, only to be lost.

58

Six weeks after sailing the tender into the down-at-heel and French-loyal Norwegian port of Christiansand, where Crow had simply walked up to the captain of a noisome Archangelsk frigate bound illegally for England with sealskins and whale-fat in barrels, and demanded to be taken home, Hester found herself once more in the fish-scale-spangled chaos of the Port of London. For weeks, she had touched Crow only when she must, and now he steadied her as she walked down the gangplank in the damp skirts of a muslin gown worn thin at the seams, feeling about as far from respectable as she had ever done in her life. Her body betrayed her as it so often did where he was concerned, and the warmth of his touch, his fingers lightly holding hers, actually brought tears to her eyes, even as he steadied her the moment her threadbare boots touched the cobbles. He stood still for barely a moment before leading her with purpose away from the wharf towards one of the side-alleys where hackney carriages could be hailed. The streets were unnaturally quiet, with none of the usual mudlarking, bun-selling, pickpocketing and gin-soaked women or children to be seen, only the odd gathered group of young men who watched Hester and Crow as they passed. Preserving what remained of his cigarillos, he was now chewing a wad of tobacco won from one of the crew of the Archangelsk frigate in some rum-soaked night-long congress she had not been party to. For the duration of their voyage, she'd confined herself to the silent cabin they shared; he had insisted on surrendering the bunk to her and when he slept at all, she would find him with his black hair in a dishevelled mess, tumbled in his greatcoat and pressed against the cabin wall with the seaman's ability to cling like a limpet. She longed to be alone once more, to never have to see him again.

'I don't like this,' Crow said curtly, as though the atmosphere was all her fault: it was threatening even for London.

'Well, what now?' she demanded, twitching her skirts away from the runnel of green-tinged human ordure streaming down the middle of the cobbled alleyway, all shadowed by buildings in various states of disrepair.

'I'm taking you to Dorothea Lieven,' Crow spoke without looking down at her, staring straight ahead as seagulls tossed and wheeled in a flat grey sky. Without waiting for a reply, he hailed a hackney; the driver's features were mostly concealed by a greasy checked muffler, but his eyes were sharp and appraising, and Hester felt unpleasantly naked and vulnerable, knowing that the name she shared with Crow was more likely to lead them into danger than shield them from it. Crow handed her up into the carriage so that she breathed in a miasma of onion-tinged human sweat left behind by the previous occupants.

'What of my wishes?' she demanded when he had followed her in and was leaning across to close the door, so that she could not but be aware of the heat of his presence; indeed the air itself seemed to grow so hot between them that it was difficult to breathe. 'What have you to say to my own feelings about what happens to me? Or will you just continue to order everything as you please?'

He sat opposite her, leaning back against the unclean cushions in a way that reminded her momentarily and with breathtaking clarity of Kitto. 'And what else should you wish me to do? I presume you want to live? You'll be safe with the Lievens. Castlereagh won't dare try to reach you there: he can't chance antagonising Russia any more than we already have.'

'To be honest, I have no particular desire to live, because I have nothing left to live for, but I should just prefer not to give Lord Castlereagh and the English government the satisfaction of taking my life in some shameful fashion on the scaffold.' Hester snapped.

Crow did not reply and, in truth, she only wanted to be managed by him no longer, to be free of him for ever, because to be near this man was far too dangerous: she couldn't allow herself to feel such extremes of joy and pain, to risk losing again what she had lost before at such unbearable cost. She could find no words to explain this tangle of emotion and so kept her own counsel, staring unthinking at the drizzle-soaked streets of London – undersized children sweeping crossings, emaciated veterans of the Peninsular and American campaigns still clad in their ragged uniforms as they begged on crutches, and the occasional prostitute driven to walk the streets in rouge and stained satin. They reached the Lievens' in silence, greeted by servants astonished at their down-at-heel appearance, but were immediately received by both Count Lieven and Dorothea, who came running from teatime in the drawing-room with their gaggle of sons and their small daughter, Lieven still holding a peg-doll with woollen hair even as they were all shown into his candlelit library. Hester curtseyed with precision at their condolences for Morwenna, but Crow only lit one of his few remaining cigarillos at a candle and went to stand by the window.

'Hester will be quite safe with us, but what will you do, Lamorna?' The count cast a worried glance at Dorothea, who was doing her best not to look astonished at the fact Crow had forgotten himself so much as to smoke in her presence, as though she were some common woman from the street. Hester certainly no longer cared enough to remonstrate with him. 'Castlereagh still holds a great deal too much sway in the Cabinet, in my opinion. In your absence, there have been hangings every day, and not just in Cornwall. What of this mission to bring the tsar's bastard to England? Certainly, it was nothing but a ruse to have you killed well beyond the public eye, but had you succeeded Castlereagh would have been outmanoeuvred. Where is the girl?'

Crow turned to face them with a humourless smile. 'My brother found her first,' he said, 'and he has served me the turn I deserved. Kitto and Nadezhda Kurakina chose not to accompany me to England, despite the danger to her in remaining in Russia.'

'Alexander's brother Nicholas will fear any possible rival to his succession,' Dorothea said quickly, glancing at Hester. 'The tsar is still young, but with his brothers as heirs, no child of Alexander's can consider themselves safe. I have it on fairly good authority that Grand Duke Constantine has no interest in becoming tsar, but Nicholas is quite another prospect entirely. All of the Kurakina girl's foster-family are now dead – queen or not, she would have been safer in England.'

'Perhaps,' Crow said; he was alive with unnatural tension, his eyes constantly travelling between every door and window in the room as if he saw and heard things that others did not; Dorothea and her husband exchanged a silent, horrified glance.

'What will you do, Lamorna?' Count Lieven asked again. 'Do you mean to retreat to Cornwall? Surely Castlereagh will issue a warrant for your arrest wherever you go.'

'Oh, I don't intend to run from him,' Crow said. 'I go to Duke Street now, in point of fact. I only ask that you shelter my wife, and ensure that no harm comes to her. No blame for any of this can be attached to Hester, and under your protection I'm confident she'll be safe.'

Dorothea and the count stared at him in silence. Dorothea actually put both hands to her mouth. 'No,' she said. 'You can't mean that, Jack – really, you can't. How on earth could Kitto have put you in this position – to actually aid and abet the escape of the only person who might have kept you from Castlereagh's reach?'

'We need discuss that no further – I have reaped what I have sown, that's all.' Crow finished his cigarillo and cast the glowing end out of the window left ajar to admit a rose-scented breeze rising from the small garden below.

'What on earth are you actually talking about?' Hester said calmly. 'Duke Street? You can't mean that you go to Castlereagh himself? He'll have you hanged by morning.'

'I shouldn't think so.' Crow spoke still with that disarming lack of expression in his features, as though he wore a mask of his own face. 'He'll want a much larger audience when the time comes. You forget: according to his telling of this story, I've committed high treason.'

'Oh my God,' Dorothea said quietly, and stood a fraction closer to her husband.

Lieven shook his head. 'Lamorna, the man needs to be challenged, not appeased. He holds a great deal too much sway – he's more a despot than a prime minister.'

'Oh, come on,' Crow said. 'Castlereagh will find reasons to keep hanging the innocent Cornish and English alike until he has satisfied whatever demon drives him, and considering he's been given to stringing up supposed recusants since 1798 I doubt there'll be an end to it soon. But with my life extinguished perhaps he'll then be content long enough for the rest of the Cabinet to oust him.'

'No,' Hester said, furious tears springing to her eyes; she could not begin to imagine this insufferably proud man hooded on the scaffold, his lifeless body then hanging for all to see. 'Kitto is so young – he might have been foolish and angry with you, but do you really wish him to have this on his conscience for the rest of his life?'

'Well, we can't have everything, can we?' Crow said. 'You and I both know that by now, my dear. Please don't make a scene by trying to stop me.' He gave her one of his twisted, most devastated smiles, and spoke then in Cornish, so that only she could understand: 'Or worse, by not doing so, my dearest and only love.' And he took Hester's hand in both of his, and raised it to his lips, one last time. She called his name, but he only carried on walking to the door, past the silent footmen who had borne witness to all this, and then Hester was only conscious of Dorothea guiding her to a chaise, and Lieven's voice raised into almost a shout, even though she could no longer understand anything that was said to her, or near her.

59

Two weeks after his arrest in the incongruous surroundings of Lord Castlereagh's drawing-room, where he had noticed odd little details like the very ugly gilded porcelain shepherdess on the mantelpiece, and the oppressive green of the botanical wallpaper Emily had chosen in a fit of passion for Sir Joseph Banks, Crow was taken from his private cell at Newgate and escorted under heavy guard to a barge on the Thames, and from there to the Tower of London, watching the grey river and the gulls tossing above, and coal-smoke drifting against a blue sky. He walked across Tower Green flanked by two guards; they led him over dandelion-studded grass towards the timbered Queen's House, late morning light striking off the multitude of mullioned windows in a way that reminded him acutely of Nansmornow at that same time of day. The light changed as they walked, and he was taken into an entrance hall plastered above and wainscoted below. This house had been built for Anne Boleyn in her early, triumphal days, he knew, but it was here also that she had been condemned to die on her scaffold, and Lady Jane Grey, too, who had been no older than his brother. He remembered sitting cross-legged on the Turkey rug in the schoolroom at Nansmornow listening to a tutor who had always smelled of pear drops and tobacco tell him that before Lady Jane went to her own beheading she stood at the window of her tower-prison, watching her nineteen-year-old husband go by cart to his execution and then return, his head wrapped separately in a cloth. Crow was conscious of being escorted upstairs, and of the mingled scents of beeswax polish rising from three-hundred-year-old oak and one of the gaolers, who released a particularly sharp underarm stink every time he moved. He was led into the Council Chamber where it was said Guido Fawkes and his co-conspirators had been interrogated, and light streamed in through the tall mullioned window at one end, illuminating a high-ceilinged timbered room: white plaster, oak beams, bare floorboards, flames hissing and spitting in a cavernous medieval fireplace. Sitting at a long table of scrubbed oak were most members of the Cabinet, last seen as guests in his own home: Castlereagh himself, fair-haired and handsome and well groomed as ever, contriving to look faintly amused, Sidmouth, old and worried, Nicholas Vansittart, Camden, Westmorland, Mulgrave; the fact that their faces were all so familiar from the earliest days of his youth only added to the dreamlike sense of unreality.

'The duke is too busy to join you all in condemnation?' Crow said, even as the noisome gaoler thrust him into a high-backed wooden chair at the table. His voice sounded queer and cracked; he hadn't spoken to anyone since the start of his incarceration.

Castlereagh replied without even bothering to conceal his hatred. 'Now is hardly the moment for insolence, Lamorna. I'm sure you know quite well that Wellington is in Austria lying in wait for Napoleon's retreating army – for which

Britain and Russia both have you to thank, if we're to take your word for it. Now, after some time to reflect, can you explain to us exactly why the whole of Petersburg is buzzing with gossip that you have sworn yourself to Napoleon? You were sent to Russia to bring us an heir, and yet you returned empty-handed, trailing nothing but unfortunate rumours that question your integrity, your loyalty to England. After the Cornish uprising, surely you can see how bad this all looks, how damaging the cost of your influence is and even your presence to the very fabric of society?'

'Perhaps it would help,' Crow said pleasantly, 'if Englishmen and Cornishmen were treated like the free men they once were? If you had not suspended habeas corpus and the right of the weak not to be incarcerated without charge by the mighty, the population at large might be less inclined to riot, and perhaps then there would not be so much insurrection to actually crush?'

The tension in the room rose palpably. No one could look at him: Vansittart, Sidmouth, not a single man. Westmorland and Harrowby, though both staunch Tories, had been friends with his father since they were all at Eton. Westmorland flicked an invisible fleck of dirt from the cuff of his blue jacket of superfine. Harrowby steepled his freckled fingers together, staring fixedly at a commemorative panel listing the participants in the Gunpowder Plot and their accusers. Crow ignored them all, facing Castlereagh across the table.

'You sound very like a completely unrepentant revolutionary, Lamorna, you must own it,' Castlereagh said.

'Indeed, I'm just a landowner in need of a monarch, Lord Castlereagh. If we want things to go on as they were before the Occupation, we men must at least seem useful to those whose welfare we are responsible for. And it seems to me almost as if the search for an heir has been drawn out to a quite deliberate extent.'

Vansittart nodded. 'It's gone on long enough, I agree, but you were the one meant to bring us an heir, Lamorna, and you failed.'

'And yet the assassin I faced in Russia was no Russian set upon me by the tsar, and not even a Frenchman, but a damned fool of an English boy. How is that, my lord?' Crow was drowned out by an uproar.

'Nonsense,' Camden called out. 'I've never heard such a Banbury tale. You're telling stories just to save yourself, Lamorna – do grow up. And God knows how we are to deal with the frankly appalling mess of your killing Cathcart's son.'

But Westmorland, Harrowby and Sidmouth were all watching Castlereagh, who was still smiling.

'Indeed, my only witness is my wife, and you're unlikely to believe her,' Crow said, and he wished more than anything that there was a way he might secure Hester's safety. No matter how much she had come to loathe him he owed her that, at least. It was surely too late for any other way out of this: he had always been a gambling man, and now it seemed he had gambled and lost.

Castlereagh smiled. 'But there is another mystery here, Lord Lamorna. Do you think we have no intelligence in St Petersburg at all? We know that the Russian chit was last seen with your own brother. So where is she now?'

'I don't know,' Crow said, smiling back.

'Then I think you must be persuaded to remember what happened in perhaps just a little more detail,' Castlereagh said, and Crow saw that although Castlereagh was a dissembling liar who didn't want Nadezhda on British soil at all, neither was he about to pass up an excuse to make Crow endure the extreme end of what a man might bear. Still smiling, Crow wondered what he had done to make this person abandon all reason just in order that he should suffer, and he prayed for the courage to endure what was to come.

60

The cell at the Tower of London they called Little Ease was pitch-dark and too cramped to sit or to lie in, and Crow could only crouch there even as time lost all meaning. Every limb now twitched with agonised convulsion while images of Morwenna's drowned and rotting corpse chased memories of Catlin Rescorla's steady, freckled hands as she poured tincture of opium into a cup of small-ale: he had failed in his most sacred duty, to protect those who depended on him, those who were the most helpless of all. He had a strategy, though: one must count to four hundred, counting through the agony of constricted limbs and twitching, tortured muscle, and only then might one give in and let out the beast-like roar of a man running into battle. At the back of Crow's disordered and destroyed mind, he saw his father in the library at Nansmornow on the day he had come home on leave after the Battle of Vitoria. Papa sat at his desk, just watching Crow through the forest of tall white candles arrayed beside his scattered piles of letters and accounts. *Never forget that your duty is to care for these people, to pass on this name, to steward this land. Let it all die on some battlefield with you if you must, but you will then have betrayed not only generations of your own family, but all those who depend on you.*

Nothing I could do was ever enough for you, was it, Papa? Crow asked in the darkness of his cell, but now in the back of his mind he only saw his father as he had been on his deathbed, gaunt and emaciated, ravaged by the fever contracted as he searched the battlefield at Waterloo for Crow's own remains. *God knows it should have been I who died and you that lived, but here we find ourselves, regardless. Is this enough, Papa, is this enough? I have destroyed it all; how can I even pass on such a tarnished name to the boy?*

Crow's father vanished from his imaginings, replaced by Hester, visible but turning from him in this relentless darkness; she was no more able to bear Morwenna's loss than he was, but surely Hester would be better off without him, free to live alone as she'd wanted to when she'd been a young heiress with a mind of her own. He couldn't stand the thought of her marrying again, of another man so much as taking her hand, ever, and he reached the count of four hundred and began to scream, again and again and again. But by the time the cell door at last opened with a grating crunch of heavy oak scraping across filthy wet gravel, Crow had long given up screaming. He heard muffled voices as he was manhandled from confinement, his limbs stretching with such unbelievable agony that he called out in a cracked and broken voice to the mother of God.

Ignoring the sweaty reek of stale linen last slept in by a dead man, Crow watched the grey chink of sky just visible through the narrow lancet window in his tower cell, anything to eclipse the darkness so recently left behind in Little Ease; so ruined was his flesh that they'd had to half carry him up the winding stone steps to his new quarters. He listened to the rhythm of footfalls outside, boots on damp, hard stone. A key scraped in the lock, and the heavy door swung open, but Crow didn't look around, not even when Lord Vansittart came in with a jaundiced and balding priest.

'You can send the padre away, sir,' Crow said. Why should he confess his sins when God had already punished him with such an acute lack of mercy? He ignored the hurried conference behind him and waited for the spare-featured and balding peer to pull out one of the plain chairs set beneath the lancet. Grey light puddled on the desk; someone had left paper and ink there, a quill.

'You're drunk, Lamorna,' Vansittart said, crossing one booted leg over the other. 'I heard you had been refusing nourishment, but obviously the thirst for wine goes unabated.'

'I count myself lucky to have been born with the sort of name that grants me terrible claret in the White Tower. I feel so distinguished – I must be the first Cornish rebel to be held here since Michael An Gof met his unfortunate fate in 1497. Or – forgive me – am I a French rebel, or just a common traitor? Has anyone actually decided yet?' With all the care of a man nursing cracked sinews and cramped joints, Crow got up and took the seat opposite, pouring the last of the wine into two tin flagons.

'At the moment, Lamorna, you're all three,' Vansittart said. 'Your execution as a traitor and defector to Napoleon himself is exactly the sort of sideshow to quell serious uprising. Why don't you simply give me an excuse to stop this happening?'

'Well,' Crow said, stretching out his legs, 'why would you want to?'

Vansittart sighed. 'You're not the first young man to adopt an attitude of contemptuous levity in the Tower, but I don't doubt you'll feel rather differently on the scaffold. I find Castlereagh so ubiquitous at the moment: what do we want, Castlereagh as another Cromwell? What would you wish, for some grubby Luddite to wrest control from him and put an end to all technological innovation, all industry, condemning us to the fate of an irrelevant island backwater? It might yet happen if we don't play a well-thought-out hand. Your death would be a distraction, but an acceptable heir to the throne even better – at least a chance of getting the country back on to a remotely even keel. Where is Nadezhda Kurakina? Why did you fail?'

'As I've explained to so many people so very many times: my brother found her first,' Crow said, casting around the room for a way to hang or cut himself before he was committed once more to Little Ease. 'What do you want me to say? No matter how long you confine me in that place, I can say no more.'

'You must understand that we do actually need to find a way of ousting Castlereagh.' Vansittart leaned back in his chair, shaking his head, looking every one of his sixty years even as he failed to show the slightest sign of discomfiture at admitting to the torture of a man whose father he had played bridge with every third Thursday, even if his motives were at least rationally political, unlike Castlereagh with all his obscure hatred of anyone who bore the Lamorna name. 'Why will you not cooperate?'

'In truth,' Crow said, 'I no longer care about any of it. You can all go to the devil, and I've no more to say. My child drowned on the *Curlew*, all for Castlereagh's suspicions, and my own very sorry reputation. She lived scarcely more than a year, and she died in utter terror: what have I to live for? Take me to your gallows whenever you please, I don't care.' Raising the cup, he drank the last of his wine.

It was easier to consider how morning light struck the curving silvery sides of the bowl, and how the dull silken peach-coloured petals seemed almost to absorb light, than it was to imagine Crow enduring the final weeks of his life, his final days, and yet still he would not see her. Hester was painting a pewter dish full of shade-loving roses when she heard Dorothea's butler approaching at a hurried pace and the door swung open, bringing cold air.

'Lord Castlereagh,' said the manservant, and Hester froze in her chair, horrified to see that he had come in alone, tall and fair and well dressed as ever, and most decidedly without Dorothea.

'Oh no, Lady Lamorna – don't trouble yourself to get up.' Castlereagh spoke with all his usual slow, lazy ease, quite as though he hadn't ordered the slaughter of her innocent servants at Nansmornow, and her husband were not now awaiting execution at his command, and her child and her dearest Catlin not drowned as they fled the long reach of his vengeance. In her seat before the fire, Hester turned to look at him, still holding the brush. He smiled, crossing the rug towards her, and she stood, pushing back her chair so swiftly that it shrieked across the waxed floorboards.

'Come now, my dear,' Lord Castlereagh said, 'is there really any need for you to look at me as though I were a monster? You have nothing to fear from me. In point of fact, I have a proposition for you. Well, perhaps more a reminder of a bargain I once suggested we make.'

'A proposition?' Hester said coldly. He might as well have killed Catlin and Morwenna with his own hands. He deserved to suffer; he deserved to die, and she began to notice odd details about the room – a childish watercolour of a boat at harbour propped on the mantelpiece, pale blue cornflowers drooping in a copper vase on the windowsill: anything not to look at him, this murderer.

Lord Castlereagh advanced upon her and drew out one of the other Queen Anne chairs set near the table. Still smiling, he sat down, leaning closer to her, so close, in fact, that he laid one warm hand upon her leg, as though she were a servant, a slave, a concubine, his for the taking. 'I'm sure you must be so very concerned about your husband,' he said.

'Kindly remove your hand' – Hester spoke with quiet, furious calm – 'before I scream.'

'I really would recommend you don't do that.' Castlereagh leaned closer still, sliding his hand further up her thigh towards her groin. 'I'm sure you're wondering how you might possibly aid Lord Lamorna. He's in quite a terrible plight, isn't he? I'm afraid he won't escape justice for treason, but with a little forethought – a little consideration – you might ensure that his execution takes place in private, sparing him the humiliation of a public hanging. You know, I heard quite the most ridiculous little rumour that it was actually you who shot the French guards on the day that young Captain Helford escaped his own hanging, all those years ago now. You can be sure there will be no such opportunity this time.' He smiled. 'You know, I'm sure, the bodily effects of a hanging. So unsavoury.'

Hester swallowed hot bile. 'If you'll receive me,' she said, 'I'll call upon you at home.' It didn't matter what happened to her now, after all.

Castlereagh smiled again. Tucking his forefinger beneath her chin, he turned her to face him. 'Good girl,' he said. 'I'm glad to see that you begin to understand. No, no – don't get up. *Adieu* then, Lady Lamorna.' He patted her cheek, bowed and went out, as though they had just discussed no more than the arrangements for an excursion to Hyde Park, and Hester was left alone. It was a long time before she schooled herself into at least the appearance of calm, and her hands had stopped shaking so that she was able to pick up her paintbrush once more, but by that time the light had changed, and all colour had drained from the rose petals.

61

Two hundred miles from Dorothea Lieven's white stucco Mayfair townhouse and thirty miles from the Cornish mainland, summer reigned over an archipelago of rocky, windswept islands with silvery beaches, stone houses and bounteous vegetable gardens all hidden from the north-easterly wind behind hedges of tangled broom and dog rose. Fishermen mended nets on the great stone quay at Hugh-town on St Mary's, idly watching sun-browned children row kists of salted mackerel to aged relatives stubbornly crofting the off-islands. A mile and a half across open water, Catlin Rescorla was knee-deep in the monks' herb bed at the Priory of St Nicholas on the holy island of Trescaw. It had been a dry summer, and leggy dandelions colonised the comfrey; beyond the reaches of the garden, the marram grass was blue with those exotic flowers one of the brothers had brought with him from foreign parts before taking the cloth. They'd gone wild since Catlin's girlhood on Bryher across the water, those bright flowers, seeds blowing on the wind away from the grey bulk of the priory, so that now they grew in violet swathes right down to the wide white sands and the glittering sea beyond.

'Cat, see!'

'What is it, maid?' Catlin winced as she straightened her back, idly passing her weeding fork to the child lining up pebbles in the dust at her feet. Brother Anselm was hurrying down one of the steep paths, looking for all the world like a purposeful rook in his dusty black Benedictine robes, even though he was a young lad of no more than twenty. It had been Anselm who'd found Catlin and the maid hiding in the watery cave at Piper's Hole across the far side of the island. Till she lay on her deathbed, Catlin would never forget the sheer cold terror of seeing a man in dark robes approach across the distant heath, of scrambling down among the rocks with the child in her arms and white surf crashing below before they gained the cave. She'd crouched in the dark, clinging to the maid. But in the end it had been only Brother Anselm, stumbling and slipping on the black rocks in his long robes and salt-stained sandals, first of all just leaving cloth-wrapped parcels of bread and hard cheese and last year's wrinkled apples.

'Mistress Rescorla!' Brother Anselm stopped now a few paces away from the herb garden, sweat fairly dripping down his great beak of a nose. 'Father Thomas wants to see you.'

Catlin stared at him. So this was it. They'd lured her in from Piper's Hole with promises of safe harbour all that time ago, but in the end the monks were just as afraid of Lord Castlereagh as everyone else. She swooped on the maid, picking her up, holding her close.

'Nothing to be afraid of,' Brother Anselm said, smiling but nervy. 'There's no English soldiers, nothing like that.'

'Then what is it?' Catlin said. The child waved the gardening fork with such wild abandon that she nearly crowned Brother Anselm with it, and Catlin had to prise it from her grasp. 'Hush now, maid. Don't fret.'

'I don't rightly know, Mistress Rescorla, but a message came across from St Mary's when we were at morning prayers, and Father said you must see him without delay. I'll finish this patch of weeding.'

'Ansom!' The maid reached out for him, and Brother Anselm popped his finger in his cheek at her; he'd left eight younger brothers and sisters behind in Essex, so he said. Morwenna was growing hale and heavy, and Catlin set her down gratefully, leaving her to run unsteadily to the young monk, her woollen skirts whisking through the dust. Hester had never seen her run. Leaving them both behind, Catlin hurried up the sandy, rock-strewn path to the priory with tears in her eyes, sure that she had done wrong in hiding for so long, but without the smallest notion of what she could have done instead. Lord Lamorna was like to be hanged, it was said: they'd heard that much out here on the islands. He'd go to the gallows thinking his child and wife had drowned on the *Curlew*, never knowing that Hester had fled Hugh-town all those months ago, or that his daughter was safe here on Scilly. He'd never know of Catlin's own awful quarter-hour hell of indecision on the quayside as folk started to board the *Curlew* with all those English soldiers milling about, poking their noses into everything, sniffing around like so many dog foxes. And then Catlin had gone and done it, made this choice she'd never since been sure was right, even when news of the wreck came: she had marched straight up to the *Curlew*'s purser with Morwenna in her arms and signed her own name on the passenger manifest, alongside Lady Lamorna's, and Lady Morwenna Helford's (infant), before losing both herself and the maid in the crowd at the quayside, climbing straight down the granite steps at the far end of the quay, and rowing hard across the sound from St Mary's to Trescaw in a dinghy that had belonged to Hester's father, left on its mooring from affection to him. It hadn't even been stealing.

Catlin found Father Thomas not in his cell, but in the little rose garden just outside the refectory where the brothers took their meals. He was a tall old man, broad-shouldered and with a shock of white hair – some sixth son of a nobleman who'd pledged his life more closely to God than his aristocratic family ever intended, giving up a rich living in Rutland for the quiet of this far-flung priory. He was deadheading the yellow roses with fingers thick and gnarled as oak, so absorbed in his task that he didn't at first look up as Catlin approached. 'Father?' she said. 'You sent for me.'

He looked up and smiled, frowning a little. 'Mistress Rescorla. Forgive me – I find it's easier to speak to God in this garden than anywhere else, and I confess I was lost in thought. I hope you know that you and the child are welcome to sanctuary at the priory for as long as you so choose. I see no possible reason for a serving-woman and a child to be embroiled in accusations of aristocrats fomenting revolution, or of treachery, but I have this morning received news which may change your position.'

Catlin couldn't look away; she felt small and powerless in the face of his fierce blue eyes, and that ridged nose. 'What is it, then, Father?'

'You've been much troubled over Lord and Lady Lamorna believing that the child drowned in the wreck of the

Curlew – as, I confess, have I. Lord Lamorna we know is certainly in prison in London; his wife's whereabouts is still uncertain.'

'I daren't write to him, Father,' Catlin said. 'Even in Cornish – even in cipher. Surely every letter is read by his guards? There's nothing to be done that I can see, wicked though it seems, not without putting the child at risk. Lord Castlereagh is that cruel, I'd put nothing past him.'

Father Thomas snipped a withered rose, letting the head fall into the basket. 'What if I were to tell you, Mrs Rescorla, that Captain Helford has been seen disembarking from the *Brieuze* in Fowey, in the company of a Russian soldier, and took the fast mail coach to the capital?'

'I'd say he's like to be arrested the moment he sets foot in London,' Catlin said: she'd long ago learned that hope could be a very foolish indulgence.

'I'm afraid it's very likely he's in town already,' Father Thomas said. 'This news must be close to a week old: we heard it by chance when the mail-boat came this morning.'

'But if he's not, and I write to him, there's just a chance Lord Lamorna might hear the maid's safe before they hang him?' Catlin said. 'And Captain Helford will never tell a soul save his brother where she is.'

'It would be an act of mercy, my child, would it not?' said Father Thomas, and even as Catlin knew there could be no doubt he was right, she couldn't help but be afraid that the cost of easing the last days of one man's life might be a heavy burden to his daughter, and to herself.

62

'Hester?' Dorothea came into the morning-room trailing her shawl, her gown hanging in graceful folds down to her blue kid slippers, and although she was obviously full of news, her smile swiftly disappeared. 'Why was Lord Castlereagh here?' She stood at Hester's chair, frowning at the unfinished painting, white canvas biting into the soft warmth of half-painted peach-gold rose petals. 'I was quite distracted by the children – if I'd only known he planned to visit in such an unannounced and odd fashion, I should never have left you to face him alone. What on earth did he want?'

Hester drew in a long, shuddering breath. 'I'm not at all sure. To gloat, perhaps? I think his senses are quite disordered. How are the children? Is Paul's fever any better? I'm so sorry.'

Dorothea shook her head, distracted. 'He's much better, I thank you. But that's not it at all— Hester, there's someone to see you – someone else – we're only lucky that Lord Castlereagh left when he did.'

'Dorothea, you're not making any sense,' Hester said. 'Please, I can stand no more mysteries.' She suppressed a wild flame of hope: had Crow been released?

Dorothea shook her head. 'Oh, but you're quite right – indeed I hardly know what to do with myself.' She turned to the footman waiting by the door. 'James, perhaps it's best if you just bring them in.' Her lips twitched into a sudden smile that Hester wanted to slap off her face. 'In fact, our visitor has come to see you in particular, Hester.'

'I don't at all comprehend—' Hester began, but Dorothea's butler came in, and before he even announced the callers, Hester saw a sharp-featured boy with curling hair and an expression of shielded hostility, accompanied by a tall, filthy and unshaven young officer, so travel-stained that his uniform of the Coldstream Regiment was almost unrecognisable. She got up, pushing back the chair with undisguised violence; she had to cling to the edge of the table.

'Hets?' Kitto said, standing very still, staring at Hester as though she had risen from the grave. '*Hets*.'

'You look an absolute disgrace,' Hester said, battling tears. He was here, here at last. 'Kitto, how could you?'

'It wasn't his fault.' The strange young man at Kitto's side looked from Hester to Dorothea and back, quite undaunted. 'Kitto only did what he thought was right.' With the flickering intensity of a battle-seasoned soldier, the boy glanced around Dorothea's drawing-room, assessing his distance from every door, every window.

'Nadia, leave this to me,' Kitto said quickly. He looked so sorry, and so exhausted, that Hester longed to cross the room and shake him.

'Nadia?' Hester said instead, his words only now sinking in. 'Nadia?'

Kitto and the boy looked at one another with equally unspoken meaning, and Dorothea stepped forwards, smoothing out her gown. 'Lady Lamorna,' she said, 'might I introduce Nadezhda Sofia Kurakina? Your husband, I should imagine, will be so glad that she has chosen to visit London.'

Hester summoned every ounce of composure she possessed, and held out her hand for the boy – this girl – to shake. 'I'm delighted to make your acquaintance.'

'Indeed I'm quite sure you're not,' the girl said quickly, and Hester could see how this child had passed for so long as a young soldier, with her spare features and narrow, boyish frame, but now she knew the truth it was immediately obvious: of course she was a girl, a wiry, tousled girl, but a girl all the same, and despite everything Hester felt a burst of shocking pity for her because she looked so frightened, so unhappy, and so young.

Dorothea smiled as though she'd just been forced to introduce someone's wife to his mistress. 'Please be assured that my husband is already in possession of all the documents and correspondence pertaining to your parentage, Miss Kurakina. It's fortunate that your parents wrote to each other frequently. Before your mother's murder during the French Occupation of England, the tsar and Princess Sophia exchanged letters, portraits and sketches with your adoptive parents; we anticipate no challenge to your identity. We have papers legitimising your birth as a result of a secret marriage between Princess Sophia and one of Alexander's deceased cousins. Captain Helford, you and Miss Kurakina will both reside here in the embassy until this matter is resolved. I think that seems best, no?'

'We must go,' Kitto said, desperate. 'We must go to Jack at once.'

The boy – the girl – gave only a curt nod.

'I'm afraid Count Lieven has said exactly the same thing,' Dorothea went on with all her usual smooth assurance. 'Miss Kurakina, we can hardly present you to the Cabinet in your current condition. Pray come with me. I'm sure Lady Lamorna and Captain Helford have much to discuss.'

Nadezhda exchanged another pregnant glance with Kitto, not displaying the slightest sign of enthusiasm at the prospect of hair tongs, ribbons, corsets or any amount of snowy muslin. Still without a word, she was first to look away, setting back her shoulders as she followed Dorothea to the door. Kitto took great interest in the window, and in the shifting green leaves of a beech tree that cast shade over the railed, oval garden in the middle of the square, and Hester realised with complete exasperation that they were both, in a quiet way, entirely broken-hearted at leaving one another. Only when Nadezhda had gone out with Dorothea did Kitto turn back to her, his face resolute.

'Hester, indeed I'm sorry,' he said. 'You mustn't blame Nadezhda. She never wanted to come to England or to have any part of this at all, but she told me that I couldn't do this to Crow on her account. I was so—'

'So desperately angry with him?' Hester supplied, and she did not say the rest: *So desperately angry with him, and so in love with her.* Instead, she put out her arms, and Kitto held her so close that for a moment it was hard to breathe, the nearest he had to a mother, as she knew very well.

'For the longest time I thought you were dead as well,' he said, speaking into her hair, and she knew that he knew about Morwenna, that she was gone. 'Hets, I'm sorry.'

Hester could do nothing but hold him: soon, very soon, he would be all that remained. Crow was lost to her, and Morwenna, too, and she knew very well there would be no life beyond her assignation with Lord Castlereagh; even if she might buy a less hideous death for her husband, she had no intention of living with the shame of what she was about to do. She hoped that God would forgive her.

63

Kitto battled a vivid and dizzying sense of unreality as the carriage drew up outside the Byward Gate at the Tower of London, the Kentish ragstone walls pale and bright in late summer light that winked off the stinking, gull-blown waters of the Thames beyond. He fought a sickening broadside of dread and panic at the prospect of facing Crow as a condemned prisoner, glad only that Hester would remember her husband as proud and as insufferable as he'd always been. She'd scarcely looked at him as they left the Lievens', almost as though she were afraid to, or she had wanted to conceal something from him in those agonising moments of farewell, when words had fallen like stones to the marble floor. Wouldn't it be worse for her and Dorothea, with nothing to do but sit in that quiet drawing-room and wait? Nadezhda herself sat in silence, almost unrecognisable in a pale muslin gown, so vulnerable with her thin brown arms and a ribbon carefully threaded through her cropped curls, and still with the ever-alert posture of a partisan soldier. Count Lieven smiled at her, and spoke reassuringly in Russian, but she only nodded, looking as though she wanted to crawl out of the window and disappear into the Thames.

You're sacrificing yourself for my brother, he'd said to her as they lay beneath the night in the Nogai camp, only their fingertips touching. *You hardly know him.*

I'm not doing it for him, Nadezhda had replied, giving him an odd look that would haunt him in all the years that came afterwards. *I'm doing it for you. And I don't care what anyone says, but that's the truth.*

The carriage drew to a halt, and they all sat speechless. 'Very well,' Lieven said at last, nodding at Kitto, 'I'm sure I need not tell you to leave this to me, Captain Helford.'

'I betrayed him,' Kitto said. 'What else is there to say?'

Lieven frowned and, without another word, climbed out of the carriage as his liveried postillion held open the door, helping Nadezhda out afterwards. She tripped on her gown, steadied by the ambassador's gentle touch at her elbow. She stood frozen on the cobbles in the heat of the sun like a rat trapped by an adder making ready to strike, and Kitto knew that she felt as naked and vulnerable without a weapon as he did. Goose pimples rose on her lean, muscled arms exposed to the wind by the short muslin sleeve of her dress as liveried guards crossed Tower Green to meet them, all tramping feet and creaking leather; it felt like a fevered dream.

'This is grotesque,' Nadezhda said quietly. 'I feel grotesque. Oh God.'

'It's all right,' he said, unconvincing even to himself, 'it's going to be all right,' and then they stepped from the light fresh morning into the Tudor gloom of the Queen's House. There really were never any half-measures with Crow. *Only you would end as a prisoner in the Tower of London,* Kitto thought, incomprehensibly furious. With Lieven and the guards bringing up the rear, Kitto followed Nadezhda up a wide staircase; she clutched at the encumbering muslin skirts with her horsewoman's fingers, so quick and deft, and what would they find in the Council Chamber, where the Cabinet had agreed to meet Lieven? Crow already sentenced to die? Kitto couldn't fight a growing certainty that Nadezhda's sacrifice wouldn't make any difference when all was said and done, that she'd given up her freedom for nothing. By not immediately surrendering her into Crow's jurisdiction, Kitto himself had given Castlereagh the ammunition he needed to ensure Crow's downfall: this was about nothing so much as appearances, and now it was too late. Kitto heard an unfamiliar voice announce Lieven, and then his own name, but even as they were ushered forward into a high-ceilinged timbered hall, Nadezhda herself was not mentioned, as though she did not matter at all. Blinded by sudden light pouring in through a tall, mullioned window, Kitto's eyes adjusted to the sight of a long table flanked on either side by powerful men in carefully tailored coats and cravats – Vansittart, Castlereagh himself, indeed half the Cabinet sat here, men who had been friends with Papa, who had slept night after night at Nansmornow, taking their meat and claret at Crow's own table.

Crow himself sat in the middle of them all, facing the fireplace, casting no more than a single disinterested glance in Kitto's direction, and Kitto had to fight not to cry out, because he looked so much older. His dark hair was now even seamed with silver above one ear, although he was only twenty-eight. Kitto longed to demand what they had done to him, but knew he couldn't, and he endured a rush of shame and sorrow so intense that for a moment it was hard to remain standing in that room. *Hester is dead,* Crow had said, there in the woods as they fled Chudovo, and Kitto had left him, he had walked away and left him, knowing. Nadezhda and Lieven were ushered to seats at the table; Lieven had unfolded his leather document case and on either side of him Lords Vansittart and Camden both frowned over a drift of unfolded letters yellowed with age.

Everyone else was watching Kitto, expectant, all except Crow, who just looked momentarily even more exhausted and said, 'For God's sake, boy, sit.' He turned to Castlereagh, who was now leaning back in his chair, looking at Nadezhda with a complete lack of expression. 'What's wrong, my lord, isn't this exactly what you wanted?' Crow went on, gently. 'Nadezhda Kurakina is here, as you requested.'

'This speaks only of your brother's loyalty and sense of duty, not your own,' Castlereagh said smoothly. 'That, or the ambition of Miss Kurakina.'

'I have no desire to be your queen, or even your political pawn, but I have even less desire for another man's life to sit on my conscience,' Nadezhda said. 'I am here, and so Captain Helford's brother should go free.' She spoke in French but she might just as well have spoken in Russian, for the men only glanced at her as if she were some sort of mechanical curiosity like one of the clockwork monkeys from Astley's Amphitheatre.

Kitto caught the warning in Crow's expression and said nothing.

'It can hardly be suggested that the girl came of her own free choice,' Lieven said quickly. 'I'm sure you'll all appreciate that this is going to be difficult enough to smooth over with the tsar as it is – but in the interests of keeping our friend Napoleon in check, I'm naturally willing to make the effort should the Cabinet be agreeable to it. Miss Kurakina's disappearance is already causing great consternation in Petersburg. Even more so than the death of Lord Cathcart's son, in such suspicious circumstances. Nevertheless, we must also appreciate the fact that it was Lord Lamorna's quick action that enabled the safe evacuation of Petersburg, even as Napoleon retreated.'

'Not just that!' Kitto could no longer contain himself. 'He told Napoleon that Alexander had sworn himself to Britain finally and irrevocably even though he hadn't yet even done that – Napoleon only retreated because he thought he'd be outnumbered.'

'And if you can get them to believe that,' Crow said lazily, 'you'll have my eternal respect.'

Kitto knew then that Crow walked towards his own death with open arms.

'Oh, pull yourself together,' Crow said to him in Cornish, but he was smiling, and Kitto found that he couldn't breathe. Vansittart passed him a cup of wine, but he got up and fled to the window and stood facing it in a vain attempt to collect himself.

'Quite,' Castlereagh said. 'Regardless of all this messy business about the French, given the disturbance Lord Lamorna elicits everywhere he goes, does it not seem wisest to make an example of him, whether or not we have an heir who might be made acceptable to the populace? Captain Helford, come and sit down.'

Kitto put his hands to his face, then clasped the cold stone windowsill, and went to take his seat once more, his distress so clearly visible to everyone in the room that he was sure he would never forget the shame. Beneath the table, Nadezhda took his hand in her own.

'Well, it's gratifying at least to have the measure of one's own brother,' Crow said, incomprehensibly. 'Make sure you don't give in to Thomas Simmens about the lower farm. The man's entirely a chancer – the Trewarthens have held it well enough since the 1650s. And don't listen to Greaves about the copper seam at Wheal Barn, either. Or marry before you feel you must.'

'No—' Kitto said, quite winded with grief, but Lord Sidmouth interrupted, holding up one liver-spotted hand for silence.

'What did you mean, Lamorna, when you said that you were glad you had the measure of the boy?'

'Only that he did exactly what I hoped, and what I expected of him, knowing him as I do.' Crow looked at Kitto then, but his expression gave nothing away. 'It's true – you behaved just as I knew you would when I harangued you in the unsporting way that I did, south of Chudovo. You left, taking Miss Kurakina as far from me as you thought you could get. I would've been disappointed had you acted in any other way, you hot-tempered, entirely unmanageable young malcontent.'

Kitto stared at him with everything to say but no power to speak, as did every other person in the room.

'Jack,' Lord Vansittart said wearily, 'what do you mean by this? You actually intended Miss Kurakina to come to London under Captain Helford's escort instead of your own?'

Crow sighed. 'It's not as complicated as you all seem to think.' He turned to address Sidmouth, Camden and the others, ignoring Lord Castlereagh. 'I was meant to fail in my mission. Why else was my account at Coutts embargoed by Castlereagh himself? Why else was I followed and shot by a damned fool of a young man filled with delusions of grandeur by people far more intelligent than he was? God knows I pity his poor father, who will never get over it. But in those circumstances, how far do you think I'd have got with

Miss Kurakina? I could offer her scant protection. I should have led her only into danger, and perhaps to her own death as well as my own.' Crow turned to Kitto. 'By the time I found my brother, I was a wanted man. It's only fortunate for you that Captain Helford's loyalties are so bound to England that having encountered me in Napoleon's camp, he didn't trust me to bring Miss Kurakina to London, and did it himself. The use of my visit to Napoleon you must decide for yourselves.'

Kitto opened his mouth to speak, but fell silent at the look on Crow's face.

'Well, that seems incontrovertible, at least,' Lord Vansittart said, to a low-voiced rumble of agreement from up and down the table.

Castlereagh smiled, sitting still as a spider, and Crow watched from the far side of the table, with just the same wholly deceptive nonchalance as if he were about to destroy him at hazard or faro. 'You can argue about what I said to Napoleon for as long as you like, and in whose interests, but the facts remain that he ordered Davout into retreat, and Petersburg was saved, and the entire North Sea isn't at this moment full of French warships. Doesn't anyone else care why Lord Castlereagh is so reluctant to find an heir that might be acceptable to Britain that he should send me to Russia to die in pursuit of the one still-living royal offshoot not tainted at some stage by association with Napoleon?'

Kitto could only watch him, along with the entire Council Chamber, so winded by outrage and relief that he couldn't speak. Crow just sat back in his chair as though he were waiting for someone to suggest they join the women in the drawing-room after dinner.

'Well, this at least leaves us in no doubt as to Captain

Helford's loyalty,' Lord Vansittart said, at last. He turned to Castlereagh. 'Robert, I'm afraid I wholly reject the notion that the boy is complicit in anything Lamorna might have done. He brought the girl to England.'

Kitto only looked at Crow. 'You did it on purpose?' he demanded in Cornish, because this was between he and his brother alone. 'You deliberately made me so angry that I ran away with Nadezhda?'

'It was really quite easy,' Crow said. 'Actually, it was indefensible, and I'm sorry. Do try and be less foolish, won't you?' He turned to Lord Vansittart. 'Might I beg the favour of a moment alone with my brother before returning to my cell?'

'A young officer allowed to meet alone with a traitor – is that really wise?' Castlereagh said smoothly, and Kitto wondered what on earth they had all done to make this man loathe them so much.

'It's surely better that you don't, for the boy's sake, Jack,' Lord Vansittart said, and Crow only shrugged.

'Let me, damn it,' Kitto said.

'Now then, you must do as I say, even if you won't listen to anyone else,' Crow said. '*Va-t-en, Christophe*. Go.'

Lieven and his father's friend Lord Vansittart walked beside Kitto to the door, with Nadezhda behind them, and he remembered very little after that until they reached the carriage. With Count Lieven watching them both, Nadezhda couldn't touch him, or he her, and Kitto realised that Lieven had been talking to him for some time, and he hadn't heard a word.

'Well,' Lieven went on, 'whatever one thinks of your brother, Helford, he comprehensively exonerated you there. I'm sure there'll be no difficulty about rejoining your regiment when the time comes.'

Kitto found that he could not reply, and was only glad that the slight pressure of Nadezhda's little finger against his as they sat side by side allowed him to rein in every shattered emotion. Soon she would be gone, drawn into a world of palaces and court intrigue, where he could never follow, and they would never again ride with the wind in their hair, or at least not together.

64

Hester knew quite well that walking alone through London at night from the Lievens' to St James's Square was by far the most dangerous thing she'd ever done, more likely to kill her even than shooting people, which, she thought grimly, had become almost a habit since her marriage. She gripped the pistol even now, primed and ready to load, held at her side and concealed in the folds of the walking habit of ombre serge as she made her way down the wide pavement. The moon had risen and was nearly full, and on reaching the wide square she kept to the shadows cast by the houses. The Castlereaghs' windows were dark and shuttered, just as he had promised. She had only a scant few hours between the time the servants finally went to bed and rose again; the Lievens' had been wreathed in thick black silence as the house slept, Kitto so silently inconsolable that evening that he could neither eat nor see anyone. Hester was sure that had it been remotely possible for him to be alone with Nadezhda, she would have known how to comfort him. Supper had been taken on a tray in her room, a soup of fresh peas and cream, honeyed strawberries in a dish; Nadezhda had dined alone with the Lievens, and Hester had heard the occasional burst of rapid-fire Russian rising up the stairs from the dining-room. Nadezhda seemed to be on far more intimate terms with their hosts than one would suppose for a girl who had only just met them, and dressed as a soldier.

Crossing the silent square, Hester at last reached the house, and swiftly went down the ill-swept steps at the front, treading on last autumn's dead leaves. The scullery door had been left open, as Castlereagh had promised in his note, and Hester turned the cast-iron handle, stepping into a corridor black as the bottom of a coal scuttle. This unlocked door was her only way in, but she was sure it could easily also condemn her; Castlereagh had surely not gone into his own servants' quarters to turn the key himself: there was already at least one witness to her visit. But she couldn't think about that now, about what the consequences of all this might be. Now, all she could do was to hope that Castlereagh's Emily really had gone to their Kentish retreat at North Cray, and that he was alone. The entire London house would be in darkness, every lamp and every candle extinguished, all except one, as he waited for her.

Hester closed the door, one hand on the wall, flakes of damp whitewash loosening beneath her fingertips, seized by a sudden childish terror of wolf spiders and rats, and in the back of her mind she heard Catlin's voice: *Don't be daft.* Catlin wouldn't have been afraid, and even if she had, she would have continued regardless; one could always count on Catlin to do what needed to be done. Hester forced herself to place one jean-booted foot before the other, to carry on walking – more than once, her fingertips brushed doorframes and cold brass doorknobs, but after striking her head hard on a shelf of jars in what turned out to be a larder, she sensed her way towards the heart of the house – first towards the warmth of the kitchen, still lit with the warm yellow glow of the banked-down fire, then on up the stairs. There would likely be a mastiff dozing somewhere in the family quarters of the house, and she dared not leave this dark warren of servants' passageways.

One step at a time, unable to see even her own foot, she counted the narrow, winding flights of stairs until she came to the third floor. The servants' entrance to Castlereagh's bedchamber was likely through his dressing-room, which would be in darkness by now, and indistinguishable. Now there was no choice: feeling her way along the wall until she touched a baize-covered door, Hester turned the handle and stepped out into a wide hallway, moonlight spilling across Indian rugs from a tall window. She caught the faint scent of potted tuberose and crossed the hallway in silence; one door was outlined with the faintest glow of candlelight, as though it had been drawn with witchcraft or marsh-light. Hester shivered: she felt oddly weightless, as though blown along on a rising wind like a puff of white dandelion seed, all quite beyond her own control, because surely she could not be about to offer herself to Lord Castlereagh. When she pushed open the door, she found him in an armchair near the fire with a quilted vermilion smoking jacket over his clothes, legs crossed, in idle contemplation of the flames. With mocking courtesy, he stood up as she closed the door behind her.

'My dear,' he said, 'how happy I am that you came. Such a privilege.'

There had been no choice, as they both well knew. He gestured to the chair before the fire and Hester sat, numb, breathing in the lingering scent of his presence: stale tobacco and port. He had been drinking, he with his head like a marble

Greek statue, and well-moulded, wine-stained lips, and she wondered how so fair and handsome a face could belong to a man with so wicked a heart.

'I've looked forward to this for a long time.' He smiled, standing before her. 'If only we could have done this sooner, Hester, so much sorrow might have been avoided. Claire was just the same. She refused me, too. Such a sad waste. She would have been better with me than Lamorna, instead of bleeding to death in that terrible fashion, bearing a child to a man who sired them upon his servants.'

Claire. Hester understood with a cold jolt that he was talking about Crow and Kitto's mother and father, just as he had done before. He was really very drunk, she realised. He held out one hand, as though he had asked her to dance at an assembly. She took it, recoiling at the light pressure of his touch; never again would she take Crow by the hand as he had surely taken Countess Tatyana Orlova's, and as Castlereagh himself had perhaps once led the previous Lady Lamorna down some long-ago dance, when the men had worn white powdered wigs and the women hooped dresses of satin and brocade, and French soil was red with the blood of revolution. Standing in the firelight, Castlereagh pulled her close to him.

'My dear,' he said, 'there's no need to cry.' He bowed slightly, leaning closer, and very gently kissed her neck. 'Didn't I tell you I've always had a yearning to taste such exotic fruit,' he went on, and Hester had to remind herself to breathe as he placed one hand on her shoulder, running it down her arm, then spreading his fingers across her corseted breast, brushing naked skin. 'You're not the Lady Lamorna I thought was mine, but perhaps it's better this way. I wanted her so very badly, you see,' he whispered. 'My Claire. She was mine.'

Hester forced herself to speak. 'My lord, I think we'd be more comfortable upon the bed, no?'

'Of course, you're right,' he said, and Hester's fingers shook as she unlaced the silken cord of his smoking jacket, easing the heavy embroidered silk from his well-made shoulders so that it fell to the polished floorboards at his feet, leaving him standing before her in breeches, waistcoat and shirt. She was quicker with his cravat, although the heat of his breath against her face churned her stomach: he was closer to her height than Crow's, and they were face to face. Smiling, she unbuttoned his shirt, just a little.

'Ah,' he said, 'so you like to take control, you well-taught little slut?'

'Indeed I do,' Hester said, and allowed him to kiss her on the lips although his hot, wet, pressing tongue sickened her. Stepping closer, she pushed him lightly on to the bed, so that he lay on his back. He had really left her with no choice but to do this. Hester leaned forwards, kissing him again, and even as Lord Castlereagh held her in his arms, she allowed the small knife to slip from the long sleeve of her gown until it lay beside him on the counterpane, quite unnoticed even as she placed all her weight on the other arm in order to free the little pearl-handled blade from the leather inlaid sheath. Reaching low, between his legs, with her other hand, Hester said, 'Are you ready, my lord?' And when he said yes, oh yes, she pushed the blade with extreme precision into the side of his neck, severing the artery even as his hot blood splashed into her face.

65

Crow no longer slept for any length of time; after all, he was soon to rest in perpetuity. He lay on his back upon the narrow bed, contemplating the slow dance of dust motes caught in afternoon light streaking in through the tall lancet window. He thought of the family chapel at Nansmornow, and Reverend Tregarthen alternately boring and terrorising his congregation in the village church, and the Methodists singing in Newlyn before Captain Wentworth had given the command to fire at will into their chapel. He was not at all sure he believed in the concept of heaven but wished that he did, and in any case he'd scarcely earned a place there: Morwenna had died so cold, and so afraid, and he would be as far from her in death as he now was in life. He had always been painfully surprised at how the very young might be comforted by nothing more than one's presence and one's embrace: first Kitto, then Morwenna. It was so exactly like Castlereagh to make him suffer by waiting to hear the date and time of his execution that Crow didn't move when he at last heard footfalls in the stone passageway outside his cell, and that metallic scrape of a key in the lock, and bolts drawn back, one after another, until the door swung open. He couldn't bear the thought of Castlereagh's satisfied smile were the man to hear that he'd been even slightly disconcerted, but it wasn't one of the prison guards who now came in. Instead, Lord Vansittart walked in alone and looked down at Crow in ill-disguised exasperation.

'Quickly,' he said, 'get up and come with me.'

'Indeed I'm not going to the gallows like this. Wait for me to shave, and I'll have a clean shirt, at least.'

Vansittart sighed. 'Much as you were born to be hanged, Jack, and much as I believe you would actually welcome the prospect of extinction, I'm afraid I must disappoint you. Castlereagh has beaten you to it.'

Crow didn't move, allowing himself to feel nothing at all. 'What?'

'It's only fortunate for you and Captain Helford that your whereabouts can be unequivocally attested – yours in particular, boy.' Vansittart walked to the table, surprisingly limber for a man of such advanced years, taking Crow's jacket from the back of the chair with an impatient twitch of his spare, fleshless fingers. 'Put this on, and don't waste any more time. Castlereagh was stabbed last night. I've no desire to learn what in God's name Sidmouth holds over Castlereagh's doctor, but so far he has the damned fellow swearing on a heap of bibles that the man was insane, and took his own life. This country is volatile enough without more murder at the highest level of government.'

Crow got up then and took his jacket, fighting the bizarre sense that this was some kind of waking dream, as though he had smoked opium. 'But then who did kill him?'

'I haven't the smallest notion, and in any case it's a matter of complete irrelevance – the very streets of London are hot with unrest as though we were some damned republic. To be frank I call it good riddance, and I am not the only one. Jack, the Cabinet is united behind this course of action: with Castlereagh dead, we're free to clear the way for public acceptance of Miss Kurakina as Queen Sophia. It's long since time that you went home to Cornwall and stayed there for a very considerable period, I feel.'

'Your pretty young figurehead with all that Hanoverian blood,' Crow said, shrugging on his jacket; privately certain that once she had been invested with the crown, Nadezhda was going to give these men a lot more trouble than they predicted.

The journey from the Tower to Mayfair was undertaken in a closed carriage, as fast as it could be managed on a clamouring, noisome London afternoon. Crow sat opposite a fastidiously cross-legged Lord Vansittart, accompanied by an armed guard consisting of two leather-clad thugs from the Tower with clubs and pistols.

'Such company for a free man, sir?' Crow leaned back in the seat, grateful that they had found him a clean shirt and let him shave after all.

Vansittart only pursed his lips. 'I knew your father, and I've known you long enough to be quite certain that you have absolutely no idea what's good for you. I'll get you to Dorothea even if I must have you marched in with a pistol to your kidney – the woman might be a scheming hussy, but if anyone knows how to smooth over a mess of this magnitude it's her.'

On reaching the quieter environs of Mayfair, Crow found himself walking up the front steps to the Lievens' front door, Vansittart at his side, passing serried pots of lavender on every marble step; he had come here for some damned musical recital in the Little Season with an unwilling Hester on his arm, and he longed with a breathless physical ache to see her, if only she would consent to receive him.

The Lievens' butler admitted them with a complete lack of surprise or emotion impressive even in the most top-ranking of London society's upper servants. 'If you will come this way, my lords. His lordship and her ladyship have just returned from their customary ride in Hyde Park; Captain Helford and the young Russian lady accompanied them.'

Crow was just conscious of Lord Vansittart's name announced at the drawing-room door followed by his own – something he'd thought never to hear again. Now here was Dorothea crying out at the sight of him, pressing both hands to her mouth, Vansittart rocking backwards and forwards on the balls of his feet and Lieven smiling into his brandy; even Nadezhda looked pleased to see him, so gamine in a muslin gown she clearly despised with all her mountebank's heart. Dorothea kept repeating that Hester was indisposed in her bedchamber, ringing the bell for a footman to send her maid to Lady Lamorna's room at once. Moving like a school of fish, the three of them stepped forwards as one to reveal Kitto, who stood at the hearth watching the fire, almost a stranger in buckskins, top boots and an exquisitely cut jacket. Dorothea must have moved heaven and earth to render the boy decent in such short order: she was, after all, a master manipulator, and understood the importance of appearance. Even so, there was still so much of their mother about him, and Crow could never be sure if it was the set of his eyes, or his mouth.

Turning to look up only cautiously, as though he mistrusted the evidence of his own ears, Kitto saw Crow at Vansittart's side and immediately dropped his glass of Rhenish. It smashed on the hearthstone in a bright explosion, stem flying away from the bowl, flames caught in the broken glass. And then, as Crow watched, his young brother extinguished every last pulse of violent, fleeting and conflicted emotion from his expression. He turned away then to look at Nadezhda standing in her gown and shawl at Dorothea's side, and Crow knew in that moment Kitto had understood it all for the first time. Kitto didn't voice his outrage or slam the door, as he would once have done. He only stood and allowed his cold grey gaze to travel from Crow to Nadezhda and back again, with all of that devastating and wholly well-bred control.

'I know what you're thinking, and it wasn't like that, not entirely,' Nadezhda said, quickly. 'Kitto—'

'I beg that you will excuse me, sir,' Kitto said to Crow. 'Now that you've all got what you wanted from me, my presence in this house is scarcely necessary.' He turned to Dorothea and the count, bowing. 'My sincere thanks for your kind hospitality.' Then he walked straight past Crow and went out, leaving sunlight to stream into the room casting diamond shapes on to the Maratha carpet where he had been standing.

There was a moment's roaring silence in which no one seemed able to move, let alone speak, and then Nadezhda shrugged Dorothea's hand from her arm and ran to Crow, crashing into his chest. 'Stop him!' Her voice was thick with tears and he held her as he hoped he would once have had the kindness to hold his own daughter in forgiveness if she'd lived long enough to disappoint him. Encircled in his arms Nadezhda shook, this girl who could ride wild horses, and who killed anyone who got in her way. 'Oh, please—' Nadezhda broke off, unable to speak the truth before the Lievens which, Crow suspected, was that she had run away with Kitto really wanting only to be with him, to no longer serve her father the tsar. He would probably never know who had recovered a sense of duty first, Kitto or Nadezhda herself. 'I never wanted to lie to him,' she said, soaking Crow's jacket with her tears as he absent-mindedly smoothed the curls at the nape of her neck with the edge of his thumb. 'I just wanted to stay with him.'

'I know,' Crow said, 'but it was a fairy tale that couldn't be sustained, was it not? Get her something decent to drink.' Flinging the order over his shoulder to the silent Dorothea and her count, he set Nadezhda to one side with all the gentleness he could summon, which was not much at that point, and left them. Kitto could not be ignored, but he still had not seen Hester – why had she not come? Surely she must know by now that he was here?

Kitto was already out in the street. Professionally ignored by the Lievens' butler, who closed the door after them, Crow ran to catch up and fell into step at his brother's side, fighting a barrage of exasperation and acute guilt.

'I'm sorry,' Crow said. 'I really am. Sometimes I wonder what I've become.'

'Oh, don't bother,' Kitto replied, determinedly not looking at him; he was pale, only the ridge of his cheekbone stained with colour, another trait he had inherited from their mother. 'Really – go to the devil, Jack. I don't want to listen to it.'

'What a shame.' Crow steered him from the walkway to the Lievens' stable-mews. 'Let's enact melodramas for one another amongst the carriage traces and feed sacks instead of in the open street.'

In the cobbled stable-mews, a Lieven stable-lad doggedly continued shovelling filthy straw into a barrow and Kitto at last turned to face his brother.

'What do you want? It's lucky I didn't expect an apology at all, let alone to receive it without one of your verbal assassinations. So what have I done now?' Kitto demanded in rapid Cornish, the hollows beneath his eyes bruised almost purple with sleeplessness: he was as angry as he was exhausted. 'Was I not courteous enough? I haven't forgotten what you always taught me, you know – that appearances are more important than anything else. I could blow up a French garrison and you'd just be filthily sarcastic, but you only threatened to horsewhip me when I was uncivil to that bitch of a stepmother.'

'Kitto—' Crow began.

'And now somehow you're out of prison and free,' Kitto said, flushed and hot. 'Is this another of your deceptions? I don't know what to believe. Did you do all that just to teach me a lesson, or will they come and take you away again, and hang you after all?' He had grown more incoherent with every word, and moved as if to push past Crow and walk back out into the street.

'No, no, it's going to be quite all right,' Crow said, for want of anything else, and thank God Kitto submitted to his hard and unforgiving embrace: neither need acknowledge that the boy was weeping in a way Crow had not seen him do since he was a young child. 'You'll find another girl,' Crow told him.

'It isn't just that,' Kitto said. 'You know it isn't. I'm sorry.'

'What a bacchanalia of apology,' Crow said, and Kitto laughed. 'If it helps, try and understand that Nadezhda would have felt as though she had no choice,' he went on. 'She's always known that her people's regard and care, including the tsar's, is completely dependent on her efficiency as their own political tool. It's conditional.' He paused. 'I make no excuses for myself: I've been despotic, indolent and occasionally unforgivably violent. I'm sure I've given you far too much money, and absolutely nothing in the way of principles, but I hope you knew that, if it were humanly possible, I would always have shifted to get you out of a hole.'

'I know. Let's not pretend you wouldn't have been absolutely bloody about it, but yes. I bet she wept all over you as well.' Kitto wiped his face on his arm and shook his head like a young hound rising from the river. 'For a terrifying, cold-hearted, lying bastard, you've got the most convincing manner – as if it's in your power to just sort of resolve everything. Christ, I'd as lief cut my throat before sitting through supper.'

'Quick, then, before they untack your horse,' Crow said. 'Go out and gallop up Rotten Row. Dine at White's and get drunk. Better yet, go to Clarges Street and get yourself a very expensive whore.'

'No,' Kitto managed, dry-eyed.

'Come now.' Crow still spoke in Cornish, giving him a slight shake.

'It's Hester,' Kitto said. 'She hasn't been out of that bedchamber all day – Eames told us just before you came in. I asked one of the maids and she didn't even open the door to let them come in with her chocolate. I would never have gone out if I'd known that. I should have gone to sit with her.'

Crow briefly closed his eyes and remembered what Hester had told him in Petersburg. *What have I to live for, now that she is gone because I left her?* Above all, Kitto must not witness what Crow feared he was about to find. 'Never mind that,' he said. 'Go now and ride off all this spleen – must I tell you again?'

Kitto obeyed, walking out of the stables without another word, and Crow ran indoors through the servants' quarters, ignoring Eames, who passed him with a tray of iced champagne on his way to the library. None of them understood that there was no victory to toast, and Crow sprinted up the stairs; by the time he reached the first floor he had lost all equilibrium, calling his wife's name, suddenly furious that he didn't even know which bedchamber she was in, and had been in all day. He cornered a maidservant emerging from the second-floor stairway that led up to the nursery. 'Where is Lady Lamorna?' he demanded, only half aware of how frightened she looked.

'Down at the end, your honour,' the girl gasped, and Crow left her, calling Hester's name, to which he received no reply. He reached the door and knocked, calling again and again, answered only by silence.

'If you're there,' he said, 'just answer, and if you don't want me to come in I'll walk away now, I promise.'

The silence stretched on until Crow barged the door with his shoulder, once, twice, three times: exquisite agony after his incarceration in Little Ease, and then the door burst open inwards, but he couldn't see Hester at all, not on the bed, not anywhere. Surely the damned maidservant hadn't sent him to the wrong room? He would take the girl by the shoulders and slap her scrubbed pink face so hard that she fell. He took hold of the mantelpiece, appalled at himself, ashamed of this unbearable anger. It was true what he'd said to Kitto: what had he become? That was when he saw Hester's discarded jean boot, and surely all air had been sucked from the room? He found her on the floor on the far side of the four-poster bed. She sat leaning against bedframe and tumbled counterpane, quite still, stinking like a butcher's shop, her gown spattered with dried blood, her face smeared with it. Whispering her name like a prayer, he crouched at her side, not daring to touch her; she didn't move, wouldn't look at him.

At last, she did turn to him, tears standing in her eyes so that he couldn't bear it, and he longed to hold her even as he knew he'd forsaken the right.

'My love,' he said, 'what happened to you?' He saw that she was holding a small glass bottle and lost all concern for keeping his distance if that was what she wanted, immediately snatching it from her unresisting fingers, holding it up to the light, removing the stopper. He dared not touch her. '*What have you done?*'

'*No!*' Hester said. 'Put the stopper back in. I thought it best not to take it here: it would be a shame to leave Dorothea with a scandal. I'll take it at home.'

'No,' Crow said, 'you'll do no such thing.'

'Why not,' Hester demanded quietly, 'when you let yourself go to the gallows? They might have released you now, but I should think I'll be next.'

With a bright burst of understanding, Crow took the vial and went to the window. The casement was already slightly open; he pushed it up and flung the poison far across the rooftops, where only gulls and ambitious rats might be harmed by it. He went and sat on the floor at her side.

'It was you,' he said, 'wasn't it? You killed Castlereagh.'

'Of course I did, and now thanks to you I shall be hanged for it as I expect I deserve, instead of being allowed to take my own way out.' Tears began to slide inexorably down her blood-smeared cheeks and then he took her hands, at last, at last.

'No one shall harm a hair of your head. Even if Vansittart hadn't this afternoon told me that the entire Cabinet sees his death as a blessing, I should let no one hurt you, Hester.'

'Oh no,' she said, 'only you are allowed to do that.'

He didn't insult her by mounting a defence to that

accusation, but instead rang for hot water and waited by the door to receive it, ensuring that he thanked the maid he'd frightened, and that she could not see into the room no matter how she tried to peer around his shoulder. Crow carried the steaming jug to the wash-stand and filled the rose-patterned bowl, and all the while Hester still sat by the bed, not moving, staring sightlessly at the wall. When he held out his hand to her, she didn't take it, so he crouched at her side.

'There's no relief like stripping off one's uniform after a battle,' he said, 'and you have fought a war.' She didn't move; he was forced into underhand tactics. 'The boy is completely overwrought, you know – I had to send him out on his horse to collect himself. He was so worried about you.'

Still she said nothing, but she consented to take his hand and stand up. He unbuttoned her gown down the back, dizzy with the scent of her beneath that of stale blood, longing to let his touch linger on the naked skin at the nape of her neck. She stood immobile as the gown slipped from her shoulders and down to the floor, automatically stepping out of it, all that bloodied mauve-grey muslin; it was an Indian print, and evening sunlight glinted from the silver threads woven through the heap of ruined fabric; he would get her another one, as many as she wanted. The blood had soaked through to her petticoats; he unlaced ribbons and lifted more ruined fabric over her head; he would serve her however she pleased until the last breath left his body. When at last he unlaced her corset, and she stood in only her shift, she let out a shuddering sigh, and went to the bowl of warm water, washing her own hands, her own face with brisk dexterity that told him he was not needed, that she had never needed him, and certainly did not now. She turned to face him and drops of water clung to her eyelashes like seed pearls, and he was reminded with shattering force of the first moment he had ever seen her, soaked to her skin on the beach at Lamorna, and he was quite defenceless.

'Please,' he said, 'Hester, please.'

Afterwards, he was never quite sure how precisely it happened, but at last she was in his arms, held tight against his chest; he had just enough presence of mind to kick her bloodied clothes so far beneath the four-poster that no servant could retrieve them without waking him, and as one they moved to the bed, he still wearing his boots. Holding Hester close to him, Crow felt himself plummeting along with her into a dark and dreamless sleep, her fingers twined around his on the pillow. But before dawn, before they were both really awake, he reached for her and she for him and he was glad that she could not see the tears of relief start to his eyes as he ran his hands down her back, pulling her closer as he had longed to do for so many weeks. Even as he did so, he realised that she herself wept uncontrollably.

'No,' she said, pushing him away, 'no. It can't happen again, do you see? I loved her so much, and it must never happen again. Why do you not understand?'

And so Hester turned her back; and Crow saw that she was quite irrevocably destroyed by the life he had led her to, and he lay awake watching the room fill with unrelenting sunlight.

66

The sun had long since risen above the jumble of London rooftops one saw from the morning-room at the Russian Embassy. Dorothea always ordered breakfast to be served there for those who wanted it, claiming that no one could bear the gloom of the dining-room so early in the day. Still wearing the clothes he had ridden out in the night before, Kitto came in and pulled out the chair furthest from Nadezhda's, who had been breakfasting alone at the polished walnut table beneath the window, early sunlight striking off the silver knives and forks.

'I suppose you've been out all night,' Nadezhda said over the rim of her coffee cup, watching him spread greengage jam on fresh bread: he was astonishingly hungry. 'I, on the other hand, was sent to bed after supper. Countess Lieven told me I must keep my good looks for when she introduces me to London society.'

'It sounds like a dead bore,' Kitto said, tossing the letter he had found in the holland-covered quiet of Lamorna House on to the table; doubtless it was only another bill he hadn't a cat in hell's chance of paying until the next quarter of his allowance was due. 'At least you don't have the headache I've earned for myself.' He let Dorothea's footman pour his coffee, pushing away an alarmingly distinct series of memories: the inside of White's, scant details of a disreputable supper party in Will MacAllen's rooms at the Albany where Crow's name had been liberally toasted and Castlereagh recommended to eternal damnation; after that, there had been powdered limbs, bare feet and perfumed hair, crumpled linen, and not Nadezhda lying at his side on the grass beneath a vast Russian sky.

Frowning, Nadezhda tugged at the tight, puffed sleeve of her gown as she pored over that day's copy of the *Morning News*. 'It says here,' she said, 'that some Archbishop of Canterbury has proclaimed that the Royal Marriages Act ought to be contravened in the light of the current constitutional crisis invoked by the French Occupation. He says my mother's marriage should be declared legal, and myself legitimate. Who is the Archbishop of Canterbury? Should I care what he has to say? And how absurd it all is when she was never even married in the first place.'

'It means they're turning public opinion towards you,' Kitto said. 'I don't know how they'll do it, but they will.'

'Lord Lamorna said they won't claim the tsar is my father, but one of his cousins who died, and that he and Princess Sophia were married in secret. I suppose I'll have to give up my own church and join yours, but I'd say a grand duke would do just as well for you all as the tsar.'

'Something damned Gothic like that, I should think,' Kitto said, 'but anything's better than Castlereagh.'

Nadezhda put down her coffee cup with a rattle of china

against gilded saucer. 'Oh, let's not,' she said, looking at him, her nut-brown face alive with tension. 'Please let's not just pretend none of this has happened, Kitto.'

He remembered her standing before him in the meadow outside Chudovo, saying that she would marry him. She must have known then that she could never do so. 'What in Christ's name do you want me to say?'

'*I don't know.*' She grasped the handle of her knife, sawing distractedly at the edge of the table, then let it fall to her a plate with a discordant clatter of silver and ivory.

They both fell silent at the sounds of footsteps in the marble-tiled hallway outside, and for a moment she held his gaze, and Kitto knew he would soon have to say goodbye to her, this riddle of a girl he had ridden with across the great Russian steppe, and that in all likelihood it would be years before they met again.

'I'm sorry,' she said, quite suddenly. 'Whatever happens, I want you to know that I loved you first, more than anyone.'

'I know,' Kitto said. 'Nadia, I know you did.' He leaned forwards across their coffee cups, crooking his forefinger beneath her chin, turning her face up to his. He kissed her, one last time, beneath the stunned gaze of Dorothea's footman, and they broke apart just moments before the doors were opened and Dorothea herself came in, staring with icy disbelief from one to the other, as though she had seen them through three inches of lacquered oak – perhaps it had been the expression on her footman's face that gave them away so comprehensively?

'Tea, if you please, James,' Dorothea said in her scarcely accented English. 'I suppose you won't have heard the news about Prince Volkonsky and Countess Orlova, Kitto? Nadezhda, you won't know him, although of course you know the countess.' Her voice cracked. 'Tatyana and I were at the convent together – more years ago now than I care to recall.'

'Volkonsky?' Kitto said, and Countess Orlova's gilded ballroom felt like a half-forgotten dream here in London with the grey skies and familiar streets, and the swift exchange of insults between the link boys and a butcher's lad delivering rolled joints of beef and hams along the street.

'He's dead,' Dorothea said. 'They're both dead. My poor husband was quite distraught this morning – Sasha was a cousin of his, you understand. It's said he led a suicidal rearguard attack on the French as they reached the border with Sweden, all because he was grieving for my dear Tatyana, who died only the week before, quite by herself, with only her maid. The grand duchess may write me as many letters as she chooses, but no one will ever convince me that Tatyana didn't take her own life – it's appalling. People can be so cruel, and so hypocritical, and I'm sure she was no worse than anyone else, but without reputation a woman is nothing.'

'I'm sorry,' Kitto said, for want of anything else, not sure what other part he was to play in this tragedy that had moved even Dorothea Lieven to tears.

'Well, love is a game for children and idiots, they say. And usually both.' With that pointed utterance, Dorothea sat down and began to peel a pear from the silver dish with her knife and fork, and had quite recovered herself by the time Hester came in alone, clad in a half-mourning gown of light grey silk.

'Will you only consider this?' With a surprising dose of her old crispness of manner, Hester let a folded letter fall on to the linen tablecloth. 'There's one for you, too.' She tossed one on to Kitto's plate, and he began to sincerely wish that he'd never come in to breakfast.

'Where's Crow?' he asked, wary. 'What's he done?'

'You may well ask!' Hester stabbed at slices of preserved oranges in honey, and let them fall one by one on to her plate as if each were slaughtered prey. 'He's gone.'

'Oh, for goodness' sake,' Dorothea said, looking up sharply from her tea, which she still drank with lemon and honey in the Russian fashion, even after so many years in London. 'Really? What has he done now?'

'He has behaved with his usual high-handed disregard for anyone else's feelings.' Hester spread butter on to her bread with savage flicks of the ivory-handled knife. 'Kitto, read yours.'

He had already unfolded the letter, staring down at his brother's familiar, untidy handwriting, listening to the clock on the mantelpiece tick with methodical unconcern as he read. *You'll perceive that it will be better for Hester—*

'Blame myself for his death?' Hester snapped, and Kitto guessed that her own letter had mirrored the entirely breathtaking contents of his own. 'I'd be more likely to help him on his way. I'll scalp him. I'm completely serious.' She passed her own letter to Dorothea. 'Go on, read it, I don't care.'

'But he's giving up everything for you.' Dorothea stared down at the folded sheet. 'He grants you permission to divorce him, Hester, with you to retain your title and possession of Nansmornow until Kitto marries, at which time as you would become the dowager, with Borlaze, Hexham or Oakhurst at your disposal, should the small dower house at Nansmornow not please you.' She paused, as if it were a struggle to choose the right words. 'My dear, he is behaving as no man ever does. He's extinguishing himself in every way that he can without actually taking his own life.'

Nadezhda just watched them all in silent astonishment, and Kitto let his letter fall to the table and stood up, dizzy with mounting fury. 'He's renouncing the title so that I inherit,' he said. 'I'm going after him.'

'Of course he can't renounce the title,' Dorothea said sharply. 'That's not even possible. It's not legal. He's raving. The only way Crow can cease to be Earl of Lamorna is by dying.'

'Which is what he's been trying to do for weeks – can't you see that?' Kitto said. He couldn't bear to repeat what Crow had written to him, not before Dorothea, not even before Nadezhda:

> Left to my own devices I would put period to my existence; however, I have been brought to realise that this would cause distress to those whose regard I scarcely deserve. Instead I must content myself and look after the interests of all those who depend upon me by organising affairs so that my life appears extinguished.

Kitto crumpled the folded paper. 'He'll get all his papers in order and that'll be it. He speaks six languages, you know. Six at least. He'll join some foreign regiment as a sell-sword and get himself killed just like Prince Volkonsky did. I'm going after him.'

'But how do you know where he's gone?' Nadezhda said.

'Cornwall,' Kitto said, looking at Hester. 'He needs the attorney. He'll have to go to Nancarrow's in Penzance before he does anything. Who in God's name does he think he is, moving us all about the place as if we were his knights and pawns, without any consideration for what any of us might actually want? Are you coming? He travels damnably fast – it won't be a comfortable journey if we want to reach Isaac Nancarrow before Crow gets to him.'

'Do you really think I care how comfortable it is?' Hester spoke with measured rage. 'You're escorting me to Cornwall after breakfast whether you like it or not.'

The tsar's daughter stood by Dorothea's side at the library window overlooking the street below. Together, they watched the carriage roll away and Nadezhda remembered Kitto mounting the golden Turkoman mare behind her, and the warm heat of his body against hers, the hard muscle of his belly and the strength in his arms on either side of her as he had clung to the mare's mane. She knew quite well that the moments of greatest freedom in her life had come and gone, now all quite unattainable like so many dandelion seeds blowing away on the wind.

Sighing, Dorothea passed her a handkerchief. 'He's just a boy, darling. I don't promise anything about who you'll one day have to marry, regardless of whether we get you on the throne or not, but there will be others. Pretty ones too, as long as you're careful about them.'

'I've told what feels like such an awful lot of lies,' Nadezhda said, 'but the worst one was when I said I'd marry him.' She turned to Dorothea, as fierce as she was tearstained. 'It wasn't completely a lie, you know. I did want to, in my heart.'

'I'm afraid that with your parentage you would never have been given a choice about something so important as marriage, any more than I had a say myself. Captain Helford was only so incensed about being treated as a chess piece because he has always expected to order his own existence. You, my dear, must learn as I did to direct the course of the game even as others move you about the board. I'm only sorry you had to endure Ilya Rumyantsev,' Dorothea went on. 'But we women must learn greater strength than men ever suspect. You performed this duty with your father's blessing, and it will all be to the greater glory of Russia.'

'Poor Countess Orlova, though,' Nadezhda said. 'Did she really kill herself, do you think?'

Dorothea turned to her with a considering expression that made Nadezhda suddenly afraid. 'Perhaps it was just as well Lord Lamorna plunged Tatyana into a scandal. Did you not know there were rumours that she and Sasha Volkonsky associated with the Green Lamp? That even Alexei Pushkin does, too? Those people might seem like only silly, romantic fools, but they are rebels who seek to undermine your father, Nadia. Sometimes even a tragedy is for the best.'

Nadezhda looked down at her feet, so unfamiliar in stockings and slippers of pale satin, filling in the yawning space between what Dorothea said and what she meant. 'Countess Orlova wasn't a wicked woman,' she said firmly. 'What if she'd told all of St Petersburg that I was riding around dressed as a boy? Then even my father couldn't have saved my reputation.' Just how would she have then been disposed of? Strangled or stabbed, and put into the cold Neva? She wished with all her soul that she had ridden away down the street with Kitto and the sister-in-law he loved so much.

'Darling, you were such a clever girl. Don't upset yourself by thinking Tatyana acted out of any concern for your happiness.' Nadezhda stood very still as Dorothea caressed a loose curl near Nadezhda's ear. 'But let me drop you a hint,' the countess went on. 'You know your papa loves you. Wouldn't he be saddened to learn that you of all people felt sympathy with someone like Tatyana Orlova, who had no self-control or respect for her own honour, let alone for her tsar? Are you not obedient to him at all times?'

'Yes, madam. Of course I should never feel sympathy for such a person.' Nadezhda closed her eyes against the warning and thought of Kitto standing behind her in the green waters of the River Kerest, and of the moment she had turned to face him when it seemed that she was no longer acting out a part ordained for her by others, but living just as she wished, free as a bird on the wing. And so she had done, even if only for a little while.

67

It was early in the morning yet, with seagulls wheeling and skrailing in the grey sky, but everyone on the cobbled quay stared at Catlin as she stepped off the mail-boat with Morwenna in her arms, the maid sucking two fingers: a bad habit in a child, but after so many months of hiding and then keeping quiet and out of the way of the brothers at the priory, what choice had there been other than to let the maid soothe herself as best she could?

One of the old boys from the mackerel-boat alongside the quay limped over after a muttered consultation with his fellows. 'Word was you'd drowned on the *Curlew*, maid,' he said, eyeing Catlin critically from the crown of her head down to the worn-out toes of her boots. 'You and the little tacker.'

'Well, you can see that we're still living and breathing, Mr Simmens,' Catlin said, wondering just how many times she would have to have this conversation.

Unperturbed, he jerked his head at the cart, half loaded with creels of shining mackerel. 'Word from London is that his lordship is still like to hang,' he said. 'But he'd want to be sure you'd got home safely, Mistress Rescorla. Nat's driving the trap over to St Buryan directly: he'll take you to Nansmornow, my dear.'

Catlin found herself thanking him even as she wondered if her letter had ever reached Master Kitto; in fact, she longed to walk alone along the coast path, with the ocean turquoise beneath and all this heavy wide grey sky above. Catlin wouldn't have minded the rain in her face, but the maid was tired, pushing her round head into the hollow beneath Catlin's chin as she clung to her fichu. And so Catlin was handed up into the cart and sat between two creels of mackerel with the child in her lap, the skirts of her gown spangled with scales, and her lungs full of the fresh-fish scent of salt water. The boys on the quay stared at her as though she were St Piran come walking smack up the beach, clean out of the sea. As the cart rolled away everything she saw seemed to pass all mixed up together, as though someone had swirled a brush through the middle of one of Hester's paintings before it had dried. It was all a whirl of grey granite walls speckled with lichen, and cobbled streets, and the honeyed scent of gorse flowers when they left Penzance behind and came up on to high ground above Newlyn where all the little fields were split with flower-strewn hedges: cornflower, yarrow and crimson sea campion. They passed the turning down to Lamorna Cove and the village of Nantewas, and up the hill past the Rosemerryn cottages just within sight beyond the trees, and the lane snaked around to the right-hand side, leaving the coastline and tacking inland to St Buryan. Here were the gates of Nansmornow, just where the lane began to creep inland. The cart rolled to a halt, and Nat Simmens helped her down, so that Catlin stood by the grey granite bulk of the lodge-house, hefting Morwenna against her hip, watching the cart roll off down the lane.

'Where, Cat?' Morwenna asked, and Catlin ignored her nerves. After half a year apart, would the child even remember her parents? Not that she'd see his lordship again, but Hester might yet be safe. Perhaps there was even a letter waiting here at Nansmornow, perhaps there had been a little bit of good to come out of these months, which had been like living through a succession of fevered nightmares: just as you thought one was over, another began, and no matter how much a body sweated and wept it never seemed to end.

'You're home, maid,' Catlin said, wishing she'd had half an hour to wash the child's mucky linen cap, even as she wondered where she herself would go, in the end. Who could be housekeeper to a dead man and a missing woman? In reality, Hester would not be here, could not be here, and yet the maid belonged to Hester and his lordship. Catlin herself would not be allowed to keep her: there would be letters, and attorneys, and testaments, and the worst outcome would be the child sent to Hester's mother's family, the Dukes of Albemarle, who would treat her as less than human and doubtless clap her up in some seminary as they had done with Hester's beautiful, half-Irish mother. Innocent of all that lay in store, Morwenna sat down on the carriage drive and began to play with sycamore seeds drifted into the grass as Catlin stood like some kind of mazey fool, gazing at the great wrought-iron gate. She had no notion what would even happen to Nansmornow: surely it would pass to Master Kitto, but a wild boy away at war would not want to keep up a family seat the size of this place. It would be let out, or all the furniture sheathed in holland covers and most of the staff laid off, and Mr Hughes would be gone, off back to London, she supposed, to work for another fashionable family. He'd doubtless left months ago.

Somehow Catlin couldn't face the old gardener and his wife who lived in the lodge-house, so she just pushed the gate open and urged Morwenna to walk beside her, her small hand warm and sticky in Catlin's own. The rolling lawn was deep green and quiet, the ancient house long and low in the afternoon light, white rhododendrons in flower along the east wall, and there was no one scything the grass or window flung open to admit the scent of the hedged rose garden, and with the little maid in tow Catlin was not sure whether to take her straight to the front door, or around to the back. What if this whole house had been requisitioned by the English and no longer even belonged to Lord Lamorna? What then?

'Chicks, Cat?' Morwenna said.

'Oh, there's chickens, maid,' Catlin said absently, and whisked the child up into her arms and carried her around the side of the great house till they came to the gate in the high wall of the kitchen garden.

'Egg, please.'

'We'll see.' Catlin wasn't at all sure they'd even be admitted to the house. The kitchen garden was quiet too, ranks of onions and carrots and turnips standing to attention like soldiers on the parade ground and no one weeding, and the laundry-yard quiet, too, sheets still on the line even though it was Thursday, but perhaps they'd had weather, and Morwenna had a strand of Catlin's red hair loose from her cap and was winding around her finger, and it was all Catlin could look at as she pushed open the scullery door and walked into the house for the first time since Beatie and Lizzy had been killed there by the English soldiers, since she had run into the night with this child in her arms. She heard voices from the servants' hall along the passage, but she kept going as a body always must keep going, and pushed open the door.

68

Not far from Truro, on the road that led upcountry from Cornwall and into England, the parish of Mitchell lay hemmed about by moorland and wilting in the sun. In the courtyard at the Plume of Feathers, Crow leaned on a wall feeling the heat of the bricks even through his jacket and shirt, watching the innkeeper who crossed the courtyard, bowing as he came, licking his lips before he dared speak.

'Medway will have the horse shod in an instant, your honour.'

'Good,' Crow said, and watched Jennings hurry back to the taproom in his mud-splashed gaiters and jacket greasy at the elbows, with flakes of dander littering the shoulders. What it would be like when he was just an ordinary man, and could no longer command such treatment; would unkempt innkeepers still be afraid of him then? He heard the dull rhythm of hoofbeats in the lane, and the more distant grinding of carriage wheels in stone and mud. Soon he would be riding south once more; soon he would be a man with no name, and not Lamorna at all, or even Crowlas, all of his titles passing to Kitto, first by means of deception and, before long, by means of his death honourably in battle so that no one need enact tragedies over it. Across the yard, a child of indeterminate sex traversed the cobbles with a basket of brown hen's eggs, dragging patched skirts in straw and mud, stopping only to stare at Crow, wary but still wondering whether to try him for a penny.

'I should look where I were going if I were you,' Crow said, ignoring the commotion kicked up by the arrival of a mud-splattered outrider outside the gates, 'because if you don't, either you or I will end wearing the eggs.'

The child only stared at the gate, clinging to the basket with none-too-clean hands, and Crow took the flint from his waistcoat pocket to light a cigarillo, watching as his own brother rode into the yard on one of Count Lieven's grey horses. Still in civilian dress, and liberally mud-splashed, Kitto called with impressive hauteur for the child to send for a stable-boy.

'Oh, come now,' Crow said, 'can't you see the infant is already busy?'

Kitto looked at him with a creditable lack of surprise and dismounted, gentling Lieven's grey with swift and unconscious expertise. The child had enough native self-preservation to disappear into the dark cool of the tavern, leaving them both alone.

'What's a few days here and there between us, after all?' Kitto said, advancing on him. 'You'll have everything signed off with Nancarrow before long, I don't doubt. Why don't I just give you orders to stable the damned horse?'

'I suppose you could always try it,' Crow said idly. Kitto stopped where he stood, sketched him a mocking bow and walked off towards the stables himself with the grey at his side, leaving Crow to smoke and watch as his own carriage rolled into the courtyard with his own driver and groom on the box, both of whom had the good grace to look horrified at the sight of him.

'Carry on, Phelps,' Crow said, grinding the end of his cigarillo beneath the heel of his boot, 'don't mind me.'

He walked over to the carriage and opened the door before his groom had the chance to, and handed Hester out into the yard; she didn't betray the slightest shock at the sight of him, clad in mauve muslin half-mourning for their daughter, a loose spiral of hair grazing the soft hollow of skin at her décolletage, and the touch of her fingers against his sent a bolt of heat straight up his arm. A maidservant he didn't recognise scrambled out after her and hovered on the cobbles, terrified.

'Ellen, go into the inn and bespeak a parlour,' Hester said and without looking at Crow she relinquished her hold on him. 'You, my lord, may accompany me.'

Crow obeyed, suppressing a frisson of anger at her tone; he wondered if he would ever get used to being addressed by this woman as though he were a raw recruit on his first outing at the parade ground. But he would not have to get used to it, because she had to let him go, she must understand that he would only ever make her miserable. Jennings appeared even before they had got into the tavern, bowing and wiping his hands on his apron, leading the way to a dim parlour with faded green damask curtains at the window and dust motes suspended in silvery light puddling on ill-swept floorboards.

Jennings had scarcely closed the door, bowing and backing out before Hester stalked across the room and bolted it from the inside.

She turned on Crow, her dark eyes flashing as she answered his unspoken question. 'I'm never setting foot across the threshold of Nansmornow again – the extraordinary notion that I should possibly want your house or the title you inflicted upon me—'

'Then why are you here?' Crow said.

Furious at being interrupted, she approached him with alarming speed; he let her back him up against the table; four uneven oak legs shrieked across the floorboards. The black woollen travelling cloak was flung back across her muslin-clad shoulders; she had already dispensed with her gloves, exposing forearms of a rich golden brown. 'Why am I here? Because if you so much as go near the offices of Isaac Nancarrow, I'll skin you alive. I will flay you. How dare you?' She took hold of his jacket in both her hands. '*How dare you?*'

'I'm sorry.' It was all he could say but, judging by her expression of untrammelled fury, it wasn't enough.

'You're an autocratic, infuriating and entirely hopeless person,' Hester said, 'and I hate you.' And she kissed him with such merciless force that even he was momentarily stunned by the sweet salty taste of her and the sheer ferocity of it. She pulled away, one hand on either side of his face. 'You cannot just *arrange* other people's lives for them, do you understand?'

He broke away, no matter how much he didn't want to. 'Hester, I must leave you, I must let you go.'

She reached out and slapped him with shocking speed and surprising strength.

'Jesus Christ!' he said. 'Have you quite done, you hoyden?'

'I'll be the judge of that,' Hester snapped, and he took hold of her wrist before she could strike him again – there were, after all, limits – and now he had her backed up against the door, one arm lightly pinned above her head, her breasts heaving from the confines of her bodice, and he longed to ease them free of it and take one nipple after the other in his mouth, to divest her of those skirts and those petticoats and to serve her until she was quite beyond reason.

'Look what I've done to you,' he said, quite seriously. 'Hester, *look what I've done*. You deserve better than this.'

'Oh, I should think that I do,' she snapped. 'Much better! It would be so refreshing to be married to someone respectable and possibly even considerate, if such an unlikely combination even exists. But it's you that I have. Can't you see that we got into this misery together and God knows that's the only way we'll get out of it.' She kissed him again, but with such gentleness this time that he nearly wept, and just for a moment he dropped his head so that his forehead rested upon her shoulder, and he dispensed with the cloak with one expert manoeuvre so that, as one, they dropped to the floor. In a froth of muslin and linen petticoat, she straddled him with a profligate ease that made him cry out with longing and he put up his hands to her face, looking up at her as he tucked his little fingers behind her pearl-strung ears. 'Hester,' he said, 'I love you, my God, I love you.'

This was not the Plume of Feathers's finest bed, but it was the cleanest. Hours after getting into it, Hester woke among crumpled linen to the sound of rainfall, with Crow asleep beside her. A servant must have come in, because the fire had been banked down. The curtains had not been drawn, and the room was flooded with the pewter light of a Cornish full moon, illuminating the tattooed, muscled expanse of Crow's back as he slept on his belly, his face turned towards her, even as raindrops silvered the mullioned windows. Poised to trace a line down between his protruding shoulder blades with the tip of her finger, she paused. It was never a good idea to surprise Crow out of sleep. Instead, she leaned closer.

'Wake up.' They were nearly forty miles from Nansmornow, but Crow kept horses at every staging-inn from here to Penzance. They would ride through the east gate long before suppertime, but even so it was still rather an unforgivable thing to do to one's servants: there would be lower kitchen-maids frantic in the bean rows, and the larder would be ransacked for bacon pie and hastily thrown-together orange creams, and spinach with nutmeg. Hester leaned closer still. 'John, wake up. It's time to go home.'

He started and turned over, smiling at her, still half asleep, those extraordinarily long thick black lashes almost brushing the winged ridge of his cheekbone. She saw the shadow pass across his face as he thought of Morwenna, and Hester recalled the weightless feeling in her arms when she had passed her daughter to Catlin at the quayside on St Mary's.

'Time is cruel,' he said, reaching up to smooth the tear from her cheek with the edge of his thumb and drew her close so that she rested her head upon his chest. 'We see it all so clearly and nothing can be altered. We should break our fast, and someone may have to drag the boy out of bed by his heels. I left him in a temper to either drink every quart of rum within five miles or lose an entire quarter's worth of blunt at hazard. Not that he has a quarter's worth, God take his eyes.'

But when Ellen had dressed Hester, and Crow had assembled his toilette for the day with all the efficiency of a soldier who had spent years in the Corps of Guides with no batman to assist him, they found Kitto already in the parlour, lounging in the corner at a table laid for breakfast by a serving-girl with a smear of ash on her apron, and an expression which betrayed her opinion of people who rose at ungodly hours of the night. Kitto's hair was extremely dishevelled, dusted with hayseed.

'Coffee?' Crow asked his brother gently.

'You haven't been to bed,' Hester said, 'have you?'

'I thank you, yes, and not exactly, no,' Kitto said, eyeing a dish of hard-boiled eggs with distaste. 'I've been thinking – Jack, I suppose I can have my allowance, can't I? God knows what's to happen about my pay.'

'Are you actually absent without leave?' Hester said, taking the coffee pot from the serving-girl who had almost poured coffee into the eggs. Kitto leaned his head back against the tall settle and groaned.

'I wrote to Wellington before I left Petersburg,' Crow said. 'You'll be back with your regiment before Christmas, I should think. But you can have all the ready you want, although God knows what you'll find to spend it on in Cornwall.'

Refusing cream, Kitto drank his coffee, wincing. 'The thing is, I thought I might go back to London instead. There might have just been the slightest difficulty in the village last night about the smith's daughter, although believe me she was very willing. And anyway, MacAllen told me there's a new hell opened – he's had the most astounding run of luck at E.O.—'

'No!' Hester and Crow both spoke at the same time; Crow, extraordinarily, failed not to laugh.

Kitto stared at them. 'What?' He drank more coffee, staring at them both over the chipped rim of his cup. 'I tell you what, I'm damned if I'm going to Nansmornow to play gooseberry for you two.'

'That's exactly what you'll do,' Hester said, passing Crow the cream. 'We'll entertain for you – you won't be bored. But you must come home.'

'Listen to her, boy,' Crow said. 'It'll only be more trouble if you don't, let me assure you.'

'You both hate entertaining, sir,' Kitto said with calculated respect.

'We leave in less than quarter of an hour, and if you don't get into the carriage I'll pull you off that horse,' Hester said conversationally. 'You may think I won't, but I will.'

'Don't try her,' Crow advised, switching to French as the serving-maid came back in with a dish of hot bacon. 'It's not worth it.'

Kitto did eventually get out of the carriage, though, after falling into a dead sleep against the window for five hours. He woke with a start when they changed horses at the forge nestled among the scattered granite houses of Treswithian and sprang out on to the grass verge thick with sea campion, replacing the hired groom on his horse.

'Don't break your neck,' Crow told him. 'You're still half drunk.'

'Nonsense. Do enjoy the carriage ride, old man,' he said, grinning at them both over his shoulder as he spurred the mare and rode away at a gallop, leaving Crow alone with Hester. She leaned back against his chest so that he felt as though he had the entire world encompassed in his arms, and together they watched the grey sky with trails of blue, and the moors yellow with broom in flower. The horses were changed for the last time at the toll gate north of St Erth, and the carriage sped from Rose-an-Grouse and Canon's Town, and through Crowlas itself, where fields of ripening wheat lapped against moorland, and the post-road passed Longrock, circling Gulval, Penzance and Newlyn. Mount's Bay spread out before them like glittering cloth and beyond it the Cornish sea, all the way to Scilly. After Newlyn, some of the wheat had already been cut, and there were hayricks in the fields, and the sheep had been clipped, thank Christ, but once they had passed the outskirts of Mousehole, moorland and field alike gave way to the green wooded Lamorna Valley that Crow knew more intimately than anywhere else on earth. They had been talking of commonplaces up until now, of Kitto clattering into the stable-yard at Nansmornow louder than an artillery wagon to warn the servants of their approach, but now with the coming of the wooded valley a hush fell between them. Crow knew that because this was the last place he'd seen the maid alive, there would be no help for it, and the past would flood the present with blood-soaked memory. Knowing him as she did, Hester reached for his hand, sitting as she was in his arms, and his hand held in both of hers rested on her thigh where the cloak fell away to reveal the crisp, clean muslin of her gown, their fingers twined together, his pale, hers rich brown. The east gate was open, and Crow fought the urge for brandy as they rolled along the carriage drive past the parkland; with the wind in this quarter, he could hear the rolling crash of the sea that had called him away from this place when he was a boy, and now welcomed him home. He closed his eyes briefly and thought of all the times he had come from Eton, and after that on leave, and then as a broken man made gradually whole, only to be smashed clear from his mooring again. He glanced out of the window, and at late afternoon shadows stretching across the lawn, and even as he breathed in the muddy scent of the lake he saw a woman running across the grass with a child in her arms and her cap askew. *Please, just be one of the women from Nantewas,* he silently begged. The pair grew closer, crossing the lawn, and he saw a flash of pinned and braided red hair as the child pulled off the woman's cap, waving it aloft. Hester was searching in her reticule for something, and had not yet seen. Not that she would, because how could she see what was only a trick played by his own mind? Catlin Rescorla and the maid, his daughter, his own Morwenna. Catlin set the child down on the grass, stooping to speak to her, and they ran hand in hand towards the carriage, the maid stumbling on her skirts and steadied by Catlin's hand. She had barely been able to walk when he saw her last. Thank God Hester didn't have to endure this, what might have been.

'John.' Hester took hold of Crow's arm, and her reticule crashed to the floor, sliding beneath the rear-facing seat, spilling hairpins and a tin of clove pastilles, and her handkerchief. '*John*,' she said again. 'Look out of the window.'

An Historical Note

This book took place during a period of history that never happened: Joan Aiken's *The Wolves of Willoughby Chase* begins with a preface that ignited, long ago, the beginnings of *Wicked by Design* and this world inhabited by Hester, Crow, Kitto and Nadezhda. The alternate universe of *Wicked by Design* is however populated by several characters who owe a debt to real people. People used to say that Napoleon thought of his divorced wife Josephine as his lucky star, and so according to my flexible logic she had to survive beyond 1810 for him to have beaten Wellington at Waterloo in 1815. Dorothea Lieven will be an old friend to anyone familiar with Regency history, and Hester's late father was inspired by Captain John Perkins. In the course of my Russian research, I stumbled upon Captain Nadezhda Durova, a young Russian woman who disguised herself as a man and served as a cavalry officer in the tsar's army. Tsar Alexander discovered her secret, and awarded her the Cross of St George. Like my Nadezhda Kurakina, she had a gift for communicating with horses, and was charged with the responsibility of delivering a herd for use by the army. Her biography, *The Cavalry Maiden*, is a joy from start to finish. It's said that the Prince Regent's sister, Princess Sophia, really did give birth to an illegitimate child around 1800, but the truth about that child's true identity in *Wicked by Design* is entirely my own invention.

Acknowledgements

I am indebted to Karen Wallace for all those Fridays of looking after my youngest son, and also to my editor Rosie de Courcy and my agent Catherine Clarke for their unfailing support. I am so grateful to everyone at Head of Zeus, especially Lauren Atherton and the eagle-eyed Richenda Todd. In particular, I owe sincere thanks to Stephenjohn Holgate and Lisa Glass for their thoughtful commentaries on the manuscript, and also to Janice Lobb for the Cornish translations – and for her very kind help at an early stage with my research into Cornish history. My sincere gratitude also goes to Oliver Bullough for sharing his considerable knowledge of Russia and for gently pointing out that there are no mountain ranges this side of the Urals. A huge thank you to Jade Stock whose feedback at a critical moment was an absolute lifesaver, and all those who read *Wicked by Design* in the process of creation and pitched in with suggestions when I could see no way to proceed – Leila Rasheed, Ruth Warburton, Rachel Ward and Emma Pass all gave me crucial bits of advice at crucial moments. Heartfelt thanks are due to all at Waterloo Uncovered for the unparalleled insight into warfare, particularly to David Ulke and Mark Evans. Thanks also to the Coldstream Guards, re-enactors from His Majesty's 33rd Regiment of Foot, who were so generous with their knowledge. My eternal gratitude to John for our lively discussion just before Christmas about whether the ball would fall out of a muzzle-loading pistol if you were running under enemy fire (apologies to everyone else who was caught in the crossfire of this minority interest but enthusiastic discussion). Thanks are also due to Dr Anna Collar and Dr Stu Eve for answering my last-minute-panic questions about muskets. Thanks, too, to Dr Claire Shevlin for her excellent advice about being shot in the stomach. Last but by no means least, thank you to Laura and Rob at Rosemerryn for their kind hospitality on my reconnaissance trip, and the local residents who gave me such a warm welcome in the Wink, and to the kindly lady who stopped to give me a lift up the hill from Lamorna Cove because it was raining. Any errors in this book are my fault and, as writers always should, I hope to learn from mistakes that I have made.